Something

to

Navigate

By
Suzanne Pederson

This book is a work of fiction.
All characters and events portrayed are fictitious.
Any resemblance to actual people,
living or dead, is purely coincidental.

Cover Design by Susan Krupp

Thank you for respecting the hard work of this author.

Acknowledgements

Thank you, as always, to my beta readers and editors. You give me the vital feedback and support that I need! You're the best.

Dedication

This book is dedicated to my readers. If you've read *Something to Remember* and *Something to Cherish*, then *Something to Navigate* is dedicated to you. Thank you for coming back for more, for having faith in my writing, and for staying on this journey with me (and with Ian and Mary!).

Chapter One

Ian glanced at his watch as he ushered his son and granddaughter into their pediatrician's office. He was running about ten minutes late for their appointment and he hoped that the doctor wouldn't make him reschedule. His wife had already rescheduled the kids' kindergarten wellness check-ups twice in the last month due to professional obligations. He and his wife were both busy attorneys; Mary had a small but demanding employment law practice in town and Ian was a shareholder at a large firm where he primarily did insurance defense work, and their demanding schedules had played havoc lately with the kids' appointments.

His wife was supposed to bring them to this third attempt, but Mary called him on the way home from her office to let him know that she had gotten a flat tire. So, Ian dropped what he was working on at the law firm to rush home to pick the kids up from Karen, their nanny, who remained at the house with their youngest child, Skylar, who was a year younger than her brother, Philip.

"Sit in those chairs, guys…" Ian pointed across the room to where four miniature chairs in various colors were situated around a small table that was filled with Lego bricks. "And don't fight over the Lego. There's enough of it for both of you."

"Okay, daddy." Philip went to sit in the only blue chair, but Ellie pushed around him to land her bottom on the seat before him.

"Hey, I was going to sit there!" Philip tried to push her out of the chair but Ellie managed to hang onto her seat.

"Knock it off, guys…" Ian scolded them from across the room as he stepped in front of the receptionist's counter to check them both in for their appointments. "Powers, Cinderella and Philip." He turned to watch the kids as Ellie elbowed Philip in the chest and Philip shoved her backwards with both hands.

"Stop it, Philip."

"But she took my chair, daddy!"

"He pushed me first, poppee!"

"The doctor will be with you in just a few minutes." The receptionist drew Ian's attention away from the squabbling kids.

"Thanks." Ian left the counter to stop the kids from fighting. "You sit here," he moved Philip into a red chair on the opposite side of the table from Ellie, "and you sit here…" He moved Ellie into a green chair that was next to the one they were fighting over. "And nobody sits in the blue chair. Okay?"

"That's not fair, daddy! I saw it first!"

"It's totally fair." Ian picked up a magazine to distract himself from the bickering kids, he glanced at the cover in boredom, and set the magazine back down on the table beside him. "Why did you push Philip away from the blue chair when you knew he wanted to sit in it, Ellie? Was that very nice of you?"

"I like blue, poppee, and I got there first." Ellie answered him with an adorable pout, reminiscent of her mother's adorable childhood pouts.

Ian frowned with disapproval. "He likes blue too. And you only got there first because you pushed him away from it." Ian turned to face Philip to include him in the scolding.

"You know better than to push her back. What if I shoved your mom around like that? Would that be very nice of me?"

"She pushed me first, daddy." Philip stuck his tongue out at her.

"Put your tongue back in your mouth…" Ian glanced at his watch. He did not have time today to be sitting in a doctor's office playing referee to two fighting kids who thought a blue chair was worth a noisy quarrel. He had a big trial that he was preparing for and a shareholder's meeting in two hours that he was surely going to miss now.

"I noticed that your twins call you by different names. That's so cute…"

Ian turned in the direction of the female voice that effectively distracted him from the stress of his conflicted thoughts. "I'm sorry?" He had barely noticed the young mother who was sitting in the waiting room with a sleeping baby in her arms.

"Your twins… they don't call you by the same name. How did that happen?" She tossed her hair in a self-conscious way and shot him a flirty smile, something for which Ian had no interest in noticing.

"Ahh…" He glanced their direction, thankful that they had stopped fighting with each other, at least for the moment. "The boy is my son. The girl is my granddaughter."

"Oh, my goodness. I never expected that! They're the same age?"

"I know..." Ian bit his lower lip at the surprised response that he always got whenever he answered that particular question. He was not inclined to continue chatting with the girl, but sitting here alone with her in the waiting room with only the distraction of the two very quiet kids who were now thankfully engaged in their Lego play, didn't provide Ian with an easy way out of the conversation. He shot her a friendly smile with the realization that he was trapped in this dialog, and offered her a short explanation. "It's a second marriage sort of thing…"

"Oh…" She returned another smile. "So, that makes you a flaming hot poppee dealing with stressful dad obligations and demanding granddad duties too, huh? That must keep you pretty busy…" Her question landed between them with a flirty giggle that begged for further conversation as Ian's phone rang in his pocket, providing him with a perfectly timed exit strategy.

"Hey…" He thankfully answered his wife's call with a goodbye nod to the girl. "Where are you?"

"I'm at the tire store… they said I should replace all four tires, so that's what I'm doing now… waiting for them to get that done. Did you make it there on time?"

"I did. We were ten minutes late but we're checked in and waiting to see the doctor. Are you going to be able to relieve me before 3:00 pm? I've got that shareholder meeting that I need to attend."

"I guess it depends upon how fast they can get the tires done."

"Cinderella Powers?" A nurse dressed in playful looking medical scrubs stepped into view through a doorway across the room. "And Philip Powers?"

"I gotta go…" Ian hung up his phone as he stood to usher the kids towards the nurse in friendly scrubs.

"How is everyone today?" She shot him a smile from across the room as Ian picked two Lego bricks up from the floor.

"We're good." He reached for Ellie's hand because she was the wild one who always needed the most guidance when it came to acting appropriate in public.

"Let's go, Ellie…" He removed a Lego brick from her hand that she didn't drop on her own.

"Let go of me, poppee! I'm not done playing!"

"Yes, you are." Ian pushed the rest of the Legos out of her reach. "Come on, Philip…"

His son dropped the bricks in his hands and reached for Ian's other hand.

"Are we getting a shot today, daddy?'

"I don't want a shot!" Ellie tried to wiggle her hand free from Ian's palm so Ian let go of Philip's hand to scoop Ellie into his arms. "Let's not worry about getting shots until the doctor tells us that's what's happening today, okay?"

Ellie's mother had cognitive issues and so did her husband, Ricky, so much of Ellie's parenting came from Ian and his wife, Mary, who gave birth to Philip only a few months before his daughter gave birth to Cinderella – aka Ellie. Jenny wasn't supposed to get pregnant, but against Ian's instruction, her husband suggested that she stop taking the pill so they could have a baby. When Ian learned that Jenny was pregnant, he and Mary made the decision to hire a nanny to care for their son and also Ellie, who lived with both of her parents in a flat that was attached to Ian's large farm house through an internal kitchen door. It was a perfect set-up for the two cognitively impaired adults – they were living on their own, but under the direct supervision of Ian and Mary. Ricky's parents lived in town in a smaller home, so they could indirectly stay involved in Ricky's life as well.

Ian had a ten-acre farm in the hills of Vacaville, California which he purchased before he and Mary got married about seven years ago. He and Mary were childhood sweethearts through high school. Both of their fathers were in the Air Force, deployed to Vietnam when the two of them met as ten-year old's. After Ian's father was killed in action, his mother remarried another Air Force officer and the two kids were forced to part ways in high-school, when Ian's step-father was transferred to Omaha, Nebraska.

Ian returned to California after he graduated college, and while in law school, he met his now ex-wife Elizabeth, his granddaughter's grandmother. Their marriage wasn't happy, and Elizabeth had an affair when Jenny turned three. Unbeknownst to Ian, Elizabeth often visited her boyfriend while Ian was at work, and one day when she was at the boyfriend's house, Jenny fell into his backyard pool and nearly drowned. The fall and subsequent oxygen deprivation left Jenny cognitively impaired. When Jenny was only four, Elizabeth left Ian and married the boyfriend. That was when Ian became by default, the single parent of a special-needs child.

Elizabeth, by her own choice stayed absent from Jenny's life except for an annual lunch date that Ian coordinated each year when he took Jenny to Disneyland for special father-daughter time. Elizabeth resurfaced as an active parent in Jenny's life after Mary insisted that Ian invite Elizabeth to Jenny's wedding, because Mary felt that Elizabeth had a right to be there. At the time it seemed like the right thing to do, but Mary later regretted that decision. When Jenny got pregnant, Elizabeth unexpectedly divorced her husband and moved from Los Angeles to northern California, to become more involved with Jenny and her baby – and also, as a byproduct of that involvement, with Ian.

Elizabeth was conniving and self-centered, and when she first returned to Ian's life, she was determined to suck Ian back into her arms. Her manipulative shenanigans drove Ian and Mary crazy when she first returned. But after a rocky period of adjusting to her being present all the time, Ian set some ground rules that allowed Elizabeth, who worked remotely from home, to stay at Jenny's flat three nights a week so that she could help with Ellie. The weekends and holidays were reserved for Ian and Mary, though they were flexible, and willing to accommodate Elizabeth if she wanted extra time on those days, though she rarely indulged their flexibility.

It wasn't a great situation for Ian and Mary, having Ian's ex-wife living off and on in Jenny's attached house, but after a rocky first year, most of the conflict was resolved, and the co-parenting thing was seemingly working out for everyone. Except that Elizabeth was not always dependable, she often had a hidden agenda, and rarely thought about others as much as she thought about herself. Added to those inconvenient truths, Elizabeth was as gorgeous as she was self-serving, which sometimes made Mary feel incredibly insecure. Ian was, however, blind to Elizabeth's beauty, and barely tolerant of her presence, so for the most part, Mary rarely seemed to feel threatened by her anymore.

But of late, the insecurities seemed to be resurfacing, and Ian's patience with Elizabeth was definitely eroding.

****

When the doctor visit was over and both kids were buckled into car seats, Ian called his wife to get a feel for her status. "Hey, we're through at the doctor's office. How's it going with you?"

"Not as good as it's going for you, because there was a mix-up with the tires and they put the wrong ones on, so the car is now back up on the lift getting the wrong tires pulled off, and the right tires put on."

Ian exhaled with frustration as he started his truck. "How does a tire shop put the wrong tires on a car and stay in business?"

"I know…" Mary gave him a neutral answer, as she often did, to keep him from blowing a fuse.

Ian glanced at the clock on his dash as he backed out of the medical office parking space. "Are you heading home when the car is done, or going back to your office?"

"I'll head home."

"Okay, I'll drop the kids off with Karen and let her know that you won't be too long behind me."

"That works. But I'm bringing work home."

"Of course, you are." That was part of being a lawyer. There was never enough time in a single day to finish everything that needed to be done at the office, *but thankfully,* because he and Mary had both become lawyers they were married today. They may otherwise never have reunited. Ian and Mary were by chance, representing opposing parties in a wrongful termination lawsuit when they unexpectedly met in court, after not seeing each other since high school. Ian was defending the employer through his insurance coverage, while Mary was representing the plaintiff, a former employee of Ian's client. He and Mary got married two years later and despite the complications of life in general, and Elizabeth in particular, they had a respectful and fun marriage. Ian couldn't be happier with anyone else. He loved Mary today as much as he loved her when they were infatuated kids in high school, and even farther back to when they first met as fifth graders in elementary school.

Ian had always loved Mary. And he knew that she felt the same way about him. They were soulmates from the very beginning and he felt confident that they would die as soulmates. They were completely compatible, and regardless of life challenges, they both willingly accommodated each other without complaint.

Ian eyeballed the traffic as he waited to pull out of the parking lot. "So, how long do you think you'll be? Maybe an hour from now you'll be home?"

"Your guess is as good as mine, Ian." Mary's distracted comment warned Ian that she was working on her laptop right now, getting a jump start on her evening workload, while she was waiting on the tires and chatting with him. Finding time to actually get the evening workload done once they got home was always the tricky part of the equation because they were kept so busy with their parenting obligations that included maintaining their own household and also managing Jenny's household. Plus, they had four horses and a pony, a number of goats, an old rabbit, some chickens, various birds, two pigs, and a number of cats and dogs.

"I'll let you get back to whatever you're working on…" Ian eased into the heavy traffic with another glance at the truck's digital clock. He might be able to still make his meeting if the hand-off at home went quickly. "I'll probably stay late at the office tonight. Can you get dinner started and barn chores done without me?"

"Sure." Mary's voice distractedly came through the phone. "When you drop the kids off with Karen, can you tell Jenny and Ricky to get the barn chores started?"

"Yep." Ian chuckled at what his wife rolled downhill. He had no doubt that when he finally made it home tonight, the chores would be done, and dinner would be ready. Mary was one of the most capable women he had ever known. But Jenny and Ricky were also pretty good about helping out with the barn chores.

Ian dropped the kids at home with Karen, he gave his four-year-old daughter, Skylar, a quick hello, he ordered the two adult kids to start barn chores, then he quickly returned to his office to slip into the shareholders' meeting only ten minutes late.

****

When he finally came home later that night, Mary met him at the front door.

"Hi there, frazzled baby-daddy… crazy day, huh?"

Ian chuckled at her greeting and kissed her hello. "Did the barn chores get done?"

"They did." Mary returned his hello kiss. "I've got dinner ready for you. The kids and I have eaten."

"How about a glass of wine?" Ian closed the door behind him as his two young kids clamored into the entryway to greet him with noisy squeals of excitement.

"Daddy's home!" Skylar jumped into his arms as Ian handed his briefcase to Mary.

"Hey, cupcake… how are you today?" She was barely older today than Jenny was when she had her pool accident. It was a comparison that always came to Ian's mind these days. She was precocious and silly, intelligent, and stubborn. She was a lot like her older sister at this age, but mentally, she was moving beyond where Jenny was at this age. Ian gave her a kiss and a big squeeze hello. He absolutely adored her.

"I'm bigger today, daddy." She wrapped her arms around Ian's neck and happily gave him a silly kiss in return to his fatherly greeting. "Because I helped mommy in the barn tonight."

"You did?" Ian shifted her in his arms. "What did you do for mommy?"

"I turned the water off."

Ian chuckled at that. "Well, I guess that was helpful enough."

"Hi daddy!" Philip waited by his side for his fatherly greeting. "I helped her, too, daddy. I pushed the hay into the hay nets and pulled the string tight so mommy could hang the nets up for the horses to eat their hay."

"Well, that *was* a big help for mommy, Philip." Ian tousled his son's hair. He was a lot like Ian at this age. Responsible, playful; obedient and curious. Ian adored him as much as he adored his girls.

"They both helped me." Mary stood patiently by his side watching the children's' greetings.

Philip kept talking. "But Ellie didn't help mommy. She was bad because she wouldn't listen to mommy when mommy told her to stop stomping in the water from the hose." Philip added to his tattle-telling in a conspiratorial voice. "My sister had to yell at her to stop splashing in the water but Ellie was being bad and she did a big jump in the water and got mommy's pants all wet. Mommy had to put her in time out and Ellie kicked and screamed and said she hates mommy. And my sister told Ellie that Santa Clause won't come if she doesn't stop being a bad girl. But Ellie said she didn't care and then my sister started crying."

It was always a little weird for Ian when he thought about his two youngest children being siblings to Jenny – his oldest child and Ellie's mother.

Jenny's childhood felt like a lifetime ago and now that she was well into her twenties, Jenny seemed so much older than Ian's two youngest kids. Except emotionally and mentally, Jenny didn't seem that much older than them at all.

"It sounds like Jenny and your mom had their hands full today. I hope you two didn't add to the trouble…"

"We were good, daddy." Philip answered him in a serious voice. "And mommy hugged my sister and told her it would be okay. So, she stopped crying."

Ian glanced at Mary to give her a silent thank you. She was an amazing step-mother to his special-needs daughter – a better mother than Jenny's biological mother.

Skylar joined the conversation. "And I told Ellie, I'm not being bad like her because I want Santa Clause to come. So, I'm being a good girl."

Ian smiled at that. "As long as you weren't teasing Ellie." He set his daughter down and moved his attention onto his wife. "I'm afraid that Ellie's going to be as difficult to raise as her mother was, but for different reasons. I also fear that I don't have the energy anymore to deal with all that."

"I know." Mary nodded at his concern. "She is definitely more challenging than our two kids. And Elizabeth doesn't help considering how she always lets Ellie get away with everything, including her tantrums. And, she encourages her oppositional behavior."

Ian completely agreed with Mary's assessment of Elizabeth's parenting style. Elizabeth never backed Ian and Mary up when it came to raising Ellie, and she was not a disciplinarian – at all. She allowed Ellie to do whatever she wanted, whenever she wanted. Manageable bedtimes were disregarded on Elizabeth's overnights, bad table manners were ignored, tantrums were rewarded with bribery, and in a contrary way, Elizabeth encouraged Ellie to stand up for herself – even when that meant saying no to parental authority – including Jenny's timid parenting… *like who did this five-year-old think she was, getting sassy and stomping her foot down in protest, defiantly saying no to all of them?* It drove Ian crazy.

When Elizabeth and Ian were still married and raising Jenny together, Elizabeth did the same thing with Jenny. She never said no to her – and she'd get Jenny to do what she wanted by threatening her with… *when your daddy comes home…* which used to drive Ian nuts. Like he was supposed to be the mean parent so she could be the nice parent. Elizabeth was now doing the same thing with Ellie – she was casting herself as the nice grandparent, so Ian and Mary came off as the mean grandparents.

"By the way, guess who called me today?" Mary turned away from their chaotic greeting in the hallway to step into the kitchen to microwave a plate of food for Ian. "Wally…." She glanced over her shoulder to catch Ian's reaction to the change in conversation.

"*Kick the can Wally*?" He was Ian's arch nemesis all the way back into grade school, because Wally had always liked Mary, and Ian knew it.

Mary nodded and continued with her story. "Completely out of the blue, he called..." They hadn't seen him in years. Not since they all ran into each other at their last high school reunion about eight years ago – right after Ian and Mary started dating again.

"No kidding?" Ian followed Mary into the kitchen. "Why is Wally calling you all of a sudden?" When they were kids growing up in their tight neighborhood community, they had all played together in the hills and streets, and in the summer time they would stay out after dark, long after the street lights came on, and one of their favorite summer time games was *Kick the Can*. And Wally was always there for the game, kicking the can and flirting with Mary – openly challenging Ian's hold on her.

Mary set the plate of food in her hand onto the clear tray in the microwave to start it cooking. "He's expanding his research on childhood brain injuries and he wants to meet Jenny. He remembered you talking about her at the reunion. He was surprised to learn that she's now married with a child of her own, which goes right to the point of his latest research. He's studying how people who got childhood brain injuries are functioning as adults. And he's incorporating in his research the functionality of children of cognitively impaired adults."

Ian slid out of his suit jacket and dropped it over the back of a kitchen chair. "Why didn't he call me for permission to talk to her?" He loosened his tie so he could pull it out from under the collar of his shirt. "You'd think that a doctor would recognize that consent for a cognitively impaired adult to be included as a data subject in his research project would have to come directly from her father, not her step-mother."

Mary chuckled at his self-righteous question. "Well, he called my office phone, maybe because it was easier for him to find my number on-line than it was to find your direct number on-line."

Ian smirked at that. "Or maybe he just wanted an excuse to call you…" He chuckled at what he was thinking as he added to his teasing observation. "Because my firm's number is on-line too, and it's not that hard to get ahold of me. All he had to do was leave his number with the receptionist…"

Ian went to their wine chiller to pull a bottle of wine out of it. "Who would pass the message onto my secretary…" He reached for the bottle opener. "Who would give the message to my associate, who would ultimately pass it onto me buried beneath a lot of other more important messages… which is why she will then have to follow up with me the following week to make sure that I returned all of my calls. And it's possible that she might not even give me the message without first calling the person herself, to make sure that it's a call I will want to take."

Mary laughed at the complexity he was outlining. "So obviously, much easier for him to connect with you through me. Because my receptionist immediately transferred the call directly to my desk where I picked the call up myself, and instantly started chatting with Wally."

Mary shared an office space with two other attorneys, both of whom were law school friends. The small firm arrangement meant that she made less money than Ian who was a top earner at his firm, but it also meant that she was under less pressure, and she had more freedom with her daily schedule. Which is why she would usually take the kids to their doctor appointments.

Ian poured them both a glass of wine. "So, Wally wants to interview Jenny as a data subject in his research?" He handed Mary her wine glass and lifted his own to his mouth. "Why would I let him do that? As Jenny's conservator tasked with maintaining her privacy, I am not at all inclined to let him talk to her."

Mary shrugged off his counter opinion as she offered more details about Wally's request. "Actually, he also wants to follow Ellie too, now that he knows about her. And Ricky."

Ian huffed. "I don't want *any* of them becoming a curious line-item entry in a voyeuristic article disguised as an analytical piece, written by a kid I knew in grade school who thought he was being funny when he scorned me with his *Loser Powers* moniker."

Mary laughed at what Ian pointed out to her. "I'd forgotten about that."

But Ian hadn't forgotten. "And then there was his *Lover Powers* taunt..."

Mary chuckled at his recollection.

Wally spent a lot of time in high school mocking Ian's love for Mary like it was nothing more than a teenage infatuation. And that used to really bug Ian.

He huffed at his own memories and fell into a perfect mimic of Wally's teasing. "Someday *Loser Powers* she's going to recognize your *Lover Powers* as being nothing more than a bumbling, immature and selfish lust for her body. And then she's going to find herself a real man – someone like me – to fall in love with."

Mary laughed at Ian's condescending mimic. "And look how you proved him wrong." She opened a drawer to get a knife and fork out for Ian. "Not only are your lover powers pretty damn smooth and not at all bumbling, but there's also never been any other man in my life who mattered as much to me as you. So, Wally was wrong on all accounts."

Ian tapped his wine glass into hers in silent appreciation of her compliment. "Likewise, for me. You're pretty damn good in bed, yourself, Mary Edwards, and you've always been the only woman that mattered to me."

"As your raunchy, promiscuous and dismissive past with other women might suggest..." Mary brought that point up as a further tease.

Ian chuckled with self-deprecating humor. "Guilty as charged." In college, he had become quite the ladies' man, and he had definitely taken advantage of that before he got married, and before he reconnected with Mary. By his own admission, he slid in and out of relationships way too easily back then.

"So..." He humbly accepted Mary's observation. "I guess there's some truth in Wally's taunting when it comes to my previous immaturity and self-serving, bumbling love pursuits."

Mary chuckled at his honesty and returned to the point of their earlier conversation. "I'm sure Wally will anonymize the identity of the participants in his study, so, why not let him meet them? I mean, he's an MD and a PhD for goodness sake! He out doctors both of us… so that should earn him some respect!"

"Damn it…" Ian sipped his wine as he teasingly recognized Wally's academic achievements. "Regardless of his uber-education, it just doesn't feel right to me, to let *Polly Wally* turn my kid into his next research subject. And I don't want him getting access to Ellie either. Because the road in front of her is going to be tough enough when her friends meet her parents and she starts realizing how different they are to her friends' parents. And that in itself is going to make her journey harder than it should be. I know this for fact, because I was witness to how mean kids could be when Jenny was little. And Ellie doesn't need to grow up knowing that on top of all that, she was a data subject in some freaky study about a vulnerable population that doesn't get much respect from the rest of the world. I mean, someday Ellie is going to be old enough to pick up Wally's article and read all about herself. And I have to wonder if that's something we want for her?"

"Daddy…" Jenny knocked on the internal kitchen door that was closed between the two houses.

"Come in, Jennifer…" Ian opened the door for her and Jenny stepped into the room with them. She was a beautiful, sweet, funny, and determined young lady. As a little girl, she was a difficult child to raise because the brain injury made her emotionally unstable, and the oxygen deprivation made it difficult for her to process information. But these days she was doing just fine, and Ian loved her as much as he loved his other two kids. She was special in his heart because for many years she was the only reason he got up in the morning to face another day. "What's up, buttercup?"

"You and me and the birds and bees…" She giggled with her normal return of his tender greeting before telling him what was wrong. "Cinderella is being bad. She won't listen to me, daddy. But I didn't spank her because that's mean. And I don't want to be a mean mommy. I want to be nice like you. But she's being mean to me. I told her it was bedtime. It's seven-thirty. But she won't stop playing on her tablet and she told me to go away. And then she said she doesn't like me. She said gammy says she doesn't have to listen to me. But I want her to listen to me, daddy, because I'm her mother. But she hit me when I told her she has to do what I say. And Ricky won't help me."

Gammy was what Ellie called Elizabeth, and it burned Ian that Elizabeth would allow Ellie to believe that she could say no to her mother – *ever* – because it was hard enough for Jenny to try and reason with Ellie, who was a very bright and stubborn child.

Ian glanced through the open kitchen door, into Jenny's flat to see if he could see Ricky or Ellie in the living room of their attached home. "What in the hell happened to your kitchen, Jennifer? It's a mess!"

"I know, daddy." Jenny gave him an apologetic shrug. "Cinderella spilled her dinner on the floor. It's spaghetti leftovers that Mary gave us from last night. And Ricky won't clean it up. It's his turn to cleanup. I cleaned up last night. But he won't do it tonight because he's playing his game. He said I have to clean it because I don't have a game to play. But it's not my turn."

"Ricky?" Ian hollered out to him. He could see the boy on the couch playing a video game. Ellie was sprawled out on the carpeted floor in front of him, surrounded by various toys and stuffed animals.

"Ellie…" Ian called out to her too, as he stepped through Jenny's kitchen, into their living room. "How about picking your toys up now and getting ready for bed?" He moved a glass of milk that was dangerously close to being knocked off of the coffee table.

"I don't want to go to bed, poppee… I'm still playing."

"Well, it's bedtime. So, it's time to stop playing and start cleaning up your mess. Okay? And when your toys are picked up, you need to get your pajamas on and brush your teeth. And next time your mother tells you to do something, I want you listen to her and do what she tells you. Can you do that for me?"

Ellie didn't answer him, so Ian let it go for the moment, so he could move his frayed attention onto Ricky instead. "Hey…" He tapped him on the leg.

Ricky distractedly glanced up at him. "I'm winning."

"That's great, Ricky, but Jenny said it's your turn to clean up after Ellie. So, I need you to stop playing your game so you can get the kitchen cleaned up. Come on… it's your turn to do the cleanup. So, be the man that I know you can be, and help Jenny out a little bit. Okay?"

Ricky didn't take his eyes off of the television screen. "I'm playing my game. Jenny can do the cleanup. She doesn't have a game to play."

"Nope." Ian took the control panel from Ricky's hands.

"Hey!" Ricky yelled in protest and tried to grab it back from him. "That's my controller!"

"Nope!" Ian held it away from him. "If today is your cleanup day, you need to do the cleanup. So, that's what I need you to do right now."

"That's not nice, Ian. You grabbed that away from me."

"And how nice are you being to Jenny, Ricky?" Ian had established the rotating schedule for the adult kids a long time ago as a way of helping them stay on top of their parenting chores without them having a fight every night over who had to do what. In many ways, they were still kids themselves, though they were both in their mid-twenties. "Come on… it'll only take a few minutes to clean up the mess while Jenny helps Ellie get ready for bed. Then you can go back to playing your game."

"But I have to finish it now. I can't pause it."

"You want me to turn it off for you?" Ian stood firm against Ricky's objection.

"No!" Ricky yelled back at him. "Don't do that!"

"I won't turn it off if you do what I'm telling you to do." Ian held the control panel away from Ricky's reach. "But if you don't get up right now, I'm turning it off. One… two…"

"That's mean, Ian. And you can't be mean to me."

"Three…" Ian stood firm. "Four…" The countdown always offered the adult kids, both of whom had short fuses, time to throttle back from their current trajectory so they could catch their breath and hopefully reset the course of their behavior so they would do what was expected of them. The few extra minutes was usually all that Ian needed to regain control over them. If he got to ten, the game would be turned off – and Ricky knew that. "Five…"

Getting the adult children to do what he wanted them to do was often more difficult than getting the little children to comply with his orders. Because truth be known, Ricky was probably stronger than Ian at this point; he was also heavier and taller, and both adult children were very strong willed. So, compliance mostly came down to them respecting Ian's authority, and if that was ever truly challenged by Ricky, Ian wasn't quite sure how he would be able to maintain control over him.

"Remember when you told me before Ellie was born that you would have to clean up her toys when you wanted to play video games? Remember how you told me you would do that? So, that's what I want you to do, Ricky. Right now. Pick her toys up and clean the kitchen mess, and then you can go back to playing your game. Show me how adult you are…"

"Okay, Ian." Ricky thankfully gave into Ian's fatherly scolding. "Don't say number ten..." He dropped to his knees and reached for Ellie's toy basket.

"You have to help me pick up your toys, Cinderella. Ian said so." He scooped up her little fairy figurines and tossed them into the basket.

"Give those back to me, daddy!" Ellie screamed at his intervention. "I don't want to pick my toys up."

"Ellie…" Ian levelled an intimidating stare her direction. "Come on… help your dad. Otherwise, we're going to take your tablet away for a few days while you think about minding us… Right, Ricky?"

"Right, Ian." He turned to give him a high five that Ian returned.

Jenny backed him up, too. "That's right, daddy. We're going to take Cinderella's tablet away from her because she's a bad girl. And you can't hit me anymore, Cinderella. Poppee said so, because that's not nice."

"Hey, Jenny don't tell her she's a bad girl." Ian softly corrected Jennifer's scolding with a parental tutorial. "Ellie's always a good girl," he glanced his granddaughter's direction, "even when you aren't acting nice. Right, Ellie?" He gave her an encouraging smile and returned his attention to Jennifer. "There's a difference between being a bad girl, and acting bad, Jenny. Like I've said to you. You're a good person even when you're having a tantrum, you're just having a bad, out-of-control moment. Right?"

Jennifer nodded at his instruction. "Right. Daddy." She moved her focus onto her daughter. "Act like a good girl, Cinderella… not a bad girl." Jenny followed Ian's lead with a redirected scolding that she took further on her own. "When you hit me and don't mind me, that's acting bad even though you're a good girl. And if you act bad, I'm going to take your tablet away from you until you can act good again. Right daddy?"

"Okay, poppee…" Ellie tossed her tablet onto the couch to help her dad with the toy clean up. "I'll act like a good girl, mommy."

"Thank you, Ellie." Ian exhaled with relief as he stood over his granddaughter and son-in-law, watching their cleanup effort with visible enforcement authority. "And I want you to stop hitting your mother, Ellie. You got that? No hitting. We don't hit you… and you don't hit us."

"Okay, poppee. I won't hit her again."

"Thank you." Ian moved his attention back to Jennifer. "Why don't you get Ellie's pajamas and I'll help you get her ready for bed?" If he didn't stay and help Jenny, he knew that chaos would return and he'd ultimately be called back in here. Ellie would throw a tantrum, Jenny would fall apart in despair, and Ricky would return to his video game and completely tune-out the domestic distraction.

"Okay, daddy." Jenny left the living room to fetch Ellie's pajamas as Mary joined Ian from the kitchen in the main house.

"Your dinner is warm. Why don't you let me take over in here, so you can eat and catch your breath? I can wrap this production up on my own."

"Thank you…" Ian stretched with fatigue at Mary's suggested release. "Are our kids already in bed?" The evening obligations felt so much longer these days now that there were little kids in the house. But at least with Mary here to help with the parental obligations, his evenings didn't feel as overwhelming as they did when Ian was a single dad, raising Jenny on his own.

"Yep." Mary shot him a happy smile. There was such a difference in the way the two households functioned. "With night lights on and books in hand. They're waiting for you to read them their bedtime stories. But eat first… and FYI, it's going to be *Go Dog Go* again for Philip, and *Green Eggs and Ham* for Skylar…"

Ian shook his head with amused frustration. His kids made him read those two books practically every night. He could not get them to move onto other books. "Thanks for the warning. I'm ready to toss those two books into the garbage." Last night he read *The Little Engine that Could* to Philip, but Philip still insisted on *Go Dog Go* before he would agree to go to sleep.

"So, where's Elizabeth tonight?" It was Monday night and she was supposed to arrive by 5:00 pm and stay at Jenny's house through Thursday morning to help with Ellie. Ian and Mary covered Thursday through Monday, from whatever time Elizabeth showed up.

"She called Jenny this afternoon to tell her that she was sick. She said she'd come over tomorrow if she was feeling better."

Ian huffed with cynicism that he filled with audible doubt. "It's more likely she's got a date tonight. I'd put money on that if I was a betting man…"

Mary chuckled at his lack of trust in Elizabeth. "Maybe she's honestly sick?"

Ian shook his head with learned disbelief. "Nope. She's either got a date…" He added an alternative possibility. "Or she had a date last night and today she's hung over… Because nobody who is as healthy as Elizabeth, naturally gets sick as often as she's been getting sick lately. I told you when she popped back into our lives that she wouldn't have the attention span to stick around for too long. And my guess is that we're starting to see the unraveling of her unpredictable maternal dedication. I've seen how this kind of obligation works for her in the past and I recognize where we are on her timeline."

Mary nodded at the plausibility of Ian's observation. "You're probably right."

"Mark my words…" Everything that Ian had predicted so far in the past about Elizabeth had come true, and Ian expected that what he was seeing now would also come true. He handed Mary the game controller and gave her a kiss.

In the six years that Elizabeth had been back in Ian's life, Mary had witnessed more than one episode of Elizabeth's excessive drinking. She had tolerated Elizabeth's brazen but unsuccessful attempts at wooing Ian back into her seductive arms. And she had openly pondered, as a mother of little children herself, how Elizabeth could walk out of Jenny's life when she was only four years old, to leave her solely in Ian's hands, rarely seeing her, except for Ian's mandated annual lunch visits.

Nonetheless, Mary stayed neutral tonight when it came to weighing in on Ian's predictions. "Regardless of the reason for her absence tonight," She picked up the half-full glass of milk to take it to the kitchen. "I let Karen know that she'll probably have all three kids again tomorrow."

"Okay." Ian went towards the door between houses to retreat into his own household where at least the evening would feel a bit calmer. "I love how Lizzy keeps raising my daycare bill without any thought or consideration about the cost to me." Ian frowned with his thoughts. "She wants a day off, and poof… I pay for extra day care…"

"Well, fortunately we can afford it." Mary buffered the tension and Ian left her in the kids flat to monitor their evening efforts so he could change out of his work clothes, choke down his dinner before it got cold again, and say goodnight to his own kids before they fell asleep without a story.

"Give me Wally's number tonight," Ian hollered out to her as he stepped out of sight, "And I'll call him tomorrow morning."

Chapter Two

"Hey… *Polly Wally…*" Ian finally connected with Wally Thursday afternoon between meetings and clients. "I hear you've been phoning my wife behind my back… dropping her number into your speed dial… When are you ever going to accept that I indelibly inked her soul a long time ago, and won her devoted loyalty for life? You haven't got a chance in hell with her. So how about doing the dignified thing, and step out of the competition before you make a fool of yourself?" He chuckled with the tease that had started years before when they were both trying to woo Mary into their arms.

Wally laughed with Ian's joking. "That's just like you, *Loser Powers...* always trying to flaunt your non-existent, adolescent *Lover Powers*. But just so you know, I've caught a few good fish of my own over the years… so keep that in mind while you're boasting about your immature successes. You aren't the only one with persuasive lover powers, you know. I've got a few slick moves of my own."

Ian chuckled with him. "Fair enough…"

Wally was an okay guy and his wife was attractive enough. She was a therapist who seemed like a smart lady. Not that Ian really knew her as an adult. But their paths had crossed in high school. Betty Jo was a year behind all of them in school, but she was in band like Ian and Mary, so Ian had faint recollections of her from back then, though she had never really moved in his crowd. She was a wall flower who was easily overlooked in a room full of friends, and like a lot of other teens who were too cool for their own good, Ian had certainly paid her no attention. And Mary's only recollection of Betty Jo from high school was that she played second clarinet in band, which meant she wasn't good enough to play first, and she hung out with a giggly group of goofy girls that rarely mixed with Mary's more sophisticated girlfriends.

Wally, on the other hand, was always hanging out with them in school because he lived on their street, and he inevitably landed in many of their classes. So, Ian and Mary both shared a lot of memories of him. Wally wasn't someone that Ian would hang out with as an adult. Wally was always a bit nerdish, somewhat boring in personality, slow to read social cues, and desperate to maintain superficial friendships as a way of boosting his own lacking ego.

Ian was more of a ring leader at heart, and he was always quite popular and engaging even at a young age. Admittedly, he was overly self-assured, and somewhat of a cool cat, even though it wasn't intentional on his part. He just knew that people saw him that way and he wasn't going to deny it for the superficial reason of being humble. But it also wasn't something Ian cared about flaunting. He was just being himself... good or bad… this is who he was.

"So, tell me about this study you're doing…" Ian took charge of the phone call, because it wasn't in his nature to give up control. Plus, as a high-powered attorney, he was calling Wally from his office, and he was aware, as was always the case, that time was money, and Ian wasn't one to waste time or money. "Give me the reader's digest version because I've only got about five minutes to give you, and if it's something I might be interested in, I'll listen in greater detail later…"

Wally chuckled off Ian's dismissive request, and eagerly provided more detail than Ian really wanted, but he convincingly explained his intentions for the study, and the benefits that he hoped would be obtained through it, so Ian gave him tentative consent in an effort to wrap the conversation up.

"We'll talk more later when you come by the house. And Ricky's folks will have to weigh in, and so will the two adult kids."

They wrapped up the conversation, and Ian returned his attention to his work.

****

When he came home from work later that night, Ian shared with Mary that he had given Wally tentative consent for the kids to participate in his study. "He'll swing by this weekend to meet them, and I'll explain to them what he's trying to do and we'll let the kids give their own consent."

Mary nodded with surprise. "So, *Polly Wally* gets to use them as data subjects after all, huh?"

"We'll take it one day at a time." Ian added an explanation on Wally's intentions. "He wants to follow the kids over an extended period to observe how they all interact with each other. He's researching how cognitively impaired adults, parent their unimpaired children. Concurrently, he's interested in how unimpaired children thrive in homes where their parents are cognitively challenged."

"Interesting." Mary was working on dinner preparations. "He knows that we help the kids with Ellie, right?"

"He does."

All three of the little kids were playing in the family room in the main house, so Ian went to greet them in there. "How are my kids and grandkid today?"

Ellie pushed her way into his arms before the other two could get their first. "Hi poppee! I was a good girl today."

Ian chuckled at that. "Well, good for you, Ellie. That makes poppee very happy."

"I was good too, daddy!" Skylar reached for him to pick her up.

"Except Skylar peed her pants today, daddy." Philip hovered for attention.

"You did?" Ian frowned at his daughter. "What happened?"

Skylar fell into an adorable pout. "Karen took us on a long walk and I had to go pee pee! But we were too far away. I couldn't hold it inside me."

Ian chuckled at that. "Why didn't you just go outside? Wouldn't that have been better than getting your pants wet?"

"I didn't want a snake to bite my bottom, daddy. Philip said it would eat me."

"Philip…" Ian shot him a teasing scowl and Philip laughed like crazy.

"I scared my little sister, daddy. It was funny!" He fell on the floor with laughter and added a silly confession. "And then I went pee outside."

Ian shook his head with disapproval. "Well, it's easier for boys to pee outside, than girls. And I hope you were polite about it." He moved his attention back to Skylar. "If you have to pee outside just look where you're going before you squat down. And don't squat in tall grass." He gave them each a hello hug and kiss before returning his attention to Mary.

"I also called Ricky's parents today after I talked with Wally and they're fine with Ricky's participation in the study. And also, Ellie's participation."

"That's good." Mary went to the dining room to set the table. "Does Elizabeth get to give consent?"

Ian huffed. "Not a chance, because she has no legal ground to withhold consent for any of them." He finished setting the table for Mary and called out to the kids. "Dinner's ready. Go wash your hands and faces guys."

Mary stepped back into the room with two plates of food. "Ellie, can you please go into your house and get your mom and dad for dinner?"

"Okay memaw…" Ellie left to go to her house to bring her parents back for dinner. Most nights when Elizabeth wasn't there, the two families ate together.

****

Wally arrived at Ian's house Saturday evening and parked in the driveway between the house and the barn.

"Hey… *Polly Wally…*" Ian greeted him with the old nickname as his friend got out of his car.

"*Loser Powers…*" Wally returned the favor. "How you doing?"

"Ahh… no." Ian smirked at his name calling. "Look around you, dude… Does it look like I'm a loser to you?"

He confidently waved his arm towards his beautifully landscaped home, his well-maintained barn with its attached covered riding arena, and the fenced in fields, all of which were situated on his nicely-manicured ten-acre farm.

Mary joined them from the house and Ian turned to watch her approach. When she was a few feet away from them, he reached out to her and when his fingertips connected with hers, he clasped his palm around her hand and drew her closer to his body. "Definitely more like *Powerful Powers* these days…"

He wrapped his arm around Mary to tuck her under his shoulder in a secure hold, and shot a confident grin at Wally. "And that's in addition to *Lover Powers…*"

His eyes returned to Mary with an intimate twinkle. "Right?" The arm he had wrapped around her shoulders slid down her torso until his palm landed on her mid-drift where he squeezed her flush against his own hip so he could slow kiss her lips with a seductive affirmation for Wally.

Mary held his stare with a longing gaze when he ended the kiss. "Definitely, *Lover Powers…*" She shot him a happy grin as Wally laughed off his boastful claim.

"I didn't think you had this kind of staying power in you back then. And I definitely didn't expect you to rise to this level, Ian. You were more of a simple guy. Easy come, easy go. You're happy if everybody else is happy. No big aspirations, no need to succeed. Just leave me alone and stay out of my way so I can do my own thing…"

Ian chuckled at that. "Well, you don't always know what you have inside you until you're challenged to find it."

Mary joined their conversation. "And he's still a simple guy who is happy if everyone else is happy…" She held her hand out to Wally. "Nice to see you again."

"Likewise." Wally shook her hand with enthusiasm. "I just don't understand why you're still hanging out with this guy…"

They all chuckled at his teasing until Ian took charge of the conversation to stop the silly banter. "Let me show you around, then I'll introduce you to the kids…" He gestured towards the barn and stepped that direction. "Jenny and Ricky have both learned how to care for their animals. And they both show their horses in Special Olympics… in fact, that's how they met."

"Interesting." Wally followed behind him as Ian led the way to their barn. "How long have they been married?"

"Just over six years." Ian opened the barn doors to show him the horse stalls.

"And how's their marriage working for them?" Wally stood in the doorway and looked around. "Nice place."

"Thanks." Ian smiled at his compliment. "They seem happy enough. Like most marriages, they have their ups and downs. But Mary and I help them navigate the rough patches."

"Ricky's become obsessed with his gaming lately…" Mary added to Ian's observation with more truth than Ian wanted to admit. "So that can be a problem." She pointed that out with an additional observation. "And Jenny can get overwhelmed sometimes by the parenting challenges…"

"Well, Ellie can be a handful." Ian neutralized Mary's comment because he didn't want Wally jumping to any conclusions about the kids' marriage or their parenting abilities.

Mary added more to her summary. "And they have their fair share of arguments…"

Ian frowned at what she added. "A lot of couples argue, Mary. But for the most part, they're managing just fine. Better than I ever thought possible when Jenny first told us about the two of them wanting to get married. And better than a lot of *normal* couples who can't keep their marriage together for more than a year or two."

Mary shot him a hurt scowl and Ian winced as he realized how close his comment had swung home. He often forgot that Mary had a failed first marriage, too. Like Ian, she was briefly married after law school, but unlike Ian, she and her husband parted amicably during the second year of their marriage, without ever having children.

Ian shrugged an apology to her and moved on. "They do a great job with barn chores without much supervision." He added the extra information about the kids to erase his thoughtless gaffe towards his wife. "We can trust them completely to care for all the animals that we've acquired over the years. As long as there's nothing too out of the ordinary for them to think through, they've pretty much got the routine animal husbandry down."

"True…" Mary nodded at Ian's summation. "With minor supervision…"

They were all suddenly distracted by a black Mercedes that rolled down the driveway and stopped close to where they were standing outside the barn.

Elizabeth parked her car and opened the driver's door. "Hi guys!" She happily waved at them as she exposed a beautifully sculpted leg and small shapely foot adorned with a sexy red sandal and bright red toenails.

"What is she doing here today?" Mary watched her climb out of her car like an actress in a seductive movie.

"Good question." Ian's eyes guardedly followed her figure as she stood before them and closed the driver's side door. She was wearing skimpy shorts and a body clinging top that hugged her chest and micro waist like she was a perfectly formed *Barbie* doll. All of her curves and her flawless flesh were nicely on display for them as she turned and waved again. "I forgot my jacket here!" She swiped at a fly with her perfectly manicured hand with its red painted nails as it buzzed near the flesh of her exposed abdomen. "I'm so forgetful sometimes!" She shot them a flirty smile

Ian shook his head with a frown. “I know that’s not her only jacket, so why can’t she wait until Monday to pick it up?”

“She wouldn’t even need the jacket…” Mary backed Ian’s disapproval with a frustrated frown. “If she dressed more appropriately, like maybe in a sweatshirt and long pants with real shoes instead of the midriff exposing shirt and almost *not-there* shorts.”

Ian smirked at Mary’s observation as Elizabeth crossed the driveway on her way to the kids’ flat. She frequently disregarded the agreement that Ian worked out with her years ago that she wasn’t supposed to come by his house at all on the weekends. Those days were supposed to belong exclusively to Mary unless Elizabeth pre-arranged to have a weekend or holiday. It just wasn’t fair to Mary to have Elizabeth constantly coming over here.

She stepped back into view a few minutes later with a jacket folded neatly across her arm. “Got it!” She called out to them in a giggly voice as she returned to her parked car. “Have a fun evening!”

“Wow…” Wally came alive beside them as Elizabeth opened her car door. “Who the hell is that babe?” He couldn’t take his eyes off of her as she slid her barely covered bottom onto the sleek leather upholstery of the driver’s seat.

Ian turned his direction. “My ex-wife…” His focus moved onto Mary with an apologetic shrug. It was totally like Elizabeth to find an excuse to come over here on the weekend.

Ian returned his attention to Wally. “Jennifer’s mother.”

His eyes returned to Mary with an intimate eye exchange that Wally didn’t observe because his undivided focus remained locked on the black Mercedes that was now cruising down Ian’s driveway.

“Is she married, single, or dating anyone?”

Ian moved his eyes onto her retreating car. “As far as I know, she hasn’t permanently hooked anyone in for a while… but she’s always fishing…”

“God, she's beautiful. What a knock-out. How did you ever manage to talk yourself into giving her up? That had to be one of the hardest choices you’ve ever made for yourself. I can’t even imagine. Because I would bite onto her hook in a heartbeat… even if it hurt to bite down.”

“No, man, shut your eyes!” Ian turned a horrified expression on him. “You do not want any part of that. Don't let yourself even think about going there. Not even in your head. That enticing body is nothing more than seductive gift wrap, hiding some very expensive and addictive poison. She's a train wreck, man, and if you let her get under your skin you will live to regret it for the rest of your life. She's chaos, Wally, no matter how good she feels under your body."

"Really, Ian?" Mary exhaled in protest. "That's your wave off?"

"What is that supposed to mean?" Ian defensively turned his attention on Mary but all she returned to him was an angry scowl.

"Train wreck or not… what an eyeful." Wally couldn't keep his eyes from following Elizabeth's car as it left the driveway for the main road into town. "She's the most beautiful chaos I've ever seen. She's gorgeous, man, and I would give her a full pass to get under my skin… and I would take that ride with her all the way to hell and back!"

"No, man!" Ian gasped with disapproval. "You don't mean that. Turn your head away, right now! Because that beautiful train ride to hell and back is not worth the price that you'll pay for it. There is no passing Go with her and no getting out of jail for free. She will roll your ass straight into purgatory for the rest of your days on earth."

Ian manually grabbed Wally's shoulders and physically turned him away from her. "She will ruin your life, dude. Forget you even saw her today."

Mary huffed with disgust. "It's amazing to me, Ian, how a calculated attorney like yourself can have such a loose tongue when you surely have the good sense to know when to censor your thoughts and speak with caution! How do you ever manage to control yourself in court?"

"What is wrong with what I just said, Mary?" Ian turned to her in protest. "She *is* a train wreck who will drag his ass straight into purgatory!"

Wally chuckled at the defensive nature of Ian's retort. "Well, she looks like a joyride into heaven, if you ask me. That does not look like a trip into hell." He smiled between the two of them and laughed at his own joking before it slowly caught up to him that nobody was laughing with him.

"I'm sorry…" He stopped himself from going on and apologized with sudden embarrassment. "Obviously I was just horsing around with you guys, acting like we were all back in high school, playing around with the old rivalries..."

Ian shook his head at him. “You’re married, dude. You shouldn’t even be thinking like that.”

Wally huffed off his insult with defensive amusement. “And now I’m getting lectured by a guy who’s on marriage number two?”

Ian scowled at his charge without offering a defense for himself. Then he added to his scolding because it wasn’t in his nature to hold himself back. “Just a reminder to sit on it, next time you get the urge to talk like a horny school kid. Especially in front of Mary, because that was just impolite, dude… drooling over my ex- in front of her.”

“You’re right. It was.” Wally offered a remorseful apology to both of them. He had always been socially awkward as a kid and apparently little had changed for him as an adult. “I’m sorry, Mary.”

“Okay…” Ian tried to take charge of the rest of the conversation before the day got completely away from him. He did not want Mary hurt by Wally’s uncensored infatuation, or his own blundering tongue that had already let more out of his mouth than it should have. Mary was right to wonder why he didn’t stop himself more often. He repeatedly let his tongue roll too freely and it rarely benefitted anyone when he did that. And this particular time it was obviously offensive to Mary, though Ian had no specific recollection of what he just said.

His eyes took Mary in with that realization, and he shot her a quizzical smile. She had long ago accepted that Elizabeth was a knock-out. And Ian never insulted Mary by trying to convince her otherwise. Elizabeth was born with the kind of good looks that easily turned heads when she walked into a room. As Wally had just observed, Elizabeth was gorgeous. She was blessed with a perfect body, the kind of innocently seductive face that every girl seemingly wanted and every guy seemingly fell head over heels in love with. She also had the most enviable head full of thick wavy locks that one couldn’t help but drag their fingers through, if they were lucky enough to get that opportunity.

But Ian also recognized that Elizabeth’s undisputable beauty was superficial, and once you got that misleading quality out of your system, there was really nothing left to love about her. Elizabeth’s most notable traits included her constant need to find a better guy; her egotistical, selfish, and demanding attitude; her unreliable and incapable presence, her self-preserving behavior, and her misguided sense of entitlement. There was really very little about Elizabeth that was redeeming or endearing. Plus, she was somewhat of a drunk, which might be amusing the first time she got drunk with you, but after that, it was just plain annoying. Ian regretted ever saying hello to her the first time they met – and he wished with all his heart that she had never returned to his life.

"I'm going back to the house now to check in on the kids." Mary abruptly took charge of her own day by briskly walking away from Ian before he could call her back without Wally noticing his effort. And regardless of a real desire to draw her back into his arms, Ian could not make himself do that in front of his old nemesis. As much as Ian would like to console Mary and remind her how beautiful she was to him, he did not want to acknowledge in front of Wally what had surely become apparent to him – that Mary was mad at Ian and before the day was over, he would need to make amends to her.

Ian could recognize analytically that Wally's drooling over Elizabeth wasn't his fault, but he knew that Mary would nonetheless lay the blame on him. Ian had accepted years ago that Mary lacked self-esteem. She saw herself as an average plain Jane who at best, had an okay figure that had subsequently hosted two back-to-back pregnancies. And at worst, the wear and tear on her body left her feeling more matronly these days, than sexy. But that wasn't how Ian saw her.

Contrary to Mary's negative self-assessment, Ian had always found Mary to be absolutely stunning. There was a quiet beauty about her that glowed from within; it was a subtle attractiveness, not splashy like Elizabeth's, but it was far more alluring and seductive than Elizabeth's shallow offerings. And unlike Elizabeth, Mary was extremely competent in her career and completely capable in her personal life. She had a gentle and accommodating soul, she was patient and insightful, and she had always been as self-less as Elizabeth was selfish.

In every way imaginable, Mary was accomplished and fun and she had a wonderful personality. She knew what she wanted, and she wasn't afraid to speak her mind. She could stand up for herself, and take life on without insecurity – despite her own self-consciousness. Mary was a full package deal and Ian wouldn't trade her for all of the Elizabeths in the world. She was just that special to him.

But none of what Ian saw in Mary ever truly resonated with her, and sadly, that had always been the case. Since the first day Ian met Mary, she had lacked confidence in herself. She saw herself through a critical lens that only saw her own flaws and short-comings. She was blessed with the kind of self-critiquing mind that could index every mistake she'd ever made, and catalog in painful detail every insecurity she harbored.

Ian had prided himself lately, on the fact that she had mostly learned to accept that she was truly beautiful in his eyes; but today was an unwanted reminder of what Ian had learned over the years, beginning with their earliest days together – Mary's insecurities were always within reach, just below her skin, and sometimes he was the reason for her noticing them.

Ian desperately wanted to go after her to soften the blow of Wally's infatuation, but he couldn't leave Wally without finishing his property tour and introducing him to the kids. So, he quickly wound up the walk-about so he could take Wally to the kids' flat and hurriedly introduce them, then he left Wally alone with the kids so he could seek out his wife.

"Hey… where are you?" Ian found her in the main bathroom, bathing their kids in a tub full of bubbles.

"How come you left in such a hurry?" He reached for a bath towel for Skylar as she stood to get out of the tub but Mary made her sit back down.

"Where's Wally?" She dodged his inquiry by asking Ian a question of her own as she ran a washcloth over Skylar's face.

Ian let her guide the conversation to give himself a chance to gage her temper. "He's in Jenny's house, interacting with the kids and Ellie."

"Great." Her tone was clipped and judgmental. "So, he's doing what he came here to do."

"Yep." Ian hovered behind her, not exactly sure how to fix what had mistakenly gone wrong between them. "And what are *we* doing now?"

Mary huffed in answer. "Obviously, *I'm* bathing the kids, Ian. I have no idea what *you're* doing here, so why don't you tell me?"

Ian consciously made a decision not to react to her baiting sarcasm because he recognized it as being nothing more than a shield for hurt feelings. "I see that you're bathing the kids. And you're astute enough to know that I'm here inquiring about your sudden departure because I'm concerned that you might have hurt feelings." He knew that was the reason without her saying so, but he wanted to hear Mary express in her own words what was troubling her, because that's where he would find his best response to her anger.

She let out an annoyed huff without turning to look at him. "Yep. It didn't seem like you needed me out there for your ego pumping, *boy's club*, show and tell with Wally. And the kids were in the house by themselves, waiting for bath time. So, I went where I was needed more – *where I would be appreciated* – as opposed to staying outside where my presence wasn't wanted at all, and was perhaps in fact, unwelcome."

Ian frowned in objection to her underlying attack on him. He knew he deserved it, but that didn't make it easy for him not to respond to her bait. "So, why does it feel like I'm getting the brush off from you? I get that Wally was drooling over Elizabeth, and I recognize how offensive that might be for you, and also how hurtful, but what did I do wrong besides wave him off of her?"

Mary glowered in answer. "Where should I begin, Ian?" She blew out a sarcastic huff and dived right in without waiting for any guidance from him. "How about we start with how good she feels under your body?"

"What?" Ian scowled at her accusation trying to recall what exactly he might have said to make Mary say that. "You're going to have to help me out here…"

Mary did so in a mad voice. "She's chaos *no matter how good she feels under your body?* Gee, Ian, thanks for that visual. Like that's what I want you sharing with our high school friend! How good your ex-wife feels under your body!"

Ian flinched with regret. He *did* remember saying something like that. But not quite the same way that Mary apparently heard it. "I'm sorry. You're right. Those were poorly chosen words though I'm not sure that you actually heard what I thought I actually said."

"Huh!" Mary shot him a hurt glare. "And need I mention how her enticing body can roll your ass to hell and back?"

Ian winced with shame. "*To hell…* Mary. That was the key phrase there. That she'll drag your ass to hell and back."

"Whatever, Ian!" Mary scowled back at him with hurt anger. "But why stop there when there's so much more to discuss? Like, it's good to know that you still find her so attractive. Why not just say that she's F*ing seductive? Oh, wait! You *did* say that, didn't you?"

“Is that a bad word, mommy?” Philip interrupted her mad tirade.

“No, Philip!” Mary lowered her voice as she rationalized her defense. “Because I only said part of it.” She settled her mad eyes on Ian and let out a calming breath. “Are there any other accolades that you regret not throwing around for her, Ian?”

He frowned in self-defense as he wrestled with the impulse to say something back to her that he knew he shouldn’t say. But the urge was hard to resist and Ian couldn’t stop himself from giving into it. “How is it you can hear every single word that your opposing counsel has to say in a closing argument on the other side of a courtroom, but you can only hear half of the words that I haphazardly said in a conversation standing not one foot away from you?”

Mary blew off his accusation without even considering it. “And that right there, Ian…” She turned an insulted glare on him. “That passive aggressive observation you just made… feels like another attack on me. Thank you very much! So why don’t we agree to just let this one go, for tonight…before I *really* get offended by what falls out of your mouth?”

Ian held his mouth shut in silent answer to her accusation, then he let out a defeated sigh and agreed with her charge. “I’m sorry. You’re right. I didn’t mean to attack you.” He tentatively stepped closer to her so he could rub her shoulder in a way that might hopefully release some of her tension. “My whole approach to this misunderstanding was wrong. So, let me start over…”

Mary scooped Skylar out of the tub and handed her to Ian. “Nice you could give Elizabeth so many glowing compliments in under five minutes. That was a good roll for you, Ian. I can’t help but wonder how much better you could have done, if you had only had more time to collect your thoughts and really do her justice…”

Ian locked his mouth down. Mary was not going to be able to let this go, any more than he was going to be allowed to let it go. And the only way for him to get out of this was to just shut up. But sometimes holding back was too hard.

“I’m sorry.” He held his tongue in check, as he carefully rethought his approach. Then he gave into the need to clear his name. “Honestly Mary, I’m confused how I got myself into so much trouble with you.” He consciously stayed on guard as he tried to talk himself out of the dog house. “Because my recollection is that from the very beginning of Wally’s drooling, I called her poison.” Ian wrapped Skylar up in the towel and rubbed it over her tiny body to dry her off.

"You called her *addictive*... poison, Ian... in case you've forgotten exactly what tumbled out of your mouth." Mary moved her attention onto Philip who was silently following their argument.

"How come you're so mad at daddy, mommy?" He looked between the two of them with a troubled expression. "Was he a bad boy?"

Mary silently shook her head no as Ian let out a contradictory snort behind her back. "Yep. That's usually the case, buddy. In fact, for a good portion of my life I've been a *really* bad boy. But we'll talk about that when you're a little older."

Mary couldn't help but snicker in response to his joke that was intended for her, not their son. Ian cautiously settled his eyes on her. The fact that she could chuckle just now, meant that there was a good chance that he could turn this around and put an end to their fight.

He knew that Mary adored his bad boy presence in high school, but mostly, he admitted to himself, that was because he wasn't really as bad as he liked to portray. But after he and Mary parted ways, he did become more of a classic bad boy, when out of a sustained despair he slid in and out of intimate college relationships like a man without a conscious. But his actions came mostly out of a deep depression. What he wanted back then was the one thing he couldn't have: Mary. And though he truly tried to move on, nobody else could compare to her, or hold his interest.

He was also aware that he had a reputation for being detached from his feelings. But that was only a cover that he adopted as a boy. Losing his father and then Mary taught him at a young age that love could hurt. So, he learned how to disconnect from his feelings before the hurt ever set in, and that way he never had to get caught up in any emotional turmoil. It wasn't an image he was going for it was just a survival skill, though admittedly, he had fostered a distant and brittle relationship with Elizabeth years ago, which usually became apparent when he spoke to her in a tone that was dripping with disrespectful condescension.

But he had raised Jenny by himself and he'd done a good job with her, and his heart was usually in the right place, so Mary rarely held any of his derogatory traits against him. Except she seemed mad enough today to hold some of it against him.

"Mary…"

She was kneeling over the bathtub, so Ian lowered himself onto the toilet seat to close the gap between them and keep himself from physically towering over her. "How do I fix this?"

She huffed with condescension of her own and instead of settling down, she fed his remorseful concern with a bitterness that could rival his own adopted brittleness.

"It wasn't your selection of nouns that got you in trouble with me, Ian, so let's move on from you calling her poison. It was your use of adverbs and adjectives that made it so bad." She pulled the plug in the tub and wrung the washcloth out.

"You mean addictive?" Ian removed the towel from Skylar's body so she could climb into her panties and pajamas.

"Like that wasn't offensive enough, Ian…" Mary lifted Philip from the tub and handed him to Ian. "You threw enough descriptors around in your wave off like *beautiful, enticing,* and *seductive* to turn the whole dreadful train wreck into a worthwhile peril…"

Ian rolled his eyes as he wrapped the towel around Philip before he moved his attention back to Skylar who was pulling her underpants backwards up her legs. "They're backwards, Skylar. You need to take them off and turn them around."

"I don't want to, daddy…"

"Well, they're not going to feel comfortable, so let's turn them around anyway." Ian slid them down her legs and turned them around so his daughter could step back into them. His eyes returned to Mary to address her distorted observation.

"She was addictive at the front end of the relationship, Mary, not the back end. And now she just annoys the hell out of me. You *know* that."

"Huh…" Mary closed the shampoo and shower gel bottles and turned to help Ian with the kids. "Regardless of the timing of your addiction, it's good to know that she can still make you recall so fondly her addictive attributes." She rubbed the towel over Philip's body in silent protest and set it on the floor. "And nice to hear that you still find her so beautiful…"

Ian exhaled with patience. "I was only recognizing what Wally was observing about her; that *he* found her beautiful." Ian handed Mary his son's pajamas that were stacked out of her reach on the vanity behind him. "I wasn't saying that *I* find her beautiful. You're focusing on the wrong words, Mary. Because the most important word that I chose to say out there was poison. Elizabeth is poison. Plain and simple It doesn't matter how addictive or beautiful she might be... what matters is that she's poison. And it doesn't take much of her poison to ruin your world."

Mary scoffed at that. "Well to me the most powerful observations you made included her seductive, addictive and beautiful attributes... and let's not forget the icing on the cake... how good she feels under your body."

"Who feels good under daddy's body?" Philip joined the conversation with wide eyed innocence."

"Your mommy feels good to me, buddy..." Ian side stepped the issue with quick fatherly timing that allowed for ambiguity.

"Under your body?"

Ian chuckled at their son's focus. "Cuddled up beside me in bed, she feels good."

Skylar giggled at their conversation and happily added to it. "But not under your tummy, daddy." She climbed into his lap and wiggled into his arms. "Because that would squish mommy. And mommy doesn't want to be squished by you."

Ian laughed off her concern with adult amusement. "I promise not to squish mommy..." his eyes settled on Mary, "...unless she wants me to squish her."

Mary sighed in defeat, ready to end the adult argument, but not quite ready to stop talking about it. "I get that you were just trying to shoo him away from her."

Ian held his sorry eyes on her. "But I didn't do that very well." He pulled her into a kiss that surrendered his position to her. "My bad, not yours. It was careless and insensitive of me not to watch what I was saying in front of you. And I'll try not to do that again."

Mary let him kiss her, though Skylar still sat in his lap between them, poking them both in the face with her teasing fingers.

"I think someone's stabbing me..." Ian called her out on it and Skylar laughed with silly amusement.

Philip chuckled too. "Is that a make-up kiss, daddy?"

"It is..." Ian shot him a thankful smile. His innocent interruptions in their argument, helped to calm the tide.

Philip scowled back at him. "Did you stick your tongue in mommy's mouth?"

They all laughed at his question. "Pretty gross, huh?" Ian tousled his hair.

"*Really* gross, daddy. You have to keep your tongue in your own mouth."

Ian shot Mary a smile and returned his thankful attention to his son. "Let's talk about that when you're older, Philip… and we'll see if you still think that."

Mary laughed at his teasing. "So, how about we get these kids fed, and their bedtime stories read?"

Ian nodded at her suggestion as he pulled her into another kiss. "I'm honestly very sorry."

"I know you are." Mary forgave him without bitterness.

"Daddy loves mommy…" Philip laughingly sang between them.

Ian looked at his son and happily gave him a wink. "I *do* love your mommy…lots and lots."

"I love her too, daddy!" Skylar wiggled out of his arms to leave the bathroom. "But now I'm hungry and I want dinner!"

"Me too!" Philip yelled behind her as they both moved away from them.

Ian stood from the toilet seat. "So, let's eat some dinner and then it's bedtime."

"But stories first, daddy!" Skylar ran down the hall to go to the dinner table.

Philip ran beside her. "Before you say goodnight to Ellie because that takes too long!"

"I want *Green Eggs and Ham!"* Skylar yelled with excitement as her bottom landed in her chair at the table.

"I want *Go Dog Go,* daddy!" Philip yelled across the table from her as he also landed in a chair.

"We'll do both of those books…" Ian rolled his eyes and softly put his foot down. "And then we're moving onto other books…After tonight…"

Mary chuckled with the three of them as she pulled Ian into her arms and apologized for being angry. "I'm sorry, for making such a big deal out of nothing… I guess my feelings were just hurt."

"Hey," Ian cuddled himself around her. "That was my fault, not yours. So, no apology necessary. I own my mistakes when I make them, and I didn't need you telling me how badly I goofed today. That was just careless talk on my part… probably because Wally was there and somehow that caused me to stop thinking like *me*, and start talking like a doofus kid."

He swatted her on the butt with affection and whispered into her ear. “When these kids are in bed tonight, let’s share more than a make-up kiss…”

Mary shot him an intimate smile. “I am *so* going to make you forget about Elizabeth ever being under your body…”

Ian smiled at that. “It’s too bad the kids know those two stories so well… If they didn’t, I could skip half the pages and get myself into your bed sooner…”

“Well, that’s really dependent upon how quickly we can wrap up Ellie’s nighttime routine…”

Ian sighed with what she pointed out to him. “Yep, there’s always that tiresome routine to get through…”

Chapter Three

Across town Wally couldn't get Ian's ex-wife off of his mind and that worried him. He dearly loved his own wife, but they had fallen into a rough patch in their marriage and he knew that he was vulnerable to the befuddled way that he was now feeling after seeing Ian's ex- today. He didn't know why, but he could not stop thinking about her, and the fact that Ian so adamantly tried to wave him off of her only worked to fuel the flames inside him. She had now gotten under his skin like an irresistible itch that he desperately wanted to scratch. And he didn't think it was a purely physical reaction. From a distance he felt drawn to her for some unknown reason. He sensed a vulnerability about her and a contradictory electricity; she was captivating and enchanting, incredibly sexy but visibly fragile. And he sensed that she was more misunderstood than understood, and definitely unappreciated by Ian and his wife. Wally felt the need to protect her from Ian's dismissive attitude. And he desperately wanted to learn more about her. He was *literally* charmed by her.

His own wife joined him in the entry way when she heard him close the front door behind him. Her reception was not welcoming.

"I expected you home an hour ago. I don't know why you never call me when you're running late. Just once, it would be nice, if you did that. It's hard to plan dinner, you know, when you can't bother to let me know when you're expected home."

Wally set his brief case down as he returned a greeting that was less than understanding. "I was working, Betty Jo. And I couldn't exactly stop what I was doing to check in with you." Except, Wally acknowledged to himself, he could have called her in the car on his way home. But he didn't do that because he knew it would just give her a chance to continue the fight that she started with him before he left the house this morning. "If my arrival time was that important you could have texted me for a heads-up, right? But I guess you'd rather have a reason to be mad at me."

His wife huffed in answer. “I’m not mad at you. I’m just asking… why can’t you ever call me?”

“Fine.” Wally nodded with her surrender and forced himself to back off of her. “I’ll try and call next time.” He silently scolded himself for not giving her more of an apology than he just offered because the other reason he didn’t call her on the way home – besides not wanting to continue her earlier fight with him – was because in the solitude of driving home he was wistfully thinking about Elizabeth – which was far more enjoyable than arguing with Betty Jo. And for that moment in time today, those dreamy thoughts made him feel alive – and that felt wonderful. It reminded him of how long it had been since he felt that good. Thinking about Ian’s ex-love interest made him feel like a man again. In the fantasy of his mind, he could hold her and love her, and fill all of her needs, and more potently than all that, he could make amends to her for the wrongs that Ian had surely committed against her – and for once in his life, he could feel like he was as cool as Ian.

Of course, that kind of longing created a threat to Wally’s integrity, and that realization alone made him wince. He was not the kind of man who thought about other women. He was dedicated to his marriage and also to his wife of thirty years – despite the rough patch they were experiencing right now.

“I’m sorry I didn’t call you.” Wally tried to leave his thoughts of Elizabeth behind because he recognized that they were dangerous to his marriage. “I guess I was distracted by my research subjects.” He smiled as he said that because it wasn’t a complete lie. Elizabeth was the mother of his primary research subject, and the grandmother to his secondary research subject – and that drew Elizabeth, by circumstance, into his research. The realization admittedly lifted Wally’s spirits a little.

“Did you hear me, Wally?”

“What?” He focused his attention on Betty Jo. “I don’t think I did hear you.”

“Obviously.” His wife rolled her eyes at him. “I apologized for getting cross with you.”

“Oh.” Wally shot her a smile. “I’m sorry too.”

Betty Jo was pretty. She was a kind lady, and she had a sweet personality. But she never seemed genuinely happy with Wally anymore, or considerate of his needs. For a long time, Wally had felt like she was drifting away from him and he didn’t want that to happen but he didn't know how to stop it. He was happy being married to her. They had a good relationship, or at least they *had* a good relationship up until recently, and a successful marriage. They also had three grown children and a grandchild on the way. And Wally didn't want anything ruining his family's cohesive happiness. They were a good family.

He consciously reminded himself of that. *He had great kids and a wonderful life.* What he and Betty Jo were going through right now was nothing more than a difficult patch. Like Ian described today when they were talking about Jenny and Ricky. Something that could be navigated and resolved.

"Let's go out to dinner tonight." Wally offered the impromptu date as a way of reconnecting with his wife and maintaining his family happiness. He wanted to push Elizabeth completely out of his mind and he desperately wanted to feel like he was in love with Betty Jo tonight, because for the first time in his married life he was afraid that he might actually be falling out of love with her. And he didn't want that to happen. He wanted to keep his family intact and he still wanted to love his wife.

"I've already changed into pajamas, Wally." Betty Jo turned away from him to return to the kitchen. "I've got leftovers warming up. And the last thing in the world that I want to do is get back into nice clothing, to drive across town to wait for someone to serve me dinner when I've already got dinner cooking at home. And besides, I want to eat in front of the TV. My shows are on tonight. Plus, if we go out for dinner, you'll only spend the whole evening talking about your research and that's the last thing I want to hear about at the end of a long day at the clinic."

Wally let out a defeated sigh. "Okay. We'll stay home." He pulled her into his arms to give her a hello kiss as he pictured Ian and Mary slow kissing earlier today. As had always been the case when Wally witnessed Ian interacting with Mary, he was left feeling inadequate as a man and slightly jealous of his friend. Ian had such a suave way of kissing… of dropping his arm around Mary's shoulders and pulling her in; of reaching for her hand and grasping hold of her fingertips and closing his palm around her smaller hand; of just standing beside her and casually shooting her a happy smile that always came off as so much more. There was a sexual energy in everything Ian did that could give a person goose bumps just watching. Even his most benign moves came off as intimate foreplay. It was easy to imagine the two of them having sex… *passionate sex…* and often. You just got that feeling about them. They were a hot couple, even when they were interacting in the most innocent way. All the insecurities that Wally ever felt as a kid, seemed to return to him as an adult today just watching the two of them talking to each other.

And then Ian kissed her…

"Did you hear me?"

"What?" Wally forced himself to forget about Ian and Mary.

"I said dinner will be ready in five minutes."

"Okay." Wally let out a defeated sigh. "Aren't you concerned that we hardly ever kiss anymore? We've both been working a lot of hours lately, and doing our own thing in the evenings and on the weekends, and it feels like we aren't connecting anymore. And I don't want to lose touch with you."

"Don't be silly. Didn't you just kiss me?" His wife stepped away from him with a distracted look on her face.

He did. But it didn't feel like the kind of kiss Ian would give Mary. And Betty Jo didn't respond to it the way Mary responded to Ian's kisses – like she wanted another one, thank you very much.

"I don't know why you think we're losing touch with each other." Betty Jo went to the stove and opened the oven to peer inside it. "I'm warming last night's chili." Her focus became fully engaged on the Pyrex bowl of food that she was warming. "Are we eating in front of separate TVs again tonight? Because I want to watch my programs and I know you aren't really interested in them."

Wally frowned at her question because it proved exactly what he just said to her. They were slowly drifting away from each other, and if they didn't put a stop to it pretty soon, they were surely going to find themselves too distant to close the gap. But Betty Jo was right about her TV shows; Wally had no interest at all in her silly sitcoms – they surely had value for other people, but they just weren't for him. He'd rather work on his research. Having spent countless years studying children with traumatic brain injuries, he was fascinated now by the idea of researching adult patients who had experienced childhood brain injuries. Some of them were parents now, and seemingly invisible in a society that only saw "whole" people. The basic premise of Wally's research was that parents with cognitive issues were likely living below the poverty line, with few good role models and a high incident of victimization and isolation. They also seemed to lack good healthcare and social support systems, despite having seemingly higher incidents of psychological issues that would inevitably impact their children.

Wally had already met with a number of families that were proving his theory, but now he had Jenny and Ricky in his study, and their adorable Cinderella. That was a huge score for him. Just getting Ian to talk to him felt like a win. But getting him to allow access to his daughter and her family? Wally felt like he really scored big on that one. Jenny was as sweet as can be, and so polite. Ian had done a good job raising her. And her husband was fun – a bit of a nerd like Wally, but more engaging. They seemed to be a functioning and loving family that contradicted his research to date – but he understood them to be an anomaly, not the norm.

From what Wally could tell from his initial visit with them today, Jenny was well supported by Ian and Mary, and it was clear that Jenny felt emotionally supported throughout her life. She had no memories of her mother living with her as a child, but she was full of stories about her father. Clearly, she adored him, which was evident from the many times she referenced him as her hero. In her eyes, he was the smartest, kindest, most attentive father on earth – except for the few times that she recalled him scolding her. And then, as she put it, her daddy could be mean because he would tell her if she couldn't stop crying and throwing a tantrum, she'd have to go to her bedroom until she calmed down. But he never stayed mad at her, according to Jenny, and he always gave her ice cream to help her get happy.

From the sounds of it, Ian *was* a perfect father. Jenny could barely remember him ever raising his voice at her, though Ricky could recall two incidents of Ian yelling at them. The first time was when Ian learned that Jenny was pregnant. According to Ricky, Ian had a full-blown tantrum over that one, and he said a number of cuss words in front of the two kids. Wally could well imagine that scene. The second incident was unrelated to any particular event, but Ricky recalled Ian yelling some bad words and getting mad at Elizabeth who was there. But other than those two times, it seemed that Ian always managed to keep his cool with them.

In many ways Wally had trouble connecting Jenny's super hero, very paternal dad to the ultra-cool, untouchable dude that Wally knew in high school. And yet, as Jenny talked about him, Wally realized that the likeable father perfectly fit the character of the very likeable omnipotent friend Wally had known throughout his childhood. There was a reason why everyone loved Ian. He was steady and quick, sophisticated, and laid back. Wally couldn't remember a single time when Ian acted unfairly, or mean-spirited. He was just a really likable guy. It was no wonder that Jenny saw him as a champion.

She was also very fond of Mary, but that came as no surprise to Wally. Everybody loved Mary. She was as steady as Ian, almost as quick, classy and collected, and one of the sweetest and fairest people Wally had ever known.

Wally left his thoughts behind to refocus his attention on Betty Jo. He and his wife had done a fine job raising their own children. But unlike Mary and Ian, he wasn't sure that they had done as good a job holding onto the love in their marriage. They had definitely lost their sexual drive – Wally couldn't remember the last time they had sex – and Wally feared they were barely even friends today.

"I guess I'll eat in my office." He gave his wife another kiss in an attempt to mimic Ian's casual but potent style, but nothing felt as slick to him as Ian's lovelock on Mary – and his wife certainly didn't act like his kiss had any impact on her. Wally pushed the comparison from his mind to focus on Betty Jo. "I do have a lot of notes from today's interviews to go through…"

"Good." She shot him an obliging smile. "So, you'll keep busy without me."

"Sure." Wally left her in the kitchen while he went to their bedroom to change out of the clothes that he wore to Ian's farm.

It was hard for him to grasp that he had really reconnected with Ian and Mary so intimately after so many years of no interaction with them. They had run into each other briefly a number of years ago at their high school reunion, but other than one brief conversation that night that mostly revolved around his brain injury research and Jenny's childhood brain injury, they hadn't talked in years – until today. But now, here they were, laughing and talking and loosely hanging out like long lost friends. It felt like nothing had changed between them today as Ian and Wally bantered over Elizabeth. And yet, everything had clearly changed for all of them.

Wally had so many fond memories of the three of them as kids and later, as teenagers.

Ian was just one of those guys back then that everyone envied. Notwithstanding the fact that his father died when he was only ten years old, Ian seemed to have everything. He came off as being a jock, though he never played sports in school. He was sort of a badass, though Wally couldn't remember him ever really doing anything bad, and he was always the most popular guy in seemingly *every* crowd. He was a cool musician when being in band could make a person seem less than cool. He was such a suave student council president, that everyone wanted to be on student council; and he was always the guy that every girl wanted to date. *Nobody* had a chance at getting noticed by girls if Ian was in the room. He was just that good looking, that confident, and that likeable. It was enough to make a good friend hate him. But even that was impossible. Because Ian was the kind of guy that everyone wanted to be friends with.

And Mary was a treasure – there were no other girls like her. Wally admittedly had a horrible crush on her throughout his entire childhood. But he never had a chance with her. He remembered in sixth grade when he gave Mary a special valentine. His mother had purchased a box of valentines for him and he had purposely looked at every one of them before deciding which one would be hers. Then he carefully wrote on it, *you are the most special girl in our class* and he drew a heart on the valentine around both of their names. He had hoped the romantic gesture would at least make her look at him.

When it finally came time for the class to exchange valentines, he kept his eye on her, waiting expectantly for some kind of expression when she opened his, but it never came – he only saw her turn to goo when she opened a valentine from Ian. Not that Wally ever got confirmation about that, but when she opened a valentine that was clearly not Wally's, she kept staring across the room at Ian. And when they were finally allowed to leave their desks she went straight to where Ian was sitting and showed him the valentine. And in a very *Ian-ish* way he downplayed her gushing over him, but Wally could tell that Ian was eating it up inside. Regardless of Ian feigning that it wasn't him who gave her the Valentine she showed him, Mary was clearly in love and not about to be put off by his childhood brush off of the romantic gesture. And that was the day when Wally's rivalry with Ian really took hold. As far as Wally was concerned, Ian never deserved Mary, but she was hopelessly devoted to him. And Wally desperately wanted her, but Mary never seemed to notice him.

There was another night in high school that stood out in Wally's mind when they were all hanging out at a friend's house for a Friday night party. Ian and Mary arrived at the party together, but it was obvious that they'd been fighting before their arrival. Mary was usually very clingy with Ian, and he never seemed to mind her hanging on him. In fact, where other guys might push their girlfriends away in search of more space, Ian seemed to encourage Mary's constant body contact. They rarely kept their hands to themselves. Ian always had an arm draped around her body, they were always holding hands, and they moved through a crowd as a singular entangled unit. They were rarely ever apart from each other for more than a few minutes. It was always Ian *and* Mary, never Ian *or* Mary.

But this particular night, as soon as they arrived, Ian left Mary alone in the living room with a group of silly girls, while he went outside to where a keg was set up to pour himself a beer. When he returned inside the house he went straight to the kitchen where he hung out with a group of guys, without taking Mary a beer, and without joining her in the living room. That in itself was unusual because Ian knew how to behave like a gentleman – Wally would give him that much. He was an officer's kid and a courteous military brat and leaving her alone in the living room by herself was not the kind of gentleman's behavior that Ian would usually exercise with Mary.

But this night he was clearly ignoring her. He was completely detached from her – *except,* Wally observed, Ian's eyes were constantly on her as she moved through the party, laughing like a school girl and singing and dancing to the music with her mob of giggling girlfriends.

And that's when Wally decided to make his move on her. He went outside to the keg and refilled his own beer, then he poured one for Mary, and in a somewhat daring move he approached her in the living room like she was there on her own. Afterall, Mary didn't *belong* to Ian, they were simply dating like all the other kids in school. And if the two of them were fighting, or on the outs with each other, maybe even breaking up, there was no reason in the world, why Wally couldn't make a move on her.

Except... he should have known better.

Wally could almost laugh today as he remembered what happened next. She was sitting there on the couch innocently laughing with one of her girlfriends when he approached her nonchalantly, and offered her the beer. Mary shot him a surprised smile and happily took the beer from him, *which felt like a major coup for Wally* – except – just as she was thanking him, Ian casually appeared in front of them, and without saying a single word to any of them, *including Mary*, he took the beer from her hand and set it on the coffee table. Then he grasped her empty palm in his own hand and raised her off of the couch to lead her down the hallway, into an empty bedroom where the two of them disappeared for at least an hour.

Wally impatiently watched the clock turn as he waited for them to come out. When they did finally resurface, they were clearly back in love because Mary spent the rest of the night laughing and cuddling in his arms, and sipping beer from the cup that he shared with her. And Ian had left an obvious trail of hickeys down the front of Mary's neck that she proudly seemed to be wearing like a badge of honor. And she had given him a couple of hickeys in return.

It was all so seventies and very adolescent, but it seemed incredibly cool to a timid teen standing in a room full of virginal teenagers, many of whom, *including Wally*, had never even experienced a first kiss yet. Just the idea of kissing a girl, back then, seemed like a big deal to Wally. But, actually taking a girl into a bedroom and passionately making out with her.... The whole idea of *that* kind of action was so far out of reach for someone like Wally.

But not for Ian. He and Mary were *that* cool. They were *the* couple back then. *Everyone wanted to be them.* As a couple, they seemed hipper than everyone else; they were happier and more confident than the rest of them, and visibly committed to each other.

Where other couples' relationships were filled with teenage angst, Ian and Mary seemed to know that they were in it for the long haul – despite the occasional flare up between them. They were a *forever* couple. *Everyone knew that.* There was never any doubt in anyone's mind that they would stay together forever. Which is why Wally should have known better than to try and woo Mary into his arms. But there was always something magical about Mary that drew Wally in... and something about Ian that made Wally want to protect Mary from him, and in the process, *if at all possible...* Wally desperately wanted to one-up him. He wanted so badly to be a cool cat like Ian.

And that was the origin of Wally's *Lover Powers* taunt. It was actually Ian who first coined the phrase in a bragging way, though Wally doubted that Ian would remember it like that. Something so insignificant as a conversation with Wally was too inconsequential for Ian to remember. But Wally could still remember every word and gesture as if it all happened yesterday. It began that same night when Wally and Ian by happenstance, arrived at the keg at the same time to refill their cups after Ian resurfaced from the bedroom with an apparent powerful thirst.

He was wearing Mary's hickeys like a teenage score card and Wally was annoyed about that because he was concerned about Mary's virtue and distrustful about Ian's intentions. He knew in his heart that Ian was going to break Mary's heart one day, and he didn't want her heart broken. She was completely trusting of Ian, and in contrast Ian was such a dismissive hotshot who had an answer for everything and a personal connection to nothing.

So, as the two teenage boys were standing outside at the keg, while Mary was in the bathroom, and Ian was draining foam out of the hose before filling his cup, Wally got up the nerve to make a crack about Ian getting himself out of trouble with Mary. And in true Ian style, he boasted back at him, *what can I say, doofus? I've got some awesome lover powers. She can't help herself. So, why don't you stop scoping her out when I'm not by her side, because you're tripping if you think you've got a chance in hell with her.*

It was so annoying how Ian could be that confident when they were still only teenagers, except it wasn't something he put on as a show, or tried to pull off. The adulation he got from his peers boosted his ego enough to make him feel invincible. More importantly, he just knew who he was and what he had inside him; and he was really good at reading what other people were lacking. And no doubt, he was accurately reading Wally's insecurities that night. But nonetheless, Wally confidently stood his ground, partly because he had such a crush on Mary and he wanted to rescue her from Ian, and partly because he desperately wanted to one-up Ian. So, with as much bravado as he could muster, he answered back, *don't be the fool that you are, dude. Love is a fickle thing... if you catch my drift. And one day you're going to show her the chump that you really are... Mister Lover Powers, and your foxy mama is going to cut out on you for the last time, and the next thing you know, she'll be going around with me.*

Ian just laughed with amusement and confidently walked away from Wally without saying anything back to him, which was annoying enough in itself. But then he proved his point about his awesome lover powers, when he joined Mary across the room and drew her into a passionate kiss that lasted way too long in a room full of observers. It was wholly belittling to watch and inspiring all at once.

And then Ian unexpectedly moved away, and Wally thought for a minute that he might finally have a chance with Mary, but that was wishful thinking on his part, because somehow, even from a distance, Ian managed to keep control over her. In fact, Mary seemed to completely disappear after Ian left town. She was absent from their normal after-school life. She never went to parties anymore or school dances, or other places where her friends hung out, and she kept to herself even during the fun graduation activities. She was so withdrawn from life that Wally could barely even remember seeing her during the latter part of their senior year.

But here they all were again, falling back into their same roles from high school. Ian was still the coolest cat in the room, and Wally still worshiped the ground he walked on while hating it all at the same time. And Mary was still Mary, charming and wholesome, and as beautiful as ever, perhaps even more beautiful today because she had become more self-assured with a mature confidence, unrelated to her status as Ian's girl. It was interesting to see where they had all landed as adults. Ian still adored Mary today – that much was obvious – and she was clearly still devoted to him, though Wally suspected there might be trouble in paradise tonight due to his own banter with Ian about Elizabeth's beauty.

Wally didn't mean to go there so openly in front of Mary, he simply couldn't help himself. Elizabeth was gorgeous and even more interesting than that – *she used to belong to Ian* but somehow, *the Golden boy* had lost her – and that was an intoxicating thought to Wally – that Ian could lose *any* girl – and it made her more attractive to Wally than he ever could have imagined. And that's what made it too easy for Wally to openly ogle her in front of Mary.

Wally wondered how his own life might have turned out differently had Mary dated him in high school after Ian left town? Maybe he would be married to her now instead of Betty Jo? Maybe

Ian would still have Elizabeth but he'd be jealous of Wally having Mary?

Wally forced himself to stop thinking about all of the what ifs, and instead focused on returning his attention to his *actual* life and his sweet Betty Jo. He didn't understand why he felt so restless tonight, except now that the feeling was here, he remembered feeling this way in high school when he stood on the outskirts of Ian's mythical life. But Wally had successes of his own and he shouldn't be feeling this antsy as an adult. It's not like Betty Jo was a consolation prize. She wasn't Mary and she wasn't Elizabeth, but she was a decent wife and a good mother. She was pretty and charming – when she wanted to be – and on the rare occasion when they went to bed together, she could actually be good in bed; they just hadn't had sex in an awfully long time.

Wally exhaled with a determined reminder that his own life was good enough. He swapped his street clothes for comfortable pajamas and returned to the kitchen to re-engage his wife before she bailed out on him for a night alone with her TV. He really needed to work on rebuilding his relationship with Betty Jo before he actually got tempted to throw his comfortable life with his wife away – to chase an ego-pumping dream that he didn't really want and that he didn't really expect to happen with Ian's *Goddess* ex-wife.

"I'm back…"

"Hi…" Betty Jo noticed him as he came into the room and dutifully offered him a gin and tonic. "How'd it go today with Ian and Mary?"

Wally took the drink from her hand and consciously gave her credit for trying to take an interest in his work. "Okay, I guess…" He sipped from his cocktail and felt himself relax a little. "So, here's something unexpected." Wally took another drink from his glass as he fell into the conversation. "Ian's ex-wife came by while I was there today, and boy is she a looker, but clearly high maintenance… she's *exactly* what I would have predicted he'd suck into his arms as an adult."

Betty Jo chuckled at that. "He was so adorable in high school, everyone loved him, but he moved in a stratosphere that was way out of my league…and I guess when you move in that kind of highly selective crowd and operate at that unreachable level of elitism, you're going to draw in the kind of high velocity woman that demands a lot."

Wally laughed at what she said, because it justified his snarky feelings today and it made him feel less two-faced for talking badly about his long-ago friend who had generously given him access to his family, which Wally suspected was unusual for Ian. "Well, this one is definitely high octane and I am positive that even Ian with all of his endless capabilities, surely had his hands full trying to manage her. And I think I probably got him in trouble with Mary today when I pointed that out to him – how Elizabeth was so beautiful. Mary suddenly got pissed and walked away."

Betty Jo frowned at his story. "I don't think Mary really liked me in high school." She sipped her drink and continued voicing her thoughts. "Like Ian, she was in *that* crowd… and she didn't really have time for someone as insignificant as me."

Wally shrugged off her observation without agreeing with her because he didn't like that she was putting Mary down. He could get how Betty Jo might feel that way about her – wrong impressions could be made when you judged someone by their friends – except Mary never acted like she was in *that* crowd. And she was only there because Ian was there. Like Wally; he was never really in Ian's crowd either, except he lived on their street, so he sometimes slid in.

"Anyhow," Wally returned to his story. "Not that I meant to hurt Mary, but when I inadvertently exclaimed how Ian's ex- was hot, Mary practically had a melt-down in front of me. But Ian, as always, played it cool, like nothing was wrong between them. Only I could tell that everything was suddenly wrong. I don't think Ian wanted me to notice, but I grew up watching these two interact, and I could feel the tension rising between them. Mary was definitely annoyed with him and Ian was on edge about it."

Betty Jo distractedly shook her head as she listened to his tale. "Well, you probably shouldn't have commented about Ian's ex-wife like that in front of Mary. I can see why that would irritate her."

"I know." Wally chuckled at the memory nonetheless because he *did* like the feeling of rattling Ian's cage, though he didn't want to admit to himself that he had probably hurt Mary's feelings in the process. The whole regrettable exchange just made him feel like he had somehow one-upped Ian. And that was a first for him.

In hindsight, Wally couldn't help but feel amused as he pictured Ian frantically yelping at his heels in a desperate effort to maintain control over a situation that was out of his control – a noticeable role reversal for Ian… *being out of control…* and for Wally… *having control…* and it felt incredibly empowering to Wally.

He returned his attention to Betty Jo without acknowledging that he suddenly felt like a bigger man. "So, his ex- is truly a good-looking lady, and nobody can honestly dispute that about her. She's a knock-out. But worse than me commenting on how hot she looked, was Ian's own badly timed reminiscing about how good she felt under his body. I couldn't believe he'd say something like that in front of Mary, but Ian always did say whatever came to his mind – no matter the consequence."

"Certainly not an attractive trait." Betty Jo shook her head in silent disapproval. "But when you get a free-pass all your life, it's hard to know where the rest of us would see boundaries."

"Exactly." Wally nodded at his wife's assessment. He was feeling a little underhanded, shooting Ian down, but Betty Jo's approval of the mean-spirited conversation, spurred him on and boosted Wally up a little. "What a piece of work, huh?"

Hearing for the first time in his life, someone – *anyone* – voicing their disapproval of the almighty Ian Powers made Wally feel somehow redeemed in his own way. Not that he felt good about the mean things he was saying, but sharing a joke at Ian's expense made Wally feel a little less emasculated. And it felt good to be sharing a conversation with Betty Jo like they were friends again. "That's just how Ian operates. I remember in high school he'd be horsing around with his buddies, laughing and cutting up in class like they were jocks who didn't have to do the school work – they just had to show up – except none of them were jocks. And no matter how much he was goofing off, he never got in trouble for it. Our teachers just seemed amused by him."

Betty Jo shook her head in objection. "Some people are never held accountable."

"I know, right?" Wally nodded, agreeing. There was just something about Ian that everyone loved and it allowed him to get away with the kind of stuff that usually got other kids in trouble.

"He was overly confident like that in band, too…" Betty Jo sipped from her cocktail as she continued with her own recollection. "You could always tell that he thought the rest of us were inept. Our teacher would stop whatever song we were doing because we somehow blew it, and Ian would impatiently do a defiant drum roll before we could start over, or he'd dismissively hit a cymbal in passive protest to our cumulative stupidity. And our band teacher never called him out on it. Instead, he'd back him up and say something, like: *Exactly my sentiments, Ian...* then he'd scowl at the rest of us and say, *Come on, guys, get your act together like Ian! Is he the only one here who can read music?"*

"Yeah. Some guys just have it." Wally took a gulp from his own glass. "I'd sure like to know how he got himself out of trouble tonight. Because I'm fairly certain that his wife wanted to upend the apple cart on him."

Betty Jo chuckled at the vision he created. "Well, I hope she stood her ground with him. Because talking about his ex- like that in front of her is just plain rude."

"Yeah, well Ian never cares about his own rudeness. But Mary will put him in his place. She is not the type of woman who's going to let him get away with that."

Betty Jo stopped listening to serve their food, and when their plates were filled, she handed one to Wally.

"So, I'm going to watch my show now…"

Wally nodded at her dismissal then he decided, *what the hell*, he should just eat with her. Maybe he could get into her silly show after all, and they could laugh together about nothing – but at least that would be something – laughing together – which was obviously the true value of her seemingly nonsensical shows – to laugh and relax with each other. And if they really reconnected, maybe – *just maybe* – they could even have sex tonight… that could be a really significant turn of events for them – because Ian Powers wasn't the only one who had some awesome lover powers. Wally had some pretty slick moves of his own. He just hadn't used them in a while.

"I changed my mind. Why don't I eat with you so we can watch your shows together? You can fill me in on whatever plot I need to know."

"Really?" His wife looked shocked by his offer. "Okay… if that's what you want…"

Chapter Four

When Ian came home from work Monday evening, Elizabeth was at the house exactly as expected – but never really anticipated.

"Hi sweetie!" She happily called out to him as he crossed the front yard to go her direction.

Her top was too short and Ian couldn't help but notice as he walked closer to her that she'd gotten her belly button pierced like she was a twenty-year old urbanite looking for a meaningless date night with an anonymous drunk.

But that wasn't nice of him to think like that so he pushed the thought away before he said something he shouldn't say.

His eyes moved on in an effort to distance himself from his disgruntled thinking. Ellie was playing in the sandbox Ian had built near the side of the yard, and Philip and Skylar were playing in the sand with her. Two of their dogs were laying on the grass in a shrinking patch of sunlight, and someone had tethered the rabbit on a long leash and it was also sunning itself near the two sleeping dogs. Ian's eyes left the domestic pet scene to return his attention to the domestic human scene that felt more pressing to him.

Elizabeth was spread out in a lounge chair watching over the kids with divided interest, a cocktail in one hand and a celebrity magazine in her other hand. Ian's eyes went immediately to the pool gate. Years ago, he had finally given in to Jenny and Ricky's request for a pool. First, he put in an above ground pool to see if having a pool at his house would truly work for him. Ever since Jenny's fall into the pool at Elizabeth's ex-husband's house, Ian hated the idea of having a pool at his place. But after Jenny and Ricky got married, he finally acquiesced and got the above ground pool. A few years later he paid for an in-ground pool, but he never fully trusted Elizabeth's parenting to feel comfortable with any of the kids' safety when she was watching over them alone – even though she had raised four boys with her husband at the same house where Jenny had her accident – which should have redeemed her to some degree, in Ian's mind; but it didn't.

"Hey…" He nodded a greeting to her when he saw that the pool gate was closed. "Where's Karen?" There was comfort in knowing that Karen was at the house caring for his two kids when Elizabeth was caring for Ellie, but it didn't look like she was here now, and nobody had told Ian that Karen was leaving early today – and that annoyed him. If he had known Elizabeth was flying solo with them this evening, he would have found a way to leave his office early.

Elizabeth left the lounge chair to seductively stretch in front of him. Her belly ring caught the sunlight with the movement of her body. "Karen had a doctor appointment this afternoon, so I came early to relieve her of the kids – yours included. I figured you wouldn't mind me watching them while I was watching Ellie. And in case you're unaware, Philip has been coughing since I got here. I think he might be coming down with something. I told him to stay away from Ellie, but you know how he never listens. I swear he can be as dismissive as you sometimes. You should address that unattractive behavior with him before he grows up to be just like you. He'll make some woman miserable…" Her eyes settled on Ian's, "… much like *you* tend to make all women miserable."

Ian held her malcontent gaze without comment because Philip did not have a problem listening; Ellie was the problem child who never listened to anyone. And that was largely Elizabeth's fault because she encouraged her oppositional behavior. But Ian didn't care to have an exchange of words with Elizabeth about that.

"Where's Jenny?" She was pretty good about watching the kids and keeping them out of trouble. And strangely enough, Ian actually trusted her more than Elizabeth with keeping them out of harm's way. Because the minute one of them did something that was not allowed, Jenny would be all over it. She may not have the mental faculties to process how to correct their actions, but she would surely make their behavior known, and that in itself seemed more than what he could expect from Elizabeth.

"She's arguing with Ricky. That's why we're outside." Elizabeth sipped her cocktail.

Ian frowned at what she said because it was the second time in a week that the kids' arguing was brought to his attention; and he did not like hearing that they weren't getting along. "What are they arguing about?"

"I have no idea." Elizabeth sighed with boredom. "They're just arguing, Ian, constantly. They're a lot like you and me when we were married. I don't think they're very happy anymore."

Ian questioned that they could be anything at all like the two of them. From what he could tell, Ricky and Jenny were a good couple and well matched. In contrast – Ian and Elizabeth were never a good couple, or well matched. When he and Elizabeth were married Elizabeth was always making unrealistic demands on him, and Ian honestly tried to comply with most of them, though admittedly her selfish pursuits and grandiose ideas were often taxing to him. And when he sometimes pushed back, Elizabeth would start a fight with him – and then his mouth would usually let loose with thoughts he shouldn't share, and Elizabeth would find equally mean things to say back to him. And then all hell would break loose between them and it would be a free-for-all for who could come up with the meanest things to say to each other to destroy whatever love might remain between them.

Ian didn't think he was perfect; he knew that he shared the blame for their failed marriage. To begin with, he was wrong to marry her because he wasn't really prepared to fully give her his heart. He thought he was when he made the commitment to her, and he wanted to be a good husband, but he realized pretty quickly into the marriage that he wasn't really in love with her. He was ridiculously still in love with Mary, who he hadn't seen since high school. And that distraction in his heart was hard on Elizabeth because she could never meet Ian's expectations. And when tension grew between them his divided loyalties always surfaced and it became harder and harder to fight with respect. And with respect gone, they soon grew to hate each other.

And then she had her affair.

"I'm sure the kids' arguments are nothing like ours, Lizzy." Ian certainly hoped they weren't. If they were, the kids were destined for divorce. And Ian didn't want that.

"How would you know, Ian?" Elizabeth smirked in opposition to him. "You don't pay enough attention to them anymore to know what's really going on in their world."

Ian frowned in response to her observation. "Well, I haven't heard anything from Jenny about her being unhappy, and until I do, I'm going to assume that she's fine. Because Jenny talks to me, Lizzy. Need I remind you that I have been her only sounding board for most of her life. So, it's a good assumption that she'll tell me if something is troubling her."

"Well, she talks to me more than you these days, Ian." Elizabeth fondled the naval jewelry like a lover engaged in foreplay. "And you aren't here to see what's going on. From what I can tell, you work sunup to sundown – like you did when we were married – and when you are here, you're not really here. You and Mary live in your blissful little bubble with your second family of kids. But I'm here Monday night through Thursday morning with the older kids, and I work from their home and I'm there in the evenings, sleeping in their flat. So, I hear their arguments day and night. And these days I know more about those two kids than you do."

Ian didn't answer her charge against him, because he realized as she was talking, that he couldn't win an argument against any of what she was saying, because in part she was actually telling the truth. He *did* spend his days in an office downtown while she worked from home. And when he and Mary were helping Jenny and Ricky with Ellie, they sometimes did little more than check in with them in the evening. Partly because Ellie behaved better on Ian's rotation with the kids, than she behaved when Elizabeth was there, and because of that Jenny and Ricky needed less help with her. But Ian was otherwise quite involved with the kids, especially on the weekends when they rode their horses and did farm chores together, and he was generally unaware of any tension between them during those times of co-activity. When he and Mary were with them, they seemed happy. And on most of his nightshifts with the kids, they ate together as one big family, and the dinner conversation always seemed jolly. And both adult kids appeared to be in good spirits.

"Ian… are you listening to me?"

Ian settled his eyes on her with exasperated impatience. "If I didn't respond to you, Lizzy, I guess I wasn't listening." He moved his attention onto his youngest two kids and glanced at his wrist watch. Elizabeth had sucked the energy out of him like only Lizzy could, and he did not want to continue this conversation with her.

"Skylar, Philip? Time to go in. Your mom will be here shortly so how about we get ready for dinner and bed before she arrives?"

"No, daddy!" Philip objected to his order. "I'm not hungry."

"Not yet, daddy!" Skylar joined her brother's protest. "We're playing."

Elizabeth snarled with glee. "I told you he doesn't listen very well… and now he's got his sister following suit."

Ian ignored her observation. "Come on, guys…" He didn't want to cave into his kids' plea for longer play while Elizabeth was watching, but as he stood there waiting for them to come to him as ordered, they noticeably did not respond to his command.

Elizabeth waved her manicured palm in his face as she settled an *I told you so* expression on Ian. "So, who's the guy who was here Saturday? The one you and Mary were talking to?"

Ian returned his attention to Elizabeth. He was not inclined to tell her about Wally because common sense told him that she would use the information to her advantage – and to Wally's disadvantage. And he didn't want Elizabeth unleashing her sexual prowess on Wally because Wally had already shown Ian that he would be vulnerable to Elizabeth's attention, and Ian knew that Wally would have no idea how to resist the seductive moves in her man-eating playbook. In addition, Wally would misread her quest for attention from him for what it truly was – nothing more than her own misguided need to prove that every man on the planet couldn't help but fall in love with her.

"Don't hold out on me…" Her manicured fingers tugged on the silver and crystal studded naval ring that was pierced through her belly flesh.

When Ian raised his eyes from it, she shot him a seductive smile, visibly thrilled that he had noticed it. "His name is Wally." It annoyed Ian that he had somehow been tricked into watching her play with the damn thing. "He's someone Mary and I knew in high school. He's conducting brain injury research and he'll be doing a few interviews with the kids and Ellie. You may hear about him from the kids, but you probably won't see him again because he's only going to be here on the weekends."

"Well, that's too bad."

"Elizabeth…" Ian shot her a cautionary scowl. "Stop salivating over him. You don't need him. And he doesn't need you creating a conflict of interest for him."

"Don't be such a dream crusher." She pouted at his warning. "He's a doctor?" Her hand trailed back down to her naval jewelry but Ian consciously kept his eyes from following it down there.

"He is. *And he's married.*" Ian added that with emphasis because he could read where her mind was going. "So, if by chance your path does somehow collide with his, try and keep your hands off of him. Okay?"

She giggled at his directive. "And now you're sounding like a jealous husband…"

Ian scowled at her charge. "Let me say what I just said again because I'm not sure that you heard me, Lizzy… *he's married.* So, why don't we both try and help him keep it that way?"

Elizabeth laughed off his order. "Well, he's unbelievably cute. And I saw how he was looking at me."

Ian rolled his eyes in despair. "He's not your type, Lizzy; he's a harmless geek who is not in your league, so leave him alone. I'm sure you can easily find someone more worthy of your talents and attributes who has less to lose after you devour and discard him for your own personal amusement."

Elizabeth giggled at his put down like it was an intimate compliment. "Thank you. But I think I should at least get to know him if he's going to be interviewing my daughter and granddaughter for his research project."

Ian turned and walked away from her because there was nothing more that he could say that would rein her in. For Betty Jo's sake – and Wally's sake – he would just have to make sure that Wally never showed up here Monday through Thursday. He did not want Wally's marriage destroyed by Elizabeth. They may never have been best friends, and there had always been a childhood rivalry between them, but there was also an established loyalty, and Ian did not want Wally harmed by his ex-wife. He may be a socially awkward nerd and a bit annoying at times, but he was a decent guy, and he didn't deserve to be hurt by Elizabeth.

"Ian…" Elizabeth called out to him in a seductive purr. "Are you getting jealous of Wally now because I might like him?"

Ian went inside without answering her question… *and…* he realized, without dragging his kids in with him.

When Mary came in behind him twenty minutes later with both kids in tow, Ian greeted her in the doorway with a troubled sigh. "We're going to have a Lizzy problem."

"Why do you say that?" Mary set her briefcase down in the entryway, she shooed the kids into their rooms to put their pajamas on, and followed Ian into their bedroom to change out of her work attire.

Ian hung his own clothes up that he had discarded on the bed before she got here, and helped Mary out of her suit jacket. “She’s got the hots for Wally. She just ran me through the third degree trying to get information on him. And he’s not going to know what hit him if she goes after him. It’s going to be the brutal train wreck that I tried to warn him about.”

Mary frowned at his prediction. “Please don’t tell me what qualities and charms she’s about to unleash on him... I do not need any more of your nostalgic visuals.”

Ian held an apologetic stare on her. “I’m sorry.”

Mary peeled her shirt off and slid out of her skirt. “I’ve known Wally and Elizabeth long enough to appreciate your concern, *without you reciting the graphic erotic details,* and I recognize the obvious imbalance.”

Ian grinned without comment.

Mary continued the conversation. “What makes you think she’ll go after him? Other than her curiosity about him?”

Ian picked Mary’s skirt and blouse up from the bed where she dropped them in a pile, and tossed them into their dry-cleaning basket. “I know Lizzy. Plus, she told me that he was cute.”

“Ah oh…” Mary stepped into sweatpants and pulled on a tee shirt. “Well, as long as he only comes over on the weekends… hopefully no harm will come to him.”

“That’s my hope.” Ian pulled her into his body to kiss her hello. “We might also have a problem with Jenny and Ricky. Lizzy says they’ve been arguing a lot.”

Mary nodded at his observation. “I’ve been noticing the same thing. Not a lot, but more than before. And that’s worrisome.”

“It is.” Ian exhaled with concern. The whole Lizzy/Wally problem would be bumped into second place if there was a Jenny/Ricky problem, because Wally’s marital status was far less concerning to Ian than Jenny’s marital status. He did not want the kids falling out of love because he had no idea how he would make them fall back in love.

“I’ll talk to Jenny.” Mary quickly volunteered to help out. “I’ll see if I can figure out what’s going on with them. Maybe it’s something simple like not listening to each other and him not helping out. He *has* been absorbed with his games lately.”

Ian nodded at his wife’s suggestion as a knock on their bedroom door interrupted his hello greeting with her.

"What is it?" Ian kissed Mary's lips before leaving her arms to open the door to see who was on the other side of it.

Jenny stepped into their bedroom wearing a tearful face. "I need a new baby-daddy. I don't want Ricky anymore. I'm through with him because he's no good."

"Whoa, whoa, whoa, whoa… That is not how it works, Jennifer." Ian laid his vocal skid marks down on top of her request with parental authority that left no room for doubt about what he was saying. "When you marry someone it's for life. You work it out, buttercup, you don't quit. That's not how marriage works." He ushered her into the room with patient determination. "So, Ricky's the only baby-daddy you get, Jenny. That's who you picked. Okay? You do not get to swap him out when you're mad at him."

"That's not fair, daddy!" Jenny burst into tears. "Mom got to pick a new baby-daddy when she didn't like you anymore!"

Ian huffed at the comparison. "Well, that was your mom's mistake. Because she didn't do any better with baby-daddy number two than she did with baby-daddy number one. And that's the perfect example for what I'm saying. You work it out with number one, because number two is rarely better."

"But you think Mary's better than mom… and Mary's your number two."

Ian scowled in defense of himself. "I do. But that's not… it's more than… it's complicated, Jenny, so let's leave me out of this."

"But I don't want Ricky anymore." Jenny didn't let him off the hook. "And mom said I don't have to keep him if he's no good. She said I could dump him like she dumped you. It's my choice."

"No! That is not what you're going to do!" Ian raised his voice in anger. "Go get your mother, right now, Jennifer, because I need to talk to her…*now!*"

"No, Jenny. Do not do that." Mary intervened with quiet resistance. "First… why don't you tell your dad and me what's going on with you and Ricky?" Her eyes settled on Ian with calm determination. "And Ian can talk with your mom later about the advice that she's giving you if he feels it's inappropriate."

"Sure." Ian haltingly took her advice, though it wasn't easy for him. "Mary's right." He returned an appreciative stare towards Jenny and guided her towards his bed so she could sit down on it to talk with them. "Why don't you stop crying, and tell us what's going on?"

Jennifer lowered herself onto the mattress in a fresh wave of emotion. "Ricky isn't nice to me anymore, daddy. He's mean to me."

Ian frowned with concern. "In what way is he mean? Is he hitting you or pushing you around?"

"No. He calls me names, like stinky butt."

Ian forced himself not to smile with amusement. None of this was funny, except their name calling sounded so innocent compared to his adult fighting with Elizabeth.

"So, tell me about that." When he trusted himself not to chuckle, he moved the conversation forward. "Why does he call you stinky butt?"

Jenny wiped her eyes with the back of her hand. "I don't know. My butt stinks?"

Ian chuckled. "Are you taking a shower every day, washing yourself like I taught you when you were little? Cleaning all the cracks?"

"Yes." She giggled with embarrassment.

Mary handed her a Kleenex.

Ian sat on the bed beside her. "Then your butt probably doesn't stink."

Jenny burst into fresh tears. "But he said I'm a stinky butt. So, I called him a doo-doo head and he said he's not a doo-doo head but I'm booger brain."

Ian couldn't help laughing. Jenny and Ricky's fights were nothing like Elizabeth and Ian's fights. They were more like Skylar, Philip, and Ellie's fights. Ian forced himself to stop chuckling. "Why did you call Ricky a doo-doo head? Does he have doo-doo in his head?"

"No." Jenny giggled and wiped her eyes. "But he won't stop playing his game and talk to me. And he won't let me watch TV."

Ian nodded at what she was sharing with them. *This* was the problem that they needed to address; an apparent insurmountable problem for these two, but for adults with better reasoning and coping skills, an easily resolved problem. "So, it sounds to me like we just need to help you kids set some new boundaries. Maybe he only gets to play his games between certain hours of the day and you get to watch TV when he's not playing his games. And for the rest of the day, you guys do other things that you both enjoy."

Jenny nodded at his suggestion. “Ricky only wants to play his game now, daddy. All the time. He doesn’t want to play with me or talk to me. He said he’s not my friend anymore.”

“Those were just fighting words, Jenny. I’m sure he didn’t really mean that.” Ian pulled her under an arm to give her a supportive side-hug. It always tore him up when Jenny’s friends broke her heart. She was so sweet and innocent and because of that she never understood why they were being mean to her. “You’re going to be okay, Jenny. I am confident that we can work this out…”

She nodded at his encouragement. “Because I’m your buttercup?”

Ian smiled. “My buttercup with *Super Powers*… remember? When the mean kids hurt us, what do we do?”

Jenny giggled at his old call to action. “We bounce back.”

“And move on...” Ian tousled her hair. “We don’t stay down.”

“We stand back up!” Jenny raised her fist in the air. “And then we have ice cream. Because we are best friends. And I will feel better because you are my super hero, daddy. Aren’t you? More than mom…”

Ian shot her a grin, without confirming what she said. Then he kissed the top of her head. “What does your mom say about all this? Have you talked to her about it?”

Jenny shook her head. “Mom doesn’t talk to me. She’s not my friend. She’s only Ellie’s friend. She tells me to stop being mean and stop fighting with Ricky. Then she goes to her room and watches TV. She doesn’t let me watch TV with her. Only Ellie watches TV with mom.”

Ian frowned at what he was hearing. “Sounds like your mom and I need to talk.” His eyes went to Mary in silent fury. Then he moved them back to Jenny. “Does she ever come out of her room to tell Ricky to stop playing his games?”

“No.” Jenny started crying again. “She just tells me to stop yelling. She said I’m a bad wife. And Ricky’s going to dump me.”

“Okay, that’s it.” Ian left the bed and reached for Jenny’s hand. “Come on, let’s go talk to Ricky and your mother and see if we can sort this out.”

“Okay, daddy. I won’t dump him if you don’t want me to. I’ll work it out.”

Ian led the way to Jenny’s flat and opened the internal door between houses. “Ricky?”

He was sitting on the couch playing his video game. Elizabeth was in the kitchen serving a peanut butter and jelly sandwich to Ellie.

"That's what you're serving our granddaughter for dinner?" Ian couldn't help himself. If he'd been alone with her, he probably would have snapped even more at her.

Elizabeth turned in protest on him. "It's what she wants, Ian. And this is my time with her, not yours. So, why don't you try and restrain yourself from sniping at me?"

Ian let it go, but not entirely. "Did you by chance get the rabbit put away before you came inside, or did you leave that for me to do without telling me that Jumper is still out there?"

Elizabeth scowled back at him. "Jenny took care of him."

"Good." Ian nodded and moved on. "Ricky…"

He barely looked at him.

Ian tried again. "Please put your game controller down. I'd like to talk to you."

"I'm playing…" He didn't take his eyes off of the TV.

Ian went to the television and turned it off.

"Hey!" Ricky jumped off the couch and went to the television to turn it back on. "I'm playing my game! You can't turn the TV off."

"Ricky…" Ian calmly stood his ground. "Let's talk about what's going on between you and Jenny."

"I don't want to talk. I want to play my game."

"Nope. We're talking." Ian guided him back to the couch. "Why are you calling her a stinky butt?"

Ricky shot Ian a mean scowl. "Because she's bothering me." He moved his attention onto Jenny. "You tattle-telled on me?"

Jenny started crying again. "You're being mean to me. And daddy says you can't be mean."

Ian backed her up as he tried reasoning with Ricky. "What would you do if Ellie called you a stinky butt?"

Ricky chuckled. "I'd tell her that she has to be nice to me. And she can't call me that. Because I'm her dad."

"Okay." Ian nodded at his answer. "So, I'm telling you the same thing… it's not nice to call your wife a stinky butt, and I want you to stop calling her that."

"I'm sorry."

Ian nodded forgiveness. "So why are you calling each other names? Because that's the bigger concern."

"I don't know."

Ian guided him through the communication difficulties. "Do you still love her?"

"Of course, I love her. She's my wife."

Ian nodded with relief, glad to at least get that much out of him. "Okay, so you need to show her that you love her… unless you want her to stop loving you…"

"She can't stop loving me. I'm her husband."

Ian shook his head with the reality of what he was thinking. "She's not going to love you just because she's married to you. She's only going to keep loving you if you keep loving her. And you have to show her the love. If you don't, you're going to end up getting a divorce like Elizabeth and me."

Ricky turned a mad stare on Jenny. "You better not stop loving me."

"And you had better not stop loving her." Ian addressed his charge before Jenny could respond to it for herself.

"Did you stop loving Elizabeth?" Ricky's eyes darted between Ian and Elizabeth.

"I did." Ian unapologetically held his stare when Ricky's eyes returned his direction.

"And she stopped loving you?"

"Yep." Ian nodded his head. "So, why don't you guys start acting nicer to each other so you don't suffer the same result? Maybe stop calling each other names and start doing more things together?"

Ricky looked between them. "Okay, Ian. I can be nicer. Can I play my game now?"

"Nope." Ian shook his head in answer. "We're going to make a schedule for your gaming. From now on you can only play for two hours each day. And then you have to do something else. Things that you can do with Jenny and Ellie. Because when couples stop doing things together, they fall out of love. And then it just gets ugly."

Elizabeth huffed to his side. "Advice you could have followed to save your own marriage, Ian…" She joined them from across the room. "But that's right. Our divorce wasn't your fault, was it?"

Ian ignored her.

Ricky answered his directive. "Two hours is not enough time. I want more time for my games."

"Nope." Ian stood his ground. "That's all the time you're going to get from now on. Otherwise, I'm going to stop you playing them, all together."

"That's not fair."

"Yes, it is." Ian stood firm in his decision. "Do you want a divorce where you have to move back home and live with your mom and dad, and not have a wife anymore to cuddle in bed? Do you want to stop living with Ellie and only visit with her at your mom and dad's house every other weekend and sometimes in the summer and every other Christmas and Halloween?"

"No."

"Because that's what will happen, Ricky." Ian laid it out for him.

Elizabeth huffed to his side. "Which is more visitation than you allowed me."

Ian ignored her victimized spin on Jenny's childhood custody arrangement because it misconstrued how he was granted sole custody of Jenny.

Ricky answered his charge. "I don't want to live with my mom and dad because they will tell me when to go to bed. And Ellie's my Cinderella. And Jenny's my wife. And they will live here with you."

"That's right." Ian stayed focused on Ricky and not the distraction of Elizabeth. "And that will turn you kids into a broken family."

Ian moved his eyes onto his daughter. "And you don't want that either, right?"

Jenny held a scowl on Ricky. "Unless he calls me stinky butt again…"

Ricky laughed at her threat. "You farted last night, and that was stinky."

Ian smiled at his teasing. "Well, Mary's broccoli salad can do that to you…"

Jenny giggled with what she added. "Well, you farted too…"

Ricky laughingly started singing. "I farted, you farted, we all farted a broccoli fart…"

Ellie came into the room with them. "Will peanut butter and jelly make me fart, too, poppee?"

They all laughed at that.

"Okay…" Ian looked between them, relieved that they were at least laughing again. "So, problem solved for the moment?" His eyes took in both of the kids before he moved them onto Ellie, Elizabeth and Mary. Then he returned them to Jenny. "Anything else you want to say to him?"

Jenny moved her eyes onto Ricky. "He's my baby-daddy and I love him?"

Ian smiled. "There you go…" He nodded at Ricky. "What about you, Casanova?"

Ricky chuckled with male pride at the name Ian sometimes used for him. He understood it to mean lover-boy. "You're my baby-mama and I wanna take you to bed now and…"

"Okay!" Ian raised his hands to interrupt what he was saying. "That's a good place to stop what you were saying out loud…"

Mary chuckled at that, but Ricky said it anyway. "I'm going to have sex tonight if I can't play my game."

Ian shook his head in defeat. "Listen, Ricky, learning when to lay some skid marks down is a good thing…"

Elizabeth huffed at his lesson. "Something you still haven't learned…"

Ian ignored her. "And now," he reached for Ricky's arm to tug him his direction. "Let's you and me go outside to get the barn chores done before it gets any later. Because I'm not doing them by myself again tonight."

"Okay, Ian." Ricky gladly went along with him. "And then I can play my game for just one hour, okay?"

"Nope. You're done for tonight. But tomorrow you can play for two hours." Ian led the way towards the open door between houses, as Ricky trailed along behind him. "Come on…" His attention moved onto Elizabeth.

"You and I aren't done with this conversation, Lizzy…" He was still mad about her encouraging Jenny to leave Ricky, instead of helping her work out the problems.

"How's that?" Elizabeth threw him a flirtatious grin.

Ian stopped to impatiently indulge her. "I don't care how you want to frame our dissolution, and if that includes you telling her that you dumped me… fine. But if I hear about you encouraging her to dump him again…" Ian pointed at Ricky. "You're out of here. That is not what they need to hear from you. And I am not putting up with that. Do I make myself clear?"

Elizabeth huffed in answer. "That is so like you to insist that you're the only one who gets to set the rules of engagement for these kids."

Ian smirked back at her. "Unless something changed that I don't know about… you're here at my pleasure… and because of that… I *do* get to set the rules of engagement. And perhaps I need to remind you, that my control over her is something you set in place when you dumped her in my lap when she was only four years old which by default, put me in charge. And one more thing that's hitting a bad chord with me that I might as well get off of my chest while we're talking about the things that make me mad… how come she thinks you're Ellie's friend, and not her friend?"

"What do you mean?" Elizabeth looked surprised by his question.

Ian felt himself go a little nutty inside. "I let you back in her life because you claimed that you wanted to re-establish a maternal bond with her, and she seemed to benefit from the maternal interaction. But she just told me that you're Ellie's friend, not her friend. Why does she feel that way? You're here, but you're not really here for her?" Ian huffed in fury at what he knew was the truth. "That's right! I remember how it works for you! It's never about the people you live with, it's only about yourself and what's good for Lizzy... right?"

"That's not true."

"Yes, it is." Ian should have waited to have this conversation with her later, because he could feel himself imploding internally, but it was too late now to put the conversation off. "If you want to continue being a part of her life…" He forced a calming breath to settle himself down before he finished voicing what he was thinking, "… you had better start being more of a friend to her, because I am not going to let you break her heart again by abandoning her emotionally like you abandoned her physically."

He moved his attention onto Mary and nodded for her to follow him out of the flat. "And now, Lizzy..." His eyes returned to her in fury. "That was the talk. No further discussion needed." He stepped through the doorway with Ricky on his heels, and stopped to turn around.

Elizabeth was still staring at him as Ian addressed Mary with an idea that just came to him. "I think we should take Ricky and Jenny to Monterey for the weekend to remind them of how much fun they have with each other. Do you think you can get Karen to watch the kids this weekend?"

Mary nodded. "I'll ask her. And we'll need to see if Ricky's parents can tend the animals for us…" They usually complied with Ian and Mary's request because they rarely asked them to help out, and because Ricky lived with them, they usually wanted to return the favor.

Ian moved his focus onto Elizabeth. "And I trust you can stay with Ellie this weekend to help Karen out?"

"I guess… if that's an order…"

Ian shot her a complacent smile. "It was certainly a leading question..." He moved his attention back to the adult kids. "So, it looks like we're going on a weekend vacation. You two…" he pointed to Jenny and Ricky. "And Mary and me… let's go have some fun… a second chance for you kids to fall back in love."

"That's a great idea, daddy." Jenny squealed with excitement.

Ricky nodded at his directive. "Okay, Ian. I'll go on a vacation with you and Mary and Jenny and have fun."

Chapter Five

Wally was having a crazy Tuesday morning when he absently grabbed his ringing phone off of his desktop and spoke into the receiver without looking at the caller ID. His desk was covered with yellow tablets filled with research notes as well as his clinical practice records, and today was just one of those wild days when the demands upon him professionally were too many, and the help to relieve him personally, inadequate.

"Hello?"

"Hi there…" The most seductive voice he'd ever heard, answered his greeting. "Is this Doctor Weldon?"

Wally gave the caller his undivided attention. "It is… may I ask who's calling?"

"Elizabeth Chambers, mother of Jennifer Powers…"

"Well, hello…" Wally had no idea how she'd gotten his number but he was thrilled to have her on the other end of his phone line. She certainly didn't get his number from Ian or Mary. That was for sure.

"I hope it's okay for me to call you like this."

"Absolutely okay." Wally left his chair to stand and pace behind his desk. "What can I do for you?" He was almost rendered breathless from the surge of adrenaline that began pulsating through his body.

"Well, I heard that you were working with Jenny and Ricky and their daughter Ellie, my granddaughter. And I thought it appropriate for us to meet."

"Sure." Wally's heart was pounding like crazy from the nervous energy he was feeling. "Where would you like to meet? At Jenny's house? I'm assuming Ian will want to be there?" It was absolutely unimaginable that Ian would *not* want to be there.

Elizabeth giggled. "Assumption incorrect. Ian does not know that I'm even calling you and he would most definitely not want to be there. He and I do not interact on a social level. We barely tolerate each other on a familial level and for the most part, *on a good day…* we politely share parenting responsibilities for Ellie." She laughed with anticipation for what she was about to add to her disclaimer. "*On a bad day…*" She couldn't stop laughing. "You don't even want to be there."

Wally joined her laughter. "I've had my own verbal altercations with Ian before." He could tell already that he liked Elizabeth.

"So, you know how he can be…" She didn't stop giggling.

"I do." Wally's heart pounded harder. It was incredible to think that he was talking to her right now, knowing how Ian would react if he found out. He could picture Ian's rant if he discovered their call. He would undoubtedly go nuts on her… *and him*. "How did you get my number?"

"I asked Jenny what your name was… and she only knows you as Dr. Weldon, which I anticipated. Which was good for me… because Ian only provided your first name." She giggled again.

Wally chuckled with her. She was a woman who knew how to get what she wanted despite her ex-husband's calculated roadblocks. "I like your style, Mrs. Chambers."

"*Ms.* I'm divorced." She laughed as she corrected him. "That's two strikes against me…" She giggled with self-deprecating humor. "But I know how to land on my feet when I'm down, and I'm not afraid to get back in the ring for a third round…"

"A bad husband won't keep you down, huh…" Wally laughed with her as he paced with excitement. This was more lady than he'd ever known before. He could tell that just talking to her. She certainly seemed like a fair match for Ian. It would be so like Ian to withhold information that he alone had determined Elizabeth didn't need. But Wally loved how Elizabeth had learned how to get around Ian's efforts to stay in control.

"I was able to google you once I became armed with your first and last name…"

Wally smiled at her determination. "What did you have in mind?" He let her take charge of the conversation because he assumed that she was used to being in charge, and surely, she had a plan in mind for their meeting, or at least the ability to form one with ease.

"I happen to be unexpectedly flying solo this weekend… with Ellie. I'm staying at Jenny's house. Ellie's parents are going to Monterey with Ian and Mary for the weekend."

"No kidding…" Wally grinned at what she didn't say, but what he could read between the lines – that she was inviting him to a weekend that might include the kind of sexual play that would blow Ian's mind.

He forced himself to respond only to what she had actually offered since he had no intention of taking her up on what she hadn't yet offered. "And you weren't invited to the weekend of fun?" He fell into a tease with her. "The poor baby… all dressed up and nowhere to go?"

Elizabeth chuckled. "Definitely wouldn't be invited to a weekend with Ian and Mary. Those two love birds are nauseatingly infatuated with each other like immature teenagers who don't know better than to keep their hands to themselves. It's embarrassing having to watch them."

Wally chuckled at her imagery. "They have always been like that – overly touchy-feely. It's enough to make you gag…"

"Or vomit." Elizabeth laughed at what he said. Then she moved her focus onto Wally. "I knew I was going to like you…"

"Likewise, I'm sure." Wally thought for a minute for some other derogatory thing that he could say about Mary and Ian because he could tell that Elizabeth enjoyed putting them down. "Ian used to leave hickeys all over her neck like a kid trying to prove he could get laid…"

Elizabeth huffed with disapproval. "Well, that fits his wannabe rock-star image…"

"Yep…" Wally loved how she agreed with him. "And Mary was just as bad, advertising how she was letting him score with her…"

"Mary is too full of herself…"

Wally chuckled despite feeling secretly sad about putting Mary down. "It sounds like you could use some like-minded company this weekend…" He didn't know why he offered that, except it felt good to be talking to her.

"You read my mind!" Elizabeth confirmed his suggestion with a specific invitation. "Why don't you bring a bottle of wine and some Chinese take-out? We can chat over lunch and get to know each other."

"Sure…" Wally's heart pounded harder. What was he doing? Every bit of common sense warned him off of her – this was the kind of woman who left no man standing. *Ian said so himself* – she would take him to hell and back – and that did not sound good to Wally.

But he couldn't find the will-power to listen to his own caution. Undisputedly, what he desperately wanted to do, was stand in line to buy himself a ticket for that perilous ride into purgatory with her.

"Not that I want you to get the wrong idea…" Elizabeth giggled like a school girl – *a wave off and a come-on all at once.* "This is just a professional meet and greet for us.... Nothing more." Her laugh said otherwise, but Wally acknowledged her verbal clarification.

"Of course." He couldn't help but feel a sense of loss as he silently waved goodbye to an erotic rendezvous, while he simultaneously welcomed the relief that washed through his anxious thought process. He did not want trouble with Betty Jo. *Wally loved Betty Jo.* He reminded himself of that again to make sure that he was staying focused on what was very important to him. *He was a married man…* and he wanted to keep it that way.

"Can you come early and stay for the day so we can get to know each other while you interact with Ellie and observe how she interacts with me? I don't want you having a one-sided view of her – only seeing her through Ian and Mary's interactions…"

"Sure." That was a fair enough concern, and certainly a legitimate reason to meet with Elizabeth without Ian being involved. Why not?

"And probably best if we don't say anything to Ian or Mary…" Elizabeth spoke with a conspiratorial tone. "Not that we'll be doing anything wrong, but you know what they're like… *lawyers…* they get themselves so worked up over things the rest of us just don't care about."

Wally chuckled. "I've seen them both get riled up about silly things…" Like when Ian went nuts over Wally ogling Elizabeth… why did it even matter to him? It's not like Wally's marriage was any of Ian's business… and if he didn't want Elizabeth talking to other guys… well, maybe he should've done a better job of holding onto her. After all, he was the one who let her go… so why should Ian now have any rights over her? Who was he to dictate who Elizabeth talked to?

She laughed winding up the conversation. "So, I'll see you about what? One-thirty?"

"Sure. I'm looking forward to it. What's your favorite Chinese food?"

She giggled like he asked her what sex toy she preferred. "I'll get the food… you bring the wine."

"It's a deal." Wally hung his desk phone up, feeling like a man on a mission. *She liked him!* It was absolutely unbelievable, and thrilling to think that she was interested in him despite the almighty Ian Powers coming before him. What a hard act to follow… but here he was… following Ian's departure on his own two feet…it was an amazing revelation, and Wally had to admit to himself… it went straight to his head… And in fact, the jubilation that he was feeling was striking nerve endings all over his body.

Elizabeth, *Ian's one-time sex Goddess…* liked dumb ol' Wally, *Ian's invisible side-kick.*

****

When Saturday finally arrived after the longest work week Wally could ever remember, he woke early without an alarm clock, he went to the gym and worked out, and returned home at noon to shower and shave and dress for the meeting. Nothing too fancy. He wanted to look casual but professional since that was the context of this meeting. He grabbed a pair of Docker slacks, a button up short sleeved shirt, and splashed himself with cologne.

"You're off for your lunch meeting?" Betty Jo met him by the door as he was collecting his keys and wedding ring from a dish where he dropped both each night when he came home from work.

"Yep." He slid the gold band onto his left index finger and gave her a kiss goodbye. "I'm not sure what time I'll be home. It's a working lunch… so it may go long in the afternoon."

"We can microwave leftovers when you get here. I've got a busy afternoon too, so I may run late as well." She was also dressed nicely, but casually.

Wally barely noticed. "Are you meeting your girlfriends for a boozy brunch in Sacramento?" He said that as a tease because she often met with her sorority sisters on the weekend for girlie luncheons – in fact, a lot of weekends.

Betty Jo nodded with distraction, already moving on in her head with her own plans.

"Okay… drive safely." Wally gave her a quick kiss goodbye and left his house. He felt incredibly light and airy as he walked to his car, excited about meeting Elizabeth, and happy about feeling so alive again.

He drove into town and stopped at a liquor store to buy a good bottle of wine, then he eagerly drove to Ian's house, listening to the radio and smiling the whole way. He couldn't remember feeling so uplifted in ages.

He parked his car in the driveway next to Ian's black truck and turned off the ignition. It was hard to believe that he was about to get out of his car to spend the day with Ian's drop-dead gorgeous ex-wife – *behind Ian's back*. It was sort of a thrilling contrary thing for Wally to do. It felt daring to him, and kind of like he was scoring a big one for himself.

"Hi…"

Wally jumped and turned with a start to a tapping on his window.

There she was… waiting for him to step out of his car.

Wally shot her a grin and opened his door. She looked like an angel dressed in a flowery summer frock, barefoot, and lightly dusted with a sweet flowery scent that made him want to pull her into his body for a never-ending kiss. He couldn't remember the last time he felt that way with Betty Jo.

"I hope you don't mind… last minute change in plans. Ellie's having an overnight slumber party with Ian's kids… her aunt and uncle… I couldn't talk her out of it."

"Jenny's half-siblings…that's right." Wally nodded his head. "Jenny told me about them." But Wally had to think for a minute about how Elizabeth was describing them. "Weird family… I would have impulsively called them her cousins given their closeness in age…"

"Right?" Elizabeth chuckled. "So, even without Ellie being here, let's take this opportunity to get to know each other… since you know Ian and Mary so well and I'm as much a part of the kids' lives as the two of them."

Wally nodded at her suggestion. "Good point."

Elizabeth shot him a smile. "You'll have to tell me all of your worst stories about Ian and Mary from high school…I can't wait to hear them."

Wally chuckled. "I have the wine... did you get the food?"

She knowingly grinned back at him. "Two of my favorite things. Do you want to ask me what my third favorite thing is?"

“Sure…” Wally was suddenly feeling completely out of his league with her. She was so beautiful and self-assured – she didn’t look at all nervous about making conversation with him. She was simply oozing confidence – *like Ian* – who always came up with exactly the right thing to say, at exactly the right moment – whether it was a put down, or a compliment. The perfect comeback always seemed to be on the tip of Ian’s tongue, ready to fall out of his mouth at precisely the right moment.

Elizabeth apparently had that same talent. She was a perfect match for Ian. Except, *apparently*, she wasn’t… because she was now flirting with Wally – at least it seemed like she was flirting with him – as awkward and socially incompetent as he felt.

“What’s your third favorite thing?” He shot her a confident look that masked his inner turmoil. If he could only stay calm and cool – *like Ian* – she might think that he was in her league.

She giggled and brushed her thick wavy locks away from her movie-star face. “Actually, I’d say it’s my first favorite thing… before food and wine…”

Wally anticipated what she was going to say. “Men?” He couldn’t help but confidently guess that. And because he fit that bill, it made him feel desirable – especially since she was the one who had chased him down – not the other way around.

She laughed with a sexy wave of her hair. “Look how well you already know me…” Her beautifully manicured hand left her hair to trail down her body.

Wally watched it go down, over her breasts and down lower across her abdomen towards her nether region. She brought it back up to tuck some hair behind her ear.

“We must be destined for love… to be so in tune with each other…” She reached for his hand and tugged him along as she turned toward the house on her pedicured bare feet. Her skirt billowed from the motion of her body and a slight breeze that blew in, and she dropped her other manicured palm to hold the light cotton material to keep it from blowing. “I guess I picked the wrong thing to wear today… it seems a little windy.”

Wally could only focus on the movement of her firm thighs and her dancing feet with red painted toenails. He didn’t know what he was doing here, and he regretted coming now that he realized the power that she seemingly held over him, because he knew it could only bring him trouble at home – and he did not want trouble. But he could not step away. He was drawn to follow Elizabeth by a force he could not understand or resist.

In the back of his head, he heard Ian cautioning him… *she's chaos Wally… no matter how good she feels under your body…*

"So, I guess you've been here before…" Elizabeth ushered him inside Jenny's flat to where the kitchen table was set for two. "I stay here on weekdays to help the kids with Ellie… and any other time that Ian asks me to help out."

The place had been cleaned to a high polished gleam, and there were freshly cut flowers on the table, likely from Ian's front yard because they looked like the same roses that were growing out front. And there were two wine glasses waiting to be filled.

Wally said what came to mind in a sudden rush to save himself. "You know I'm married, right?" He didn't know why he felt the need to blurt that out, except it was the only armor he still possessed – *his marital status* – and standing here so close to her, Wally felt a desperate need to save himself. He was clearly in way over his head, and that realization scared the wits out of him because he knew if she started something with him, he would not be able to stop it.

Elizabeth giggled at his disclaimer. "I know… I've been thinking about that too – darn it. But you're so adorable… I may not be able to help myself."

Wally blushed. It wasn't a cool reaction to her compliment, and if he were Ian he would have somehow – *coolly* – blown off what she said without blushing. If only he had a small portion of Ian's cool. But he didn't. He mustered the best he had in him and shrugged off the flush of his cheeks like it was no big deal.

"I love the dress…" He tried his best to pull off an Ian type reaction by returning a casual compliment to her. "… but then… it's probably not the dress. It's you. I suppose anything you wear is going to look good on you…"

She giggled at his compliment without blushing. Like Ian, she knew what she had, and that gave her the confidence to take his compliment with grace. "You sound like Ian, when you say things like that… no wonder you two were pals."

"Really?" Wally felt himself relax with her. He never would have represented himself as Ian's pal, but her thinking he fit the bill made him feel more manly than he usually allowed himself to believe. "How about I open that bottle of wine for you?"

"That'd be great…" She fluffed her hair. "Because you know… it's my second favorite thing…" Her hand landed on his shoulder like they were sharing some whispered conspiracy. "I've got an opener over here…" She stepped away from him and Wally followed her to the counter.

"I wasn't sure if you'd want red or white…"

She laughed at his quandary. "Well, Ian would tell you it doesn't matter what you choose… I'll finish whatever you bring."

Wally chuckled at that. He could see that Ian definitely had his hands full with this one. And that probably delighted Ian as much as it frustrated him. Perhaps more of the former at the beginning of their relationship, and more of the latter at the end. "I take it he thinks you drink too much?"

Elizabeth giggled as she went for the two glasses. "I'll definitely drink to that!" She handed him the glasses. "Let's both drink to the opinions of Ian Powers that no longer matter to me."

"Here, here…" Wally poured the wine in both of their glasses and handed one to Elizabeth. "To the opinions of Ian Powers that we are both happy to prove wrong…"

And to the beauty of falling in love with her; the first of Ian's contrary opinions that Wally was already proving wrong.

She tapped her glass into his and raised it to her pouty lips. "To proving him wrong… one judgmental opinion at a time…"

Wally raised his glass to his lips. "To my arch nemesis, the almighty *Loser Powers…*"

Elizabeth blew wine from her lips… "I am so going to love hanging out with you…"

For a minute Wally was reminded of that long-ago evening when he taunted Ian that Mary would drop him one day to hang out with Wally instead. He figured it was almost as good to have Elizabeth hanging out with him as it would have been to have Mary at his side… maybe it was even better to have Elizabeth – she just might be more fun.

"So, are you happily married… or just getting by?"

It was Wally's turn to try not to let the wine in his mouth blow out. He couldn't believe she'd come right out and asked that and he wasn't sure how he should answer her. If he did the right thing and feigned happiness it would push her away, but he couldn't bring himself to lie to her to bring about the right result.

"You're not happy." Elizabeth answered the question for him. "Otherwise, you wouldn't be trying to convince yourself to lie to me."

"You're right." Wally truthfully nodded, not that he meant to – she just seemed to have the ability to draw an honest confession out of him. "But we're working on our happiness." He quickly set the record straight. "And I'm not looking to cheat on my wife..."

Elizabeth chuckled. "Nobody ever admits that they are... but it happens."

Wally gulped at the thought. "I'm not that kind of guy."

Elizabeth's grin turned wicked. "I've never known a married guy who wasn't that kind of guy..." Her smile was definitely flirting and Wally couldn't help but flirt back.

"We'll see..."

"Yep." She spoke like she already knew the answer to her unspoken proposition that hovered in the air between them.

Wally looked for a distraction. The kitchen setting had an adult intimacy to it with the table set for two, except for the scribbled coloring book pages displayed on the refrigerator doors, held up by Disney magnets. Wally knew they were Jenny's from her years of going to Disneyland with her father. The art work would be Cinderella's... except half of the pictures had been colored by a better artist – Cinderella's mother. He moved his attention around the small kitchen and into the family room where he sat last Saturday when he met Jenny, Ricky, and Ellie.

Elizabeth had pillows nicely displayed on the couch and there was soft music playing from an unseen stereo. Her intentions seemed obvious. She might as well have splayed him out on the dinner table and devoured him right there because he suddenly felt like captured prey – *her chosen entrée for this evening.*

His eyes moved back to Elizabeth and he saw that she was watching him. "I'm..." He shrugged as he looked back at her because he realized that he honestly wasn't the kind of guy she usually knew – *he wasn't a cheat* – regardless of her intentions and his own unhappiness. He just didn't belong here.

"Don't be nervous..." She read it in his expression. "I do no harm."

Wally gave her an apologetic shrug. "I can't cheat."

"Of course not."

"Seriously." He added to his apology. "I just couldn't do that to my wife… even if…" What? He didn't like her anymore? She didn't turn him on? In fact, she barely noticed him?

"I wouldn't want you to cheat on her!" Elizabeth went to the counter where four white boxes waited to be opened. "I'm not that kind of woman." She changed the subject. "I bought broccoli beef…" She turned to look at him. "Most guys seem to like their red meat…"

Wally smiled. She did seem to know a lot about men.

"And sweet and sour pork…in case you like white meat…"

Wally went to stand beside her. "How can I help?"

She handed him a serving spoon. "And there's vegetarian fried rice and chow mein."

"My favorite…" He reached for one of two plates and served himself some food from each box. Then he went to the table and set his plate down. When hers was filled, though it barely had any food on it, he pulled her chair out for her.

"Why, thank you." She smoothed her dress over her firm small bottom and gracefully lowered herself onto the seat.

Wally scooted the chair in for her and went to sit across from her. "So, tell me something I don't know about Ian…" He picked his fork up to begin eating as one of her painted toes found his ankle under the table. Wally looked up with a start.

Elizabeth answered his question like nothing startling was happening. "He can apparently sing every Disney song by heart… and he can play them all on his guitar."

Wally chuckled. "I remember what a good musician he was in high school. Drums and guitar… he was phenomenal on both. But the Disney thing doesn't fit his cool guy image…"

Elizabeth nodded. "I know. Nonetheless, part of his endearing charm." Her toes slid up his pantleg. "Just one of the many reasons why women can't help themselves with him…"

Wally smiled.

Elizabeth picked her fork up. "Your turn…"

Wally nodded trying to think of anything but the stroking of her toes on the inside of his ankle. What could he share with her besides the fact that she was sending tingles up his leg? He wanted to come up with something that was less flattering about Ian than his ability to woo women into his arms with Disney songs.

"Here's something..." Wally shot her a grin. "When Ian was moving from California our senior year of high school, a bunch of friends had a going away party for him, and he got really wasted. It was kind of funny at first because he was remembering everything that everyone had ever done wrong to him, and he started teasingly calling people out for stuff. Like he defiantly pointed to me and jocularly said, *remember that time Polly Wally in seventh grade, when you tagged along to Baskins & Robbins with Mary and me and you did not have enough money to pay for what you bought... I did not like having to pay for your triple ice cream cone and soda."*

Elizabeth giggled. "That'd just be his way of saying goodbye. A few caustic remarks as he shoves you out the door."

Wally chuckled. "Yeah, he was calling everyone out for all kinds of silly stuff."

Elizabeth nodded with appreciation for what Wally was sharing. "Ian does have a good memory when it comes to remembering the wrongs that have been committed against him."

Wally agreed. "Except when it comes to Mary, of course... he would never call her out for anything."

Elizabeth huffed and rolled her eyes. "Mary the perfect nymph..." She sighed with disgust.

Wally chuckled. "So, back to Ian's drunken night."

"Yes, please give me the details..."

Wally was happy to oblige. "At some point during the night I noticed that Ian was no longer holding center stage chewing people out for inconsequential stuff, and in fact he and Mary had disappeared. So, I went outside to the keg to see if they were out there, and I saw Ian across the yard barfing in the grass. Mary had her arms wrapped around him, trying to keep him on his feet and he was barely standing up. So, I went over and asked if she needed any help with him and she frantically shooed me away, because she didn't want anyone seeing him like that. And Ian was no longer in a playful fighting mood, he was just feeling belligerent at this point, and he turned on me, and said something like, *dude, can't you wait until I'm at least out of town before you make your move on her?* If he hadn't been puking, he probably would have swung a fist at me. So anyway, I left them alone and went back inside, and by then word had gotten out that Ian was sick and everyone was surprised about that because he could usually drink most of us under the table, without it even showing on him. But this night... he was an emotional wreck and he never came back inside for the party. He and Mary stayed outside for the rest of the night. When I finally went home around 2:00 am, I saw them still out there by themselves. Ian was laying in the grass on his back and Mary was laying on her stomach beside him and I'm sure they were both crying. Every so often as I stood there watching them, Ian would bring a hand to his face to wipe his eyes. And Mary was openly weeping with him."

Elizabeth frowned at his story. "I heard about that night from Mary once. She told me he was puking everywhere. Again, doesn't fit his cool image, but he somehow always seems to get a free pass."

"Right?" Wally ate a bite of food as her toes slid higher up his leg. It was incredibly distracting – and extremely enjoyable.

"Here's another one…" Wally liked sharing Ian's less than finer moments with her. It reminded him that Ian was, in fact, no different than the rest of them. And taking Ian down, conversely, built Wally up. "When we were sophomores in high school, we had this math teacher who was the most miserable human being… and one day Ian had the brilliant idea that he should toss a Black Jack firecracker into his classroom during one of his lectures."

"You're kidding me…" Her toes slid up and down.

"Nope." Wally forced himself to concentrate on what he was saying. "He did it during my algebra class, him and Joe Greene, this jock he hung out with. But the prank backfired on him. Joe tossed his Black Jack into the room and it made a bang under Dressler's desk. But the fuse on Ian's Black Jack was too short and it went off in his hand before he could throw it. And as the thing exploded the two of them took off running in different directions and Ian turned and ran head-on into our principal, who was coming down the hall because he heard the first bang. I don't remember if Joe got caught, but Ian got in trouble. He couldn't deny it was him because the fire cracker had burnt his hand. He had blisters all over his fingers."

"Oh my gosh, I've never heard that story. How much trouble did he get into?"

"Detention for three days, I think, but everyone thought it was a cool prank. So, he got some good yardage out of the burnt fingers except he couldn't play his guitar for a few days and that really annoyed him. When the news of what he did traveled through our school it fed his tough-guy image, but honestly, that was probably the worst thing that I ever knew him to do."

Elizabeth poked some food in her mouth as her right foot found Wally's left leg. He tried not to notice it sliding up and down from his ankle to his knee as he focused on another story. "Ian had this Chevy van that we used to all pile into and he'd drive it out onto some backroad and find a place to park it, and we'd sit around inside it drinking beer and smoking dope. Just having a teenage party. He had a mattress on the floorboards of it, so you can imagine the kind of activity that sometimes took place there…"

Elizabeth nodded at what he shared with her. "He told me about his van a long time ago, and how he and Mary lost their virginity in it, right before he moved away. Totally in Ian's character to have sex with her knowing they were breaking up. And obviously conniving on Mary's part… like maybe she could somehow trap him with a teenage pregnancy or something..."

"Really?" Wally was surprised by her revelation. "I always thought they were having sex long before he moved away. But now I'm shocked that he'd have sex with her knowing he was leaving town…what kind of guy would do that? Take the virginity of someone you supposedly love, and then leave like that?"

"Right?" Elizabeth shook her head. "He has this detached side to his personality… he can completely shut his emotions down and go absolutely heartless in a matter of seconds. He just turns himself off on command." Elizabeth leaned Wally's direction as her foot went higher up his leg. "On the other hand, you seem like a guy who is always in touch with your emotions…" She poured more wine into their glasses. "Like you could never be heartless or detached like Ian."

They spent the next two hours sharing tales at the kitchen table before Elizabeth suggested that they move to the family room where they could chat more comfortably on the couch instead.

Wally anxiously agreed, though he feared for his own integrity if they did make the move. What he *should* do right now, was go home and end this meeting that had become more of a hot date than a professional appointment, before anything more unforgivable than her sexy toes sliding up and down his leg happened between them.

Elizabeth plopped down first and patted the cushion next to her. "Don't be scared..." She giggled flirtatiously. "I promise I don't take hostages…"

Wally chuckled. "Maybe it's you who should be scared…" He didn't know why he said that, except he liked flirting back with her.

"Of you?" She giggled at the idea. "I don't think so…" Her tone egged him on as her hand pulled him down beside her. "You don't have it in you…"

Wally dropped onto the couch cushion and drew her into his arms. "You wanna bet?" Their lips met with passion and he kissed her with all of the emotion he felt inside that hadn't been released in way too long. His palm slid down the side of her torso, taking in the firmness of her frame, then he drew it back up to slowly enjoy the roundness of her plump breast. Wally moved his left palm down the other side of her body. She was the sexiest thing he'd every kissed or held in his arms. He regrettably acknowledged to himself, as his palms slid over her body, that he would definitely be taking that trip to hell and back with her if she didn't hurry up and push him off the train.

"Wow… those hands…they're amazing." She stared into his eyes with a seductive beckoning as their lips barely parted from the heat of their exchange. "I didn't think you were that kind of guy…"

Wally felt the incredible rush of a pounding heartbeat and the demanding roll of internal sexual energy that needed to be released. "I didn't think so, either." She made him feel so alive that his own actions terrified and excited him all at once. "But here we are…" He was absolutely horrified that he couldn't shutdown the undeniable rush of desire that had taken him hostage.

"Kiss me again…" Elizabeth dropped her palm on his thigh and slowly moved it higher until it bumped into the bulge at the end of her journey. Her fingers raised over it and barely touched him sending chills throughout his entire body.

"Oh God…" He desperately wanted to make love.

Elizabeth dropped her lips onto his. "I need this so badly… you have no idea. My entire body is aching for you."

Wally stopped her palm from stirring things up inside his Dockers. "Is there a bedroom in this house?"

"I think I can find one." Elizabeth pushed herself off the couch and took his hand in hers. Wally mindlessly followed her into a room and quietly locked the door behind her. He had no idea what he was doing here with her, but he couldn't find the will power to stop what was about to happen. He ached so badly for the feel of her body under the bare flesh of his own...

Chapter Six

Ian drove the approximate two-and-a-half-hour trip to Monterey Saturday morning, singing with Mary and the kids to favorite 70s hits, and a fair share of Disney songs. They had packed overnight bags last night, so they could leave early this morning. Karen had stayed the night so she was in place, and Ricky's parents had agreed to care for their livestock and other pets. Ian hated leaving his younger children out of the fun weekend adventure, but he wanted this trip to be focused entirely on the big kids. He felt like they had somehow been pushed aside lately, and because of that their happiness had been overlooked.

Elizabeth was right. He was so busy these days at work and at home taking care of the little kids that he had somehow lost touch with Jenny's happiness. And that wasn't like him. Ian had been solely responsible for Jenny's happiness for most of her life. And he didn't want to abstractly pass that responsibility onto Ricky, because as much as he thought Ricky was a good husband for his daughter, Ricky didn't have the ability to solely take on the responsibility of her happiness. And everyone's happiness was dependent upon keeping these two adult kids in love.

When they arrived in Monterey, they checked into the Portola Hotel where they had stayed before, and after they were settled in their adjoining rooms, they went to a nearby beach to stroll along the water's edge. Mary and Jenny walked together so the two of them could have a girl talk, and Ian hung back with Ricky so they could talk without Jenny and Mary listening.

"So, what's going on with you and Jenny?" Ian picked up a scorched piece of driftwood and tossed it into the ocean to watch it ride a wave.

"Nothing…" Ricky was making a trail of crooked footprints in the wet sand.

"Well, maybe that's a problem in itself, Ricky…" Ian walked along beside him, watching the water roll in as the waves pounded into the shore before sliding back out again.

"What's a problem?" Ricky shot him a confused stare.

Ian shrugged with his need for clarification. "How come you guys are fighting all the time and not having fun with each other?"

"I don't know." Ricky moved his eyes away from Ian's focused stare. "We don't fight all the time."

"Well, that's not what I'm hearing. So, let's talk about it… man to man."

Ricky returned his eyes to him. "Okay, Ian. I'll talk man to man."

Ian shot him a smile. "So how about this for openers… how's your love life?"

"I don't know what you mean?" Ricky bent to pick a seashell up from the sand. "I'm going to give this to Jenny. She likes seashells."

Ian grinned with satisfaction. He liked that Ricky was thinking that way. "Are you guys still cuddly with each other? Are you making love when you go to bed? That sort of thing?"

Ricky blushed. "Jenny doesn't let me touch her in bed."

Ian frowned at that. "How come?"

"My legs hurt her legs. They're too heavy. She doesn't like that. And she doesn't want me putting my arm on her either. It squishes her. So, I don't do that."

Ian wasn't sure if he was talking about making love, or just laying his legs on top of hers when she was trying to sleep. "You mean when she's sleeping, she makes you stay on your side of the bed? Or are you saying she never lets you cuddle her anymore?"

"I don't touch her when she's sleeping. She gets mad when I do that. So, we don't cuddle any more. I go to bed too late."

Ian nodded with less concern than he felt at the start of the conversation. He'd take a late bedtime issue over any of the other numerous reasons Jenny might have for not wanting Ricky to touch her. "Why aren't you going to bed together? That's what Mary and I do. That's how we stay connected. At the end of a busy day, we go to bed together and we talk about our day, and we laugh with each other… and that often gets us kissing… which is a pretty good thing for us."

"And then you have sex?" Ricky kept his eyes on him.

"Sure." Ian shot him a grin. "If I'm lucky…"

Ricky laughed at what he said. "I'm not lucky."

It was Ian's turn to laugh at what Ricky said. "Well, what are you going to do to change your bad luck?"

Ricky shrugged his shoulders. "I like to play my game. And Jenny gets tired so she goes to bed. And I'm not supposed to wake her up. She doesn't like that."

"Yeah, Mary isn't wild about a midnight wake up, either." Ian frowned in contemplation. "So, how does a guy your age choose to play video games when instead he could be crawling into bed with his wife to have sex? I don't get that. If it were me… the choice wouldn't be hard. I'd choose Mary any day over video games."

Ricky patted him on the back with gentle understanding. "That's because you aren't very good at playing video games. But I'm a superstar. And I like to win."

Ian laughed at that. "Still, I'm just saying… I think you're focused on the wrong thing, Ricky. Because I'm scoring at something better than gaming… I'm… we're cuddling."

"And having sex. I know." Ricky laughed with him. "I like sex. But Jenny says, not now when I wake her up. She's too sleepy."

Ian shook his head with patient understanding. "Well what time are you waking her up?"

"When I'm too tired to play my game. That's when Jenny's snoring."

Ian nodded at what he said. "Okay, so you need to stop playing your games so much. They're messing up your life, Ricky, and I'm not going to be able to fix what you're doing to yourself."

"I don't want to stop playing my games."

"You want to stop being married?"

"No."

"You want to stop having sex?"

"No."

"Then you better listen to my warning and get control over your life."

"Hey?" Mary turned to look at them.

"What?" Ian shot her a happy smile. From what he could tell, the kids had a very fixable problem. "I can't hear you over the ocean…"

Mary and Jenny were walking just far enough ahead of them that the waves crashing onto the beach drowned out her voice.

Mary stopped walking so the two guys could catch up with them. “Jenny was remembering the last time we came here when we played miniature golf. The kids had so much fun with that. Why don’t we do that today?”

“Sure.” Ian looked at Ricky to see what he thought about that. “Do you remember how to have fun without a game controller in your hand?”

“I like to play golf.” He high fived Ian. “Is that how I get control of my life?”

Ian chuckled. “It’s a start, Ricky.”

“So, let’s play miniature golf!” He left Ian’s side and went to Jenny’s side instead, and happily grabbed her hand. “I can beat you at golf!’

Jenny laughed at his teasing. “I will beat you first!”

The kids walked off on their own, leaving Ian and Mary to enjoy some alone time for their own quiet conversation as they made their way back to town to the miniature golf attraction.

“How’s Jenny doing?” Ian closed his palm around Mary’s hand and softly caressed it inside his own hand.

Mary rubbed her thumb over the back of his hand in response. “He just doesn’t have time for her. It’s like she said before… he can’t stop playing his video games.”

“Yeah, that’s what I got out of Ricky. So, maybe all we need to do is enforce some rules over his gaming to put them back on track.”

They made it back to town where they played a round of miniature golf, and they all had fun with that, even though Ricky got the worst score of his life, which he bemoaned to no end.

Ian teasingly rubbed Ricky’s back, copying Ricky’s earlier consoling gesture towards him. “You can’t be a superstar at everything, Ricky.”

He pouted only half teasing. “But I want to win.”

Ian shot him a grin. “You did win… you had a great time with Jenny. Right? So, maybe you’ll get lucky tonight…” He teasingly offered that, like they were chatting man to man.

“That’s true.” Ricky went to hold her hand and they left the arcade to walk down the street to the Bubba Gump Shrimp Co on Cannery Row, for dinner.

They ordered their food when they were seated at a table, and Ian ordered a bottle of wine. He poured some in both of the kids' wine glasses, then he poured some for Mary and him.

"Cheers…" Jenny picked her glass up to make a toast.

Ricky clinked his glass into hers. Neither of the kids ever drank much. Occasionally, Ricky had a beer with Ian when they were outside doing farm work, and both kids would sometimes have a glass of wine with dinner, but other than that, they weren't big drinkers.

"To my daddy because he's the best daddy in the world, and to Mary because she's my best mother ever."

Ian grinned at her toast as he tapped his glass into Jenny's. "Nicely stated, Jenny."

Mary smiled with them as her glass tapped into theirs. "Thank you, Jenny. And you're my best grown-up daughter."

Jenny giggled at her endearment. "Because I'm your only grown-up daughter."

They all laughed at the truth in her words.

Ricky added his own toast. "To my beautiful wife." He clanked his glass into hers. "I want to go back to the hotel after dinner and get lucky, and have sex."

Mary choked on the wine she was sipping and Ian shook his head with contained amusement.

"Ricky…"

"Honey-bear!" Jenny squealed with embarrassment. "That's not what you're supposed to say in front of my daddy!"

Ricky laughed without a care. "Ian told me to take control of my life. And I want to have sex tonight. So, I'm taking control. That's how I get lucky."

Ian chuckled off Jenny's embarrassment and Ricky's dedication to his advice. "You know what, Ricky? I might want to have sex too when I get back to the hotel. But that's not something I'm going to announce to anyone but Mary."

"Daddy... you're not supposed to want that."

"Why not?" Ian scowled in objection. "We've all had a fun day on the beach, and then we had all that fun playing miniature golf…"

"Followed by our romantic dinner…" Jenny added to his recap in a dreamy voice mimicking the kind of overly dramatic crooning she'd heard on TV.

"Yep…" Ian smiled between them. "And that kind of fun makes me feel happy inside and that makes me feel romantic. So, I may want the same thing that Ricky wants at the end of this day. And there's nothing wrong with Ricky *or me* wanting to have sex with our wives… as long as you and Mary want to have sex too. That's the bottom line…"

Ian moved his focus onto Ricky. "You need to remember that, Ricky, as you take control of your life. Because Jenny gets to say *no* even though she's your wife. If she's not into it with you, if she's not in the mood, if she's not feeling it… she gets to say no. So, if you don't want her to say no, you need to be nice to her, you need to get to bed on time, and you need to show her some loving attention to get her in a romantic mood… and if you do that…" He shot Ricky a wink. "You just might get lucky like me."

"Daddy…" Jenny squealed with embarrassment again.

"I know Ian." Ricky reached for Jenny's hand and held it in his. "I'll be nice to her and go to bed on time and show her attention to get her in a romantic mood."

Jenny giggled. "And don't call me stinky butt anymore."

Ian chuckled. "And don't you call him a doo-doo head."

"I won't!"

The two kids laughed together.

"Or booger-brain…" They said it together and laughed harder.

Their meal was served and the table conversation stayed fun. The kids laughed and shared stories about their day on the beach, they remembered stories from their honeymoon and they teased each other about their golf games. It was light hearted, and back to normal sounding, and such a relief for Ian. He'd spent the last twenty plus years of his life trying to keep his little girl happy, and he didn't want her to become unhappy now that he was treating her more like a happily married adult.

When they were through with their meals, Ricky finished his wine and moved his attention onto Ian.

"Can we have dessert?" He gulped down the water in his glass. "I need a sugar boost for more energy. Because I'm having lots of sex with my wife tonight."

"Honey-bear!" Jenny squealed with embarrassment. "Stop saying that."

Ian backed her up. “Quit it now…” He handed him the menu with a shake of his head. “That’s not how a gentleman talks about his lady…” He glanced at Mary as he ended his scolding for Ricky, and with a teasing twinkle in his eye, he leaned her direction and whispered in her ear. “You should probably pick a dessert, too… for energy.”

Mary grinned at his whispered tease. “Well, you’re feeling overly confident tonight…”

He chuckled at that and spoke near her ear. “Well, I can’t remember a time post high school when you’ve turned me down…”

Mary giggled and blushed. “True statement.”

He winked with their private conversation. “Pick whatever you want for dessert. I’ll share it with you…”

Mary nodded at his suggestion as she dropped her hand under the table to rub his thigh. “Whatever you want… *lucky strike…* is good with me.”

Ian held her palm still before she got a rise out of him. “I’ll take your hand in mine….” He squeezed his fingers around hers and took the menu from Ricky to take a look at it for himself. “How about we split the chocolate chip cookie sundae?” He handed the menu back to Ricky. “What do you guys want?”

“I want my own desert.” Ricky studied the menu. “This one.” He pointed to cheese cake.

“I don’t like cheese cake.” Jenny frowned at his choice. “Pick something else. Daddy and I always share dessert, so you have to share with me too.”

“No, he doesn’t.” Ian took the menu and handed it to Jenny. “Pick your own desert, and if it’s more than you can eat, you don’t have to finish it.”

“Or we can take what’s left back to the hotel,” Mary added an alternative. “And you guys can share it later…”

“After we have sex.” Ricky agreed.

Ian rolled his eyes.

Ricky looked at the menu with Jenny and tried to persuade her to pick what he wanted. “Don’t pick ice cream. It will melt. You have to pick the cheese cake.”

“I want the sundae like daddy.”

Ian wrapped up the discourse with a final summation. “So, two sundaes and one cheese cake. Right?”

Jenny nodded her head. "I will save Ricky the cookie for later. I'll only eat the ice cream."

Ricky kissed her lips. "Because I will be hungry after I have sex."

Jenny slapped him on the shoulder. "Stop saying that, honey-bear…" She moved her eyes onto her father. "My husband is very sexy, daddy. He loves me so much."

Ian held his adoring eyes on her with happy sentiment. "I'm glad you think that, Jenny." He flagged the waitress down and ordered their desserts and when the waitress left, he returned his attention to the kids. "I'm happy to see you guys laughing and cuddling again. You gotta remember to do that more often if you want to stay in love."

"He's my baby-daddy. So, I will always love him, daddy."

Ian grinned at her giddiness. "Even when he calls you a stinky butt?"

Jenny nodded. "Because we always love each other, even when we don't like each other. Right, daddy?"

"Yep." Ian used to preach that to Jenny when she was trying his patience with her childhood tantrums. "That's what I like to hear, Jenny." He gave them both a high-five. "For a minute there I was worried that you guys were falling out of love."

"You're crazy, Ian!" Ricky yelled it too loudly and Ian waved him down a little.

Ricky laughingly continued. "She's my baby-mama. So, of course I love her."

When they were finished with their desserts and Ian had paid for their meals, they returned to the hotel. Sunday morning, they could sleep in and enjoy a no-demand start to the day because brunch wasn't served until 11:30, so Ian told the kids to watch TV in bed, *whatever…* but they should be showered and dressed and have their overnight bag packed by 11:00.

Their room was next to Mary and Ian's room, so if they needed them, they could knock on the internal door between rooms. Ian checked that the kids' external door was properly locked, then he said goodnight to the kids and closed and locked the internal door between the two rooms.

Mary went into the bathroom to brush her teeth and Ian joined her in there. "I fear we're going to be listening to their headboard knocking into our wall tonight, and Ricky's ceremonial arrival into paradise."

Mary chuckled. "So, you'll just have to make our headboard knock louder."

Ian laughed at that. "Sure… if you think you can control your own audible arrival into paradise…" His lips covered hers and he wrapped her into his arms.

****

When Mary woke the next morning, Ian was already awake, making coffee in the hotel coffee maker. When he saw that Mary was awake too, he took her the first cup and turned the television on. "HGTV?"

Mary nodded sipping the coffee. "Thanks…"

He smiled at her gratitude. "Well, after last night…I think this is the least I can do." He started his own cup of coffee and returned to her bedside. "That was amazing sex…"

Mary grinned back at him. "As always…"

"Quiet as it was…"

Mary chuckled. "Thank goodness the kids weren't noisy."

Ian returned to the coffee brewer. "I can't remember the last time we had a Sunday morning when we could lay naked in bed without the worry of kids running in…"

"It does feel indulging."

Ian returned to their bed, coffee cup in hand. Mary opened the covers for him and he carefully slid in. Spilling his coffee would ruin the casual nature of their morning, so he held his cup carefully.

Mary reached for his body under the covers and teasingly tickled him. "Don't jump with that hot coffee in your hand…who knows what might get burned?"

Ian laughingly stopped her from squeezing his thigh. "Where's the remote?"

"Over there…" Mary set her own cup down to fetch it from across the room.

Ian whistled as she walked by. "I might want you again this morning."

Mary grabbed the remote and returned to bed. "I don't think we have that much time…"

Ian chuckled at what she said, happy to give it a try. "And now I'm just going to have to prove otherwise with a Sunday morning booty call..." He took a big drink from his cup and set it on the nightstand. Then he turned to scoop Mary into his arms to pull her into a kiss that could carry them into heaven.

They made love again, with the energy of a relaxed morning, then they showered and dressed and packed up their things. Mary knocked on the door between rooms to let the kids know they were ready, and they all went to the restaurant for their morning brunch. There was live music, mimosas, and amazing food choices. The kids filled up on waffles and Brioche French Toast, Ian had Carl's Skillet Fried Chicken, and Mary enjoyed some California Benedicts and they shared some Ricotta Cheese Blintzes. It was delicious and elegant, and they all felt special – it was the perfect way to end a romantic getaway weekend.

When they were done with their meal, they left the hotel and spent the rest of the day at the aquarium, one of Jenny and Ricky's favorite places. They meandered through the exhibits, hand in hand, until they were through looking at everything, and returned to their car for the two-and-a-half-hour drive home. It was a fun and relaxing weekend, and surprisingly, Ian felt that it had benefited Mary and him as much as it had benefited the kids.

****

When they arrived home, they sent Jenny and Ricky to their house, and Ian and Mary slipped into their own home to the excited squeals of Skylar and Philip, who climbed all over them with childhood excitement.

"I missed you, daddy!" Skylar wrapped him in a big hug. "Ellie pushed me. And I fell down."

Ian frowned at that. "I hope you didn't push her back?"

Skylar shook her head no. "I called her a poo-poo head."

"Karen put her in timeout." Philip answered Ian's question with greater detail.

Ian moved his attention onto his son. "How come Elizabeth didn't put her in time out?"

"She wasn't here." Philip climbed into his lap next to Skylar. "Did you miss us daddy?"

"I did." Ian answered his question as Mary joined the conversation.

"When did Ellie push you, Skylar? Yesterday or today?"

"Yesterday."

"Well, that's interesting." Ian moved his attention onto Mary. "Did Karen tell you before she went home that Ellie was here yesterday?"

"She did not." Mary scooped Skylar out of Ian's arms so she could start putting the kids to bed. "But I'm sure she tracked it on the calendar so we can pay her for the extra day care."

Ian stood to take Philip to bed. "We brought you guys something…"

"A present, daddy?" Skylar squealed with excitement.

"Yep."

Mary went to get the plush sea otters with pups that they had picked up for each of them at the aquarium. Ricky and Jenny also had one for Ellie.

When the kids were finally settled in bed after an extended story time, *just one more glass of water*, and a ridiculous amount of hugs goodnight, Ian and Mary retired to their own bedroom to get ready for the work week.

Mary went to the bathroom to wash her face and brush her hair, while Ian unpacked their overnight bag. His phone rang as he was tossing dirty clothes into the hamper. Ian took the call then he joined Mary in the bathroom.

"Lizzy just called to tell me she can't watch Ellie this week."

"Well, that's typical of her." Mary was unpacking their toiletry bag. "Bailing out on Ellie on her weekday rotation because she had to spend the weekend with her…"

Ian scowled in response. "That'd just be her way of raising children…" He came up behind Mary and reached for his toothbrush. "Notwithstanding her lack of commitment that you're focused on…" He shot her a smile. "You're missing the point of what I just said."

"Which is?" Mary unpacked the last of their toiletry items and tossed the bag into a drawer in the vanity.

Ian squirted toothpaste on his brush then he stuck it in his mouth. "She *called* me, Mary… to tell me that… *from the kids' flat.* She didn't bang on the door to tell me face-to-face like she usually does – she called me. And that has to make you wonder…"

"You're right. It does…" Mary grabbed her own brush and filled it with toothpaste. "Why would she do that? Elizabeth never misses a chance to confront you face-to-face… especially if she can do that in a skimpy nightgown… so why is she letting an opportunity to flirt with you slide by tonight without using it to her advantage?"

"Exactly my point." Ian's mind went to where it usually went in response to Elizabeth's actions. "She's done something she knows I'm not going to like, and she doesn't want to see me until she can put it behind her. That's a classic Lizzy sidestep."

Mary nodded in agreement. "Well, let's not jump to conclusions because we don't know that for sure. Maybe she's just already gone to bed or she isn't feeling well?"

Ian huffed. "Yeah, that's the Lizzy I know and love... innocently tucked early into bed all by herself on a Sunday night…" His sarcasm was dripping but Mary completely understood his concern.

"I get what you're saying, Ian. But we just had a great weekend with the kids, and they seem to be back in love, which you desperately wanted. So, let's not worry about what Elizabeth has done until such time as we know that she's actually done something that's going to annoy us."

"Oh, she's done something to annoy me… mark my words."

"I know. You're probably right."

"Daddy…" Philip knocked on their bedroom door.

"What is it, Philip?" Ian hollered out to him from the bathroom as he spit into the sink before going to let him in.

"Ellie has my dinosaurs." He was cuddling his new sea otter, but he slept with his dinosaurs every night – and without them, he probably wouldn't go to sleep. He stepped into the bathroom with them. "She took them with her when she went home this morning. And I want them back. They're mine and they need to sleep with me."

"Ellie stayed the night last night?" Mary spit and put her toothbrush away.

Philip nodded his head. "We had a sleepover. Ellie's gammy couldn't watch her yesterday so she played with us and stayed the night. Karen said she could have a sleep-over."

"I knew it." Ian moved his eyes onto Mary. "Why didn't Lizzy want Ellie there?"

Mary shrugged and shook her head at him and together they said what came to both of their minds.

"Wally."

It had to be.

"Shit!" Ian couldn't help himself.

"That's a bad word, daddy."

"You're right, Philip." Ian blew out his frustration. "And I'm sorry I said that. I'm just angry." He took Philip by the hand and went down the hall with him.

"Are you mad at Ellie?" Philip almost had to run to keep up with him.

"Nope. I'm mad at her gammy…"

"Ian, don't go nuts on her…" Mary followed behind them. "It's late, and the kids don't need that kind of excitement tonight. Not after the great weekend we all just had."

"I'm not going to go nuts on her… but I am going to talk to her and find out what she's up to." Ian made it to the kitchen door between houses and gave it a hard bang.

Nobody answered, so Ian knocked again. "Elizabeth?"

She finally arrived in a skimpy night gown. "What is it, Ian?"

"Don't you think it might be more appropriate to wear a robe in front of Ricky instead of traipsing around in front of him in a barely there night gown?" He couldn't stop himself from scolding her.

Elizabeth shot him a defiant smile. "Ricky's already gone to bed, Ian. So, what do you want? Because I was also in bed."

Ian huffed at her defense. "Why don't we start with your reason for not watching Ellie on Saturday when you told me you could watch her?"

Elizabeth noticeably caught her breath. "What do you mean?"

"Just what I said, Lizzy. Why did Karen have Ellie this weekend for a sleepover when you were supposed to be watching her?"

Elizabeth glanced between them, then she looked knowingly at Philip. "I got a migraine…" Her eyes came up.

"Huh…" Ian glared with doubt.

"Seriously, Ian." Elizabeth stepped away from the door. "Is that why you woke me up?"

Ian followed her into the house. "Ellie has Philip's dinosaurs. He'd like them back."

"Oh." She shot him a friendlier smile. "I'll go find them. I just put her to bed a while ago."

Mary came up behind Ian and rubbed him on the back. "Breathe…"

He turned to look at her with a frozen stare. "A migraine, my ass…"

Mary met his glare. "Whatever she's done, no matter the truth… it has nothing to do with us. The kids are all fine, and that's what matters. So, who cares what Elizabeth does on her own time, right?"

Ian begrudgingly shook his head. "It actually wasn't her own time, Mary, because she committed the weekend to us, but you're right. It's not our business as long as the kids are being cared for."

"Here they are…" Elizabeth returned with three dinosaurs in her hand. "Sorry about that. I didn't notice that she brought them home."

Ian handed them to Philip. "Go back to bed and we'll come kiss you goodnight in a minute."

"Okay, daddy." Philip scampered off and Ian returned his attention to Elizabeth.

"If you tell me you're going to watch Ellie, that's what I expect you to do. If you can't do that for some reason, then courtesy dictates a phone call. I'd just like to know what's going on with the kids in my household."

"I'm sorry." Elizabeth held her own against him.

"Fine." Ian accepted her apology, but he didn't quit scolding her. "Need I remind you that you are only here with my permission. It would behoove you to remember that, Lizzy."

"Sure." She shot him a friendly smile. "My mistake. And I'm sorry about that. I just thought if I took a nap… but I couldn't shake the headache."

Ian turned and left the flat without saying more and without listening to her excuses.

When he and Mary were back in their own house, he turned to look at her. "She's lying."

Mary nodded, agreeing. "Yep, you're probably right. So, I have an idea. Since we both went to the same place in our heads, how about we invite Wally and Betty Jo to our house next weekend when Elizabeth isn't here? We're old high school friends… he's doing his research on the kids… why not have him over for dinner so we can all get reacquainted with each other? That will give him a chance to see how the kids and Ellie interact with us and you can get a feel for whether he's seeing Elizabeth."

"Good idea, Mary. I'll invite him for a barbeque on Saturday, when we know Lizzy won't be here."

Mary nodded her agreement. "And if you think he's seeing her, you can try and intervene."

Chapter Seven

When Wally returned home late Saturday night, Betty Jo barely noticed him.

"Hi there…" She was reading a book in the living room.

"Hello." Wally nodded at her greeting. Seeing her made him feel horribly guilty and incredibly nervous all at once. He did not feel at all like himself right now, and in fact, he hated himself more than he ever could have imagined as a result of what happened today. He was a complete wreck inside, and he felt like crying and confessing the truth, but more than anything else, he just wanted to undo what he had carelessly done today.

But that wasn't possible. There was no stuffing that ugly Genie back inside the bottle. What happened today was something Wally was going to have to live with for the rest of his life.

He was now a cheat.

Ian was right. Elizabeth had taken Wally on a ride into purgatory and there was no escaping that destination.

He had cheated on his wife.

For the rest of his life, that ugly truth would be with him – though he had sincerely intended not to do that to her.

"You're awfully quiet…" Betty Jo set her book down and moved into the kitchen.

"I saw Ian's ex-wife today." Wally offered what he could without giving her more detail than he should. He felt like he somehow had to say something about what happened today, but he couldn't really say anything about it.

Betty Jo hardly paid him attention. "You were working with his granddaughter?"

"Ah, yeah." Wally wasn't sure that he could keep from telling Betty Jo the truth because sitting on this secret was eating him up inside. In fact, he felt like crying, as he had done in the car on the way home. But there was no *good* reason for him to tell her what he did, unless he thought that her knowing about it could fix their marriage – which ran contrary to common sense. Her knowing about what happened could only make their marriage worse.

Betty Jo filled two plates with food and jammed them into the microwave. "Is she as arrogant as him?"

"No." Wally poured himself a cocktail. He wasn't a big drinker, and it wasn't like him to drink all day – wine with Elizabeth, and booze at home – but it also wasn't like him to cheat on his wife. And he needed something to calm his nerves before he completely made a mess of everything by telling her the truth… and ruining Betty Jo's life. And not just her life, but the lives of their children and unborn grandchild. If only he could figure out how he was supposed to act now, but nothing felt right to him.

"Sorry I'm so late…"

Betty Jo set the microwave timer. "I barely got here myself."

Wally nodded at what she said as he forced himself to just breathe his way through a seemingly normal conversation with her. "She's actually, surprisingly nice." He exhaled his nervous energy. "In fact, they seem like a perfect match for each other. I can't figure out what went wrong between them. They're both so quick witted and confident. Kind of full of themselves, not at all humble like us. And they're both fun… but I'm going to avoid running into her again. She made me feel very uncomfortable today, and for the sake of my research… and my friendship with Ian…I'm going to make it a point to keep my distance. I'm not even sure I want to see Ian anymore."

"Well, if you think you shouldn't… that's probably a good idea." Betty Jo didn't ask him why he felt uncomfortable around her, in fact she didn't ask him anything at all. She returned to her dinner preparations, the microwave pinged, and she pulled out his plate and handed it to him. "You don't mind if I eat alone in front of the TV, do you? It's another one of my shows, and I can't begin to explain all the backfill on this one to you…"

"No…" Wally was thankful for the space; he desperately needed to pull himself together, though he recognized that this right here – *their separate lives* – was the cause of their problem. *This* was why it happened today… most of the time he didn't even feel married.

When their kids still lived at home there was so much going on that the growing distance between them wasn't noticeable. But nowadays, their empty nest made it obvious how much they had grown apart – and how little they now had in common.

Wally went to his den and pulled out his research. He could only hope that Betty Jo would do her usual thing tonight… stay up late watching TV alone, and crawl into bed long after he had fallen asleep. It would be horrible if all of a sudden, *for the first time in longer than he could remember…* she actually wanted to make love. If she did, he had no idea what he would do. He only knew that he could never go through with that tonight. That would be such a betrayal… worse than the betrayal he'd already committed – to go from Elizabeth's arms to Betty Jo's arms all on the same day.

With that thought in mind, Wally went to take a shower, then he crawled into bed with a medical book so he could easily be asleep by the time she came to bed.

Tomorrow would be a new day, and Wally was determined to start over. He was going to go to the gym and sweat Elizabeth out of his system. Then he would go home to his wife and be the best damn husband possible. He was going to learn from this mistake and fix his marriage. And as a byproduct of that effort, he was going to fall back in love with Betty Jo if it was the last thing that he ever did on this earth. And the guilt that he carried with him for the rest of his life would be a deserving punishment and a shameful reminder of how much he had to lose if he ever cheated again.

****

When Wally woke Sunday morning, he knew without doubt what he needed to do. He would have to exclude Jenny and her family from his research so he never had to see Ian or Elizabeth again. He hated closing the door on Mary, but that was a price he would have to pay for his indiscretion.

With that decision behind him, he talked Betty Jo into going out for breakfast with him, then he convinced her to go on a day trip with him – no research distractions, no cell phones, just the two of them being friends. He desperately wanted to move time backwards to a point in their past when they were madly in love.

They drove to the historic town of Columbia, a two-and-a-half-hour drive, and Wally made conversation with her during the whole trip. When they got there, they parked the car and wandered through the old western buildings and streets, then they went on a stage coach ride, and laughed like crazy after "bandits" held the coach up at mock gunpoint and threatened to steal their valuables. When that was behind them, they returned to the shops and Wally bought Betty Jo a silver and turquoise necklace and earring set that looked lovely on her. Then they bowled on an old fashion bowling lane, and visited a gold mining shop where they panned for gold in streams of running water. It became a really fun day, and for the first time in ages, Wally felt like the two of them could fall back in love. They had lunch at a nice tea house and walked hand in hand down the old western lanes peeking in shop windows and checking out old hotels and saloons until it was time to drive home.

They arrived at their house late at night and Wally hoped that despite the late hour, Betty Jo might want to make love with him, but instead she excused herself to watch TV in the family room while he retired to bed alone.

Elizabeth hit his phone up twice on Monday, but Wally let her calls go to voicemail. When Ian called him midafternoon, Wally thought about letting his call go to voicemail too, but curiosity got the best of him and he took the call.

"Dr. Weldon…" He used his professional greeting even though he knew it was Ian on the other end.

"Hey, dude…" Ian greeted him in a friendly voice. "How'd your visit go last Saturday with the kids? I thought maybe you'd call me last week to set up your next visit with them, and when I realized today that I never heard from you, I figured I'd give you a call and see how it went."

"Oh." Wally let out a relieved breath of air that he wasn't calling because he found out about Elizabeth. "I like your kids, Ian. You did a good job raising Jenny. She seems sharp considering her challenges. But her daughter is something else…"

"Yeah…" Ian agreed with his unspoken opinion. "She's a challenge for other reasons."

Wally chuckled. "I see that. She's definitely going to keep you on your toes. So, I was looking through my notes today, and I was actually thinking about calling you. I've got so much data from other families that I'm thinking of leaving Jenny out of my research. I know you were hesitant about letting me include her anyway, and she's sort of an anomaly in that she has such a great support network with you and Mary… and her mother."

Ian huffed at his inclusion of Elizabeth. "Well, her mother is at least present these days, if nothing else, which is more than she can claim throughout Jenny's childhood… but that's water under the bridge that I'm not letting myself get sucked into today."

Wally chuckled at what he said as he gave into the urge to defend Elizabeth. "Well, maybe she couldn't handle living under the constant pressure cooker of your harsh judgment and never-ending criticism, Ian."

The sustained silence on the other end of the phone warned Wally that his comment fell too close to home.

"You've been talking to her…"

"What?" Wally stumbled for a second… he needed to be more careful about what he was saying if he didn't want to accidently give his secret away. "I was just… guessing… you know… don't most divorced people have that kind of gripe against each other?"

The silence preceding Ian's response was shorter. "I can't speak to the opinions of other divorced people, Wally…" Ian answered him with a calculated chill. "But as far as *my* divorce goes, there's plenty of room for harsh judgment when it comes to Elizabeth."

Wally chuckled at his defense. "You see… that kind of insensitive attitude right there probably made life difficult for her."

"Let's move on." The chill in Ian's voice didn't thaw. "Mary and I would like to invite you and Betty Jo to the house on Saturday for a barbeque."

"Sure." Wally agreed to the invitation because he felt awkward turning it down. And he had always liked hanging out with Ian though the idea of spending any time with him right now made him nervous; but admittedly he'd love to see Mary again.

"You want to come around four o'clock? That'll give my family time to finish our barn chores and farm activities before dinner… or you can come earlier if you want, and see how the kids manage with those responsibilities."

"Sounds interesting." Wally couldn't help but be curious. "What, say maybe two or three?"

"That'll work. I gotta go. I'm running late for a meeting."

Wally called Betty Jo after Ian's call to tell her about the dinner invitation. "We've been invited to Ian and Mary's on Saturday for a barbeque. We're going to head over there about two or three o'clock, watch the kids do their barn chores, and then have dinner. You good with all that?"

"Okay. I had some other plans, but I'll cancel them. If this is important to you."

"It is. And I want you to be there with me. I want us to be a couple. I want us to do things together."

"Sure, Wally. That sounds fine."

****

When Saturday arrived, Wally felt like a bucket of nerves. He didn't want to do anything today in front of Ian that would give his betrayal away. And he didn't want Betty Jo somehow learning about his indiscretion. He desperately wanted to be happily married without a guilty conscious, but visiting with Ian today was making it hard for Wally not to think about his cheating.

He went to the gym like he did every Saturday morning, then he puttered around his home office until it was time to shower and change out of his workout clothes into something a little nicer. Betty Jo was already showered and dressed when Wally stepped into the bedroom.

"You look pretty…" She was wearing a nice pair of jeans and an attractive top.

"Thanks." She stepped out of the bedroom. "I'll be in the living room with my book when you're ready."

Wally nodded at her directive. "Thank you for doing this with me today. I know Mary wasn't a friend, and neither was Ian…"

She shrugged off his concern. "Neither one of them had any interest in me in high school, but it's important to you, and you're researching his kid, so I can make the sacrifice…"

Wally pulled her into a kiss. "Thank you."

She nodded and stepped away.

Wally showered and dressed and found her thirty minutes later, reading her book. "You want a glass of wine before we go?"

Betty Jo glanced at her watch. "Sure, if we have time."

"It'll soften the edges of our nerves…"

She nodded at what he said. “Why would you be nervous? You’ve known these two for years… and you’ve functioned in their inner circle most of your childhood.”

Wally agreed with a nod. “True. But they’ve always been…”

“*Them…*” His wife understood.

Wally nodded. “Yeah, it’s hard to explain. Being around Ian just makes me feel like I’m not cool enough.”

Betty Jo laughed at him. “Wally… you *aren’t* cool at all, and Ian *is* cool. But you’re still a decent guy. I married you, didn’t I?”

He smiled with her sort of compliment and went to open a bottle of wine. “Why *did* you marry me?”

Betty Jo followed him into the kitchen. “You’re smart, kind, attentive, accommodating, confident…”

“I am *not* confident…”

Betty Jo chuckled. “Well, you seemed confident when we first got together. And you’re good looking…”

He grinned at that. *Adorable…* that’s what Elizabeth said. Wally pushed the thought away.

“Why did *you* marry *me*?” Betty Jo took the glass of wine that he held out to her.

“You’re beautiful…” In her own way. “Bright, altruistic, funny, and driven. I thought we’d be a good match…”

She nodded at his observations and drank some wine. “Is this going to be an awkward night?”

Wally gulped from his own glass. “I hope not. Why do you ask?”

“I don’t know… just… some of the things you’ve shared about Ian and Mary make me wonder why you even want them as friends. They seem so uppity…”

Wally felt bad, hearing her say that because it was his fault that she thought that way about them. And it was only because he had a bad habit of sharing Ian’s least flattering character traits in an insecure effort to make himself feel better; and that had inaccurately cast Ian and Mary in a bad light for her. Which wasn’t fair to either of them, and it wasn’t nice of Wally to do that. Ian and Mary weren’t perfect, but they were both really nice people and Wally owed them more than what he had given them. “They’re not uppity.” He tried to correct the false image with a more flattering picture of them. “If nothing else, they’re gracious and good conversationalists. So, I’m sure the evening will be fine.”

They finished their wine and Wally walked Betty Jo to the car and opened the door for her. When she was settled in her seat, he closed the door and went around the car to slide in beside her. They both remained silent for the whole drive as they pondered their own thoughts, then Wally pulled into Ian's driveway and parked his car exactly where he parked it one week ago when he cheated on his wife – with Ian's ex-wife.

Mary saw them arrive and immediately came to greet them.

"Hi!" She approached Betty Jo first, and gave her an enthusiastic greeting as she climbed out of the car. "I'm so glad we finally have a chance to get to know you better. I must admit, in high school all of my attention was myopically focused on Ian, probably to the point of rudeness. And I apologize for that. Hopefully, you won't hold that against me."

Betty Jo held her hand out in surprise. "Of course not. We were all different people in high school."

Mary clasped her palm and stepped into a hug with her. "I'm so looking forward to learning about your family. Your kids are married with children of their own now?"

Betty Jo ended the hug, nodding her head. "Two grown boys, one adult daughter, and one grandchild on the way. We're very excited about that."

"When is the baby due?"

"Next month."

"You're almost there!" Mary shot her an excited grin. "Do you know the baby's gender?"

Betty Jo happily nodded. "It's a boy. Little Henry."

"Oh, that's so fun…"

Wally stepped into their greeting. "Hey, Mary…"

"Wally…" she gave him a big hug. "Ian's in the barn with the kids." She gestured that direction. "Shall we join him out there?"

Betty Jo held back as Mary stepped off with Wally. "We brought a bottle of wine and an apple pie… they might get too hot in the car."

"Oh, that was so nice of you." Mary stopped heading to the barn. "Why don't you go out there without us, Wally, and Betty Jo and I can take the wine and pie inside?"

"Sure." Wally stepped away from them feeling nervous without Betty Jo. With her by his side, Ian couldn't turn the conversation the wrong way on him. But without Betty Jo…

He stepped into the barn and found Ian horsing around with his little kids.

"Hi…"

"Hey…" Ian nodded a greeting. "Okay, guys… this is my friend that I told you about. So, let's finish up out here so we can have some dinner."

"Hi Dr. Weldon…" Jenny was busy in a horse stall, sorting dirty straw from clean straw. "I'm cleaning my horse's stall. It's dirty."

Ricky was in the stall next to her, hanging up a hay net. "Hi Doc." He waved a greeting. "This is my horse. His name is Shazam."

Wally went closer to see him. "Well, he's a big guy."

Ricky puffed his chest out. "Because I'm a big guy. Jenny's horse is smaller because she's a girl. She's not big like me."

Wally petted the horse's forelock. "And what's Jenny's horse's name?"

She answered him from the stall she was cleaning. "Dancer. Daddy's horse is Prancer. I named them. And Mary's horse is Boyfriend."

Wally laughed at that. "And what's the name of the pony over there?" It was a much smaller pony for the little children.

Ricky answered his question. "His name is Donkey."

Wally turned a confused stare on him. "But he's a horse."

Jenny giggled. "But Ricky named him, and he likes Shrek. The movie. And Donkey is in Shrek. That's what Ricky likes."

"I like Donkey." Ricky stepped out of the stall and closed the door.

"You done in there?" Ian came up behind him and peeked inside. "Looks good to me. Is Donkey fed?"

"Not yet, Ian. That's next." Ricky went to the pony's stall and opened the door. "Hi Donkey…"

Wally followed him over there to watch him with the horse.

"Cinderella…" Ricky called out to her. "Come help me with Donkey."

"I'm playing, daddy." The three little kids were climbing on hay bales stacked in a stall.

"But you have to come help me."

"I don't want to, daddy." Cinderella gave no indication that she was going to do as he said.

Ian stepped up behind her and scooped her into his arms to take her to the stall. "It's your turn to help. Skylar helped last night, and Philip will help tomorrow night."

"Okay, poppee…"

Ian set her down by Ricky and handed her a brush. "Why don't you brush Donkey while your dad hangs his hay net?"

"Okay, poppee…"

Ian moved his attention onto Dancer's stall. "How are you doing, Jenny?"

"I'm almost done." She moved a wheelbarrow out of the way and parked it outside of the stall. Then she went to where her horse was tied in the large aisle running down the center of the barn, and untied her to lead her into her stall. "Dancer's done, daddy. I cleaned her stall and fed her. And she has water."

Ian glanced into the stall. "It looks like we're about done, guys…"

Wally watched them finish up, then they left the barn to join the ladies on Ian's large covered porch in front of the main house. There was a long wooden table set for six adults and three children. It was covered with a blue and white checked linen table cloth. There were small vases of freshly cut flowers spaced down the center of it in between lit citronella candles that sent the smell of a summer campsite into Wally's nose. It looked like an elegant garden party but felt cozy like a family gathering.

"I need to change out of these clothes and wash my hands." Ian opened the front door and turned to face Wally. "I think Mary and Betty Jo are in the kitchen. They should be out here shortly." He looked to the front yard where the little kids were now playing on a swing set and play structure and hollered for Jenny's attention. "Hey… keep an eye on the little guys while I'm inside."

"Okay, daddy." She gave him a silly salute as she and Ricky joined them on the porch.

Ian returned his attention to Wally. "Why don't you open a bottle of wine and pour some for you and the ladies, and I'll be back in a few minutes."

He handed Wally a bottle opener and gestured towards the two bottles of wine that were left on the table. Then he stepped inside.

Wally went to the bottles and opened the one that he and Betty Jo brought. Jenny and Ricky went to the farthest end of the table where they sat across from each other and started playing a game of *Go Fish*.

Wally moved his attention inside the house as the ladies approached the front door carrying a big bowl of cut melons and a large bowl of potato salad. He quickly held the door open as they laughingly stepped through it. Wally smiled at the vision. He wanted Betty Jo to like Mary and the natural ease of their shared laughter, told him that were enjoying their conversation.

"Ian left you out here by yourself?" Mary greeted him as she set the bowl of fruit on the table.

"He did." Wally shot her a smile as he busied himself pouring wine. "He went to freshen up."

"I want wine, too." Ricky left the chair he was sitting in to get a glass from Wally.

"Does Ian let you guys drink alcohol?" He hadn't told Wally to pour them any.

"We're not kids, you know. We're parents and that means we're old enough to drink." Ricky didn't exactly answer his question, but there were six wine glasses on the table so Wally poured him some wine.

"Thank you." Ricky picked one of the glasses up. "And now I need some for my beautiful wife."

Wally smiled at that. "Here you go…" He poured some in a glass for her. "Is that about the right amount?"

"That's not enough, but that's okay. Ian pours us more, but you can learn how to do it better, next time." Ricky took the second glass and walked to the end of the table with it just as Wally noticed a black Mercedes pulling into the driveway.

"Ah, oh…" He couldn't help muttering to himself as he watched it drive closer.

"Rats…" Mary noticed it too, just as Ian returned from inside dressed in a clean pair of jeans, a designer tee shirt, a pair of nice sneakers, and freshly applied cologne.

"What is she doing here?" His eyes went to Mary with unmasked disdain.

"Your guess is as good as mine." She shrugged with obvious frustration.

Wally could only stare in silent horror as she parked her car next to his.

"I'm sure she, *quote,* forgot something." Mary shook her head at Ian and he knowingly nodded back.

"She dodges Ellie and us all week," he spoke in a soft voice, clearly intending to be heard only by Mary as he stepped closer to her. "And then she has the nerve to show up unannounced tonight…"

Wally turned to his wife in a rush to save himself from whatever might follow, and conspiratorially whispered in her ear softer than Ian was speaking to Mary. "I'm not sure Ian knows that she and I met last Saturday. She didn't want him butting in… so if she acts like we haven't met… please go along with that and don't say anything. Okay?"

"Sure." His wife shot him a suspicious smile. "Sounds a little covert to me, though…"

Wally held a frozen grin on her as he offered what came to mind. "You'd have to understand their relationship… it's icy… at best."

Betty Jo nodded with understanding. "Okay."

Elizabeth stepped out of her car and crossed the driveway to join them on the front porch. "Hi!" She scooped Ellie into her arms on the way, and gave her a big hug. "How's gammy's little angel today?"

"We're having dinner outside with friends, gammy. Poppee cooked chicken and memaw said I could have potato chips."

Elizabeth wrinkled her face into a disapproving scowl. "Don't eat too many of those chips, sweetie, they'll only turn you into a chunky monkey. And we don't want that, do we?"

"Okay, gammy."

"Lizzy… please." Ian scolded her from across the table where he stood beside Mary. "She's only five years old...how about waiting a few more years before you start body shaming her?'

Elizabeth turned to address him. "Well, we don't want her getting fat." She moved her attention onto Mary. "No offense intended."

"None taken." Ian brusquely addressed her comment on Mary's behalf. "So, what brings you out here tonight?"

She shot him an innocent grin. "I left my bag here with all my magazines and books in it. So, I thought I'd just pop by to pick it up."

Elizabeth moved her attention onto Wally and then Betty Jo. "Are you going to introduce me to your guests, Ian?"

Wally turned his eyes onto Ian, silently praying that he would do his detached ex-husband thing and dismiss her post haste. He did not want to be placed in a perilous position tonight of having to worry about Elizabeth saying something that might get him in trouble with Ian or Betty Jo.

Ian's resistance to introducing her was palpable but that didn't matter because Jenny made introductions before her father could do his brush off.

"This is my doctor, mom. Dr. Weldon. He's the one I told you about. The one that was coming for dinner."

Elizabeth turned to Wally in a perfect show of gracious surprise. "How nice to meet you." She held her manicured hand out to him and Wally noticed that the ruby red polish had been changed to a soft pink that perfectly matched the frilly pink ruffles in her form-fitting school-girl blouse that stopped just short of her flat midriff and the eye-catching naval piercing that Wally had fondled in her bed last week after they made love.

He focused on the hand she was extending and politely took it in his. "Nice to meet you." The fragrance of her perfume wafted him with a heavier dose of vanilla than he recalled from last week when she smelt like fresh cut flowers. Tonight, her scent pushed him away instead of drawing him in.

She gave his palm a meaningful squeeze before letting go of it. "And who is this lovely lady by your side?" She moved her attention onto Betty Jo with enviable social grace. "You must be his wife…"

"Betty Jo…" She held her hand out to Elizabeth. "It's nice to meet you."

"What a beautifully understated pearl necklace you're wearing." Elizabeth clasped her manicured hand around Betty Jo's palm. "I love how you've dressed the jeans and casual shirt up with it. I'll have to remember that look next time I'm wondering what to wear to an outdoor gathering. Very classy."

"Well, thank you!" Betty Jo blushed and reached to the simple white strand of pearls. "Wally gave this to me on our," she turned to look at him, "What was it honey, our 10th anniversary?"

"Eleventh." He felt incredibly awkward trapped between the two women – his dear sweet wife, who he adored more today than ever before, and this wanton creature he hardly knew who had beguiled him into her bed and now jeopardized everything dear to him.

"The traditional anniversary gift for eleven years is steel..." Wally forced himself to get a grip on his composure before he gave himself away. "But there's no way to make steel romantic..."

He dared a glance at Ian in an effort to look as relaxed as he could with the conversation. "So, I switched it up that year." His eyes went back to Elizabeth before he returned his focus to Betty Jo. "And gave you the traditional gift for thirty years, which is pearls."

Elizabeth settled her eyes on him like she was unwrapping him in front of everyone. "How cute." She kept her undivided focus on him for a minute too long, before she moved her attention onto Betty Jo. "He buys you a traditional anniversary gift every year?"

Betty Jo shot him a loving smile. "Well, Wally's sweet like that. And for our thirtieth this year, he bought me the pearl ring I'm wearing." She held her hand out for Elizabeth's inspection. "So, I still got pearls for our thirty years together."

"That's gorgeous." Elizabeth barely glanced at it before returning her eyes to Wally. "Wow..." She shot him a flirty smile. "Thirty years, huh?" The glow in her eyes turned teasingly wicked. "Congratulations on the unbreakable bond. What an accomplishment. I don't know many couples who have pulled that off. You must be totally devoted to each other."

Wally held a frozen stare on her, wondering how she could have the gall to congratulate their successful marriage knowing that she had personally breached it just seven short days ago? The thought turned his stomach and made him look at Ian out of curiosity, but when his eyes met Ian's stare, he realized with a start that Ian had been quietly studying him. Wally quickly looked away before he gave his guilty heart away. He did not want Ian reading the thoughts in his head.

"Thanks." Betty Jo was still focused on Elizabeth's compliment. "I guess we're doing something right..." She reached for Wally's hand. "Considering almost everyone we know is divorced."

"Here, here..." Mary seemed to sense the growing awkwardness and quietly saved the moment. "But I guess there's no surprise that Wally could make a marriage last. I remember back in high school he was the guy that all the girls used to talk to when they had boyfriend problems."

"Everyone but you…" Wally chuckled at his own observation as he glanced up at Ian again and noted that he seemed to be purposely letting the discussion role by without comment.

Mary kept control of the conversation. "Wally was sort of our *Seventeen* magazine teenage shrink…"

Wally shot her a grin. *God love Mary.* He went where she was going, helping to create a bigger distance from where they had just been in conversation. "What was that girl's name… the one who was always breaking up with Wayne Cartwright? Like every other week she was crying on my shoulder."

"April…I can't recall her last name." Mary chuckled. "But I remember who you're talking about. Surely someone must have written in her yearbook, *most on again, off again girlfriend in our class*."

Wally laughed at that. "She was always asking me what she should do and I always told her don't go back to him unless you're really going to stay together this time and work it out. I mean, that's the whole point of relationships, right? Staying committed." His eyes took in Elizabeth for a fleeting second to see if she was getting the point he was making. "But every time April went back to him, she would break it off again. They could never work it out."

Elizabeth chuckled at that. "Well, my best run was with my second husband… we lasted for almost eighteen years…"

Ian huffed from the sidelines. "And I don't even know how he lasted that long with you." He reached for a glass of wine and took a big drink from it.

"And there it is…" Elizabeth slow-clapped her hands for him. "Five minutes in, and the Ian we all know surfaces with biting sarcasm."

Wally moved his attention onto Ian. "She's right, you know. You didn't have to take that unnecessary dig at her..."

Elizabeth shot Wally a thankful smile. "Just one of the many reasons why my second marriage was better than my first."

Ian shrugged off their derogatory observations without comment. "So…" His attention settled on Elizabeth. "Now that the introductions are behind us…"

Elizabeth turned an *I told you so* expression on Wally. “And now we move onto him shooing me out the door, one caustic remark at a time.”

Ian stayed focused. “Did you want to get your bag from the kids’ flat?” His eyes stayed locked on hers with an unspoken order for her to do as he told her. “We don’t want to keep you from your evening plans. You’re obviously dressed for a night out with the boys. And we were just about to eat dinner.”

“Daddy!” Jenny protested his order before Elizabeth could indulge his directive. “She’s staying for dinner. I’m inviting her.”

“What?” Ian moved his startled eyes between them with silent curiosity before he settled them on Elizabeth with visible impatience. “Did you put her up to that?”

Elizabeth innocently chuckled back at him. “Of course not, but I can get my bag and leave if you’d rather me not stay.”

She moved her attention onto Betty Jo. “It was so nice meeting you.” Her eyes moved onto Wally and she held her palm out to him. “And nice to see you…”

Wally took her palm in his and she squeezed it in return.

“Are you making her go, daddy?” Jenny looked between them with a sad frown.

“I want gammy to stay.” Ellie joined their conversation.

Wally silently prayed that Ian would stand his ground. His eyes went his direction waiting for a biting remark that would send her on her way, but instead of belittling her, Ian begrudgingly reached for a bottle of wine and poured some in a glass for her.

“I’ll get another bottle because I’m sure we’ll need more now.” He handed Elizabeth the glass and turned to Mary. “You want to set another place at the table?”

“Sure.” Mary politely agreed.

Elizabeth giggled in response to Ian’s surrender. “Thank you, sweetie. I’d love to stay.”

Ian went to the front door and silently held it open for Mary, without acknowledging Elizabeth’s gratitude, and as Mary stepped through it, he stopped her for a kiss. “We’ll also need another glass for you.”

Mary nodded and stepped inside, and Ian turned to the rest of them. “Excuse me while I help her. We’ll be right back…”

“Anything I can do to help?” Betty Jo stepped his direction to go into the house with them.

"No." Ian stopped her in her tracks. "We've got this. You should stay out here with your husband and Elizabeth." His eyes bounced between them. "I'm sure the conversation will be interesting."

Chapter Eight

Ian joined Mary in the kitchen in silent fury.

"I know…" Mary tried to keep him from saying what was on his mind but Ian couldn't resist purging.

"There is no way in hell he didn't sleep with her." He looked over his shoulder as he said it to make sure they were still alone.

Mary scoped out the area behind him with equal interest. "What makes you so sure about that?"

Ian let out a mad huff. "Did you see the way she was looking at him?" He went to the silverware drawer to grab a fork, a knife, and a spoon for Elizabeth. "And he was horrified when he saw her approaching. Plus, he looked my way more than once with guilt oozing out of his expression."

Mary nodded at his observations. "He did look worried when he saw her car in the driveway, and he does seem uncomfortable and edgy with the conversation."

Ian huffed with condemnation. "And where does he get off correcting me on how I talk to my ex-wife?" He dropped the utensils that he grabbed out of the drawer into Mary's hand. "He's a distant friend to me at best, and she's presumably a new acquaintance for him… unless he's moved himself into a closer relationship with her than one would expect, considering they supposedly just met?"

Mary agreed with what Ian was pointing out. "That *was* a presumptuous comment for him to make."

Ian went to the cupboard to get a plate for Elizabeth. "I can read the guilt in her practiced expressions and in the innocent way she's talking to him." He grabbed a plate and angrily handed it to Mary. "And he's jumpy as hell." Ian slammed the cupboard door shut and turned to look at her.

"It makes me sick, Mary, and it's going to be a struggle for me not to call her out on it. She thinks she's being so slick… but there is nothing slick in a repeat performance. And this is exactly how she acted when was cheating on me."

Mary reached for his hand to settle him down. "Why are you so upset about this? Other than the fact that we both find the cheating deplorable. Has this become personal for you because she cheated on you? Or is it offensive because you don't want her with Wally because *it's Wally...* your arch nemesis who was always after me... and now he's cheating with *her*...your ex-wife?"

"Don't be ridiculous..." Ian scoffed at the very idea. "I could care less who she's sleeping with..." he reached for a wine glass. "Except when I know she's playing her game with someone I grew up with, who we both know will end up getting hurt by the games she's playing."

He handed the wine glass to Mary and grabbed a bottle of wine that he tucked under his arm. "I do not want to silently stand by as she destroys Wally and Betty Jo's marriage. And that's the only way this story ends, Mary. Because that's Elizabeth's MO. She will reel him in until there is nothing but her demanding self, left in his life. And then she'll leave him." He picked up the tray of chicken and gestured with his head for her to lead the way back outside.

Wally saw them approaching and quickly opened the door for them. "You should have had one of us help you." He took the bottle of wine from under Ian's arm and set it on the table. "What a great spread you guys prepared..."

Betty Jo helped Mary with the place setting. "Your garden is gorgeous and I love this huge front porch. It's such a great place to have a summer garden party."

"Thank you!" Mary carried the conversation. "We added the porch after Ian and I got married." She set her wine glass down as Betty Jo laid out a place setting.

Elizabeth was already topping off her wine. "Let me know if I can help..." She set the bottle down and drew the glass up to her lips without giving any inclination that she was really willing to help.

Ian set the tray of chicken down and covered it with a screen lid. "Ellie, Philip, Skylar?" He hollered out to them from the porch. "Dinner's ready. Come eat"

"Okay, daddy!" Philip was the first to run over. Ian stopped him on the porch steps to wipe his hands and face with a hand wipe that he pulled out of a container that they kept on the porch. Then he snagged the two girls as they ran by to run a wipe over their hands and faces as well.

"Sit down…" He helped them into chairs and started serving their plates as Betty Jo made conversation.

"Wally was just sharing a story with us from your childhood."

"Yeah?" Ian glanced his direction. "What story?"

Wally shot him a smile. "That day I went riding with you guys down by the creek…"

Ian nodded with the memory. "You rode Mary's horse and I rode Mary double on my horse." He smiled at the recollection as he finished serving Philip's plate.

Wally made a joke out of it as he settled into a seat at the table. "We don't want to hear about you riding Mary…"

"Wally!" Betty Jo objected with embarrassment as she sat beside him.

Mary and Ian both laughed before Mary added to the story. "I got stung by a bee that day…"

Ian filled Skylar's plate as he picked up on the story where Mary left off. "And Wally rescued you with his home remedy of putting tobacco juice on the sting to stop it from hurting." He set Skylar's plate down in front of her and began filling a plate for Ellie.

Mary nodded at his memory. "I don't remember where you got that cigarette, Wally…" She turned to look at him. "Do you?"

"Some guy coming out of the Seven Eleven…" Wally shot her a happy grin.

Ian finished the story. "We went for Slurpee's and while I was inside buying them, Wally got the cigarette from a shady character who was leaving the store."

"That's right." Mary passed the chicken tray to Betty Jo.

"Thank goodness he didn't smoke menthol…" Wally chuckled at their recollection. "That would have made the sting burn like crazy, but I'm not sure I knew that back then."

Ian laughed at what he shared. "Good thing you didn't make it worse for her… I might have felt inclined to take you down in a fist fight for hurting my girl…"

They all laughed at that.

Mary added another detail to their fun recollection. "Wally and I were holding the horses while Ian was inside."

Ian moved his eyes onto Wally with a playful frown. "And the reason I was buying the Slurpee's was because as usual…" he teasingly smiled at him. "You had no money."

Wally laughed at that and Ian shot him a forgiving smile. "But since you saved my girl from the pain of that bee sting… I guess you earned the Slurpee."

Wally nodded. "I always wanted to be a doctor."

Ian handed him the bowl of potato salad to start passing it around. "And you proved you had a natural calling for it even as a kid before you had the education or training." He lowered himself onto a chair and handed the fruit bowl to Betty Jo. "You were always the smart guy in the group, and the most studious. Much more than the rest of us. In fact, I barely applied myself in high school."

Wally chuckled at that. "You had other interests."

Ian smiled at Mary. "True statement."

Mary innocently grinned back at him. "Guitars, drums, and horses?"

Ian laughed. "That's not what I was going to say, because I was thinking more along the lines of my Chevy van…"

Mary smiled with their shared memories and offered another story. "Remember that time we all went looking for frogs?"

Ian chuckled. "Which time?"

Wally agreed with his need for clarification. "I feel like we were doing that all the time."

"We were!" Mary laughingly agreed. "But I was thinking about the time when we put all the frogs into that big wooden box so they could be a frog family, and while we were trying to find bugs to feed them, they started eating each other."

"That's disgusting, Mary!" Ricky called her out on the story that he and Jenny were following.

Mary turned to look at him. "It *was* disgusting. We didn't realize they would do that."

"What happened to the frogs, Mary?" Jenny joined the conversation.

"Your dad heaved the box over the back fence so they could all go free in the field behind my house."

"You saved them, daddy." Jenny gave him a thumbs up. "That's so nice. My daddy, the super hero."

Ian chuckled off her compliment. "I didn't save the one that was being eaten…"

Wally laughed at their shared memory. "Mary was totally freaked out about that. I remember she was almost inconsolable."

"I was. It was horrible."

Betty Jo changed the subject. "I remember when Ian was running for student council president. There were pictures of him all over campus, with all these catchy captions and phrases like: *Don't settle for less than Real Teen Powers; Vote for Formidable Powers; Elect Exciting Powers; The coolest Student Council Powers...The One and Only Ian Powers.*

Ian chuckled at that. "Wally won that election for me. Those posters were his idea and in fact, they were too over the top for me and I didn't like them, but I guess they worked since I won the election."

They all laughed at that.

Betty Jo continued the conversation. "Who were you running against? I don't remember."

Ian took a piece of chicken and passed the tray to Elizabeth. "Actually, my buddy Joe Greene. The varsity quarter-back. I figured he'd probably win the popularity vote, but I thought I could do a better job, so I ran against him anyway."

Elizabeth joined the conversation from across the table from him. "Wasn't he the same guy who did the firecracker stunt with you?"

Ian dropped his surprised eyes on her. "Who told *you* about that?" His attention moved suspiciously onto Wally.

Elizabeth looked between them in visible contemplation. "It must have been you, Ian. I don't know who else I would have heard that from. It's not like we didn't live with each other for half a decade and share stories well into the dark of night."

Ian shook his head in opposition to what she was suggesting. "No way I told you about that."

"And why do you say that?" Elizabeth challenged what he said in an effort to prove him wrong, but Ian wasn't put off by the doubt she was trying to cast.

"Because that was the dumbest stunt I've ever pulled in my life, and it got me into a lot of trouble. So, not exactly a bragging point."

Wally started eating his meal. "I thought you only got three days of detention for doing that?"

Ian shook his head in answer. "Are you kidding me? I almost got kicked out of school; they made me resign the Student Council position; and because I wouldn't rat Joe out when they knew there were two of us involved in that stunt, they gave me detention for two weeks *and* banned me from attending any after school events for the rest of the semester, which if you remember, meant that I couldn't attend homecoming or the Sadie Hawkins dance with Mary… which seemed like a pretty big overreach to me, considering all I really did was cause a minor distraction to a boring teacher's lecture."

Wally chuckled at that as Ian settled his eyes on Mary with nostalgic sentiment. "And that was just the trouble I got into at school." He reservedly continued with his story.

"When my mom got me home after being called to the principal's office to pick me up, she went totally nuts on me and grounded me for a month. I wasn't allowed to see anyone after school, including Mary, who wasn't talking to me anyway because she was so mad at me for getting myself in trouble. I thought she might even break up with me, she was so pissed – so that was a real concern to me – plus she threatened to ask you to the Sadie Hawkins dance." He settled his eyes on Wally. "Which sent me through the roof."

Mary laughed at that. "And I thought you were going to break up with me for making that threat… which obviously I only made because I was mad at you."

Ian laughed at that. "One of our few really memorable fights." He moved his attention from Mary to Wally. "Plus, my step-dad came darn close to giving me the beating I probably deserved for that silly stunt… *not to mention all the other crap I put him through.* And my fingers and hand were seriously injured and had to be treated for burns. I could barely hold a pencil or pen for days, and I could not play my guitar or drums for what felt like weeks."

Wally laughed at what he shared with them. "And here I only recalled you getting detention for like a couple of days… no big deal… we all thought that at the time."

"His usual free pass…" Elizabeth added to what Wally observed.

Ian shook his head at them. "I did *not* get a free pass for that one. It *was* a big deal. When my mom got me home from school that day, she knocked me so hard across the skull that I thought my eyeballs were literally going to fall out of my head and roll across the kitchen floor."

They all laughed at that image before Mary wrapped the subject up. "Not one of your finest moments… to be sure… but a memorable lesson."

"One of many regrettable moments in your life..." Elizabeth added her own belittling touch to the conversation. "Not unlike some of your more memorable moments with me." She continued in an uppity voice. "Especially when alcohol was fueling the bile spewing out of your mouth, like your last night in California that Mary told me about a long time ago, when you were drunkenly trying to incite a fight with all of your friends for the wrongs they'd committed against you."

Ian turned a frown on Mary. "Yet another story I don't usually share with anyone."

Mary offered him a sorry shrug. "I just told her how drunk you got that night."

Ian shook his head in silent defeat. "Well, I was a punk that night, too. So, not another bragging moment for me."

Wally laughed at that. "You were definitely a punk that night, but it was funny because you were being so playful with your tirade. With Elizabeth, on the other hand, I'm sure it was just hateful and mean."

"So..." Mary changed the subject. "We've all got moments in our past that we'd like to forget." She settled her eyes on Elizabeth. "Right? We don't want to bring up *all* the drunken memories we've experienced..."

Elizabeth changed the subject. "I'd like to hear about Wally and Betty Jo's family..."

****

When dinner was done and their company was gone, Ian and Mary settled their kids into bed and retired to their bedroom.

Ian held the door open for Mary and waved her into the room in front of him. "What's with everyone sharing my most unflattering moments tonight?" He stepped in behind her and closed their bedroom door. "Was there a point that I missed for doing that?"

Mary stepped out of her shoes. "I don't know why Wally would make unflattering comments about you, but the reason I told Elizabeth about that drunken night in high school was to neutralize her mocking of you for being so perfect. I mentioned it that night she got drunk at Jenny's house before Philip and Ellie were born. It seemed appropriate and harmless at the time, though I don't remember saying anything to her about your teasing rant that night."

Ian nodded at what she said. “Well, just so you know, I am 100% confident that Wally told her about my firecracker stunt.” He peeled off his shirt and tossed it to the laundry basket. “No way she heard about that from anyone else, and certainly not me. That’s one of those moments I don’t talk about because in hindsight, it was not my smartest stunt. Your dad even shamed me for that one and you know how I never liked to be shamed by him. So, no doubt about it, she heard that story from Wally.”

Mary peeled her own clothes off and tossed them to the basket. “So now what?” She went to the bathroom to brush her teeth.

“I don’t know.” Ian followed her in there. “I feel like I should talk to him before he gets sucked in over his head and she ruins his life.”

Mary nodded in thought as she reached for her toothbrush. “If he’s already been sucked in by her, he’s not going to be receptive to your interference. He’s going to perceive it as an ex-with an agenda, and a continuation of the teenage rivalry. It might even spur him on.”

Ian grabbed his toothbrush and squirted toothpaste onto it. “I can’t hover in silence on the sidelines and not say anything because I know how this story ends, Mary… and Wally has no idea what he’s getting into. Plus, Betty Jo doesn’t deserve the kind of wreckage that Elizabeth will leave behind in their marriage. It’s going to ruin their family.”

“Agreed.” Mary spit into the sink. “The only reason Wally is even vulnerable to Elizabeth is because he lacks self-worth.”

“True statement.” Ian finished brushing his teeth. “As long as we’ve known him, he’s been trying to prove himself to everyone. Like when he used to make me crazy in high school, constantly looking for ways to cut in on you.”

Mary smiled at their shared memories as she wiped some toothpaste off of her lips. “It still amuses me today to think about the two of you fighting over me throughout my childhood. I’m not that big of a deal…”

Ian wiped his own mouth clean and pulled her into his arms. “I wish you would stop putting yourself down and see yourself… *just once*... through my eyes. I didn't pick you in grade school, and I didn't ask you to go steady with me in high school, and I didn’t ask you to marry me as an adult because I thought to myself, *I want the ugly girl*.”

Mary blushed in his arms.

Ian continued. "I did all that because I saw all kinds of beauty in you that I realized I needed in my life every single day… just to keep breathing."

Mary wrapped her arms around him. "How did I ever get so lucky to meet you in the first place, and then… to reunite with you in the second place?"

"Let's make love…" Ian walked her across the bedroom and they crawled into bed.

****

Elizabeth stopped by Sunday afternoon.

Ricky and Jenny were riding their horses in the arena and the little kids were feeding and grooming their goats in a stall in the barn. Mary and Ian were cleaning tack in the tack room.

Elizabeth found them out there. "Hi…"

Ian glanced up from the saddle he was cleaning. "You understand that Sunday follows Saturday, and those two days together make up the weekend, and weekends are supposed to be *Lizzy free* days for Mary…"

She shot Mary an apologetic smile. "I just thought you might appreciate some forewarning that I'm going to be making a change in our childcare plans."

"What plans?" Ian immediately went on guard because this kind of declaration coming out of Elizabeth's mouth usually preceded the kind of news that could make him blow his top.

"I'm not going to be staying with the kids anymore to take care of Ellie. I've just signed a lease on my own place. It's a two-bedroom apartment and Ellie will have her own room there. So, I'll be watching her at my place from now on. And I want to move her to the school near my house since I'll be doing most of the weekday school runs. And regardless of where she attends school, I'm proposing that she stay with me from now on Monday morning through Friday evening so there's consistency in one household for the whole school week. No reason why she should have to stay here Thursday night."

"Whoa, whoa, whoa, whoa…" Ian laid his skid marks down on top of her suggested plan, with urgent and emphatic emotion. "That is not going to happen, Lizzy. We are not going to begin a custody rotation with Jenny and Ricky's daughter. Ellie is *their* child, not yours, and you are not going to body slam your way into their parenting role. That is not your right as Ellie's grandmother."

Elizabeth blew him off with quiet determination. "Don't be ridiculous, Ian. We both know that the kids aren't really raising her. *We are.* You and me. And I can't do it anymore living in your household where you can't even talk nicely to me anymore."

"I don't care where you live, Lizzy." Ian sidestepped her personal attack on him to address instead, her unacceptable child custody plan. "But Ellie is not going to live there with you. She is staying at the house where she is currently residing with both of her natural parents and you can come to the house and be a caregiver like you've been doing, and you can stay the night or just come for the day… your choice. But that's where you're caring for her. Not somewhere else."

"I am not playing around with you anymore on this, Ian." Elizabeth stood her ground with growing confidence. "I want her at my house Monday through Friday, and in fact, I was going to bring this request up later, but I guess I'll just say it now; I also want alternating weekends from now on, and alternating holidays with her."

Ian gasped in objection. "That is not going to happen, Lizzy. Ellie lives with her parents and that's who she's spending her weekends and holidays with, and if you can't be here on the days of the week that I welcomed you into her life, I'm sorry for your loss, but I am not taking Jenny's daughter away from her so that you can have a second chance raising your do-over little girl."

Elizabeth scowled in answer. "You are so judgmental and controlling. But let me remind you, I am as much her grandparent as you, Ian. And I have the same rights as you in that regard."

"Actually, you don't." Ian laid out his legal position in a confident voice. "And that's because you stood in that courtroom when Jenny was only four years old, and you told that judge that you did not want visitation rights, and in fact you wanted no rights *at all* with her. I clearly recall you confirming to him *twice* that you wanted me to have sole legal and sole physical custody of Jenny. Do you remember that day when you stood there and said that to him? Because I certainly do. And when Jenny turned eighteen, because she can't care for herself, I was granted conservatorship rights over her and her assets. And my legal status over Jenny and her assets flows downstream to the needs of her minor children. And Ricky's parents, having similar rights over Ricky and confidence in my caregiving ability, have endorsed my rights over Ellie on their behalf. So, as a matter of fact, I *do* have rights over Ellie that you do not enjoy for yourself."

Elizabeth held his glare with dwindling confidence. "You miserable excuse for a human being."

Ian shrugged off her frustration without apology. "That's the landscape that you're stuck with. And I will continue to allow your visitations as long as Jenny wants you to visit, and as long as Ellie benefits from the contact with you. But Ellie is not going to live with you, even on a rotating basis. She's going to continue living with both of her natural parents until she's old enough to decide on her own that she no longer wants to live with them. And I'll remind you that her other grandparents are also involved in her life. And they are not going to endorse you taking their grandchild away from them or their son. So, you will not be battling me alone. I am confident that they will launch a protest against your proposed custody plan, as well."

Elizabeth crossed her arms in fury. "I've been helping to raise her since she was born, and I've been more involved than all of you. And I am not giving that up now, Ian. I want balanced access to my granddaughter." Her voice became shrill as she fired back at him with rising emotion. "I deserve the same amount of time with her that I've been exercising for the past five years. And I don't care if you have guardianship or conservatorship over Jenny and Ellie – whatever it is that you've finagled out of the courts. I'm sure if we put Ellie's current situation in front of a judge, he'll give me visitation and shared custody. Because I am confident that my daily involvement in Ellie's life since the day she was born will count for something in the eyes of the court, and I am not intimidated by you, Ian. I will legally enforce my grandparenting rights over her."

Ian shrugged off her threat with a dismissive frown. "Actually, I don't think grandparents have enforceable visitation rights, Lizzy."

Elizabeth growled with growing frustration. "You mean, unless they're apparently you, right?"

Ian returned his attention to the saddle he was cleaning in an effort to end the conversation. "That's what you get when you're the parent that stands up for the child that's been abandoned by its other parent. But regardless of my superior rights over Jenny and her minor child, you're welcome to visit Ellie the same as you've been doing. But we're not going to establish a rotating custody schedule. Ellie has an intact home with her parents, and they are going to continue raising her as an intact family. I'm pretty sure that's their legal right."

"Well, I guess we'll have to see about that in court, Ian." She turned and huffed away from them, so Ian quickly stood up to follow behind her to make sure she didn't try to talk to Jenny about her idea, or worse, take Ellie with her.

Elizabeth saw him following her, and deliberately made a point of stopping to talk to Ellie, but Ellie paid her little attention. She was busy with Skylar and Philip, brushing the goats in the stall. Elizabeth tried calling her over, but Ellie didn't go to her, so Elizabeth defeatedly left the barn.

Ian followed her outside and watched her stop at her car to grab some flattened boxes out of it and some large rolls of tape, then she went to Jenny's flat and disappeared inside.

Ian returned to Mary's side.

"Did she leave?"

"No, she went inside the house to apparently pack her things."

"We should go monitor that."

Ian nodded with dread. "She's going to create trouble and now I'm not at all comfortable with her being around Jenny or Ellie anymore."

"I know." Mary shared his concern. "She'll definitely try and manipulate them."

"Yep." Ian stepped out of the tack room to keep an eye on the kids. "I don't trust her as far as I could spit."

Mary joined him outside the stall. "Are you sure about her not having enforceable grandparent rights?"

"Nope." Ian exhaled with frustration. He was not used to feeling like an ex- under siege. "Because family law is completely out of my wheelhouse. But if my bluffing her like I know what I'm talking about slows her down long enough for me to get up to speed on this, that's good enough for today."

Mary nodded, agreeing with his tactic. "What if she has enforceable rights?"

Ian had no idea what he would do. "Whether she does, or not, the one thing I know for sure, is that I do not want her visitation case winding up in court. So, I need to talk her down from her custody grab before she files something that brings this matter in front of a judge. Because then I'm standing next to her in a courtroom, arguing my case like a powerful and heartless attorney who's beating up on his vulnerable, well-meaning waif of an ex-wife, who will undoubtedly be dressed for persuasion and pulling out all of her emotional and pouty, *please help me... somebody,* expressions that will suck the judge in, and slap me down for being the mean, insensitive bad guy. And then it's out of my hands… and the judge falls on her side and I become the bad actor. And I do not want to lose control like that. There is way too much at stake for Jenny and Ellie here, and I cannot let my ego or inexperience in family law screw this up for them."

Mary completely agreed with his summation. "Why don't I go back to the house to keep an eye on her in there, and you can stay out here with the kids and finish up?"

"Good idea." Ian gave her an appreciative kiss. "Thanks for being you."

****

Ian called the estate and family law attorney that he used for Jenny's conservatorship Monday morning and told him what was going on. "So, I just need confirmation that she doesn't have grandparenting rights that can throw me into a custody rotation with her, or worse, that she can enforce in some way that will remove Ellie from Jenny's home."

His attorney offered Ian a cautionary confirmation. "The good news for you, is that generally grandparents can't file for visitation if the child's parents are married and living together."

Ian smiled with relief. "That's what I wanted to hear."

"But of course," his attorney presented the downside for him, "Like most things, there are obviously some exceptions."

"Which are?" Ian braced himself for bad news.

"Generally," his attorney offered his summary in a thoughtful voice. "A grandparent can ask a court for reasonable visitation when certain circumstances are present, most of which are not applicable to your situation, but there's wiggle room. But even then, for most of the situations it is not a given that the court will grant the visitation, unless… and here's where it's going to get tricky for you… there's a pre-existing relationship between the grandparent and the grandchild that has "engendered a bond." In which case, the court might very well find that it's in the best interest of the grandchild to grant the visitation."

"Shit." Ian couldn't help himself.

"I know." His attorney offered a counter point. "But there's also a best interest of the child balancing test. And the court isn't going to want to interfere with Jenny and Ricky's parenting rights to make decisions about their own child."

Ian didn't see that as a very persuasive or positive fact. "That's not helpful for me, Brian. Jenny can easily be manipulated by her mother into telling the court that she wants her mother to have visitation. And even if she isn't manipulated into saying that, the court may find Jenny and Ricky lack capacity to make those kinds of decisions on their own. And then it's Lizzy and me fighting it out, grandparent against grandparent, and I'm going to lose that argument because the court is going to want to maintain a status quo, and grant her visitation, barring a good reason not to."

"That's the vulnerability you're facing."

"Shit." Ian ended the call.

****

He unbelievably received a text message from Elizabeth later that day, asking for a favor, despite the fight that she just started with him.

> BY CHANCE WOULD YOU LET ME BORROW YOUR TRUCK SO I CAN MOVE THE BOXES I PACKED IN ONE TRIP AND NOT MULTIPLE TRIPS? I'M NOT GOING TO FIT THEM ALL IN MY CAR.

Ian ignored her text.

****

When he came home from work that night, his kids were watching TV in the family room with Ellie, and Mary was in the garage working out on his old elliptical machine.

"What are you doing out here?"

She was pushing hard on the steps and burning up a sweat.

"Trying to make myself…" she had to catch her breath to keep talking. "…. feel better…"

Ian came to look over her shoulder at the elliptical machine dashboard. "How long have you been out here?" The machine indicated that she'd already gone 7.22 miles with ten minutes remaining.

Mary let go of a handlebar to wipe the sweat from the palm of her hand. "I can get dinner started in a few minutes." She puffed an answer out, but not the answer to his question.

"I'm not worried about that." Ian had spent plenty of years cooking for himself and Jenny, and if need be, he had no doubt that he could pull an evening meal together, probably out of nothing. "Why are you beating yourself up at 6:30 in the evening after a long day at the office and a long evening in front of us? By the time we get barn chores done and the kids fed and bathed…"

"I carried two babies inside my body in the space of two years, Ian." Mary breathlessly cut him off. "And it shows on me."

"Yep," Ian cautiously agreed with her, but with a disclaimer. "Creating life, especially in such a short time span is a pretty amazing workout in itself, Mary. You should be congratulating yourself on such a remarkable accomplishment. Look what you did for us… you created life and brought Skylar and Philip into our world and made us a family."

"Yeah," Mary huffed in opposition. "And Elizabeth had four boys plus Jenny in her belly, and she looks like a seventeen-year-old virgin compared to me."

It was Ian's turn to object with a huff. "Elizabeth doesn't look that way naturally, Mary. She gets work done… plus, she barely eats."

"Still…" Mary didn't slow down on the machine. "Just once in my life I'd like to know how it feels to walk into a room and see heads turn."

Ian rolled his eyes. "My head always turns when you walk into the room. And that was certainly true the first time I saw you in court after not seeing you since high school. And my head didn't turn because I thought *holy cow, that's Mary Edwards. Boy has she changed for the worst.* It turned because I thought *holy moly, that's Mary Edwards, my high school sweetheart, and she looks as perfect today as she has ever looked.* You have a quiet beauty that only grows the more a person is around you."

Mary huffed off his compliment. “Well, I’d like that beauty to smack people in the face more noticeably on impact.”

Ian chuckled at that.

Mary didn’t laugh with him. “Everyone sees me the way Elizabeth sees me, Ian.” She fell into a condescending voice to mock Elizabeth’s putdown from dinner the other night. “*No offense intended…*”

Ian handed her the workout towel she had hanging over a handlebar. “If you’re going to throw your head around like that as you adopt her snarky tone, while I’m standing this close to you, how about wiping the sweat off first?”

Mary laughingly took the towel from his hand and wiped it over her face. Ian took it back from her and dropped it over the handlebar. “For the record, Elizabeth wasn’t saying that you’re overweight, Mary. She was saying that she didn’t like you offering Ellie potato chips.”

Mary speeded her pace up. “That’s your take on it, Ian. But my take is she was calling me fat.”

Ian went to the garage refrigerator and fetched Mary a bottle of water. “You look like you could use this.” He opened the cap and handed it to her. “And let’s just be clear here. I’ve also put weight on since the two of us got back together.” He took the bottle from her hand and screwed the cap back on. “And that’s partly because, as you well know, I am not going to let the kids’ uneaten *Mac & Cheese* go into the garbage can…”

Mary chuckled at that.

Ian added to it. “And I *do* like butterscotch pudding and ice cream…”

Mary nodded with appreciation. “But I’m not happy at this weight. Even if you’re okay with me at this weight.”

“Okay,” Ian gave into her discontent. “So, we’ll work on that together. We’ll both watch our diet and increase our exercising. But I don’t want you doing that out here in the hot garage by yourself, like you’re in some kind of dark torture chamber. So, let’s bring the exercise equipment back into the house and we’ll start working out together after we put the kids to bed.”

Mary nodded her unspoken agreement as she pumped the elliptical pedals. Then she found her voice. “Okay. Thanks.”

Years ago, before Mary reconnected with Ian, he practically had a home gym set up in his spacious master suite, and he worked out almost every night when he couldn't sleep. And his abs were like steel back then, and he had the enviable six-pack. But when the kids were babies, he moved all the equipment out to the garage to make room for cribs, bassinets, and playpens. And he could no longer boast that he was that fit. In fact, he really had more of a dad bod now.

"So, for tonight," Ian swatted her on the butt. "I'll get dinner started while you finish up out here. Okay?"

Mary gave him a thumbs up. "Thanks, I'm almost finished."

Chapter Nine

Wally and Betty Jo drove home mostly in silence after what Wally would describe as an awkward garden party at Ian's house. Awkward only because Elizabeth showed up. Wally didn't know why Betty Jo was so quiet, but he knew why he was quiet. He had a lot to think about. For one thing, he felt very vulnerable and nervous because of Elizabeth. He never should have allowed himself to have sex with her. He should have stopped what was happening long before they went to her bedroom. When her toe first hit his ankle was when it all began, and that was the definitive moment when he should have said, *please don't do that.* It embarrassed and offended him that he let that continue, and that he in fact, allowed it to go further.

It was so out of character for him to even be in that position. He had never before slept with such a casual acquaintance. They had barely talked to each other for a few short hours before they had sex. Wally could only guess that the reason he got swept up so quickly with Elizabeth was because she started at a more familiar place for him than as a total stranger – *she was Ian's girl* – and Ian had previously cleared her for landing... so to speak. But in another sense, Ian had also revoked her clearance – and that's what unnerved Wally today. In the aftermath of their lovemaking, Wally had been adamant with Elizabeth that he could not continue seeing her. He thought he made it absolutely clear to her that he was committed to his wife notwithstanding his indiscretion, and now more than ever, he was determined to do right by Betty Jo. So, why had Elizabeth so brazenly pushed her way into his life today – and into Betty Jo's life? Was she planning on creating chaos for him – *exactly as Ian had warned him?*

The other thing that was troubling Wally and making him wonder about his own integrity, was the fact that Ian only seemed to graciously tell flattering stories about Wally, complimenting him on his intelligence and studious nature, while Wally was inclined to only share unflattering stories about Ian. Why was that? It made

Wally feel bad as he contemplated the comparison. He guessed it might be because he felt the need to prove something, and Ian didn't. Putting Ian down lifted Wally up. And Wally needed that kind of superficial elevation, but Ian didn't. He possessed enough confidence that he didn't need to make himself feel good at other people's expense.

But more than that, Wally figured that Ian was probably a better man than him. He was certainly a man of noble character. That much was becoming crystal clear to Wally. As much as he'd been putting Ian down lately, as much as he was inclined to find fault with him, the reality was that Ian was an excellent role model, a better man than Wally made him out to be, and a far more honorable person than Wally, himself. And that had always been true. Wally could see that now.

Ian possessed exemplary principles, he was a man of strong moral fiber, and he had a good heart. Notwithstanding his known missteps and loose tongue, and his acknowledged poorly thought-out school boy pranks, he was a man of integrity with altruistic strength. He was also very generous and thoughtful. That much was proven in the way he raised Jenny by himself, the way he stayed true to Mary, and the way he continued living his life like a man with purpose – despite the various hardships that made his life difficult.

Wally's previous conclusions that Ian lacked empathy and dedication were painfully off base, and starting tomorrow, Wally was determined to follow Ian's good example. From now on he was going to conduct his life with a better moral compass, and with more compassion and dignity.

"She seemed nice enough…" Betty Jo interrupted Wally's contemplative thoughts.

"Who? Mary?" Wally glanced her direction. He was glad that she seemed to like her.

"No, silly! I was talking about Elizabeth. On the one hand I liked her, but on the other hand, I don't know. There's something about her that seems off. It's like I'm only seeing half the picture with her or something. I can't put my finger on it, but there's just a gut feeling I get with her. Maybe she isn't trustworthy. I don't know. Like what you see is not really what you get with her."

"Oh." Wally nodded his head, not knowing what to say in response to his wife's observation. "Yeah… I think there's more to her than meets the eye."

"That's exactly what I get from her." Betty Jo expanded on her answer. "Mary, on the other hand... she's so wholesome. I really liked her. She's charming and gracious. She's funny and kind. I was wrong about her before. Mary is very likeable. I get why you and Ian had a thing for her in high school. And she's so pretty. Though I thought for a minute there that she might attack Elizabeth when she had the nerve to imply that Mary was fat, which obviously, she isn't."

Wally turned to her with a confused frown. "When did Elizabeth imply that Mary was fat?"

Betty Jo settled her eyes on him with silent consternation. "How did you miss that? When she was going on and on about the potato chips... which I completely agreed with Ian on... don't start body shaming a little girl... there's going to be plenty of that in her future. She did not need her own grandmother starting in on her. But then Elizabeth looked at Mary, after shaming the little girl, and said, *no offense intended...* like could she have been more insulting to Mary? Why didn't she just come out and say, *you should probably stop eating potato chips, too?*"

Wally frowned at her charge. "I don't think Elizabeth meant that Mary was fat. I think she was just apologizing for speaking her mind about not wanting her granddaughter to be eating junk food... which is a legitimate concern."

Betty Jo emphatically shook her head at him. "That is not what she was saying, Wally..."

"Okay." He shrugged off the misunderstanding, not wanting to argue the point with her. He did not want Elizabeth hurting Mary's feelings, but he also didn't want Betty Jo villainizing Elizabeth.

"Overall, I thought it was an okay gathering..." Betty Jo kept talking. "A few awkward moments... you were right that obviously Ian and Elizabeth have an icy relationship. I actually thought it was a bit funny when he commented about not knowing how her ex- had made it that long with her."

Wally smiled without comment, not wanting to endorse the sentiment. Then he said what came to mind, despite his intention not to talk badly about Ian. "A typical kind of Ian remark."

"I know." Betty Jo chuckled. "He's still got a sharp tongue, like in high school. He's a little too confident, a little too smart, but I must admit... he's still adorable and sexy and so open and down to earth that you really don't notice the overly cool demeanor. When you're there in his circle you just feel lucky to be there because he's fun and engaging, and he somehow makes you feel like you made it into the right crowd."

"Yep, that's Ian." Wally agreed with what she said, though her observation made him feel the kind of jealousy of Ian that he'd felt nearly all his life. Even his own wife thought Ian was special.

Betty Jo continued with the conversation. "Did you tell his ex- about the firecracker thing?"

Wally turned to look at her, a little startled that she went there. "You know what? I may have. I don't recall. When I met with her, we did share some stories about the past… in context, you know… with getting to know her and understanding all the family dynamics."

Betty Jo nodded and reached for his hand. "I'm glad we've made it through all these years together. That is kind of special, isn't it?"

"It is." Wally stiffly nodded back at her, startled that she had reached for his hand to hold it in hers. It was the most affectionate thing she had said and done in years... or so it seemed. "I'm glad that makes you happy. It makes me happy too."

"Well, Elizabeth was right. It *is* an accomplishment, isn't it?" She shot him a happy smile.

Wally returned one to her and noticed for the first time in ages, how truly pretty she was. "It is…"

They held hands the rest of the way home.

****

Elizabeth called him Monday morning and Wally couldn't resist taking the call out of curiosity. He was confident that when he said goodbye to her after their illicit encounter, Elizabeth understood where she stood with him: that he couldn't undo what they had done, but that he never wanted to do that again. But her seemingly *unintentional* but clearly *intentional* appearance for Saturday night dinner made him wonder what she was really thinking, or secretly up to.

"Hi…" She spoke in a sexy hum. "How come you ghosted me last week?"

"I…" Wally shrugged off her question. "Like I said last Saturday, I can't do this. What happened, happened. I can't make it not happen. But it can't happen again. And the best way to make sure that it doesn't happen again is for us not to see each other or talk to each other again. We need to go our separate ways."

"So, we can't even be friends?" She sounded crushed.

Wally took a steadying breath. He did not have experience breaking up with women. In fact, he had only had a few casual dates in high school and college before he and Betty Jo started dating. So, he was totally inexperienced at ending relationships. And he did not want to be mean to her or get her angry with him.

He didn't want her to become his own *Fatal Attraction.*

But he needed to stand firm. He could not let their accidental coupling turn into a steady relationship. As underhanded as that made him feel in hindsight, he could not get sucked into an on-going affair with her. He did not want to make her feel like she was only a one-night stand to him, but in reality, that's what she had become, and he had to convince her that it was truly over for them.

"It's not like… it's exactly like I said last Saturday. I'd love to keep you as a close friend but that's not a workable solution because our friendship has become complicated. I can't be friends with you and pretend in front of everyone that nothing happened between us. And I can't convince myself that I don't like you., when I *do* like you. So, making a clean break of it is the only answer to this dilemma. Because I can't indulge that attraction again... *ever*. I never should have indulged it to begin with. Not that I want to… I don't want you to feel…"

"Like it was just about sex with me?" Elizabeth giggled as she said it for him. "*Good sex...actually.*" She giggled again. "But I promise not to let that happen again. And I just couldn't help myself Saturday. I had to see you again. But nobody ever has to know about what we did. I can keep it secret."

Wally shook his head at what she was suggesting. "I'm afraid Ian may have already figured it out."

"Well, phooey on Ian…" Elizabeth huffed through the phone. "He is the one person in this world that I genuinely could care less about. So, who cares if he's offended by my love life? That's not something he gets to be concerned about anymore. Right?"

Wally frowned at what she blew off as unimportant to her, because it wasn't unimportant to him; *he* cared *a lot* about Ian being offended by her love life because her love life involved him now – and Ian would definitely find Wally's involvement with her offensive, not to mention how offensive Betty Jo would find it. Plus, he did not want a friend anymore who was always putting Ian down. *He* did not want to be that type of friend anymore.

"That actually brings me to one of the reasons for my call…" Elizabeth fell into a seductive voice. "…besides me wanting to check in with you to see how you're doing, because I know you're troubled about what happened, and that you didn't plan on that happening."

"I didn't. And it *is* troubling."

"I know. I didn't expect that either, but honestly, I'm glad it happened, because I thought it was special. Something we can secretly hold onto inside our hearts. A gift that we gave ourselves. It doesn't have to harm anyone as long as we keep it buried. You can still stay married and buy her the anniversary gifts… and all the other romantic stuff that you like to do for her. And our secret can remain a special memory just for the two of us to indulge, knowing that we'll never share that kind of love again…"

"Sure." Wally said what he needed to say to avoid hurting her feelings.

"So, my other reason for calling you is that I need a friend, and I don't really have any friends in this area. So, I'm reaching out to you. I need some help…

Of course, she did. Wally let out a troubled sigh. He did not want to get dragged into her web but he could see how that was happening. "What kind of help?" He was hearing Ian's warning in his head... *she's chaos, Wally...* But he felt like he owed her something… because of what they did together… and he should at *least* be a gentleman and not blow her completely off – plus, she kind of scared him now. There was no telling what trick she might pull on him if he offended her.

"I need to move out of Ian's flat. I can't live in that oppressive environment anymore. It was fine the first year or so, but now… you hear how he talks to me…"

"Ah huh…" Wally stayed neutral.

"He's such an arrogant bully…and he's completely domineering. He has to be in charge of everything and it always has to be his way or the highway."

"Ah, huh…" Wally didn't respond to her observation. Ian could be a bit arrogant sometimes, he'd give her that. And he definitely liked to keep control of what was happening around him. But he was never a bully. That just wasn't in his character.

Wally returned his attention to Elizabeth. "What did you have in mind?" He was afraid she was going to somehow try and push herself more noticeably into his life and he was not equipped with any experience in knowing how to effectively push back.

"I have a room that I've been subleasing where I stay when I'm not at Ian's… and the lease is up. When I moved here from L.A. when Jenny was pregnant, I never really settled into my own place. I found this room that was only supposed to be a temporary solution while I settled in with Jenny and Ricky to help care for Ellie. But it's been almost six years now. And the arrangement worked fine for a while. But I'm ready for my own place now. I *need* my own space. So, I found an apartment in Davis…"

Wally didn't say anything. His medical office and his home were both in Davis – and Elizabeth knew that.

"It's small but it's cute and there's room for Ellie there. I'll need help moving into it, though. So, that's where I'm hoping that you come in…"

"Hum…" Wally figured he could help her move and then say goodbye one final time and be done with her. He'd pay his pittance for doing wrong with her, and then he'd never see her again.

"When did you want to do this move?"

"I was hoping for this weekend? I pick the keys up on Friday."

"Okay." Wally would help her do the move. It was the polite thing for him to do. After all, she was a small woman and no doubt, she would not be able to move furniture on her own. And Wally didn't think that Ian would be willing to help her, although, he did always seem to do the right thing by her – regardless of their icy relationship – at his own expense – which was just another sign of Ian's generous and loyal character. "What's involved in the move?"

Elizabeth happily told him. "I just have a few things; a bed, a chair, some stuff in storage… a couch and book shelf, and some items at Jenny's place that I boxed up yesterday."

"Wait a minute…" Wally wanted nothing to do with that part of the move. "I can't help you at Ian's house."

"Okay." Elizabeth let him off the hook. "If you can at least help me with the other stuff…"

"Sure." Wally nodded to himself. "Do we need a truck?" He didn't own one, but he supposed they could rent one.

Elizabeth giggled. "I sort of put a feeler out to see if Ian would let me borrow his, but he hasn't answered my text…" She laughed harder. "So, that was probably pushing it too far with him…"

"Probably." Wally chuckled with her. "So, where am I meeting you?"

She gave him the address of her sublease and they coordinated a meeting time and said goodbye.

****

Ian called Wally later that day. "Hey, dude… what's shakin'?"

Wally chuckled at Ian's use of 70s slang. "Hi…" They were talking more these days than they'd talked in years. Probably more than they talked as teenagers. "What's up?" Wally figured Ian was calling because his radar had gone off during the dinner conversation on Saturday and he wanted to follow that lead.

"I just felt like checking in with you." Ian went exactly where Wally anticipated. "I feel like there's more going on with you and Elizabeth than what's being acknowledged on the surface. And I wanted to caution you on that. It's not my business. It's your life, and your call… but I still feel compelled to sound off a second warning notwithstanding my disclaimer of non-involvement. I said it before, and I'll say it again… if you take that joyride, man, it's going to plummet your life into hell."

Wally chuckled. "Nothing's happening between Elizabeth and me, Ian. Your radar is off."

Ian's silence said he didn't believe that.

"Really…" Wally offered a stronger denial. "I'm the guy who believes in commitment, not joyrides, remember? And you're the guy who's on his second marriage… so I don't think you're in a position to lecture me."

"Fair enough." Ian stayed the course, nonetheless. "But I still feel compelled to offer a warning. Don't do it, Wally. Don't get sucked in by her."

"I'm not, and I won't."

"Seriously." Ian drove his point home. "You're married. And that *is* an accomplishment to be proud of. You're the guy that everyone is emulating… *I* want to be you, proudly boasting that I just bought Mary a thirtieth wedding anniversary present. Don't lose that special lifelong bond, man. Stay the course."

Wally huffed with more honesty. “Our marriage isn’t without problems, Ian.”

“No marriage is, Wally.” Ian countered what he said with matter-of-fact, certainty. “But whatever problems you’re facing, I’m confident that you can work through them like you’ve been doing for the last thirty years.”

Wally shook his head with unwanted contempt for Ian’s position, because Ian had no idea what *real* marriages were like. He was the golden boy, married to the golden girl. *He* was the guy that everyone wanted to be. Mister never been told, *no* before. Mister *never had to work hard for anything in his life, before*.

Wally couldn’t help going there in his head. “You would know that I can work it out, how Ian? Like you and Mary ever have fights or disagreements… or trouble in your marriage.”

“Of course, we have challenges…”

“Hard to believe.” They were an enviable couple. *Lifelong soulmates.* They had always been the perfect pair and it was obvious that nothing had changed between them. They were *still* exceptional partners perfectly in tune with each other. That came out in so many ways… the soft caresses, the intimate stare downs… So, how could Ian possibly know what Wally was facing?

With that thought in mind, Wally offered a small dose of what he was thinking. “You know what Ian, some people have such easy lives, they can’t even comprehend real life challenges, and how the rest of us suffer.”

Ian audibly gasped at Wally’s observation. “Well, that says a lot about what you think of me as a person.”

He let that sink in for a minute before he offered a contrary opinion to Wally’s unflattering judgment. “I’m not going to air all of my dirty laundry as a counter argument for you, Wally, but as a contrary point, I’ll offer this one fact: Mary lacks self-confidence. She always has. And I have a hard time convincing her that she’s beautiful, which makes no sense to me. But she honestly believes that she’s overweight and unattractive. She continually beats herself up about this and because I don’t get it, I have to constantly remind myself that this is a real thing for her. And I need to be sensitive to that, which I sometimes forget… and that can cause conflict in my marriage.”

“That’s crazy.” Wally couldn’t believe what he was saying. Mary was gorgeous.

"I know." Ian didn't back down on his example. "But there it is. And that's a challenge for me. And to prove a point, she went nuts on me that day Elizabeth came to the house and I tried waving you off of her, because obviously, my uncensored effort lacked sensitivity to her insecurities."

Wally chuckled at his confession. "I thought she might be a tad annoyed with you that day."

"A *tad*?" Ian huffed with affirmation. "She was definitely more than a tad pissed at me. But we worked it out. And that's what I want to help you do with Betty Jo. Whatever the challenges, let's help each other power through them. Because I don't want you letting go of someone special like Betty Jo for an illusion of someone better, when I know for myself, she won't be better. She will make your worst days with Betty Jo seem like a carefree hayride."

Wally couldn't help but feel annoyed at Ian's insistence. "Why don't we clear up what's really going on here, *Lover Powers,* because I feel like this has more to do with your teenage rivalry with me, than a sincere concern about my happiness. Like what you're really saying is hands off because she used to be mine." Which honestly, only fueled Wally on, though he didn't admit that.

"You know what…" Ian answered his premise with a dismissive surrender. "Take her. I could care less."

Wally chuckled at his retreat. "I just feel like it used to be Mary we fought over, now it's Elizabeth. Like Elizabeth is the new Mary for you…" Wally realized as he made the allegation, that a certain amount of what he was accusing Ian of, applied to his own interest in Elizabeth. Had she not been Ian's girl at one time, he might not have been so intrigued by her. Perhaps his only real interest in her was because of that: Ian had her first and now Wally had taken her for himself. *Boom.* He was leveling the playing field.

Ian scoffed at what he suggested. "Elizabeth isn't even close to being Mary. And my concern about you being sucked in by her has nothing to do with an old rivalry between kids. We grew up together, *Polly Wally;* you've been a friend since grade school. And bottom line, I don't want to see you getting hurt... and I don't want your wife getting hurt. That's what troubles me. And I know how this story ends. It doesn't feel good, Wally. It hurts."

"Your concern is noted."

"Great." Ian huffed with his dismissal. "So, when the flames reach your house, you'll remember… I told you so." He ended the call without saying goodbye.

****

When Wally went home that night, he told Betty Jo about Elizabeth contacting him. "I got a call today from Elizabeth."

She barely paid him attention. "Ian's Elizabeth?"

Wally chuckled. "I don't think he'd like us referring to her that way, but yes. Ian's Elizabeth." And also… *Wally's…* Elizabeth – but he kept that to himself.

"What did she want?" Betty Jo was preparing dinner for them and that's what consumed her interest.

Wally shared what Elizabeth wanted, to try and keep what he was doing with her above board. "She's apparently moving out of Ian's house this weekend and she wants me to help her move furniture."

"Wow… that was presumptuous. Assuming you'd want to help." Betty Jo moved around him to get butter out of the refrigerator to drop it into a pot of boiled potatoes. "I don't see Ian being too keen on helping her, though. So, maybe her options for male helpers are limited."

"Apparently." Wally was glad that she went there on her own. "So, I told her I'd help, assuming you won't mind."

Betty Jo started mashing the potatoes. "Well, I've got my sorority get together this Saturday… we're going wine tasting in Apple Hill. So, the timing is good."

"That's quite a drive…" Wally went to the cupboard for two plates so he could help her serve dinner. "How much wine tasting will you be doing?"

Betty Jo finished mashing the potatoes and went to the sink with the potato masher. "You know me… I won't taste much. It's more for the comradery."

"Well, don't try and drive home if you think you've tasted more than you should."

Betty Jo nodded her agreement to what he suggested. "Do you want to get the pork out of the oven?"

"Sure." Wally picked up the pot holders and pulled the pork chops out of the oven. It had been a while, he realized since the two of them had conversed over dinner preparations. In fact, it had been ages since the two of them had fixed dinner together.

"Are you eating in front of your TV, or are we eating together?" He hoped for the latter.

"Do you mind?" Betty Jo scooped some potatoes onto his plate, then she scooped up some peas and put a slab of meat down beside them. "This is my night for my shows…"

"That's fine." Wally took his plate, a fork and knife and retreated to his den.

****

Ian called him the next day. "Hey… *Polly Wally…*"

Wally took the call only because yesterday's call didn't end well, and he didn't want that to become their last conversation. "I can't sit through another lecture about Elizabeth, Ian."

He laughed at that. "No lecture today."

"So, why the call?"

Ian chuckled off his suspicion. "Mary and I were talking last night, and we thought it might be fun if you and Betty Jo came over to the house Saturday to do some riding with us. You guys can ride Jenny and Ricky's horses. Our nanny can watch the kids for us, and we could ride up in the hills – have some adult fun. Maybe do dinner after that *without unexpected visitors."*

Wally chuckled at his disclaimer. "We both have plans for Saturday."

Ian wasn't put off. "How about Sunday?"

Wally grinned at his perseverance. "You're really trying to pull us under the almighty Powers wing, aren't you?"

Ian was quiet in response for just a second. "I'm just trying to be a good wingman, dude."

Wally nodded with appreciation that Ian was truly concerned. "Thanks. Sounds fun. I'll have to confirm with Betty Jo to make sure we don't have other plans."

"Sure. Just let me know so I can line up some childcare."

Wally laughed at that. "I don't envy you, still raising little kids."

Ian laughed at his own predicament. "Yeah, not something I thought I'd ever be doing at this point in my life, but there it is… *Daddy Powers…*"

Wally chuckled at his humor. "So, we'll plan on seeing you Sunday. Unless Betty Jo has something else already planned."

"Great. We'll see you then."

****

When Wally woke Saturday morning, he skipped the gym to have breakfast with Betty Jo before she left for her day with friends, then he showered and dressed for his moving day with Elizabeth. It was a crisp November morning, and he hoped they would be done with the move early enough for him to return home to watch the Warriors play the Clippers.

He drove to her house and picked her up in his car and together they drove to a U haul place to pick up a truck. Elizabeth drove his car back to her house and Wally drove the truck. When they got back to the house, Elizabeth took him inside and introduced him to her female housemates.

"This is the guy I told you about…" She shot him a friendly smile. "He happens to be a good friend of my ex-." She was dressed today in form fitting jeans, a skin tight shirt and an expensive looking pair of *Gucci* sneakers.

Both girls chuckled. "That's a good way to get back at him…"

"Right?" Elizabeth giggled as she reached for his hand to drag him along behind her. "I'm on the second floor…"

"Great." Wally chuckled, following her as she scampered up a flight of narrow stairs. "Is the new place a ground floor apartment, or is it upstairs too?"

"It's on the second floor…"

"Perfect."

She opened a door at the end of a hallway and pulled Wally in behind her, into her bedroom. There were a dozen boxes stacked neatly along one wall, some plastic bins piled beside them, and numerous large garbage bags filled with clothing and linen. Wally eyed the work-out in front of him with an experienced appreciation for what lay ahead. Her double bed had been stripped but not disassembled – he'd likely have to take care of that himself. And a recliner chair in the corner of the room would be a monster to get downstairs, and then upstairs at her new place.

"I know..." She giggled looking up at him. "We have our work cut out for us today."

Wally brushed off her stated concern with an upbeat smile, ready to make small work out of it. "Let's start with the chair. It's going to be heavy, so let's get it downstairs first. But we'll load it onto the truck last, so it can be the first thing we unload on the other side."

"I wouldn't have thought of that!" Elizabeth shot him a happy smile. "Good thing I got you to help me. You clearly know what you're doing here."

He chuckled at that. "Well, I've moved a few kids out of my own house, and into dorm rooms and apartments..."

They spent the day hauling bags, boxes, bins, and furniture first from her sublet, and then out of a storage unit and into her new apartment. They laughed and joked as they carried items down the stairs and into the truck, then out of the truck and up the stairwell to her new place. Twice she dropped something, hurting first her hand and then her foot. Wally showed concern, as she fought tears, but he kept himself from getting sucked in on a more emotional level.

When all of her possessions were finally in her new place, they returned the truck to the U haul dealer and Wally drove her back to her apartment.

"So..." he parked his car next to where she had parked her car earlier and turned to look at her. "We did it!"

She held a thankful smile on him. "Thanks for the help. I couldn't have done it without you."

His phone rang, and Wally shrugged an apology to Elizabeth. "I need to answer this..."

"Sure..." She shot him a patient, understanding grin.

"Hi..." It was Betty Jo and Wally figured she was calling to say that either she was on her way home, or she had tasted more wine than she had intended, and she was not coming home.

"How's the move going?"

Wally gave her a quick summation. "I think we're just finishing up, actually."

"That's great. Perfect timing for you if you want to watch the Warriors play the Clippers tonight."

"My thoughts exactly. Shall I order us a pizza?" Wally smiled at Elizabeth, secretly thankful for his wife's interruption in their conversation because it provided him a perfect exit strategy from Elizabeth. And it was giving him the perfect opportunity to show loyalty to his wife, not Elizabeth.

"Okay with you if I stay with friends?"

"Oh…" Wally held a frozen stare on his face. That was not what he wanted to hear. His eyes went to Elizabeth and he could tell that she heard that too.

"I guess if you think you should…"

"I just don't want to take any chances…"

"Of course not."

"I'll be home early tomorrow morning."

"Don't forget we have plans…"

"I know. I won't be late."

"Okay." His eyes went to Elizabeth as he said goodbye to his wife. "I love you, Pookie…" He wanted to make his loyalty clear to her… *to Elizabeth*… as much as he wanted to send a loving sentiment to his wife. And he hadn't called her that in ages.

She giggled with his use of an old term of endearment and returned an equally long overdue greeting to him. "Me too, Boogie bear."

Elizabeth chuckled.

Wally avoided her stare. "See you in the morning."

When he ended the call, Elizabeth said what she was thinking. "Well, that's convenient." She shot him a flirty smile. "Why don't you stay and watch the Warriors with me? I could use the man power to move some furniture around during commercials, and I can have pizza delivered for dinner. I promise we'll keep our hands to ourselves. Just platonic friends."

"I can't." Wally was smart enough to know that her suggestion was a bad idea.

"I promise nothing will happen. We've been good all day… right? So, why do you think we won't behave ourselves this evening?"

Wally didn't know. Except he was shrewd enough to know that he should stand firm in his position, and quickly drive away from here.

"Come on…" She opened the passenger door and stepped out into the parking lot.

Wally turned the ignition over and rolled his window down. "I really need to call it a day." He deliberately stayed in his seat to avoid the temptation of staying for pizza, as Elizabeth stepped up onto the sidewalk in front of the car to come his direction.

"Please…" She shot him an enticing smile as her foot missed the curb down and she tumbled to the ground.

"Shit." Wally turned the car off and opened his door. "Are you okay?"

She pushed herself up from the asphalt with tears in her eyes, as she looked at her wrist and held it in her other hand. "I think I broke it…"

"Damn it…" Wally went to help her off the ground. "Let me see it." He took her wrist in his hand, manipulated it just a little, and immediately confirmed her fears. "Yep. It's broken."

"Okay… I'll drive myself to the hospital…"

"No, you won't." Wally pulled her into his arms and helped her around the car. "Get in… I'm not leaving you alone to drive yourself to the hospital when you're obviously in pain and in need of medical care." He ushered her into the passenger seat and helped her buckle in. "What hospital do you use?"

"Kaiser."

Wally nodded and closed her door. Then he walked around the car and hopped into the driver's seat. "It looks like I'm staying for pizza after all; and the final half of the Warriors at your place." He was not going to abandon her now with a broken wrist and furniture and boxes piled around her house. She wouldn't even be able to find a toothbrush tonight.

They made it to the hospital and were immediately ushered into a treatment room. Wally explained what happened, and what he thought was injured, they took x-rays, shot her wrist up with pain killers for the reduction, and realigned the bones in her wrist. Then they put her in a temporary cast and sent her home with Wally.

He helped her back into the car, and they drove back to her place, stopping briefly at a liquor store so Wally could buy a six pack of beer. The game had already started by the time they got home, so Elizabeth immediately called for pizza while Wally set her television up so he could catch the second half of the game. When the television was up and running, and the game was going, he opened some boxes at her direction and unpacked a few things for her.

The pizza was delivered, Elizabeth took a pain pill with soda, and Wally had a beer. Her couch was a small loveseat, and it was somewhat hard and dusty, but they sat side by side on it and cheered the Warriors on as they won over the Clippers, 114 to 110.

"That was so much fun…" When the game was over, Elizabeth left the couch to clear away the pizza box with her good hand. Wally scooped up his empty beer bottles. He had only finished two of them as they watched the game because he did not want to drink too much before driving home.

"I should help you set your bed up before I go…"

"Thanks!" Elizabeth set the carton on the kitchen counter and gestured for him to follow her into the bedroom. "I feel so helpless now…"

He shot her a smile. "Keep taking the pain meds so it doesn't get uncomfortable. You don't want to have to chase the pain down. Stay ahead of it."

She nodded at his wise counsel. "I feel lucky that you were here when I fell."

He smiled at what she said because he couldn't help but feel protective of her. "Why don't you sit over there while I set this up for you?" She did as he suggested, and Wally set her bed up. Then he searched through some garbage bags for bed linen so he could make it for her. When the sheets and comforter were nicely made on it, he located her pillows and dropped them into pillow cases. "Will you be okay by yourself?"

"Sure." She said it with doubt.

Wally admittedly felt conflicted about leaving her. He did not want to abandon her while she was dealing with pain and immobility issues, and trying to manage her medications alone – all in the middle of a move with boxes she wouldn't be able to rearrange on her own, piled around her.

Elizabeth read his mind. "You could crash on my bed, and I could sleep on the couch…"

Wally scoffed at that idea. "Your couch is uncomfortable. And it's too short for even you to stretch out on. Plus, you won't be able to rest your arm comfortably on the couch."

She held a vulnerable smile on him. "We could both sleep on my bed, fully clothed. I promise not to touch you."

Wally smiled at her suggestion. Considering how her wrist looked on the x-ray, he could certainly believe that she wouldn't be up for any fooling around tonight.

"Okay. Fully dressed. And I'm only staying to get you through this first night with the broken wrist and new pain meds. You'll feel better tomorrow, and you'll be able to manage the pain meds on your own. And that's when we say goodbye for good, because I have plans that I can't cancel tomorrow, and we can't keep seeing each other. It's just creates a distraction in my marriage that I positively refuse to indulge."

"I understand." She dutifully nodded. "You're just staying tonight to provide medical care. I get it."

Wally nodded his head. "That's it. Nothing more."

He helped her locate her toothbrush, he found dental floss to use on his own teeth, he swished around mouthwash and figured that was good enough for tonight.

"Can you help me with my pants?" Elizabeth set her brush down on the bathroom counter and turned an innocent, but seductive pout his direction. "I need to pee… and I'm not going to be able to wiggle out of these jeans with only one useable hand…"

Wally shot her an amused smile, thinking to himself that… *this*… was how she sucked him in. Her beguiling innocence and vulnerability.

"Sure." He stepped over to the toilet and opened the lid for her, then he took her by the hips, he backed her up towards the toilet, and opened the button and then the zipper on her jeans. She was wearing incredibly sexy, red lacy underwear.

Wally tried not to notice. "Here…" he took hold of the waistband of her pants with both hands to try and shimmy them down her legs. "Let me push these lower for you…" It was a struggle, even for him to accomplish the task because they fit her like a second layer of skin.

Elizabeth giggled. "For the second time with you, I've made a poor choice in clothing…"

Wally chuckled; doubting that any of her clothing choices were accidental. Elizabeth did nothing by accident. That much was becoming clear to him. She was probably the most calculated woman he'd ever met. For a minute he even wondered if her fall was deliberate.

Her pants made it down to her ankles and he reached back up to slide her underpants the same direction. Then he helped her drop lower, over the toilet and stepped away from her. "So… do what you need to do in here, and when you're finished, give me a holler, and I'll come back in to help you out of your pants and into something you can manage on your own."

She giggled at his suggestion. "Okay, doc. Thank you."

Wally left the bathroom and went to the living room to text his wife.

> ELIZABETH TRIPPED OFF THE SIDEWALK AS I WAS LEAVING HER HOUSE TO GO HOME. DISTAL RADIUS FRACTURE EXTENDING INTO THE RADIOCARPAL JOINT, WILL PROBABLY NEED SURGICAL REPAIR. I TOOK HER TO THE HOSPITAL AND NOW PLANNING ON STAYING THROUGH THE NIGHT TO ASSIST HER AS NEEDED. JUST WANTED YOU TO KNOW.

His wife texted back:

> GOT YOUR MESSAGE. THANKS FOR THE HEADS UP. HOPE SHE FEELS BETTER TOMORROW. I KNOW SHE'S IN GOOD HANDS TONIGHT. SAW THE WARRIORS WON. YIPPEE FOR YOU! XO

"Hey doc…" Elizabeth called out to him. "I'm ready for your assistance."

Wally went to the bathroom and pushed the door open. "Do you know what bag or box we'll find your pajamas or other comfortable clothes?"

"I'm not sure." She tried to slide her feet out of her pants to kick them out of the way, but she could only get one ankle partially free of them. "Can you pull them off the rest of the way?"

"Sure." Wally went to pull them off for her and Elizabeth stood to pull up her lacy red panties.

Wally looked away as he helped her slide them up. "So…" He imagined she was also wearing a similarly sexy, lacy red bra that she might want him to remove before bed. He doubted that she would really want to sleep in it.

Elizabeth stepped away from the toilet and led the way to her bedroom. Wally tried not to notice her small firm butt cheeks moving before his eyes inside the sexy red panties that didn't fully cover the flesh on her bottom. *God,* she was so damn alluring. It was all he could do to keep himself from reaching out to touch her firm butt cheeks.

"Maybe in this bag?" Elizabeth leaned over it to try and untie it with her one good hand.

Wally moved his eyes off of her firm derriere and a flash of what she possessed between her legs. "Let me do that for you." He moved her to her bed and eased her down onto it so she could sit there and watch him, instead of him watching her.

"What am I looking for?"

"I have a pair of black satin pajamas with white ribbing…"

"Okay…" Of course, that'd be the type of evening wear she'd want him to find. Elizabeth was not a flannel pajama kind of girl.

"The pants are shorts… not long pants."

"Of course." Wally nodded with expectation as he dug through bras, underpants, some satin slips and camisoles… "Here they are." He pulled them out to hand them to her. "Can you dress yourself?"

"Sure. I think so." She nodded with an uncertain shrug as she reached for the pants and fumbled through what looked like a painful effort to pull them on one-handed over her lacy red panties. "Oops…" they fell to the floor and she giggled trying in vain to reach for them.

"Nope… I can't do it alone." Her eyes danced up at him. "I guess I'm going to need help. And that's going to include my bra… if you don't mind?"

Wally stepped closer to her body to peel her shirt from her torso and maneuver it over the cumbersome cast and sling. When it was over her head and free of the cast, he discarded it to the floor. Then he reached behind her back and carefully unfastened her bra without looking down in front or in back. He did not want that kind of temptation.

When the clasps were undone, the material slipped from his hands and he accidently glanced down to catch her bra from falling open. The bare form of her back was beautifully shaped like an ancient sculpture, carved to perfection. Wally's hand drifted down her spine to take hold of the sexy red material to bring it around her body to the front of her torso so he could move the strap from around the cast and sling, so her breasts could fall free from it.

Elizabeth reached for his palm as it crossed over her chest.

"Thanks…" she lifted herself up from her bed and stood to kiss his lips.

Wally wrapped his arms around her and passionately kissed her back. "We can't do this…"

"I know."

He stopped the kiss to manipulate the bra out of the tangle of sling and cast material and over her broken wrist. Elizabeth lowered herself back down to sit on the bed and Wally followed her to the mattress and dropped down around her. Her bra fell to the floor and he helped her scoot backwards so she could stretch out beside him.

"What are we doing?" His hand slid to the lacy red panties and he peeled them down her thighs. He needed her to stop him from what he was doing because he would never be able to stop himself.

"I can't wrap my arm around you… but I want to hug you so badly."

Wally peeled off his own clothes and dropped himself over her. *Ian was right. She felt so good under his bare-naked body.*

He kissed both of her breasts and then her pouty mouth. "You need to hold your arm perfectly still… and leave the rest in my hands."

****

When they were through making love, Wally rolled to his back and silently started crying. He did not want to cry in front of her, but he felt like such a shameful failure. He had been determined not to do that again, but now what? Obviously, he was a horrible disgraceful cheat. In hindsight, with the wash of his sexual release behind him, he couldn't figure out why the urge to have her was so uncontrollable.

"I'm sorry…" Elizabeth rolled to her side to quietly stare at him. "Don't be sad…doc; it couldn't be helped. We have such a magnetic attraction to each other."

Wally wiped his eyes with the back of his hand. "You don't understand. I really didn't want to be that kind of guy. I don't want to cheat on my wife. I don't want to be… *him*… the cheating husband. I want to be the dependable man who would never do that to my loved one."

"I understand." Elizabeth dropped her hand on his chest and stroked it with affection. "My second husband cheated on me, so I totally get what you're saying."

"He did?" Wally stopped crying to listen to what she was sharing. It was hard to believe that anyone could ever find a reason to cheat on her. She was a perfect bed partner, beautiful and sexy, and incredibly passionate.

Elizabeth sadly nodded and continued in a soft voice. "So, I get why you don't want to be ... *him,* and I know you don't want to cause your wife that kind of pain."

"I don't." Wally's eyes filled with fresh tears. He did not want to even think about Betty Jo right now because he couldn't handle the guilt that came with it. "So, what happened with your husband?" He shifted the focus from his own crumbling marriage to Elizabeth's failed second marriage.

She sighed with her own memories. "We just grew apart. We stopped doing things together. After raising four boys together, we suddenly had nothing in common. And that slowly eroded our relationship until the only thing we had left were a lot of reasons to argue."

Wally nodded with a frown. "That's my wife and me. We've grown apart. I'm trying to reel her back in... but she doesn't seem interested; and that causes arguments."

"I get that." Elizabeth added more from her own experience. "Ultimately my husband just tuned me out. Then one day he came home from work and announced that he wanted a divorce because he'd met someone new... a *younger* version of me."

"I'm sorry." Wally felt her pain as he imagined his own wife's grief if she ever found out about him cheating with Elizabeth... not just tonight... but *also* two weeks ago. If only he could say it was just the one time. That seemed so much more forgivable than what he would have to admit after tonight... a *repeat* performance – which basically turned his one-night affair into an on-going relationship. What else could he call it? A meaningless, *meaningful* fling?

Elizabeth nodded with understanding that came from her own grief. "My boys are exceptionally close to their father – and they like his new me. So, it gets complicated when we're all together. So, I came up here to help Jenny with her baby. She texted me at just the right moment to tell me she was pregnant, and it seemed like the timing was meant to be."

Wally reached for her hand to hold it in his. "What do I do now?" His life was suddenly spiraling out of control. *Chaos... that's what he was facing... Ian's description, once again came to mind.* "I've screwed up my whole life."

Elizabeth nodded at what he said. "Probably. That's exactly how I felt when Ian and I broke up. Like my world was in chaos and spinning out of control."

Wally nodded at her description. "So, what ruined it for you guys?" His curiosity about what happened between them – *the unraveling of the almighty Ian Powers love connection* – was definitely more intriguing to Wally now that it was seemingly merging into his own history with Elizabeth.

She shifted by his side.

"Is your wrist okay?" Wally turned to her with concern. His sweet vulnerable angel. He didn't want her feeling any pain.

She shot him a weak smile. "It's fine. Thanks." But her discomfort showed on her face.

Wally pulled her closer to give her a kiss. He was incredibly conflicted. He absolutely adored this waif in his arms who was making him fall head over heels in love with her, but he couldn't leave his wife of thirty years who he still loved deeply, for what he had to admit, was a woman he barely even knew today.

Elizabeth began her story. "When I met Ian, he was dating my friend, but nonetheless, I fell hard for him. I could not get him out of my mind. I was thinking about him non-stop. So, when he finally broke up with my friend, I quickly moved in on him. And we seemed to get along well, especially since neither of us wanted kids. So, I thought we were a perfect match. We were going to live a big life, travel a lot and enjoy our freedom, unencumbered by parental demands, and blissfully undistracted from each other. But he *was* distracted... all the time. He was working incredibly hard, putting in long hours at his firm, trying to make partner, and honestly, he didn't have a lot of time for me, and that was annoying. And I don't think I realized how tired he was or how stressful his job could be. I just wanted him to have fun with me. So, I probably pushed too hard to try and get him to lighten up, and honestly, he was usually a pretty good sport about it. But my desire to have fun all the time, and his focus on his career began to erode our relationship… *that* and his obsession with Mary which he could not shake. And ultimately, all of the conflicting stressors caused a lot of tension between us until we couldn't even remember why we ever fell in love. We just kept having these nightly, hair-raising fights where we both acted like we couldn't stand each other, until we ultimately realized we really couldn't stand each other.

Wally nodded with the picture she was creating for him. It wasn't that hard for him to imagine their passionate fights. "So, how did you end up having Jenny?"

Elizabeth shot him an adoring smile. "My idea and he only went along with it to make me happy. I thought having kids might draw us closer together and make him fall in love with me again. You know… mother of his child."

"But then she had her accident…" Wally nodded as he merged the new details that she was providing with the few facts that Ian had previously shared with him. "And that coupled with all the other stressors made Ian kick you to the curb."

Elizabeth smiled in defeat at his blunt summation. "Something like that. But I don't want to talk about Ian anymore. I just want you to hold me in your arms, and make me feel whole again, even if it's only for this one night."

"It *has* to be just for tonight, Elizabeth."

"I understand." She cuddled into his body. "But honestly, I wish you would move in with me and help me raise Ellie. We could be happy together. And you of all people would totally understand Ellie's needs, considering how much you know about her parents and brain injuries in general, and how to help children of brain injured parents thrive."

Wally let out a shocked breath of air. "You're planning on raising Ellie here?" He had not heard anything about that from Ian, and it seemed like an awfully hard sale for her to pitch to him. Wally did not see Ian giving into her request.

She nodded with confidence. "I just have to convince him that I deserve that chance, and that I'll do a good job with her."

She kissed him on the chest and closed her eyes. "He's got his own kids to raise now, so he shouldn't really care about raising Ellie. And I don't have anyone. So, it *should* be me raising her… not him. And that's where you can help me. Ian values your opinions… I mean… you're a *doctor…* and he would trust your ability to parent her. And if you were living here with me, we could raise her together, and you could make me the happiest girl in the world. Happier than Ian ever made me…"

Wally nodded his head without encouraging that train of thought. He had no interest in helping Elizabeth raise her grandchild, and for the first time since the two of them hooked up, he found himself wondering if she actually liked him for himself, or for what she thought the *doctor* in him could do for her. Because it sounded tonight like the only reason she came after him was to get back at Ian for leaving her, and to use Wally's friendship with Ian to advance her own underhanded cause against him.

Chapter Ten

When Ian answered his phone Sunday morning, Wally was on the other line.

"Hey, Powers…"

Ian chuckled at his greeting. "What's shakin', dude?"

"We're running a little late. Maybe one o'clock instead of noon? Will that still work for the horse ride?"

"Sure." Ian glanced at the alarm clock on his night stand. For once, he and Mary had gotten to sleep in on a Sunday morning. It was already ten o'clock and nobody had banged on their bedroom door yet, or clamored into their room unannounced to climb into their bed.

He tapped Mary awake beside him and pointed to the clock as Wally continued talking in his ear.

"Betty Jo was out of town yesterday and she's stuck in slow traffic, so that's why the delay."

Ian closed his eyes to passively listen to him. "Not a problem."

"Okay, we'll see you then… around one o'clock." Wally ended the call and Ian dropped his cell phone onto his nightstand without opening his eyes.

"You don't suppose something's happened to our kids, do you? Like they've been beamed up to Mars, or something?"

Mary chuckled at his teasing. "Was that Wally on the phone?"

"It was." Ian opened his eyes to look at her. "Betty Jo's returning from somewhere out of town and she's stuck in traffic. So, they're running late this morning."

Mary grimaced at what he shared with her. "I hope he's not killing time with Elizabeth, while she's out of town."

Ian frowned at the idea. "I don't want to hear about it if he is."

Mary changed the subject. "What time is Elizabeth coming for the stuff she boxed up last weekend?"

Ian let out a tired sigh. "She was insistent that it had to be today, so I told her she had to be here and gone before noon or wait until a weekday to pick her stuff up. I do not want her slinking around our property when Wally's here."

Mary agreed with him on that one. "She knows we're going riding at noon?"

"She doesn't know it's with Wally and Betty Jo, but I did tell her we were going riding, and I wouldn't be here to help her load her car if she came after twelve. And I know she'll need me to help her load those boxes, because I moved them yesterday from where she had them stacked, and some of them are pretty heavy."

"She sure accumulated a lot of stuff over here." Mary rolled away from him to climb out of bed to face the day. "I suppose we should get up, feed the kids and get some barn chores and yard work done before they get here."

"Yep." Ian tossed the covers off of his body and went to the bathroom. "I'll have Ricky mow the lawn before we go riding." His phone rang as he closed the door behind him.

"Hey, Ian…" Mary called out to him. "Elizabeth is calling."

He finished relieving himself as his phone stopped ringing.

Mary tossed it across the bed to him as he stepped out of the bathroom. "She's probably got some last-minute change in plan for picking her stuff up."

"Yep." Ian scooped his phone up. "No doubt it's because she picked up some hot date last night and she's still in bed with him, trying to remember his name."

Mary scowled at his mean lamenting. "Stop it. That doesn't do anybody any good when you talk that way."

"Yeah, she just brings out the worst in me." Ian hit Elizabeth's number in his contact list and paced the floor, waiting for her to answer his call.

"Hi…" She breathlessly greeted him.

"You called?" Ian stopped pacing.

Elizabeth meekly addressed his curt greeting. "Good morning to you too, sweetie… welcome to your Sunday."

Ian exhaled with patience. "Good morning, Lizzy. What did you want? Just get to the point because I've got a busy day and I'm not interested in playing games with you."

"I'm only asking you to be cordial, Ian." She answered him in a soft voice. "But if that's more than you can handle this morning, fine. I'm calling to let you know that I can't come get my stuff today, after all."

Ian exhaled less patiently. "Lizzy, it's boxed and ready to go, and taking up space in the kids' house. And they can't be tripping over it all week while you get your act together. So, I need you to come get it. And if you can't do that without borrowing my truck, fine. You can borrow it."

"I fell and broke my wrist last night. I'm in a cast and may need surgery."

"You what?" Ian sat on the bed to listen more patiently to her. "How much did you have to drink before that happened?"

Elizabeth scoffed at his accusation. "Of course, you'd go there…"

"Well…" Ian bit his lip while he consciously tried to throttle back his impulse to say what he wanted to say… instead of what he knew he should say.

"I'm sorry. You're right. That was uncalled for." He *did* need to back off of her. Mary was right to scold him earlier. But it was going to be hard because she had gotten under his skin so badly lately, with her brush off of Jenny and her minimizing the kids' marital vows, plus her new demand for a custody rotation with Ellie. Ian couldn't help but get testy with her. In fact, he felt a lot these days like they were reverting more and more into their old caustic pattern of hateful marital communication.

And Ian didn't want that – as annoying as she could be. "Are you okay?"

She let out a tearful breath. "I'm fine. A little sore, mostly immobile, and pretty helpless right now. So obviously I can't..."

"Of course not." Ian winced at his own insensitivity. "I can bring you your stuff. No problem. Is there anything else you need?" He glanced at his nightstand clock. *Now* his morning was a little more pressing, and Wally's extended timeline more welcome. "Let me get showered and dressed and I'll grab a bite to eat, then I'll load the truck up and bring your things to you. If you need me to pick anything up from the store for you on the way, just text me a list."

"That'd be great. Thanks. And maybe when you get here…"

Ian shrugged an apology to Mary as she joined him on his side of the bed to wag a disapproving finger at him.

"You can check out Ellie's room…" Elizabeth was still talking in his ear. "And reconsider letting her stay with me a few days each week… once my arm heals?"

Ian returned his attention to Elizabeth. "That is not going to happen, Elizabeth. Ellie belongs to Jenny and Ricky, and you and I are only the back-up caregivers; we are not on the frontline for her; we are standby support only."

Elizabeth let it go. "What time will you be here?"

"I'll need about an hour, plus drive time."

"Okay. I'll text you the address."

Ian ended the call as he settled his eyes on Mary. "You're right, I'm wrong. I should have greeted her nicely before I fell into my disgruntled attack on her. So, let's move on without the scolding because I don't have time for it. I'm going to have to really kick it into gear to get to her place and back by one."

Mary let him off the hook, and Ian returned to the bathroom to hop in the shower while Mary made him some breakfast. Then she helped him load Elizabeth's boxes into his truck, and he took off to Elizabeth's house while Mary fed horses and prepared the kids for the day.

Ian stopped at the store on his way to her place, to buy her toilet paper, laundry soap, orange juice, tampons – of all things – and shower gel.

He knocked on her door when he got to her apartment, and Elizabeth answered it in a black satin pajama set that flattered her body and showed off a lot of skin. Ian stepped in without paying her looks any attention, and went straight to her kitchen to set the grocery bags on the counter.

"Can I get you a robe?"

She shrugged off his offer. "I don't know where it is, Ian. I haven't unpacked anything yet."

He nodded at that and looked away from her. "Looks like you had help moving in…" There were two empty Budweiser bottles on the counter, which was not her choice in beer. "Unless you're drinking Bud, now?'

She shook her head in answer. "I need to get a recycle bin for the kitchen."

A pizza box was also on the counter. Ian scooped the bottles up and peeked in the box; he saw it was empty, and scooped it up too. "I'll take 'em to the community bin for you. Do you know where it is?"

She shook her head at him. "I just picked my keys up Friday night. I didn't move in until yesterday."

"Okay. I'll find it." Ian glanced through the room. Her television was set up. "Where am I putting the boxes when I bring them up?"

"I'm not sure." She looked around and went to her coffee table to awkwardly reach with her unbroken wrist to pick up two soiled napkins. "I guess when you bring them in, I'll figure it out."

Ian took the dirty napkins from her and left with the recycling. There was a fenced pool that he passed on his way to the community bins. Ian dropped the bottles and pizza box into the recycle bin and tossed the two napkins into the garbage, then he returned to his truck to start packing in her boxes.

She met him at the door when he returned to her apartment. "How about stacking them along that wall by the TV?"

"Sure." Ian went to where she pointed and set the two boxes he was carrying down against the wall. "I noticed there's a pool…"

She nodded at his observation. "I know. That won't help me persuade you."

Ian shook his head in answer. "Nope. It won't."

He made a dozen trips before her boxes were all stacked along the wall in her apartment. Ian studied the four-box-high stack for a minute and turned to look at her. "How are you planning on unpacking these boxes when you can't unstack them by yourself?"

She shrugged off his question. "I'll have to get help, I guess."

Ian nodded feeling torn about leaving her so helpless. He glanced at his watch. It was twelve-thirty. He'd barely make it back in time if he left right now. "What can I do to help? I can't stay long but I can shift some of the boxes for you, if that will make it easier for you to go through them."

"Thanks." She nodded and looked around. "I guess… if you don't mind. Can you maybe move some of them to the spare bedroom… *Ellie's room…* so they're not stacked up? Then I can look in them without moving them."

"Sure." Ian picked up two boxes and turned down the hallway to move them to the back bedroom. As he went down the hall, he glanced into her bedroom. "I see you got your bed set up. Is there anything else you need help putting together?"

"Not right now, but thanks." She followed behind him and when he set the boxes down and turned to get more, she followed him back out to the front room.

"I sent my boss an email this morning to let him know what happened, and that I can't use a keyboard for at least six weeks, and that I probably need surgery to fix my wrist and that will probably mean additional recovery time, and he emailed me back to say he's reconfiguring his work force and will probably let me go. So that's a new problem I wasn't expecting."

Ian scooped up two more boxes. "They can't fire you for having a disability, Elizabeth. That would be a discriminatory adverse employment action that can be addressed in court."

She nodded at his legal advice. "I wondered about that. Can Mary represent me if I take them to court?"

Ian scoffed at the idea. "No, my wife is not going to represent my ex-wife in a lawsuit. That scenario would be fraught with conflict, at least on the surface, if nothing else. And it would certainly provide fodder for an ethics complaint that she is not going to risk. But if they *do* let you go and you want to sue them…" He turned to look at her before finishing what he was about to say. "Are there any other reasons for them letting you go?"

She held his inquiring stare. "Why do you always expect the worst of me?"

Ian shrugged without apology or denial.

Elizabeth answered his question. "I haven't done anything that would get me fired if that's what you mean."

Ian couldn't help but walk her through the blanks to see where the checkmarks might fall. "Absences? Late mornings? Missed deadlines… Sloppy work…" He knowingly settled his eyes on her. "A sassy mouth…"

Elizabeth pouted at his lack of faith in her. "No. Nothing. Why do you ask? You don't even trust me to be a good employee?"

Ian held her gaze with unmasked doubt. "I ask these questions because those are the facts that might allow your employer to legally terminate you notwithstanding, your apparent disability. As defense counsel, all I would have to do to win that lawsuit is prove that they let you go for those reasons, and not because of the disability. When there's dirt in a personnel file, that's what we use to build our case.

And that's what your employer's counsel will do to win the case against you."

She nodded at his explanation. "My annual reviews have all been okay."

Ian set the boxes down. "Good. So, let me know if you need a referral and I'll give you a few names."

"Will you pay the attorney fees for me?"

Ian smiled with patience. "No, I'm not going to pay your legal fees, Lizzy. I already did that when we got divorced. But your attorney can recover the fees for a wrongful termination lawsuit from the employer… if you win your case, or it settles out of court."

"Okay." Elizabeth nodded at his advice.

"How about helping me pay my rent if they let me go?"

Ian shook his head with patient frustration. "Why don't we wait and see what happens, Lizzy, before you start reaching into my wallet again."

She chuckled at that. "Thank you for your help this morning."

"Yep." Ian eyed the boxes on the spare bedroom floor then he turned to face her. "You need anything else before I go?" He needed to get moving.

She shook her head, then she remembered one more thing. "Can you move my bookcase? I realized before you came that it's blocking a socket."

Ian glanced at his watch. "Sure." He was definitely going to be late, now. "Where is it?"

She went into her bedroom and pointed at the wooden bookcase. It was visibly heavy and would be awkward to move. Ian stepped into the room. "Where do you want it?"

Elizabeth eyed the wall where it was already placed, then she moved her focus to the other side of the room as she contemplated her options. Ian followed her surveillance with his own curious eyes. Her bed was unmade and clearly slept in; two pillows on the bed had been used by seemingly two people; his eyes moved on. Lacy red bra and underpants tossed to the floor; her discarded shirt thrown off beside them.

Elizabeth broke his silent focus. "Maybe over there on the other side of my bed?"

"Sure." Ian dragged a box that was in the middle of the floor, closer to the closet out of the way, so he could push the bookcase that direction, then he used his foot to brush the discarded under clothing out of the way so it wouldn't get caught up in the motion of the sliding bookcase.

Elizabeth chuckled. "Sorry… I would've picked them up but I'm a little off balance and bending over to reach them…"

"I get it. So, don't worry about it." Ian shook his head at her apology. "I've certainly seen your discarded bra and underwear before."

She laughed at that as Ian stabilized the bookcase where she wanted it.

"Okay…" he turned to look at her. "Is that it?"

She moved her eyes through the room and nodded that it was. "Thanks."

"Sure." Ian pulled her into a friendly goodbye hug in an effort to show more sensitivity than he had shown her at the start of the morning. "Let us know if you need anything."

****

When he drove into his driveway, Wally was already parked there, and he and Betty Jo were chatting with Mary.

"Hey…" Ian joined their conversation. "Sorry for running late. Elizabeth is moving out of her rental unit and Jenny's flat and she apparently took a fall last night. I have my doubts about the seriousness of her injury, but nonetheless, I ran some things out to her since she couldn't come get them herself."

Wally shot him a hesitant frown. "Actually, it's a distal radius fracture extending into the radiocarpal joint. So, it *is* a pretty bad injury because she'll probably need to have a titanium plate and screws surgically implanted in her wrist to stabilize it."

Ian dropped his jaw in surprise. "How do you know about her injury?" His eyes traveled knowingly to Mary. "You were with her when it happened?" His eyes moved onto Betty Jo to read her expression before he returned his focus to Wally. "Or you've been talking to her?"

Wally shrugged with obvious nervousness. "She asked me to help her move…" He continued less apologetically. "It seemed like I was her last hope for some much needed man power…"

"Interesting…" Ian settled his eyes on Mary as Betty Jo came to Wally's defense.

"He was helping her when she fell…"

Wally nodded at his wife's explanation. "She tripped on the curb as I was leaving, and when I checked her wrist out, I could tell it was broken." His eyes settled on Ian with nervous energy as he added more information.

"So, I took her to the hospital and stayed at her apartment last night to help her out since she didn't have anyone else to look after her."

"Really…" Ian looked his direction as a mental inventory of evidence filled his mind: the beer bottles, the pizza box, the unmade bed and discarded under clothes.

Wally buried his nervousness with more explanation. "I figured she needed someone to help her with the boxes she couldn't move by herself… and the furniture." He looked between them with an obvious anxiety in his expression. "And I set up her bed and a bookcase for her."

"He didn't want her overdosing on pain meds," Betty Jo added what she knew about it, "…or under medicating herself. So, he also stayed to help her manage the medications…"

Ian moved his eyes from Betty Jo back to Wally. "Well, I'd be concerned about Lizzy taking *any* pain medication considering her drinking habits…"

Wally shook his head at him. "She didn't have any alcohol yesterday." He held a nervous smile on him. "But she *was* in quite a bit of pain so I crashed on the floor in her room to monitor her condition through the night and help her stay comfortable."

"Well, that was nice of you." Ian held a knowing stare on him without offering any contrary evidence for where Wally *actually* slept last night. Then he admitted with ambiguity that he might have contrary knowledge about that. "I was in her bedroom this morning." He kept his eyes on Wally to watch him for a reaction. "She had me move the bookcase you set up for her."

"She did?" Wally fidgeted with the keys in his pocket. "It's pretty messy in there…"

Ian nodded. "Yep, it is." And this particular mess told Ian exactly where Wally slept last night – and it wasn't on the floor. And regardless of her alleged discomfort and her presumptive need for pain medication, Ian was confident that he also knew what happened in that bed last night.

Wally held his focus with a more visible consternation. "The whole apartment is a mess… I'm not sure how she's going to clean it up while she's convalescing...."

Ian held his stare for a minute longer, then he dropped what he couldn't discuss in front of Betty Jo. "Yeah, not my problem anymore."

He moved his eyes onto Mary to change the subject. "She thinks her boss is going to terminate her because of the fracture."

Mary wrinkled her face in protest. "They can't do that *because* of the fracture."

"I know that." Ian nodded at what she said. "But if there's a lot of garbage in her personnel file and they're letting her go for those reasons, the timing might look suspicious but..."

"They'll get away with it." Mary nodded at the legal argument he was making on behalf of the defense. "And… seeing how it's Elizabeth we're talking about…"

Ian nodded.

Mary voiced what they were both thinking. "Not wanting to be mean, but knowing her like we do… I'd be hesitant to represent her as a plaintiff's counsel because undoubtedly, there's a good employer argument to be found in her personnel file, and that's going to make for a very small plaintiff settlement, if any."

Ian chuckled. "I'd take the employer's case though, if there wasn't the obvious conflict of interest, because just a hunch… it's going to be a very defendable case and somebody's going to make good money throwing around all that evidence."

Mary laughed at that as she left the topic behind. "Let's go for that ride now."

They moved into the barn and Mary and Ian helped Wally and Betty Jo groom and saddle their horses. Both of them had ridden before, so they felt pretty confident about riding on their own. When they were ready to mount their horses, Ian gestured for Mary to join him in the tack room.

"What's up?" Mary stepped in beside him as she looked over her shoulder to ensure they were alone.

Ian quickly shared what he was thinking. "The evidence in her bedroom told a different story than him sleeping on the floor… so, if you can make it happen, give me a chance to talk to him alone on our ride."

"Yep." Mary left the tack room and Ian followed her out.

They mounted their horses and Mary and Betty Jo took the lead and Ian and Wally followed behind. They rode two-by-two along the potholed road that dissected the property, then they turned into an unfenced field to ride through the back hills of Ian's ten acres. When the guys were a good distance behind the ladies, Ian cautiously broached what he wanted to discuss with Wally.

"Dude…"

Wally turned to look at him with a very sorry expression. "I know."

Ian nodded at his unspoken acknowledgement of guilt. "So, what are you going to do?"

Wally shook his head with visible indecisiveness. "I don't know."

Ian winced. "You can't fix your marriage?"

"I want to, but now… what if she won't have me?"

Ian nodded with firsthand knowledge from his own life. "That's a chance you're going to have to take. And one way or another, you need to find that out. Just lay it out there, man. Face the elephant in the room. Tell her what you did and tell her you're sorry. And then it's in her hands. If you're lucky, she'll forgive you. And if she does, you cannot *ever* do this to her again."

Wally nodded. "I also slept with her when you were in Monterey."

"I know." Ian shook his head with disappointment. "I already figured that out."

"I knew you did."

Ian nodded. "So, make a clean break of it, and move on."

Wally turned to look at him. "That was my intention after the Monterey mistake." He surrendered to Ian's suggestion with a meek excuse for his behavior. "But my departure isn't working like I planned."

Ian held his apologetic stare. "What's that supposed to mean? *You* went back for more, or *she* came back for more?"

Wally gave him a hopeless shrug. "She showed up for dinner at your house… and it wasn't by accident, and then she called and asked me to help her with the move. I figured I owed her the help, so I agreed to that. But I initially told her we couldn't see each other at all after that first weekend. I emphatically told her that we were over. But… she keeps showing up after I say goodbye."

Ian smirked with an intimate understanding of what Wally was up against. "Elizabeth does that. In fact, it's what she does best. She gets off on playing the field and straddling relationships."

Wally nodded. "I realize that now. You were right. I'm in over my head."

Ian turned an understanding grin on him. "I tried to warn you that the flames were going to lap up your house."

"I know. I should have listened to you."

Ian nodded. "So, break it off with her again. The sooner, the better. And make it a clean break this time. There's no going back to her."

Wally nodded at his instruction. "I thought I already did that. But I guess… well, you know how she is… I'm afraid she didn't get the message."

Ian blew off his quandary with impatient detachment. "Just get an exit strategy down, Wally, and stand firm. Otherwise, you're going to freefall into divorce court with Betty Jo, and when you're emotionally and financially ruined there, you'll crash and burn with Elizabeth who will not have your best interests at heart … and trust me on this… you do not want that ending to your thirty years of partnership with Betty Jo. And your kids aren't going to want that, and neither will your grandkids want it."

Wally nodded. "I don't want that, either. But get this…" He settled his eyes on Ian. "Elizabeth is pushing me to move in with her because she wants me to help her raise Ellie. She thinks we'll be good together, and she believes that I'll be able to persuade you to let her have custody of her."

Ian huffed with determination. "That's never going to happen, dude. Ellie is not my child, and she's not Elizabeth's child. And I'm not taking her away from Jenny. Ellie is her miracle shot at motherhood. And she gets to raise her, even if I have to help her. That is *her* baby, not Elizabeth's baby."

Wally nodded. "I get that. But Elizabeth says since you got to raise Jenny on your own, you owe it to Elizabeth to let her raise Ellie."

Ian shook his head with emphatic emotion. "Elizabeth has a knack for rewriting history, so how about, *no* to her version of events… because I didn't *get* to raise Jenny on my own. I was *forced* to raise Jenny on my own. And because of that, I have a *right* to help Jenny raise Ellie on her own. And I'm using that right to keep Ellie in Jenny's hands and out of Elizabeth's hands. And I will fight Elizabeth over this issue like I have never fought her before. She does not know what she's up against. And if she dares to turn this into a legal battle, I will drain her financially and beat her up emotionally. I will embarrass her, and kick her so hard to the proverbial curb she won't know what hit her. I will fight her on Jenny's behalf 'til there is no fight left in me. I will keep her from stealing that child away from my daughter, if it's the last thing I do. I will drain my own finances to do it."

Wally grinned with understanding and slight amusement at Ian's explicit determination. "Well, just so you know, I have no interest in moving in with Elizabeth, or in helping her in that fight with you, or in raising Ellie with her. I don't even know how that conversation got started."

Ian chuckled at that. "Oh, I get how that happened, Wally. One minute you're politely returning a non-committal hello to Elizabeth, and the next minute you're putting a ring on her finger and taking the trash to the curb while she's drying her ruby red nails at your kitchen table."

Wally laughed at that. "Yeah, that about sounds right." He turned a humble stare on Ian. "I just got sucked in. I'm sure you won't get this, but she made me feel cool, like I could snag a girl who liked someone like you."

Ian laughed at that. "Dude, I never wanted to be *that* guy."

"I know." Wally shot him a smile. "But you can't help being him. And for a minute… I felt like I could be *him* too."

Ian shook his head not fully understanding Wally's feelings of inadequacy, but completely understanding how he got sucked in by them. "Elizabeth knows how to hit buttons. And she was just hitting all of your buttons."

Wally nodded. "So, between the two of us, I'm sorry about all of this."

Ian shrugged it off. "As far as Elizabeth goes, I'm *so* over her. But please… don't do this to Betty Jo. Whatever you're going to do about all of this, *just do it.* Get it over with. Cut someone loose, and then stay the course. Do not waiver back and forth between the two of them, because that's just uncool, and it's only going to unravel everybody's lives. And people are going to be left permanently hurt in the aftermath. There's no way around that sad truth. Whatever you do about this, somebody is going to be hurt. You included."

"I know." Wally nodded with understanding. "The more I got sucked in by Elizabeth, the more I realized how much I love my wife. The conflict is that I'm falling in love with Elizabeth too. But I think I made it clear last night and also this morning, that we're through. That's it. I am not doing this anymore. *I can't.* And I think she got the message."

Ian smirked with doubt. "Listen… I don't care how clear you think you wrapped it up for her last night and again this morning, my best guess… that message never made it inside her ears. She does *not* give up."

Wally chuckled with him. "No, I'm pretty sure she got the message."

Ian shook his head with doubt. "Yeah, well I thought I made myself pretty damn clear too, about twenty some years ago… and yet… she's been living in my house for the last five or so years…" Ian settled his eyes on Wally with slight bemusement as he finished his thought. "And that's without me getting bedroom benefits that I know she'd let me indulge, if I had the slightest interest in pursuing those benefits."

Wally laughed at that. "She *has* made reference to your endearing charm…"

"Well, we haven't started that custody battle yet… so there's an opportunity for me there, to change her mind."

Wally chuckled at that.

"Okay…" Ian was done talking about it. "So, it's agreed… You won't go back to her no matter what tactic she uses to try and suck you back in. Right?"

Wally nodded. "I won't. That's a promise."

Ian trotted up to the ladies and teasingly hollered out to them as he approached them from behind. "Are you girls purposely leaving us behind so you can talk about us, or what?"

Mary shot him an intimate smile. "I was telling stories about lost virginity and your Chevy van…"

Ian chuckled at that as he glanced over at Wally. "More unflattering tales from my past... because that selfish act could have unraveled a *lot* of lives… me potentially getting her pregnant as I roll out of town like a guy without a conscious. *Boom. Daddy Powers*... what a nice guy…"

They all laughed at that.

Chapter Eleven

Elizabeth called Wally the next day between patients and other phone calls. “Hi…”

“How are you?” Wally kept it professional. “Is the pain getting more manageable?’

She let out a sad sigh. “The pain is tolerable, but guess what just happened? I got fired. I don’t know how I’m going to survive financially. I mean, I just moved into this apartment, and…now what? I get evicted before I even have my surgery?”

Wally winced at the idea. “I heard you might find yourself in need of a new job.”

She sighed with emotion. “So, what am I going to do now? I can’t even do job interviews if I’m wearing a cast. Who would hire me knowing I’m not capable of doing any work?”

Wally nodded at her predicament. The accountant at his clinic had surprisingly just given him notice this morning that she was moving out of state, and she was therefore quitting her job, and it was hard for him to hold that information back from Elizabeth, knowing she was an accountant, herself. But bringing her into his office was not a good idea. Ian would agree.

“Are you still there?” She broke his concentration in a vulnerable voice.

“Ah, yeah…” Wally resisted the urge to tell her about the position. “Why did they fire you?” He could hear Mary and Ian’s brief legal discussion in his head, and that made him pursue an inquiring train of thought. “Were there other reasons for them letting you go, besides the broken wrist?”

“No, I mean… nothing big. A few late mornings, some absences… but my work is good and usually on time, and they know it.”

Wally nodded. Everyone could fall prey to a few late mornings and the occasional unexpected absence. And there were probably some good reasons for the late work.

“Are you a CPA?” He couldn’t help himself.

"I am." Elizabeth followed his thinking. "Do you know of something? Someone who might need a CPA… despite me having a broken wrist?"

"I don't know how it would work…" Wally wanted to give himself an out, now that he had opened the door for her. He needed time to think before he committed himself to a bad idea. He did not want to encourage her romantically. He needed to stay focused on Betty Jo, and fix his marriage without distraction. He was absolutely never going to cheat again.

"I just found out my accountant is leaving in two weeks." He heard himself making the offer before he had really gotten there in his head. "So, maybe there's an opportunity for you here…" He just couldn't help himself. He wanted to help her out so she wouldn't get evicted.

"Oh, my God! That's wonderful."

"No. It's not, actually." Wally wished he hadn't told her because her enthusiasm about the offer made it clear that she was only thinking for herself. And he was smart enough to realize that her myopic vision could put him in peril. "My accountant is fantastic, and I hate that I'm losing her, and even more concerning to me, I don't want any personal doors opening for you and me. *I'm married, Elizabeth*, and I want it to stay that way. I do *not* want us seeing each other again on a personal level… I cannot do anymore Saturday nights with you."

"Of course not. I understand, and I respect that."

"Do you?" Wally doubted that she did. In his mind, he could hear Ian spurring him on to challenge her the way Ian would dismissively challenge her. Wally took Ian's silent advice to heart. "Because I'm not sure that message has made it into your inner ear canal. And I need you to fully hear what I'm saying. We. Are. Done."

"I definitely understood that, Wally. We're through."

"Okay." Wally could only hope that she understood what he was saying since he had mistakenly allowed her back into his life… *professionally.* Wally made a point of reminding himself of that. If Ian could have her living in his house and never get tempted by her, why couldn't Wally have her working in his office without getting tempted by her? At least here, he wouldn't have to see her firm butt cheeks sashaying around inside those sexy red panties.

The vision that was created in his mind made him offer an afterthought. "I'll need you to dress professionally, hands always to yourself, no flirting…"

"Understood…"

"Okay. We'll talk salary and benefits and start date once you've had your surgery and we have a better idea on how long your recovery will take."

"Thank you. Thank you so much! I promise you won't regret it."

Wally would just have to wait and see about that. "Let me know if you need rent money between now and then… or anything else."

"Thank you!"

Wally ended the call and immediately called Ian. "I just fucked up. The flames are going to burn down my house and my whole family is going to disintegrate beside me. Just like you said."

"Dude… what's wrong?"

Wally let out an emotional breath. He was afraid he might actually start crying.

Ian seemed to sense that. "Wait a minute… let me close my office door."

Wally waited for him to tell him to continue, and when he did, he shared what he just did. "I offered Elizabeth an accountant position at my clinic. I didn't mean to, but…"

"She sucked you in."

"She did."

"Shit."

Wally nodded at his assessment. "Yep. That accurately sums it up. I'm so in over my head. I don't know how to fix it. I haven't said anything to Betty Jo yet about what I did with Elizabeth, because I needed to wait for the right moment. But now I'm scared to even bring it up because how do I tell her that I made the mistake of a lifetime sleeping with Elizabeth, not once, but twice, and I promise I'll never do that again, but gee, not to worry, honey, I just offered her a job at my clinic."

Ian chuckled at that. "Yeah, dude. That conversation is not going to go well for you."

"No, it isn't, Ian." Wally didn't share his humor. "It's going to blow up my whole fucking world."

"Yep." Ian agreed with him on that one. "It's going to be explosive, for sure."

"So, what would you do? With all of your worldly, detached, womanizing, dismissive experience, you must have some advice you can give me? How would *you* fix this?"

Ian chuckled at Wally's description of him. "Let me first argue against your portrayal of me, Wally." He did so in a thoughtful voice. "Because I'll admit that I've had a lot of women in my past, many of whom I would not recognize if they passed me on the street. And I admit that I sometimes cut these women loose without enough sensitivity or thoughtful process, but I've never cheated on anyone or been with anyone under false pretenses. Every woman I've been with knew what she was getting with me at the front end. So, I disagree that I was ever a womanizer. And personally, I avoid this kind of emotional conflict like it's the plague. But I guess if I somehow found myself in this unpleasant situation, I'd hit my kill switch immediately and unambiguously shut Elizabeth down. Just get rid of her. Lay it out there and unequivocally walk away from her before she can say anything in response that draws you back in. You do not need her in your life. Cut her loose over the phone if that's easier for you than doing it face to face. Call her back right now. Tell her you changed your mind, and stand firm in your commitment to end it with her. Just be done with her for once and for all, man, before she ruins your whole life."

Wally nodded at his advice. "Just like you got rid of her, right? Because it's *that easy* to be mean to her... which is why she's obviously still deeply embedded in your daily life. Right?"

Ian didn't respond right away. Then he offered an excuse for himself. "She's my daughter's mother and Ellie's grandmother. So, it's a little more complicated for me."

Wally burst into tears.

"Oh, man… please don't do that." Ian quickly offered a distraction in an attempt to give Wally some cover. "Remember that English teacher we had in 9th grade? The one who was nine months pregnant when her husband was killed in that small plane crash?"

Wally pulled himself together, thankful for Ian's well executed pivot. "Yes."

Ian kept him focused. "Remember how she said at his funeral, don't wait for the right moment to say what you need to say to loved ones because the right moment may never come… Remember how she told us about her and her husband having an argument that morning, and she was going to say she was sorry to him, but she wanted him to say it first… so neither of them said it before he left that day… and then he died."

Wally nodded through the phone. "I think I only wanted Elizabeth because every girl I've ever fallen in love with has fallen for you… or someone else. And you have no idea how it feels to be the guy who always loses the girl… but all of a sudden, *I was the guy who was getting the girl*. For a minute, *I was you*. It was stupid that I felt that way, and dumber still that it mattered to me. But it did. And now I'm going to lose my wife, *the love of my life… the girl I really want to hold onto… the one that really matters*, because of some stupid ego trip that isn't even long lasting, or worth the personal cost in the end."

Ian exhaled with patience.

"I know…" Wally voiced what Ian had to be thinking. "You tried to warn me…"

Ian refrained from going there. "You don't know that you're going to lose her, Wally. But you need to have that conversation. And you need to break it off with Elizabeth. Don't worry about what happens to her on the other side of the break-up speech, because the one thing I can guarantee you is that Elizabeth will land on her feet and in no time at all, she'll be sucking in some new guy."

Wally figured that was true, but he still didn't know how he could ever be so mean to her. He did not have Ian's experience being an insensitive, jilting lover. He had never really broken up with anyone before. And he didn't know how to do that. "I don't have a heart of stone like you, Ian, and I can't dump Elizabeth the way you dumped her. I don't want to hurt her like that. I'm just not like you. I can't go through life discarding people as if they don't matter to me."

Ian huffed through the phone at him. "I didn't dump Elizabeth, Wally. She dumped me long before I opened the door for her to walk out of my house. And it hurt like hell when she left me."

Wally gasped with surprise. "Elizabeth left you? I thought it was the other way around. I didn't think someone like you ever got dumped."

"Are you kidding me?" Ian set him straight. "I've been dumped at least as often as I've dumped someone. My fault for not being emotionally available for the women I was dating, but that never made the break ups less painful. Even though I could rationalize that I deserved to be dumped, and regardless of me having mastered the art of a detached goodbye. It still always felt like a hard kick in the gut."

Wally grinned with appreciation for what Ian was giving up. It wasn't anything he ever expected Ian to share with him.

Ian continued with his vulnerable purging. "When Elizabeth left me, it was like I'd been sucker punched. I felt lonely after she was gone and guilty for everything that I'd ever done wrong that led to our split, and I was mad at myself for everything I did right but way too late in the game to make a difference. And I felt like a failure in my dad's eyes because he was a really good guy who never would've let his own marriage end in divorce – and that made me feel shame that I could not shake for years. And as I watched Lizzy walk out of my house for the last time, I felt like a blindsided fool for not realizing sooner that our marriage was beyond saving."

Wally silently thanked him for shedding his outer layer. He never would have thought before today that Ian was capable of feeling so deeply, or sharing so honestly. "I guess I feel a lot of those same things today, Ian." He also felt a lot calmer and less alone with his troubles hearing Ian's take on things, even though his own problem remained the same. "So, what do I do now?"

Ian offered the same advice he'd been offering. "You suck it up and find the strength to dump Elizabeth once and for all, then you go home to Betty Jo and you apologize for doing her wrong, and you talk to her man to man like you've been talking to me. Don't give her anything less than that. Lay it all out there for her. And if you're lucky, she'll take you back. And if you're not lucky, do not let yourself go back to Elizabeth. You move on. And understand that Elizabeth will be fine without you. If there's one thing that I know about Lizzy, it's that she doesn't stay down for long. Because this is what Elizabeth does best. She's like a vulture who flies in for the kill, then she innocently opens her wings and catches the next wind gust out of there before she ever gets damaged by her own destructive actions."

Wally laughed at that. "Sound advice. I'll see what I can do.

Chapter Twelve

Ian called Elizabeth after he ended his call with Wally.

"Hi, sweetie…" Elizabeth cooed through the phone at him. "Thanks for your help Sunday."

"I heard you got a new job offer." Ian tried to maintain a calm voice as he bypassed a friendly greeting to go straight to the point of his call. "What happened to your old job? Your boss fired you?"

"He did."

Ian nodded to himself. "And now you're going to conveniently be working for Wally." His tone became uncontrollably more hostile as he matter-of-factly spit that out at her.

Elizabeth went audibly on guard. "Stay out of it, Ian. It's not your business."

"He's my friend, Lizzy, so I'm making it my business." Ian lost his ability to maintain a calm demeanor. "Do you care at all that he's married? Are you at all concerned about his wife, who you met at my house, and conversed with at my dinner table, and manipulated into believing you were a friend? Because Wally cares about her and he cares about his marriage. *He loves his wife, Lizzy,* and he does *not* want to be involved with you on a personal level. *He does not want that relationship.* He wants to stay married!"

"Wally's a big boy, Ian…" Elizabeth noticeably braced herself against Ian's tirade. "And he can fend for himself. He does not need you interfering on his behalf."

"Well, I think he *does* need my interference, Lizzy, because Wally has never harmed a flea in his life, and he can't figure out for himself how to end this sordid affair without hurting you. So that's a roadblock that I'm willing to knock down, to save him that heartache..."

"Not something that you would ever be able to relate to… *a heartache…*"

"Huh!" Ian ignored her charge as he fell into an emotional rebuttal against her. "For once in your life, why don't you think about someone other than yourself and do the right thing here? Help

Wally out by letting him off the hook before he completely destroys himself with his naïve effort not to hurt you. There is nothing to be gained by you ruining his life, Lizzy, unless your sole purpose in being with him is to end his marriage for your own personal gratification."

Which was exactly what Ian suspected. "That's precisely what's happening here, right? You're getting off on the unsavory idea that Wally's entire life is about to evaporate for no better reason than you need a self-serving ego boost. Whoop, whoop for the nefarious Elizabeth Chambers!"

"And now I'm being doused in holy water by *Saint Ian…*" Elizabeth was finally able to interrupt him with a self-righteous defense that included an underlying attack on him. "*Mr. Sensitivity…* yay for me. The self-proclaimed easy lover with his heart of stone who has never cared about the people he was hurting… has somehow convinced himself that he's earned the right to take the high ground over me."

Ian scoffed at her accusation without offering an apology to her. "I'm not perfect, Lizzie, but at least I've never broken up any marriages. So, how many, marriages besides our marriage have you decimated? Because breaking up even one marriage is one too many, Lizzy. You do not need to improve your track record in that regard. So, please… just let him go. Let Wally be the one who got away…"

"And I thought you were calling to be nice..."

Ian cussed under his breath. "Tell him you changed your mind and you can't take the job. Damn it, I'll help you make ends meet while you find something else. *Please.* Just do this one thing for him. Don't destroy Wally's life like you've destroyed other lives… don't do that to his wife and kids. *I'm begging you…*"

Elizabeth ended the call without warning.

"Shit." Ian moved his focus onto his desktop in silent fury to visually absorb the work that he was supposed to be doing. There was no way in hell that he could concentrate on any of it now. Not when he felt this mad inside. "Damn it…"

He left his chair and paced across the floor, then he returned to his desk and slammed his laptop shut and dropped it into his briefcase. He could barely think right now, he was so mad. He grabbed two files from a stack on his desk and jammed them in beside the laptop.

His suit jacket was hanging on the back of his office door, so he grabbed that off the hangar and pulled it on. He might as well go home and try and burn some energy doing farm chores for a while. Then maybe, after his kids were in bed, he'd be able to concentrate in the quiet of his home office, and get some of his legal work done.

He grabbed the power cord for his laptop and jammed it inside his bag before leaving his office and briefly stopping by his associate's office to tell her that he was leaving. Then he left his firm and drove to Mary's office. He needed to talk to her before he literally exploded.

When he got to her office, he greeted her receptionist with a resolute smile. "Is she in?"

"She is. Was she expecting you?"

"Nope." Ian walked on by without offering an explanation or confirming Mary's ability to meet with him.

"Hey…" He tapped on her partially opened office door and stepped inside. "You got a minute?"

"For you? Any time." Mary's face lit up with a smile. "What brings you here?"

Ian closed the door behind him. "Wally offered Elizabeth an accountant position at his clinic. And of course, she accepted it."

"That is not good." Mary lost the smile on her face.

"No, it isn't good." Ian dropped himself into a chair opposite her desk. He literally felt like he might violently implode before nightfall. "I called her when I found out about it, and as expected, that conversation went well…"

Mary chuckled at his sarcasm. "I can imagine."

"I'm just sick about this." Ian exhaled with emotion. "And I don't know how to fix it. And it's tearing me up inside."

Mary left her chair to come sit beside him. "It's not your problem to fix. It's Wally's problem."

Ian nodded his head, then he dropped his face into his hands and exhaled with emotion. "I never should have agreed to let him interview the kids. That's how this whole ugly thing got started." He did not want to cry but he felt like he might. He desperately wanted to stop what was happening. He did not want Betty Jo getting hurt the same way he had been hurt by Elizabeth years ago. "I feel like this is my fault."

Mary rubbed her palm across his back with unspoken understanding. "I'm assuming you've talked to Wally?"

Ian nodded. He was feeling too choked up to speak, but he made the effort anyway. "He's conflicted."

Mary nodded. "I wonder if Betty Jo is as blind to what's going on as she seems?"

Ian shrugged his shoulders. "If I could be fooled by Elizabeth… Betty Jo, blessed with maybe half of my acuity, can surely be fooled by the two of them."

Mary nodded at that. "True." Her phone rang and she left her chair to pick it up from her desktop. "Hello?"

It was Jenny. "Daddy's not answering his phone and Karen went to pick Ellie and Philip up from school. She took Skylar with her. And I cut my hand. There's blood everywhere."

"Oh no!" Mary looked to see if Ian was listening to what Jenny was saying.

"Let me talk to her." He reached for her phone and Mary handed it to him.

"What happened?"

"I cut myself, daddy."

Ian left his chair so he could head home, except he was on Mary's phone – so he couldn't. "Is Ricky with you?"

"He said I'm going to bleed to death."

Ian winced at what she told him. "Well, that wasn't a good thing to say to you." He exhaled with frustration. "I'm sure it's not that bad, Jenny. It probably looks worse than it is. How did you cut it?"

"I opened a can of peaches. And my hand got cut on the lid."

"Okay." Ian couldn't imagine that it was as bad as she thought. "How big is the cut?"

"I don't know."

"Look at the finger next to your thumb and tell me if the cut is as long as your finger, or only half as long, or maybe just as long as the space between two knuckles."

"I think it's two knuckles, daddy."

"Okay." Ian wanted to get to his truck so he could go home, but he had to end the call first. "Hold your hand up over your head and put pressure on the cut to stop the bleeding. I'll be there in a few minutes. Put Ricky on the phone."

"Okay, daddy."

Ian listened as she told Ricky to come to the phone.

"There's a lot of blood, Ian." He spoke into the phone in an excited voice.

Ian nodded with his thoughts. "I need to hang up this phone. It's Mary's phone. But I'll call you right back on my phone. Okay?"

"Okay, Ian."

"Have her sit down."

"Okay."

Ian ended the call and handed the phone to Mary. "I'll call you when I get there."

He left her office and fled to his truck, trying to call Jenny repeatedly as he jogged that way, but her phone was continually busy, so Ian moved onto Ricky's phone instead, even though Ricky often forgot to charge it.

"You answered it…" Ian silently thanked him with relief. "Who is Jenny talking to?"

"Her mom."

"Okay." Ian started his truck. "How is she?"

"She's sitting down like you said."

"How's the cut look?"

"It's bleeding."

"Okay, I'm on my way. Keep pressure on it, and keep it over her head."

"Okay, Ian. I'll take good care of my wife."

****

When Ian arrived at the house, he parked his truck and dashed into Jenny's place. "Hey, I'm here…"

She was sitting on the couch, holding her hand above her head like he had instructed, and Ricky was holding a bloody paper towel over the cut.

"Let me see it…" Ian took her hand and moved the towel away. "Well, that doesn't look too bad." He exhaled with relief and wiped the blood away. It was little more than a deep paper cut, maybe a half inch long at most, but not deep enough to need stitches. "There sure was a lot of blood, huh?"

Jenny nodded her head. "A lot, daddy. I was bleeding to death."

Ian shot her a reassuring grin. "I'm sure it felt like that, but it's actually not that bad. Let's clean it up, put some antiseptic ointment on it, and cover it with a band-aid and see how it looks tomorrow. Okay? I think it will be okay if we do that."

Jenny nodded at his instruction. "I called mom, but she said to call you."

Ian frowned at what she shared with him. *Even now*, after five years of living here, Elizabeth was still never *really* available for Jenny. "Well, your mom's not up to coming to see you anyway, right now."

Jenny nodded at what he told her. "I know. She broke her wrist."

"Yep. She did."

"I told her you were coming and she said good."

****

The following day Mary called Ian as he was stepping into a conference room for a meeting.

"What's up?" One of his more important clients, and three of his client's employees were sitting around the huge mahogany table in the room, expectantly waiting for Ian to join them for a complicated trial prep, and he did not have time for a conversation with Mary.

"You're going to go completely batshit crazy when I tell you this." She filled his ear anyway, without asking if he had a minute to talk like she usually did. "But you're going to have to hold it together and resist the urge to blow up, and promise me you'll take a few cool-down breaths before you say or do anything."

"I can't talk right now, Mary." Ian glanced into the conference room and stepped farther away from the open door so he could end the call more privately. "Can I call you back later? I was just stepping into a…"

"No, you can't call me back." Mary's voice became more excitable. "It's an emergency."

"What's wrong?" Ian paid her more attention. "Is someone hurt, or is it worse than that?"

Mary exhaled excitedly. "Nobody is hurt. But we have a big problem. Social Services is at our house, and an investigator wants to talk to Jenny, Ricky and Ellie. I guess she actually wants to talk to all of us. Karen called me when the investigator arrived, and I just got here myself. We let her into the living room, but we haven't let her talk to anyone yet…"

"I'll be right there." Ian ended the call as he popped his head into his meeting and begged out of it with a quick explanation that he had a family emergency and that his associate would have to take the meeting for him. Then he fled to his truck without stopping in his office for his briefcase or laptop.

****

When he arrived at his home, he calmly walked inside and politely greeted the lady he found sitting in his living room superficially talking to Mary.

"Hi…" He stepped their direction and introduced himself. "Attorney Powers…"

The lady stood to shake his hand. "Jennifer's father, not her attorney, right?" She corrected him with a nervous laugh.

Ian let go of her hand. "Actually, I'm both, right now. Her father and her attorney. I'm also, her conservator. Do you need to see my letters of authority? I have fairly broad powers over her person and also her estate."

The lady nodded. "I may need to see those. Your wife was just telling me about that."

Ian glanced at Mary and returned an authoritative stare to the lady. "That would be attorney Edwards to you. Also, for this instance, Jennifer's attorney."

Mary nodded. "We're actually Ricky and Ellie's attorneys as well." She added that to his greeting.

"Correct." Ian nodded at her addition.

The lady smiled between them. "I get your point."

"Perfect." Ian gave her a more relaxed smile. "So, what brings you into my home? Is there a problem?"

The lady shot him a timid smile. "As you probably are aware, I'm with the Department of Social Services, the Children and Family Services Division, and we oversee various statewide programs for at-risk children. Our efforts are aimed at safeguarding, preserving, and strengthening families. Part of our service involves intervening in cases of child abuse and neglect. And what brings me to your house is a report that there might be some child endangerment here. So, obviously, I need to investigate that. So, I'd like to talk to…"

"I'm sorry…" Ian interrupted her. "I didn't get your name."

"Geraldine Smith."

He nodded with authority. "And I'm assuming you have official identification you can show me?" Ian shot her an intimidating smile.

"Of course." She fumbled with her ID to quickly put it into his hands.

Ian nodded as he looked at it, and handed it back to her. "You were saying…"

Philip barged into the room at that exact moment, and stole all of their attention as he yelled at Ian. "Ellie stole my F*ing dinosaurs, daddy and I want them back right now!"

"She stole your, what?" Ian turned to look at him with a start.

"My dinosaurs…"

"No, what did you say before that?" It was hard for Ian to believe that Philip would choose this precise moment, in front of a social worker to swear for the first time.

"F*ing?" Philip timidly answered him.

"That's the word I'm talking about!" Ian scowled with parental disapproval. "It is not okay to say that word, Philip. That is not something we say."

"But mommy says that word!" Philip turned to look at her as he offered a defense for himself. "And she said it's not a bad word if you don't say the whole word."

Mary bit her tongue as Ian glanced between her and their son before saying anything in response. "So, mommy also stands corrected."

Mary nodded at his scolding. "My mistake. I'm sorry."

Ian shook his head at her with ill-timed amusement.

"Philip…" He returned his attention to his son when his humor was less visible. "If you hear mommy say that word again, you get to pick a punishment for her. Okay? So, let's figure out right now what that punishment will be." He glanced her direction. "Make it a good one so she doesn't say that word again."

"Yikes…" Mary chuckled.

Philip giggled at her mock concern that he mistook for real apprehension. "If you say that word again, mommy, you will have to eat *all* my vegetables for a whole week! Especially all the carrots!" He laughed hysterically at the punishment he was dolling out to her.

Ian fought a grin as he settled his eyes on Mary, then he managed to hold a disapproving frown on Philip. "And if *you* say that word again, I'm taking your dinosaurs away for the whole week."

"No, daddy." Philip didn't laugh at that. "Not my dinosaurs!"

Ian gave him a dismissive shrug. "It's in your hands what happens to them. I'm not going to take 'em if you don't say that word again. But if you *do* say that again… they're mine…"

"Okay… daddy, I won't say that again."

"I'm sorry…" Karen came in behind him. "We're having a little squabble over toys this afternoon. But I've got this under control. Sorry for the interruption." She took him by the hand to lead him out of the room.

Ian returned his attention to the social worker. "Do you have kids?"

"I do." She shot him a smile. "And I know what you're thinking. They sure do say the darndest things at all the worst moments, don't they?"

Ian nodded at her observation. "Exactly what I was going to point out." He shot her a relaxed smile. "So, who did you say made this report that you were mentioning?" He knew without confirmation that it had to be Elizabeth.

"It was anonymous."

"Of course, it was." Ian nodded at that. "Well, I'm sure we can ultimately discover who it was… should there be any adverse action taken by your department."

She smiled less confidently. "So, the concern that was brought to our attention was that there are minor children living in the care of parents in this household who are mentally challenged, and perhaps lacking sufficient parenting skills which might ultimately put the children in danger. So, that's what I need to determine. If there are children in this house who might need the support of social services."

Ian shook his head at her. "As you can see, contrary to your anonymous report, the children in this home are being well cared for by our nanny, and also by my wife and me. And clearly neither of us are mentally challenged. And despite my son's apparent new favorite word and his badly timed use of said word, neither my wife nor I lack parenting skills. And if your anonymous caller offered details that are more substantive than an ambiguous accusation of child endangerment, I'd like to hear them."

"The concern is for Cinderella Powers."

Ian knowingly nodded. "Her grandmother, my ex-wife, wants grandparenting time and she's threatening to remove Ellie from her parents to accomplish that. So, I'm sure your anonymous report is intended to help my ex- win that custody battle. You don't suppose that's what this is about, do you? Because I have no doubt that your anonymous caller is Elizabeth Chambers. Am I right?"

"I can't..."

"Divulge that information. I got it." Ian nodded. "What do you need from us to wrap this false allegation up?"

She smiled at his attempt to take charge. "I just need to interview her parents, maybe talk to you and your wife a bit, and also the child in question – in fact, I'd like to talk to all of the children in the home, and also the nanny."

"Sure." Ian nodded his compliance. "Why don't I give you some background, first? And then I'll round up whatever witnesses you need to interview." He began an opening argument without waiting for her to agree to his suggestion.

"Ellie's parents have been married for about seven years, and they reside together as an intact family with their child, in their own separate quarters of this house, but for all purposes, in the same home as my wife and me. There is a nanny here every day when my wife and I are at work, and she cares for all three children; our two children, plus Ellie. And in the evenings and on weekends this household operates largely as a single household with four adults, and three children. We do dinner together, after school activities, evening play, and usually bedtime. We also spend weekends together when Ellie has farm chores and activities that she enjoys doing with our two kids. And I am confident that you'll find that there is an extensive support system in place for her parents' child rearing duties. I don't know how anyone could find that lacking here. All three of these kids are smothered in love and parental supervision."

"Well, that certainly doesn't sound like there's a problem..."

"Because there isn't a problem." Ian shot her a persuasive smile. "Would you like to meet Ellie?"

"That'd be great."

He left the front room to find the kids in the family room with Karen. "Ellie, can you come here, please?"

"Okay, poppee..." She left time out, where she was sucking on her thumb."

"Please stop doing that, Ellie... princesses don't suck their thumbs."

"Gammy says I can suck it if I want to."

Ian took her hand in his without acknowledging what she said about Elizabeth. "And now you're touching me with your wet thumb! That's gross!" He teasingly laughed at her and she giggled back.

"But it's my princess thumb, poppee, so you like it!"

He squeezed her little hand in his. "I want you to meet somebody. And I want you to be very polite, okay? It's very important to me. No tantrums."

"Okay, poppee."

They returned to the living room and Ian introduced her. "This is Ms. Smith, Ellie…"

"Hello, Ms. Smith." She held her hand out to her and Ian chuckled with a teasing caution.

"That thumb is pretty wet…"

Ms. Smith laughed at that. "Are you a thumb sucker?"

Ellie nodded her head. "Only when I'm in time out. Because Skylar wasn't playing nice with me. And I hit her so Karen made me go to time out. But Skylar had to go to time out too, for being mean. But she doesn't suck her thumb. Only me do that."

Ms. Smith frowned at her story. "Well, sitting in time out doesn't sound very fun."

"It's not." Ellie climbed into her lap. "But mommy says we have to sit in time out when we need to calm down. And that's why I suck my thumb. So, I can calm down and be a good girl again."

Ms. Smith nodded at her story. "Why don't you tell me about your mommy?"

Ian went to the couch to sit beside Mary.

"Mommy's bigger than me. She's a grown up. But not like poppee and memaw." Ellie happily started talking about her. "She's funny because we laugh at things. And she's my best friend. We color. And we play games. But she's tired of *Candyland*. So, we didn't play that laster-day. And we watch Disney movies together. She likes *Cinderella*. That's why she named me Cinderella. I like *Little Mermaid*. That's my favorite. Daddy likes *Lion King* and *Aladdin*. And we have sleepovers when daddy's playing his game. Mommy and me. We read stories in bed. And sometimes we make up the words when mommy doesn't know how to read them."

"Well, that sounds fun." Ms. Smith glanced at Ian and Mary.

Ellie continued. "And daddy plays video games with me. We are champions."

Ian reached for Mary's hand and softly caressed it in his as he tried to sit through the interview with detached patience.

Ms. Smith stayed focused on Ellie. "Well, good for you. It's fun to be a champion."

"Because we are winners. All the time. Me and daddy."

Ms. Smith nodded her head. "Are you ever home alone with just your mommy and daddy?"

"Oh no…" Ellie shook her head with dramatic emotion. "Only poppee and memaw are by myself with me. And nanny Karen."

Ms. Smith chuckled at her mixed-up sentence. "I think what you were trying to say just now, is that when you're with your mommy and daddy, someone else is always here? Is that what you meant? You're only alone with your poppee and memaw and nanny?"

Ellie nodded her head. "'Cause mommies and daddies don't take care of little girls by themselves. That's silly. Poppee and memaw have to help them. Because that's what poppees and memaws do. They help parents take care of their little girls so they don't get hurt. And sometimes poppee tells daddy that he has to help me clean up my toys. Because that's what poppees do. They make daddies help their little girls."

Ms. Smith smiled at Ian and Mary. "I think you're a lucky girl to have a poppee and menaw who help you and your mommy and daddy like that."

Ellie giggled. "That's because I'm a real princess like mommy. We are two princess girls. And poppee is our prince. That's what mommy says. Poppee is our super hero."

Ms. Smith wrapped it up with Ellie and asked to chat with Skylar and Philip, so Ian left to fetch them. When he returned with both of them, he introduced them to Ms. Smith.

"You're the little boy who likes dinosaurs…"

Philip giggled. "And daddy can't take them away from me unless I say a bad word. But I'm not going to say that word. No way."

She briefly chatted with both of them, then Ian went to fetch Jenny and Ricky so she could meet with both of them.

He quickly tried to prep them as he walked them back to the living room. "This is just like your deposition, Ricky, when you had your car crash." Ian offered some quick examples. "Think about what you guys are saying before you speak and ask her to repeat any question that confuses you, or any question that you might need to think about before answering. And if you don't understand what she's asking, just say so. There's nothing wrong with that. Okay?"

"Okay, daddy." Jenny saluted him with a smile.

"Here they are…" Ian waved them into the room in front of him. "Jenny, Ricky… this is Ms. Smith. She wants to ask you a few questions about Ellie… and about being her mom and dad."

"Hi…" Jenny confidently walked up to her. "I'm Jennifer. I'm a mother. I have a Cinderella daughter. She's my best friend. She listens to me when I tell her what to do. And we eat ice cream and play and have fun together. And we watch Disney movies."

Ms. Smith stood to greet her. "And this must be your handsome husband?"

"He's my honey-bear." Jenny giggled. "But sometimes I call him doo-doo head because he calls me stinky butt."

Ms. Smith chuckled at that. "I call my husband peek-a-boo because every so often, he jumps out from behind a corner and scares me."

Jenny and Ricky laughed at that before Ricky took the idea on for himself. "I am going to scare you tonight when you are brushing your teeth. I will peek-a-boo you from the hallway."

Jenny laughed off his threat. "Don't do that to me, honey-bear. I'm your beautiful wife!"

He laughed and kissed her mouth. "But that would be funny."

Ian hovered across the room watching them talk. He did not want to leave them alone with her, but he expected that any minute now, she would ask him to leave. She was tolerant enough about Mary and him staying in the room when she was talking to the little kids, but he suspected she would want to interview the big kids alone. And he knew he would have to leave if she asked him to go, because refusing to do so would only cast doubt over all of them even though they had nothing to hide. But letting the kids talk freely without being there to provide an explanation for an awkward comment that might need to be articulated better, was unnerving.

"Would you mind if I chatted with them alone?" Ms. Smith went exactly where Ian feared.

"Of course not." Mary stood from the couch to join Ian across the room.

"Not at all…" He reached for Mary's hand as she came his way and they stepped down the hall to walk away from them.

When they were alone in their bedroom, away from the living room, Ian spoke his mind. "They're going to say the wrong thing and I won't be there to fix it. And if that somehow allows Elizabeth to steal Jenny's daughter away from her…" Ian held his eyes on Mary. "I am literally going to lose it. You know that, right?"

Mary wrapped an arm around him. "They're going to be fine because there is nothing at all that they might say that could give social services a reason to take Ellie away from them."

Ian nodded with doubt. "My gut is wound tight."

****

When Ms. Smith was finally finished talking to Ricky and Jenny, she chatted for a bit with Mary and Ian, first about Jenny's childhood history, her brain injury, and her adult capacity. Then they talked about Elizabeth, her recent departure from the house, her previous involvement at the house, and their new routine without her. She also asked about Ricky and his capacity.

After talking to them, Ms. Smith met with Karen, who had patiently been keeping the little kids busy. And finally, when she was through talking to Karen, she was ready to leave. She told Ian that when the case was closed, he would receive a closing letter, but before that happened, Ms. Smith would probably have to talk to some school officials and maybe a few other witnesses.

Ian thanked her for her efforts as he walked her to her car, and politely said goodbye to her; then he watched her drive off of his property and turn onto the main road. When she had driven completely out of sight, he returned to the house and grabbed his phone out of a pocket to madly call Elizabeth.

"Hi sweetie…" She purred into his ear as though nothing had been wrong between them. "Sorry for hanging up on you the other day. That was rude of me."

Ian bypassed her friendly greeting and her insincere apology to go straight to the point of his call. "You reported us to CPS?" It was a good thing she wasn't standing before him, because he might seriously feel the need to strangle her.

"What are you talking about?" Her feigned innocence was transparent to Ian.

"Don't pretend that you had nothing to do with CPS showing up at my house today to investigate child endangerment allegations!" He blasted her with rage he could barely contain. "Because we both know that the only person in the world who would make that kind of anonymous report on my family is you."

"I honestly have no idea what you're talking about." Elizabeth denied his accusation with calm determination.

Ian cussed under his breath. "Is that how you're planning on getting custody of Ellie? By making false charges against your own daughter so CPS will remove her from Jenny's care?"

"I don't know why CPS was at your house Ian." Elizabeth rebuffed his tirade with emphatic resolve. "But regardless of who sent them there, I am not going to leave Ellie in an unsafe environment. And Jenny's cut hand and her hysterics on the phone with me, coupled with her inability to know what to do about a simple injury offers a good example for why she should not be raising my grandchild."

"Shit." Ian cussed with more emotion. "And maybe you walking out on your four-year-old daughter, with never a look over your shoulder to see how she was doing in my unstable hands is a good example of why *you* shouldn't be raising *my* grandchild! How do you think that's going to play out for you in front of Social Services when they start investigating *your* parenting skills?"

"Don't threaten me with old news, Ian. That was more than twenty years ago. And I've raised four successful boys since then. And I am certainly capable today of raising my granddaughter successfully. So, don't try and intimidate me with your high and mighty, contrary argument."

"Fuck you." Ian couldn't help himself. "I thought you had slipped about as low as you could go when you abandoned your child for your illicit lover, but this hits such a new low, *even for you Lizzy*, that I am completely dumbfounded by your actions. I am stupefied by how low you are willing to go. And I'm warning you right now, if this is an example of how you intend to win custody of Ellie, using dirty tricks and false allegations of child neglect, I will rip you to pieces in court. I will drag your ass through the kind of hell that you can't even imagine. So, I am asking you right now to back off. Do not get me started down that track with you because I am not going to be able to throttle back. And this kind of legal battle will only get ugly for both of us. It will ruin you financially and there are no recoverable attorney fees at the end of this kind of legal spat. So, long story short, when you have your day in court, it's going to be just you and me battling it out. And let me forewarn you while I am still kind enough to talk to you… you aren't even close to being a fair match for me in court. I will easily run you into a defensive corner that you will not be able to escape despite your most conniving, self-serving ploys. I will rip you to shreds, Lizzy, make no mistake about it."

Elizabeth huffed with defiance. "Don't threaten me with your almighty legal power, Ian. Because I am not afraid of you. And what you don't realize, is that I have some money stashed away from my divorce with Steve. And I can use those funds to pay for an attorney to fight you for the grandparenting rights that you are trying to keep from me. I've already talked to an attorney and he agreed to represent me, and in fact he said I have a good case. So, I will not be fighting you alone and you will have to burn up some costly attorney fees too, just to try and stay in the race with me. Because this time around I am prepared to go all out for Ellie. I will let you keep Jenny without another legal battle, but I am definitely going to fight you for Ellie, and I am determined to win that fight. And when I do, you're the one who will be coming to me, begging for a chance to see her. So, why don't you think about that before you start swinging your almighty legal sword, threatening me like the bully you are."

"You are about as despicable as they come, Lizzy." Ian madly fired back at her with unchecked hatred. "And you have no idea what you're going up against. So, bring it on, because I am in this fight for my daughter, and I am in it to win it for her. So, go ahead and lawyer up if that's what you want to do, because I can do the same. And when we meet in court this time around, it won't be anything like the last time we were in court together. Because I will rip your ass into so many unrecognizable pieces, that it will be impossible for anyone to put you back together. You fucking bitch!"

He ended the call without saying goodbye and in an uncontrollable burst of fury, he flung his phone into the wall across the room with the kind of enraged madness that was impossible to hold back.

"Shit!" He let his mouth fly with a string of bad words.

"Well, that was effective." Mary stepped in behind him as his phone boomeranged off the wall and ricocheted into the corner of a cabinet, screen side down, on its way to a hard landing on the tile floor.

"Damn it!" Ian spun her direction to tersely warn her off of him. "I am not up to the challenge right now of appropriately channeling my anger, Mary, so back off. Because I will wrongly follow you down that rabbit hole and I will fight it out with you, if you take me there. So, please… give me some space for a few minutes so I can pull myself together."

She crossed the room without comment, and picked up his shattered phone from where it landed on the floor. "Well, maybe you can use some of that uncontrollable energy you're feeling, and the time out that you're requesting, to drive yourself across town to the Verizon store to have the screen guard on your phone replaced because it's badly cracked and probably un-swipe-able now."

Ian defeatedly lowered himself into the deep seat of a leather recliner and closed his eyes to try and settle himself down. His heart was pounding like crazy and he literally felt faint. "I haven't been this mad at her since the day she walked out of my house for the last time, when in response to her departure, I took my dad's baseball bat to the wedding memorabilia cabinet, and smashed the hell out of it." He almost couldn't breathe his heart was pounding so hard.

Mary handed him his damaged phone. "I suppose having you throw your phone across the room is better for all of us, than having you smash furniture. So, I'll give you that…" she settled her eyes on him with patient understanding. "Breathe… please…. Just take a deep breath…" She stood before him to rub her palms into his shoulders to try and help him relax.

Ian inhaled with resolve to settle himself down, and slowly released the air in his lungs. "I'm sorry." He reached for her hand and held it in his own. "She's just making me crazy. I am literally losing my mind with her."

Mary nodded at his assessment of the rocky situation. "We'll get through this, Ian. You always have before."

He nodded at what she said because that's what she expected out of him, then he closed his eyes and exhaled with a focused steadiness in a desperate effort to calm himself down. He did not feel nearly as confident as Mary, that he would really survive this one. If

Elizabeth was lawyering up, he'd have to do the same. And in the end, nobody ever came out the winner in child custody battles. Certainly not the child. And that's what really bothered him, because in this case he would actually have two damaged children when the battle was over; Jenny and Ellie – three if he included Ricky. And somehow, Ian would have to figure out how to put all of them back together again.

Chapter Thirteen

Wally glanced at his watch as he left his clinic at the end of the day. He had wanted to talk to Betty Jo Monday night after work, but she had worked late, so the timing wasn't good by the time she got home. And when he tried to call Elizabeth to rescind the job offer, she didn't answer her phone. So, that conversation was still hanging over him. And he couldn't let another day go by without having either conversation. He had to talk to Betty Jo tonight, and he needed to resolve his Elizabeth problem before he had tonight's conversation with his wife. He wanted to know that his relationship with Elizabeth was definitively over, before he had his confessional with Betty Jo.

He slid into his car, filled with angst as he mentally committed himself to stopping at Elizabeth's apartment on his way home. The singular realization looping through his mind was that by day's end he might very well be facing the end of his marriage. But first – before that crisis was upon him – he had to get through this other crisis – his final conversation with Elizabeth.

He pulled into her apartment complex and determinedly made his way to her apartment door, channeling as best he could, a detached *Ian-ish* mode of thinking. He desperately wished he could adopt Ian's heart of stone for at least the next few minutes.

"Hi..." Elizabeth answered his knock with her cell phone in hand and tears streaming down her face.

"What's wrong?" Wally stepped into her apartment and closed the door behind him, completely losing his detached composure and precarious heart of stone.

Elizabeth burst into tears. "I just had the worst fight of my life with Ian. He gets me so upset sometimes that I find myself saying the dumbest things to him. And now he's so mad at me I'm never going to be able to walk him back from the fight I started with him. He's going to come after me with everything he's got and he's going to completely annihilate me. First, he's going to beat me up in court, and by the time he's finished with me there, I'm going to be financially insolvent. And then he's going to ruin my personal life. He is not going to stop until I'm completely defeated. And it's all my fault. I never should have started this fight with him."

Wally chuckled at the vision she created in his mind of Ian going nuts on her, because it brought to mind a frantic comic strip scenario of spinning arms and legs as the two of them went at it.

"It's not funny, Wally."

"I know." He forced himself to stop smiling. "Regardless of whatever you said to him, I'll help you walk him back from a fighting position. Ian's a sensible guy and I'm sure his legal acumen will hold him back from having an ugly legal battle with you. I can't see him really wanting to go there professionally. His image is too important to him. And as much as he may feel like ripping you to pieces, I'm sure that will pass once his wife talks him down. Because he's going to listen to Mary; he always has, and she'll keep him from going there."

"Mary the golden child…" Elizbeth spat out her feelings in that regard as she wiped her eyes in an effort to pull herself together. "Ian will always be the love of my life… but Mary will always be the love of *his* life."

Wally shrugged off the importance of what she was feeling. "I could similarly say the same. Mary has always been special to me, but she's never had eyes for anyone but Ian."

Elizabeth woefully nodded her head. "So, what brings you here today? More bad news for me?"

Wally hated having to add more to her bad day but he had to get this over with as Ian had advised, once and for all.

Elizabeth anticipated what he was going to say. "I've already heard it from Ian and I know what you're going to say."

Wally went where she guided him. "I need to rescind the job offer." He said it with unfaltering determination – a robotic, unemotional, unequivocal shut down – that's what he needed to do. "I can't have you working at my clinic. That was folly for me to even think that I could."

Elizabeth nodded, clearly expecting him to say that. "I knew he'd make you do that."

Wally shrugged off her observation without denying Ian's influence. "He's right. I can't do this anymore. We're not *just* friends. We've slept together behind my wife's back. And I can't be *that guy* anymore. I can't cheat on my wife and pretend it didn't happen. And going forward, I need to make sure that there are no distractions or temptations outside of my marriage. As much as I'm in love with you, *and I am…*"

Wally slid that in to help buffer the hurt feelings. "I've got to stop seeing you, even if we would only be seeing each other professionally. I can't live with this kind of dishonest turmoil eating me up on a daily basis. I've got kids to think about and a new grandchild on the way. And I need to try and put my family back together. I need to be the kind of husband that my wife deserves. And she deserves the best. Someone much better than me. And I want to try and be what she deserves… if she'll still have me."

Elizabeth nodded her head. "I understand what you're going through, Wally. You're torn up inside."

"I am." Wally exhaled with relief that she wasn't going to make this hard on him. "This is so difficult for me. I don't want to hurt you. I'm not that kind of guy."

"I know." Elizabeth reached for his hand. "Come sit with me so we can talk." She led the way to her couch and gracefully sat down despite the awkwardness of her broken wrist and cast. "You're always so sweet to me."

Wally sat beside her. "My wife won't think that I'm sweet once she learns what I've done."

Elizabeth smiled with appreciation for what he was saying. "No, she won't. I completely understand how your wife will feel, because I've been in her shoes *the spouse who's been cheated on*. But I also understand how you're feeling, because I've been in your shoes too, *the cheating spouse…*"

Wally turned to look at her in surprise.

Elizabeth offered an explanation. "When Ian and I were falling apart, I met a man – my second husband – who was the kindest, most understanding person in the world, and I had an affair with him and that's how Jenny had her accident. I was at his house and we'd been secretly seeing each other for quite a while, and I was feeling guilty for cheating on Ian. So, I was trying to break it off with Steve and instead of breaking up, we ended up making love and that's when Jenny fell into his pool. There was an alarm that was supposed to go off if the back door was opened, but it didn't go off, and the pool gate wasn't shut, and I didn't realize she had gotten out of the house until I went to check on her."

Wally gasped at the new information she was providing. “Ian never told me how her accident happened. He just said she slipped and hit her head and fell into a pool.”

Elizabeth shrugged off the truth. “He wouldn’t want to tell you the rest because he never likes to share anything but his homeruns. And my cheating on him wouldn’t exactly be a homerun for him.” She let out a big sigh. “After Jenny had her accident, Ian found out about Steve…”

Wally shook his head at what he never expected about their past. “That must have been an ugly scene.”

Elizabeth nodded her head. “After his initial angry outburst passed which was pretty bad, he graciously forgave me and offered me the choice of staying with him and working things out between us, or staying with Steve and amicably calling it quits. I couldn’t believe how generous Ian was being. So, I chose to stay with him and we tried to work it out. But I was still in love with Steve, and we began seeing each other again behind Ian’s back. I couldn’t help it. I was in love with both of them. But I knew all along that I would have to end it with one of them, so, I finally decided that I should end it with Steve… as hard as that was for me to do. He was just so sweet.”

Wally nodded his head, completely understanding her turmoil. “That’s how I feel right now. I want to stay with Betty Jo because we’re married and we have a family together. And I *do* still love her. But I’m still attracted to you.”

Elizabeth nodded with understanding. “It wasn’t fair of me to keep Steve around when Ian was trying awfully hard to fix what went wrong between us. So, I called Steve and asked him to come over to my house so we could talk. Ian had a trial that was keeping him busy so I knew he wouldn’t come home until late that evening. So, Steve came to the house and it got emotional between us, and one thing led to another and we ended up in my bedroom.”

“No! You didn’t!” Wally gasped at what she admitted.

“I know.” Elizabeth blushed with shame. “I didn’t plan on that happening, but it happened and there was nothing I could do to make it *unhappen*. And after we made love, I couldn’t force myself to end it with Steve, as much as I knew I had to. *I could not let him go.* He was the kindest person in my life at that time, notwithstanding Ian’s sincere efforts to repair our broken marriage.”

Wally nodded with understanding. "I can appreciate the conflict."

Elizabeth continued. "I was an emotional wreck after we made love, so he laid there in my bed with me, trying to help me figure out what I should do, and without ever making a decision, we finally got dressed and said goodbye to each other, literally minutes before Ian unexpectedly came home from work early. It was so close in timing that they had to have passed each other on the road in front of my house. I didn't even have time to strip the bed and put clean sheets on it before Ian arrived."

Wally winced at the intimate details he didn't really want to hear. "That's just gnarly, Elizabeth."

"I know." She nodded with shame. "And in a weird turn of events, Ian was in a really good mood when he got home. His case had settled, and he had stopped on his way home to get flowers for me." Elizabeth continued with her story. "It was the craziest day of my life and all I could do was play along with Ian's celebratory mood, because what else could I do? So, when he suggested that we take Jenny to the park to let her play with the neighborhood kids for a while, I happily agreed. And he was unusually talkative and playful with me as we watched her run around. If he had been that sweet with me in the days leading up to me meeting Steve, I never would have had the affair with him."

Wally nodded at the image she was creating of Ian and her as a happy and loving couple; a *beautiful* couple – a *golden* couple. It made him think of his own unfortunate situation. If Betty Jo had been more attentive with him recently, he was confident that he would have been less vulnerable to Elizabeth. Not that it was Betty Jo's fault. *It wasn't.* It was completely Wally's fault. He knew that, and he accepted that. But he realized now, in hindsight, that the reason he cheated with Elizabeth had nothing to do with Betty Jo, or even love. Elizabeth simply came at him at the wrong moment in time – when he was feeling down and vulnerable to her persuasion.

She continued her story. "When we returned home from the playground, Ian made Jenny a peanut butter and jelly sandwich and we sat in the backyard with her while she ate it, and we laughed together about her messy face, and it was blissfully sweet and intimate. Then Ian cleaned Jenny up and put her down for a nap, and all of a sudden, I found myself back in my bedroom, between those same soiled sheets that Steve had just left, only this time I was there with Ian, not Steve."

"Yikes…" Wally scowled with disapproval.

"I know." Elizabeth shrugged with shame. "And Ian was being such a charmer, intimately teasing with me, which he hadn't done in a long time, giving me compliments, even going so far as to suggest we have another baby."

Wally shook his head, only imagining what was coming.

Elizabeth kept talking. "I could have loved him forever if only he could have always acted that way with me."

Wally nodded his head. He could appreciate that. "And then?" He couldn't help prodding her along.

Elizabeth finished her story. "I was so conflicted inside. I couldn't stop thinking how I just had sex with Steve, as I tried to focus on having sex with Ian. It was horrible, and I couldn't get into it physically or emotionally. And Ian finally caught on that something was bothering me, and when he asked me what was wrong, I couldn't help myself. I had to get what I had done off of my chest. So, I blurted out that I was still seeing Steve and that I had called him to the house that morning to break up with him, but instead of breaking up, I had mistakenly let him make love to me in our marital bedroom right before Ian came home."

"Oh my God, you did not tell him that."

Elizabeth nodded her head. "I know. I'm as unconscionable as him. We deserve each other." She dropped her head in shame and wiped an eye that began filling with tears. "It was the worst day of my life and the meanest thing that I have ever done to him. I could see the horror of what he was hearing as it ricocheted from his face to his heart, and back up to his head again."

Wally could only imagine Ian's shock. "What did he do after you told him?"

"Surprisingly nothing." Elizabeth wiped an eye. "It was the most tortured silent moment of my life. He just stared back at me in frozen disbelief as his mind tried to process the words that he heard. Then he silently pushed himself off of my body and walked into the bathroom and pushed the door shut behind him."

"That's it?" Wally shook his head in utter disbelief. Ian's composure was beyond applaudable.

Elizabeth nodded. "I know. So, I followed him in and asked what he was doing, and he turned to me with revulsion and calmly but emphatically stated, *I'm washing you and your boyfriend off of my body. Get out of here. I cannot talk to you right now."*

"Wow..." Wally gasped at her story. That was the kind of cool that made Ian who he was. Anybody else would surely have blown their top.

Elizabeth added more. "So, I went back to the bedroom to wait for him to come out so we could talk through it, but while he was showering, I realized that I had ruined it with him and he would never forgive me again. So, I packed some bags so I could leave without drama just in case that's how the conversation ended, and when he came back in the room, I told him that I would never cheat on him again, and I would end it once and for all with Steve, if only he would give me one more chance; but if he couldn't do that, I would leave if that's what he wanted. And he didn't try to stop me. He walked over to the bedroom door and opened it for me and waved me out without saying a single word. Not even, goodbye. So, I grabbed my two bags and left the house without saying anything to him, except that I was sorry. I have no idea what he did after that, but I'm pretty sure it involved some heavy drinking."

Wally shook his head in total disbelief. "That is the most heart wrenching break-up story I've ever heard."

Elizabeth nodded. "I know. And honestly, Ian was very generous through it all. When I returned to the house later that week to get more of my things, he wasn't there but he left me a note on the dining room table that said, *Take whatever you want, I don't care. Locks will be changed tomorrow. I'm not going to fight with you over finances, but to preserve what we have while we work through the legal process, I've moved all of our savings to another account except for $2,000.00 for your immediate needs. The remaining balance in the checking account covers outstanding checks. The account will be closed when the last check clears, so make your financial plans accordingly."*

Wally was silently awed by the precision and finality of Ian's final break up with her. No wonder he thought Wally could do the same to her. Robotic detachment. Ian's ability to shut himself down instantaneously and unemotionally was amazing.

Elizabeth finished her story. "I noticed after I read the note that this beautiful cabinet where we displayed our wedding memorabilia was gone. I had wanted to save a few things from it. But I later found it in the garbage bin outside, completely smashed up. That was the only thing that gave away Ian's emotional state. I don't know what he took to it, but it was demolished."

Wally smiled at that. The punk in Ian surely cussed her to hell and back when he smashed that cabinet. It was a little amusing to him, picturing Ian's meltdown. The vision ran in stark contrast to his usual cool façade. "What happened to Jennifer?"

Elizabeth nodded at his question. "He was always a good father to her, so I left her with him, not meaning for it to be forever. I saw an attorney the following week and filed for divorce. A few weeks after that my boyfriend was served with a personal injury lawsuit that Ian filed as guardian ad litem on Jenny's behalf. We never talked or saw each other again except when we were in court, which went by for me in a blur. The lawsuit settled out of court; our divorce became final in what felt like no time at all – I think because he honestly didn't fight me over anything. And the next thing I knew I was married to Steve and paying Ian $500 a month in child support for the rest of my life. He walked out of court with sole legal and physical custody of Jenny and for years after that our only communication with each other was over an annual lunch date when Ian took Jenny to Disneyland every summer. He wanted her to know that she had a mother, but he wanted nothing more than that to do with me – it was clear to me that just being in my presence was vile to him. And then he married Mary, and she made him invite me and my family to Jenny's wedding, and that's how we became this extended family."

Wally shook his head as he tried to absorb all of the details. "I think I owe Ian more respect than I've been giving him. He *is* the coolest guy I know, because I'm pretty sure I would have blown my top on you. I would not have kept my cool like that. And our final days together would never have ended up as an unemotional business transaction on the back side. It would have become an ugly, emotional domestic fight and I probably would have fought you with everything I had in me, for no other reason than payback for the broken heart."

Elizabeth nodded. "Well, that's not Ian – at least back then it wasn't him – because he never fought me over money or property. He just wrote the checks that he was required to write and when everything was resolved, he walked away from me without any drama. He's just like that. He can detach in a heartbeat, and once he gets there in his head, he cannot even remember why he ever loved you in the first place."

Wally shook his head with silent admiration. "Well, in fairness to Ian, you gave him a pretty good reason to detach and forget."

Elizabeth nodded back at him. "I know. I've regretted it ever since. He was actually the best thing that ever happened to me. Even when he was at his worst."

Wally chuckled. "So now what? You think he'll really come after you this time? If he walked away without drama the last time, who's to say he won't do the same this time?"

Elizabeth scowled without doubt. "We're in a different place in our lives now. And he's not going to walk away from this fight without drama. He's going to crush me with everything he's got inside him. I'm going to pay for all of my past crimes this time."

Wally smiled; he could see Ian doing that to her, despite his past composure and charitable heart. There were two sides to Ian and one side did not necessarily overlap onto the other side. As much as Ian was an easy-going lover who just wanted to keep the peace around him, he was also a savvy street punk who had learned early in life how to get by when the going got tough. And over time that hard-knocks survivor had become a polished and calculated, erudite fighter who could shore up his cause with a focused resolve and iron-clad determination.

"You really don't think he'll settle down?" Wally could see how he'd have a hard time walking away from this fight.

Elizabeth shook her head. "I'm going to have walk away without drama, just like before. It's either that or I go down fighting, because he is going to destroy me." Her eyes filled with tears again. "I pushed him too hard this time and he is not going to allow me to stay in his life, or win this fight that I started."

Wally looked away to avoid seeing her sadness. As much as she was trying to be strong, she was not nearly as capable as Ian at detaching from loved ones, though she seemed determined to give it her best shot. In many ways she and Ian were such a good match – they were both very calculated, driven, overly confident, and self-preserving. And yet, as a couple, their combined survival skills created a toxic cocktail that could only end in an explosive disaster.

"So, no worries about the job offer…" Elizabeth superficially pulled herself together. "I'll find something else. I may even return to L.A. where my boys live." She was already pushing herself into a detached mode that allowed her to unbuckle herself from her feelings. “I didn’t want to withdraw any money from my savings, but I do have some funds stashed away from my divorce with Steve that will help me get by until I find a new job. It’s supposed to be for my retirement, but… I can dip into it now.”

Wally nodded feeling thankful that she was willing to let him go without drama, and that she had money available to keep herself from being evicted. Knowing that made it easier to walk away from her. “You’ll always be a good memory for me,” he at least wanted to give her that much, “but…”

She didn’t let him finish. “It’s fine. So, don’t beat yourself up about it. I won’t hold it against you that we can’t see each other again. I get that you have to go home to your wife and family.”

Wally nodded. “I do. If she’ll have me.”

Elizabeth proudly stood to walk him to the door. “She will…”

Wally held back for just a second. “When is your surgery?” Her effort to wind this up suddenly felt like a detached and abrupt ending that he wasn’t expecting. In fact, her unemotional composure felt a little too *Ian-ish.* Wally was the one who was supposed to be definitively ending their relationship and walking away without emotion, but somehow, Elizabeth had just taken the lead from him.

“It’s later this week.” She shot him a brave smile. “I’m not concerned about it.”

Wally nodded at her masked concern as he consciously resisted the impulse to tell her to call him if she needed anything. That kind of caring comment could unravel the definitive goodbye that he was here to impose, and he didn’t want that.

“You’ll be fine.” He kept it unequivocal.

Elizabeth nodded. “I will.” She opened the door for him and waved him out. “Your wife is a lucky girl. Give her my best.”

Wally shook his head in quiet wonder. He wanted to give Elizabeth a hug goodbye, but he realized as he thought about it that *he* was now being dismissed, *not her.* And she may not want that goodbye hug from him. And that left him feeling somewhat unsettled. “No… *I’m* the lucky guy… if only she’ll forgive me.”

Elizabeth smiled with a hint of irony. “That makes you and Ian both lucky guys, I guess.”

And it left Elizabeth out in the cold. *The only unlucky one in the group.* Wally nodded and waved goodbye. “Take care.”

He stepped out of her apartment with the kind of relief that made him feel like he stood ten feet tall. *That* was a definitive goodbye. He had no doubt that she knew he wouldn't be coming back. And getting that behind him felt incredibly exhilarating. Like he'd just been given a new lease on life. And yet, he simultaneously felt deflated, like a vulnerable ant because he was terrified about what still lay ahead of him. He was incredibly ashamed of himself for his unconscionable behavior, and he was terrified by the realization of what he might now lose because of it. It was a strange and sad sensation for him to be feeling so elated and euphoric on the one hand and so horribly crestfallen and terrified on the other hand.

****

When he arrived home, Betty Jo was in the kitchen. "You're home…" She turned to him with a smile and actually stopped what she was doing to greet him with a kiss.

"I am." Wally felt conflicted kissing her back. He didn't want her kissing him under the false pretense that he was still a good husband, and until she knew what he had done behind her back, that's what he was allowing her to do. And that offended him on her behalf.

"How was your day?" He dropped his keys in the bowl in the entryway and kept his ring on.

Betty Jo noticed that when she handed him a cocktail. "You didn't take your ring off…" The routine had started years ago when he was doing yard work and he'd caught it on something that nearly took his finger off. But tonight, he wanted to keep it on.

"I didn't." Wally took her by the hand and drew her into the living room behind him. "We need to talk." His heart was pounding like crazy in fear that he was about to lose her. He was so scared about having this talk that he was afraid he might not be able to speak at all; and worse, he was terrified that by the end of the night he would have nobody left in his life who loved him. He didn't want to lose Betty Jo, but he was painfully aware that holding onto her was now out of his hands – and like Elizabeth, he may find himself forever regretting the selfish and hurtful actions of his recent past that had the potential of ruining his future.

"I need to talk, too…" Betty Jo reached for his fingers and gave them a squeeze.

Wally gulped with fear. She had likely come to the conclusion, even without knowing what he had done, that she no longer wanted him. Like Ian, he had waited too long to fix what was wrong with them. But Wally didn't want her to leave him, not now, just as he was realizing more than ever, how much he truly wanted to hang onto her. In fact, he probably loved her more right now than he had ever loved her before. She was a priceless, irreplaceable wonder – a true gem.

But none of that mattered anymore because, like Ian, his moment to turn things around, had slipped by without notice. And then… he made everything worse by cheating on her.

"Who goes first?" Wally forced himself to move forward with the kind of purpose Ian would muster. Robotic conversation; that's what Ian suggested, unencumbered by drama, emotions, or fear. Just uncensored talk… man to man… *Just do it.* Lay it out for her, get it done, and move on.

"You…" Betty Jo looked similarly stricken with fear as she suggested that he should go first. "Since you started the conversation."

"Okay." Wally nodded with the kind of internal agitation that made a person restless. What he needed to muster was calm, cool, collected detachment. He had to find the same kind of mechanical resolve that Ian found when he silently pushed himself off of Elizabeth's body to step into the shower to rinse Elizabeth's betrayal off of his vulnerable heart and soul – off of his bare-naked flesh that had only seconds ago, been enjoying the intimacy of her body.

He guided Betty Jo over to her favorite chair and waited for her to sit in it. *Mindless detachment from the emotional heartache* – that was the goal. He wanted to console her with an apology that conveyed his intention to never hurt her again. But first he had to admit that he *had* in fact hurt her.

"I…" He settled his eyes on her and swallowed his fear. He wanted so badly to kiss her… like he hadn't wanted to kiss her in years. But he realized that the kiss he wanted may never happen again for him.

Wally forced himself to speak. "I've made a horrible mistake." He heard himself talking before he was fully prepared to face the end of his marriage. The coward in him wanted to bail out and not finish what he was saying or alternatively, say something benign, but he made himself honestly continue. "If you want to leave me, I understand."

Betty Jo swallowed hard. So did Wally as he envisioned Ian's stoic handling of Elizabeth's cheating. He forced himself to continue as he silently promised himself that he would handle his own marital crisis – *whatever her reaction might be to it* – with an equal amount of humility, and dignity, and gentlemanly graciousness. He owed her that much.

"I'm…" It was so hard for him to say it. "I don't want you to leave me, but that's in your hands to decide, not mine." Wally forced himself to continue. "I will graciously accept whatever you decide."

Betty Jo nodded with unmasked concern. "This does not sound good."

Wally nodded affirmation. "It isn't," he forced the words to come out of his mouth. "I cheated with Elizabeth. Twice. I'm sorry. I knew it was going to happen, but I convinced myself that it wouldn't. I didn't *want* it to happen, but I guess I did. She made me feel attractive and whole, and as cool as Ian. And I'm so sorry that I let this happen. The first time was when I was supposed to be interviewing Ian's granddaughter. I realized immediately that it was a huge mistake going there, and I tried to end it after we were together. But she didn't listen. And she showed up for dinner that night. And I tried again to end it with her after the dinner. But then I slept with her a second time when I stayed the night at her apartment when she broke her wrist. But I promise it will never happen again. I emphatically ended it with her today. I just came from her apartment. And whether you stay with me, or leave me, it's over with her. I will never go back to her. I just want you to know that. And I'm sorry. I'm so sorry. My actions were reprehensible and unforgivable. I understand if you hate me and want to leave me. Because I'm the one who ruined us, not you. I deserve whatever happens to me in the aftermath. I am completely at fault and responsible for what happens."

Betty Jo just stared back at him in wide-eyed wonder.

Wally nodded at her silent shock, seeing in his mind how Ian must have looked to Elizabeth as he tried processing her similar confession. "I know. A lot to absorb. It's a horrible betrayal. And I can't say it enough. I'm sorry. I'm so incredibly sorry. There aren't even words to express how horrible I feel about this."

She nodded her head. "Oh my gosh… I'm sorry, too." Tears filled her eyes and she wiped them with her hand. "This is the craziest, most mixed-up night of my life."

"Understandable." Wally fought not to cry. He never wanted to hurt her, but he had, and her pain was going to break his heart. His sweet Betty Jo, apologizing to him when *he* was the one who did wrong…

Wally left his chair to take her in his arms. "Don't apologize to me for anything. I don't deserve you. This was totally my fault. My behavior has been deplorable. And I'm not going to make it any harder on you than it already is. You can take whatever you want. I'll write the checks that I'm supposed to write. I won't fight you over anything."

Betty Jo nodded at his apology and added an explanation of her own. "You don't understand…" She pushed him away from her. "I've been cheating too."

"You, what?" Wally gasped with surprise as he took an awkward step backwards.

That was not what he was expecting her to say.

She nodded at his surprise and said it again. "I cheated too."

Wally exhaled the shock that held him hostage to her words, as he tried in vain to catch up to what she was saying to him. "*You've* been cheating on *me*?" He was completely flabbergasted by her confession. The whole time he'd been trying to engage her in their relationship and reignite their love… the whole time he'd been suffering through his own shameful guilt… the whole time he was feeling disgust with himself for his own betrayal of her… *she was cheating on him?*

No, wonder she had no interest in him! No wonder she never responded to his efforts to reconnect. No wonder she never wanted to sleep with him. No wonder…Wally suddenly felt rage inside him that he did not expect to feel.

"You've been cheating on me?" His accusing rant fell out of his mouth with ugly emotion as he turned away from her to flop into the chair that he left a minute ago. "You've been cheating on me?" He was actually feeling somewhat lightheaded all of a sudden and just a little bit dizzy.

Betty Jo returned to her own chair. "I'm sorry."

"Huh!" Wally was completely blown away by her confession. He was rendered completely speechless, and he could suddenly appreciate – *first hand* – Ian's stunned processing of Elizabeth's startling news as he laid on top of her body trying to reconcile a new reality with an unreconcilable betrayal.

"I'm sorry…" Betty Jo's timid voice broke through Wally's fractured thinking. "And I understand if you want to leave *me*, now."

Wally nodded at her suggestion as he desperately tried to regroup his scattered and shattered thoughts. "I need a minute to catch up with what's happening here. So, give me a moment to process this…and switch gears… from my cheating confession…" he swallowed his emotions and settled his eyes on her. "To your cheating confession… I'm still trying to put all my thoughts back together."

She nodded at his honesty. "I understand."

Wally settled his eyes on her with anger and fear. He felt as betrayed as he felt guilty, but somehow neither feeling was able to neutralize the other. And he couldn't figure out why that didn't happen. "I tried to pull us back together, but you…" his wounded eyes fell on hers… "No wonder you kept pushing me away! You had a love interest on the side!"

He could almost cry with frustration. No wonder he landed in Elizabeth's arms! Betty Jo all but shoved him that direction. "You made me…" what? Wally closed his mouth before he said things he might regret.

Her behavior was no worse than his. He silently repeated that in his head.

They had both cheated. Neither of them was worse than the other.

Betty Jo silently nodded as he grappled for self-control. Then she said what she was thinking. "I wanted us to fall back in love, and you were trying. I could see that. But I knew you would be offended by what I had done, so I kept my distance so I wouldn't be hurt when you ultimately pushed me away when you found out about my cheating. I figured if you knew what I had done, you wouldn't want anything at all to do with me anymore. And I realized too late that what we had was worth saving. That I *wanted* to save it. But I didn't think you'd want me anymore."

Wally nodded at what she said. Before his involvement with Elizabeth, that would have been true for him. He would have left her *before Elizabeth* for no better reason, than a wounded ego. But now… He honestly wanted to keep her, *despite* his wounded ego.

He forced himself to ask about her affair, though he wasn't sure that he really wanted to know the details. "How long have you been cheating?"

Betty Jo looked away from him in silent shame. "More than you cheated. We've been seeing each other for almost a year. I haven't been seeing my friends on the weekends. And when you stayed the night with Elizabeth, I was with him."

Wally nodded in silence. He was completely shocked by her confession. "A year?" He huffed with hurt disgust. "And here I've been feeling horrible about sleeping with Elizabeth twice over what, a few weeks?"

Betty Jo started crying. "I don't know how it got started, or why I couldn't end it, even when I wanted to end it! I broke it off multiple times, but somehow it always started again."

Wally nodded at what she was saying. "I know how that happened. Because that's what happened to me. And it's not your fault for being with him. He was just filling a need that I wasn't filling, like Elizabeth was doing the same for me."

Betty Jo agreed with a nod. "So now what do we do? Get a divorce?"

Wally closed his mouth as he thought about Ian forgiving Elizabeth's affair. If Ian could forgive Elizabeth, Wally should certainly be able to forgive Betty Jo. *If she could forgive him…*

"I forgive you." Wally said that unequivocally. "I'll forget about your affair from this moment forward, if you can do the same for me. I want a second chance with you. I want you to stay with me and if you do, we'll power through this together. There's going to be some difficult conversations in front of us, and it will hurt along the way, but if we really love each other, we can figure out what went wrong and make it right. We'll work it out together, and we'll make our relationship better than ever. Please stay with me."

Betty Jo nodded at his request. "I promise I'll never do that again."

"I promise that, too. Never again." Wally left his chair to cross the room and pull her out of her chair, into his arms for a reconciling hug that felt better than any hug he'd ever had with her. It was better than any hug he'd ever had. *Period.* "We have a new grandbaby on the way… and that's something we can look forward to, together."

She nodded her head. "I don't want our kids having to navigate the awkward divorced parent thing."

"Me neither." Wally agreed. "I want them to be able to openly love both of us."

Betty Jo smiled. "I want that too."

They both burst into tears and cried together – because they hurt, because they were mad at each other, because they were scared, because they could heal, because they were still in love, and because it mattered. *All of it mattered.*

Wally wiped his tears away, then he wiped Betty Jo's tears. "So, let's start over, Pookie." He kissed her on the lips and squeezed her into a meaningful hug. The kind of hug that Ian would give Mary. One that had his love for her oozing out of it.

"Let's do that, Boogie Bear." She nodded with a smile and returned a kiss to his lips that made Wally want another one. "I want us to fall in love again."

Wally kissed her back with the kind of passion he hadn't felt for her in a long time. "I never really stopped loving you to begin with. I just got swept up in this stupid ego thing when it didn't feel like you loved me anymore."

Betty Jo nodded. "He made me feel pretty and smart, and important. He paid attention to me. And he laughed at the silly things that make me laugh."

Wally smiled with emotional pain. "Well, that's my job… to pay attention to you and make you laugh. And from now on you're not going to need anyone else to boost your spirits. Because you *are* beautiful. And you're so smart, and you're more important to me than you can ever imagine."

She smiled at what he said. "I'm going to start stroking your ego more and pay more attention to you, even your research. I'm going to quit watching my shows so that we can do things together. Like evening puzzles, and nighttime talking fests. I've been shutting you out and pushing you away, no wonder you left my side for a while."

Wally kissed her with passion. "From now on, when you watch your shows, I'm going to watch them with you. And if they're silly, that's okay. We could use the silly laughter."

They both laughed at their efforts to address and erase some of their most obvious mistakes.

"Welcome to our second chance, Pookie."

Betty Jo returned a kiss to his lips. "Let's go out to dinner Boogie bear." She tugged him towards the front door. "And when we get home…" She shot him a flirty smile. "I'm going to erase Elizabeth for you…"

Wally swatted her on the butt. "We'd better clean up your mascara before we go out …"

She laughed at his teasing. "It's a bit like fright-night, looking at me?"

Wally chuckled. "This *night* has been a fright-night in so many ways. But I'm liking how it's turning out. Even with my fright princess… looking frightful…"

She laughed at that. "I'm liking how this night is ending, too…"

Chapter Fourteen

Ian was having a crazy Wednesday, when Wally called him mid-day.

"Hey, Wally…" he glanced at his watch. "What's up?" He had an afternoon hearing that he needed to get to in forty-five minutes, and a client from hell who was giving him a hard time about what he was willing and not willing to do to settle his case. And the case needed to be settled, because it was vulnerable for a large jury award.

Wally let out a sigh with the thoughts he hadn't yet shared with Ian. "I just wanted to let you know that I've had both conversations. And they both went better than expected."

"Well, that's good news." Ian stopped focusing on his case to listen more attentively to what Wally was saying. It was kind of weird, but he'd spent so many years raising Jenny as a single parent who had no time for friends; followed by his years with Mary, where he never felt like he needed friends… that he was sort of enjoying Wally's obtrusive but simple friendship.

Immature *Polly Wally* who always got under his skin when they were kids because of his obnoxious infatuation with Mary… and grown-up Doctor Weldon, who drove him crazy as an adult with his clumsy involvement with Elizabeth… and yet, Ian liked him. It was kind of surprising.

"Which conversation do you want to tell me about first?" He realized as he asked the question, that Wally may not want to share the details of either conversation with him. Except, that Wally had called him, obviously to chat about it, so he probably wanted to talk. Ian glanced at his watch. He could give Wally about ten minutes, max.

"Elizabeth's conversation was most enlightening…"

Ian huffed with suspicion. "I'd take anything that Elizabeth says, with a massive dose of dubious salt."

Wally chuckled. "She told me about her last day with you… why you finally called it quits with her, and how that scene went down."

Ian frowned with his own recollections of that day. He did not want Elizabeth sharing their intimate history with Wally. Especially *that* history – the unwelcome memory made Ian want to distance himself from whatever Elizabeth might have told him. "Elizabeth tells a great story. But the problem with her storytelling is that at least half of what she says is fiction."

"Well, fiction or not…" Wally wasn't deterred. "…she cast you in her story as a superhero, and herself as an unconscionable villain, and it was a sad but beautiful tale in that it inspired me to be a better man."

Ian blew off his observation with self-conscious chagrin. Having no idea what Elizabeth really told Wally, he felt incredibly exposed. "Well, great…" he exhaled in thought, "If whatever story she told you helped, I guess I'm okay with her fiction."

Wally stayed the course. "I'm just saying, you were impressive as a kid, and you're even more impressive as an adult. And I want you to know that I used you as a role model for my conversation with Betty Jo."

Ian frowned with confusion. "I would've thought that my detached – *don't let the door hit you in the ass on your way out of my life – go*odbye… would have worked better as an example for getting rid of Elizabeth than as an example for hanging onto Betty Jo. But hey… it's your tangle of women, not mine. So, whatever unraveled that sticky knot for you, I'm fine with that."

Wally chuckled. "She also told me that she just had the worst fight of her life with you, and she is extremely torn up about that. So, how about making things right for her now that you've had a chance to cool off?"

Ian huffed off his suggestion. "Elizabeth and I go way back, Wally, and she knows how to navigate our fights without help." And Ian certainly wasn't interested in having Wally mediate them. "I do *not* want to discuss my relationship with Elizbeth with you." Maybe having Wally as an adult friend wasn't so amusing after all. "If you've cut her loose, I'm happy about that. But when it comes to me and her…"

"She doesn't want to fight you in court, Ian. She completely regrets starting that fight with you."

Ian could care less what she regretted. "Did she tell you that she called Social Services on Jenny and that she's trying to steal her daughter from her? Because *that's the fight.* And as long as I'm sucking air into my lungs, I'll stay in *that* fight. If I have to bury her in a legal hole six feet deep, so be it. I've got my shovel ready and I am not afraid to get covered in dirt."

Wally gasped with surprise. "You're kidding me? She actually reported you guys, for what? Neglect?"

Ian dropped into his chair to settle into the conversation. "Child endangerment." He glanced at his watch again. "And I will shred her into a million unidentifiable pieces before I let her take Jenny's child from her."

"I'm with you on that one." Wally softly agreed with him. "But just so you know, she wants me to walk you back from that fight. She does not want that court battle. So, why don't you talk to her? See what she has to say? Give her a chance to apologize."

Ian had no faith in what she might have claimed to Wally because Elizabeth had proven to Ian years ago that she could talk out of both sides of her mouth without ever revealing the contrary conversations. "When I see her white flag billowing in my face, I'll consider what she has to say. Until then… I'm lawyering up with the kind of family law experts that will beat her into an unrecognizable pulp."

Wally chuckled. "That's exactly what she's afraid you're going to do. And on a personal note, she says you're the love of her life, and she regrets doing you wrong when you guys were married, and she wishes this new conflict would go away."

Ian huffed. "Well, happily ever after wishes only come true in Disneyland. And I am *not* her prince charming." Ian changed the subject. "How'd it go with Betty Jo?"

Wally chuckled and went where Ian led him. "We're good. Funny thing is, well, it's actually not funny at all, at least not *ha-ha* funny, but here's the ironic humor… she's been cheating on me for even longer than I was cheating on her."

"What?" Ian sat up in his chair. "Are you kidding me?" That was not at all what he was expecting to hear Wally say. *Betty Jo was cheating on him?*

"I know. My reaction, too." Wally calmly fed him more details. "She ended the relationship with her guy the same day that I shut Elizabeth down. And now… we're both going to forgive and forget, and embrace our second chance. I feel lucky to have her back… and actually, we had a great reconciliation last night…"

"Let me stop you right there." Ian cut him off before he said any more. "I honestly do not want to hear the details."

Wally laughed at that. "Too much info, huh?" He didn't stop chuckling. "Sort of like me watching you and Mary saunter out of that bedroom at John's house, covered in hickeys, the night he had that party, when clearly, you and Mary had some kind of fight before you got there, that you hadn't worked out prior to your arrival…"

Ian shook his head in silent wonder at Wally's memory. "I don't remember what we were fighting about, but I *do* remember making up with her in that bedroom."

Wally laughed at that. "I honestly don't want to hear the details."

They both chuckled with the teasing, and Ian wrapped the call up. "Why don't you and Betty Jo come over again this Saturday? We'll do another ride in the hills, and then dinner."

"Sure. That sounds fun. What time?"

"Come at one, like last time. That worked fine. And I'm pretty sure that Elizabeth won't dare show up this time."

Wally agreed with him on that one. "No way. She's already convinced that you're about to rip her a new one."

"I *am* going to rip her a new one." Ian ended the call as he left his chair and grabbed his briefcase to leave for court.

When he was on the road, he called Mary to share Wally's news. "You are not going to believe what I have to tell you."

"I'm with a client." She quickly cut him off.'

"Oh. Sorry. It can wait." Ian ended the call, but he couldn't stop thinking about it. He never would've expected someone like Betty Jo to be cheating on her husband. The shock of her doing that stayed with him for the rest of the day.

****

When he finally got home from work that night, he changed out of his office attire and joined Mary and the kids out in the barn. The little kids were throwing straw around, creating more work for Ian.

"Hey, who's sweeping that up?" There was a big pile of it in the main aisle of the barn, and beyond that pile, there was straw flung all over the place.

"Sorry, daddy…" Philip stopped throwing it around and Skylar threw her last handfuls at Ellie, who pushed Skylar backwards away from her.

"Hands to yourself, Ellie…" Ian tousled all of their hair as he walked by them to go to Mary. "What time did you get home?" He popped a quick kiss on her lips and picked up a pitch fork to attack the kids' straw mess.

"About an hour ago." Mary returned her attention to the hay nets she was stuffing with hay. "What were you going to tell me earlier when you called?"

Ricky and Jenny were cleaning stalls, paying no attention to the little kids, or to Ian and Mary, so Ian stepped Mary's direction, to tell her what he learned. "Betty Jo has apparently been spinning her own sticky cobweb of love connections, because according to Wally, she was having an affair with some guy the whole time Wally was cheating with Elizabeth."

"You're kidding me." Mary stopped stuffing the hay nets. "I never would have guessed that about her."

"I know. But there you have it. Even someone like Betty Jo cheats." Ian held his eyes on Mary, as he made the conversation more personal. "Makes me wonder if we're the only couple in the world who would never cheat on each other…" He allowed himself to reveal more vulnerability than he normally showed as he added what he was really thinking. "On the other hand, maybe that's a naïve assumption on my part and it's just a matter of time before that kind of crappy betrayal creeps back into my home..."

Mary stood to share a kiss with him. "Please tell me that you aren't actually wondering if I would ever cheat on you?"

He shrugged with a learned detachment that he would have a hard time directing at Mary if it ever really came to that. "It makes me question the whole institution of marriage and leaves me wondering if monogamy isn't really doable; like maybe the cheating is just an inevitable fact in all relationships." The whole idea of that made Ian's stomach turn, which made him adopt a dismissive tone as he finished sharing his thoughts with her. "In which case, just to be clear with you, I would *not* stick around for the apologies…"

Mary laughed off his transparent armored encasement. "You would be begging me to come back, and you know it. But lucky for you, I would never put you through that. So, get over the skittish concern, because you're stuck with me forever, dude. Don't even think about that happening in this marriage."

Ian popped a relieved kiss on her lips. "And I would never cheat on you because first and foremost, setting love aside, you know how to effectively fight back, and I have no doubt at all that you would clean me out in court and I would lose everything I have today, including my kids."

Mary chuckled at his teasing reassurance. "So, keep that in mind, lambchops when you find yourself indulging a wandering eye because you're mad at me for some silly reason…"

Ian laughed at that. "Wally actually remembers that night at John's house when we had that fight before we got there, and he tried to pick you up because I wasn't talking to you…"

Mary smiled at the memory. "And we made out in somebody's bedroom…"

"Yeah, we did." Ian nodded with a smile. "He remembered the artwork we left on each other…"

Mary chuckled at his description of their passionate teenage hickeys. "Boy, you came close to scoring that night…"

"Yep. I sure did." Ian grinned at that and changed the subject. "Wally's coming to dinner Saturday with Betty Jo. I invited them to that, plus another ride in the hills…"

"Well, that'll be fun. I like Betty Jo… even if she is a cheat."

Ian nodded. "And I hate to admit it, but I kind of enjoy chatting with that doofus Wally…"

****

When Saturday arrived, Jenny and Ricky were crushed that they couldn't go riding with them, but Ian promised that the four of them would ride together on Sunday with the little kids. He and Mary would rotate riding a child in front of them, and the third child would ride Donkey on a lead line. The big kids agreed to that, and Ian suggested that they could play board games together while the four adults went riding. And when they returned, he told them, he would order pizza for all of the kids, little ones and big ones, and he'd set them up for a movie sleep-over while he and Mary had dinner with their guests. The big kids agreed to his suggestions, and Karen came over to watch the little kids while the four adults went riding.

The parched hills, yellow from the summer drought were beginning to show signs of green, although they were still dotted with wild stickers and thorns, and the ground was dry and cracked with hard dirt clods. The day was a little chilly, but it was sunny and clear.

They rode together superficially chatting about nothing, until the guys had fallen back from the ladies, and Wally brought Elizabeth up again, in a continued effort to diffuse Ian's fight with her.

"Why are you so opposed to Elizabeth having grandparenting time? It seems like a fair enough request to me."

They were riding along a trail, two by two, and Ian wished he could kick his horse into a gallop to leave Wally behind if this was what they were going to talk about. He could appreciate Wally's desire to protect Elizabeth, given his recent intimate connection with her, but Ian wished he could just let it go.

On the other hand, if Wally was still bending Elizabeth's ear, Ian recognized that talking about it with him wasn't a bad idea, if it could diffuse Elizabeth's push to take the matter to court. Because Ian didn't really want to have that legal fight with her.

He turned to look at Wally with that in mind and forced himself to answer the call of his question, without letting his own perturbed feelings for Elizabeth bleed into the conversation.

"I'm not opposed to her having grandparenting time, despite my loathing for her." Ian shot him a superficial smile. "That's why I let her take up residence in my house for the last five years, Monday night through Thursday morning – to give her grandparenting time. But she chose to leave, and frankly the timing for her departure was good now that Ellie needs less care, considering she's becoming more self-sufficient and she'll be in first grade soon."

Wally nodded.

Ian continued with his analytical perspective. "And the reason I'm not open to Lizzy's demand for a custody rotation, which is a whole different thing, is because I'm not interested in throwing Ellie into a chaotic split family type of situation that's only going to make her childhood feel unstable. For one reason, the rotation out of my house will interrupt the only sibling relationships she'll ever have. My kids are like a brother and sister for her, and they make me crazy with their constant fighting, but they care for each other like siblings and they're close to each other despite the fighting. And I'm not breaking that up. Ellie needs the best family we can build for her. It's going to be tough enough on her when she gets older and starts realizing that her parents are different; that they need *her* to care for *them* more than she needs *them* to care for *her*. And that's going to be somewhat of a lonely wake up call for her. Like suddenly finding out you don't have the security of capable parents behind your back."

Wally smiled with understanding.

Ian offered a more personal perspective. "I grew up without a dad and I know how it feels to be troubled about something and not be able to turn to a parent for advice. And that's how Ellie's going to feel about her parents soon enough, notwithstanding them being alive and available for her. Because they will never be able to commiserate as adults with her or talk through grown-up problems with her. So, for now… while she can still see them as adults who can help her out… I'd like to preserve that parental bond for her. And because it's only going to get more complicated the older she gets, I'd like to give her as carefree a childhood as possible. And making her switch homes all the time, where parenting styles will be in conflict, doesn't seem carefree to me. And Elizabeth will interrupt her relationship with Jenny, and she will work her magic so that Ellie ultimately sees her as a mother figure instead of Jenny. And I don't want that for Jenny or Ellie."

Wally nodded at what he pointed out. "Makes sense."

"It does." Ian added more to his point of view. "Plus, I'm not taking on the added burden of rotating Ellie between houses because that's going to fall on me, not Elizabeth. And I can't take on that added chaos – not to mention, there's the whole dependability issue, the distractibility issue, and her constant push to do things that are contrary to what I'd like her to do. Like it makes me crazy that she keeps encouraging Ellie to mouth off to her parents. I applaud the idea of raising assertive, strong women, but in Ellie's case, the autonomy that Elizabeth is fostering in her is only going to create more problems, than benefits. Because Ellie's perceived authority to stand up for herself is going to become increasingly problematic when she starts realizing that she can disregard her parents' wishes because they aren't capable of enforcing control over her. And then I'm forced into a battle that I don't want, with a wild teenager who has no respect for her parents, and no sense of boundaries in her life. And that's not even addressing the fact that she will undoubtedly be playing Elizabeth and me against each other."

Wally grinned with understanding. "I totally get where you're going with all that."

Ian nodded and continued. "And that only touches on how a custody rotation would impact Ellie. We haven't even addressed the impact it will have on Jenny yet, which is something that *should* be of concern for Elizabeth if only she cared half as much about Jenny as she cares for Ellie or herself. Because her power grab for custody is like stealing parenting time from Jenny and Ricky who are already facing a limited parental window. Because right now, Ellie is their friend. She likes doing the same things that they like doing, and she listens to them because she sees them as pals as much as parental figures. But that's not going to last forever, and in very little time, Ellie is going to outgrow the things her parents like to do with her, and when that happens, Jenny is going to unexpectedly lose her best friend, and find in her place, a smart-ass teen who has no interest in being her friend. And that's going to break Jenny's heart. Because the little girl she's grown to love as a best friend is no longer going to be available as a best friend. So, I intend to preserve as much of this special time for Jenny as I can, because the window for that friendship is maybe three years, tops. And after that, Ellie is going to be the lost friend of a lifetime."

"I totally get what you're saying." Wally nodded his approval. "So, all you have to do is explain all that to Elizabeth."

Ian huffed at that. "Elizabeth doesn't care about any of that. She only cares about what's good for her."

"Seriously, Ian. Just talk to her."

The trail they were riding opened up, so Ian kicked his horse into a slow canter to end the conversation.

****

When they finished their ride and the horses were groomed and fed, and put up for the night, the four adults retired to the house. Ian sent Karen home, he ordered pizza for all the kids, and poured wine for the four adults.

Wally made a toast when all of their glasses were filled. "To my wife and our second chance at marriage… I feel like an incredibly lucky man tonight."

"Here, here…" Mary joined their toast and Ian tapped his glass into hers and then into theirs as he added his own toast.

"To jumping life's hurdles and landing on your feet."

Wally gave Betty Jo a kiss and the four of them moved into the spacious kitchen to start preparing their meal. Karen had already put potatoes into the oven to start them baking while the adults were doing the evening barn chores, so Mary and Betty Jo started rinsing and chopping vegetables and making a salad. Ian had steaks ready to barbeque that he and Wally took outside.

When they were finished cooking, they brought the meat inside and Mary served everyone dinner at their dining room table. It was a relaxed and jolly gathering, and the conversation remained light as the guys and Mary shared memories from their childhood, and Betty Jo shared stories about Wally and her over the years.

As they finished their food, Betty Jo wrapped the dinner conversation up with another more personal, and vulnerable toast.

"I just want to thank both of you for being so supportive of us during this difficult time that Wally and I experienced. I'm not sure we would have survived it without your influence and support. And I want to publicly acknowledge my error in judgment, and openly apologize to Wally for my wrongful behavior because, had I not misbehaved, he probably wouldn't have misbehaved." She settled her eyes on Ian.

"And particularly, I want to thank you for just being you. I know Wally shared with you what I did, and I'm assuming it's especially hard for you to look beyond my actions and still respect me, knowing what Wally told me about your first marriage and how it ended. But hopefully…"

Ian tapped his glass into hers to bring an end to her toast before she dragged him down that *love hurts* rabbit hole. "We all make mistakes, Betty Jo, and it's not my place to judge or hold a grudge. Especially when I haven't walked in your shoes to appreciate the journey that you're on, or the road that took you there."

"Thank you." She looked around the table at each of them. "I'm sorry. To all of you. I just wanted to say that. And thank you for giving me another chance."

"None of us are perfect, Betty Jo…" Ian helped to put it behind her. "Certainly not me…" He moved his teasing eyes onto Mary. "As my wife can certainly attest."

Mary chuckled at his self-deprecating humor. "That's for sure..." She winked with her tease and Ian took it further.

"But Mary's perfect…" His eyes remained locked on hers with intimate, but sarcastic appreciation.

She laughed at his sarcasm and took the tease further. "Thanks for putting that out there. I've noted your statement against interest and also your incriminating admission – both of which I expect to be fairly persuasive in future arguments."

Ian laughed at that and tapped his glass into Wally's. "And sorry, *Polly Wally*… but arguably, I'll always be more perfect than you."

Wally laughed off his tease. "That's still to be determined."

"Daddy…" Jenny interrupted their relaxed banter as she came through the doorway between kitchens, talking without knocking. "We have a problem."

All four of the adults turned her direction.

"What's up, buttercup?" Ian sipped his wine.

Wally chuckled at his tender greeting that Jenny didn't acknowledge like she usually would.

"Mom is sick. She's barfing on the floor. She needs help. And I don't know what to do."

"What?" Ian stood with befuddled surprise, ready to help Jenny out. "Are you on the phone with your mother?"

"No. She's in the bathroom."

"*Our* bathroom?" Ian left the table to go into the kitchen to look out the front window for her car. "When did she get here?"

"After the pizza." Jenny came to his side to look out the window with him. "That's her car. It's parked beside Mary's car."

"I see that." Ian returned his attention to the dinner table. "I better excuse myself to go check this out."

Wally stood to join him. "Why don't I help you?"

"Sure." Ian wasn't going to turn his request down if Wally wanted to accompany him.

Mary stood and gestured to Betty Jo that they should go too. "This is when Ian's imperfections usually surface. Undoubtedly he will offend at least one of us when he voices the kind of sentiment that is always better left unspoken."

Ian smirked at that. “Unfortunately,” he shrugged with defeat. “That’s probably a true statement especially considering my current state of frustration with Elizabeth.”

Betty Jo stood to join them. “Well, I wouldn’t want to miss this…”

Wally chuckled. “Ian at his best.”

Jenny stepped through the open kitchen door and the rest of them followed behind her.

“She’s in there…” Ricky watched them go by from the couch where he was watching a Disney cartoon with the little kids. “She’s barfing.”

Ian stepped into the bathroom, and over some vomit on the floor.

“Why are you throwing up on my bathroom floor, Lizzy?” He lifted her up from the floor and maneuvered her limp body over the toilet. “You know how I feel about that.”

Elizabeth collapsed in his arms. “Oh look… It’s *Saint Ian*. My favorite drunk helper…did you bring your holy water?”

He smirked at her sarcastic greeting. “Wally’s here too…” Ian kept her in place with his hands and body as she drunkenly slumped against him.

“I don’t feel good.”

Ian could see that. “Well, you brought it on yourself, Lizzy.” He wiped her face with toilet paper and dropped it in the toilet. “Not the first time you’ve done this to yourself, and surely it won’t be the last time.”

Wally came up behind them. “Hey, Elizabeth,” he tapped her on the shoulder. “What kind of pills have you taken today? Anything for pain?”

“I don’t remember.” She barely looked his direction and closed her eyes.

“Hey…” Ian tapped her face awake. “Come on, Lizzy, we need to know what we’re dealing with. Is it only the alcohol tonight, or did you also take some pills?”

She giggled at Ian’s efforts to keep her focused. “There’s a doctor in the house... *and* an attorney... I can have all my medical and legal needs addressed in one drunken house call. Lucky me.”

Ian shook his head in objection. “Guaranteed, we are not addressing the legal issues tonight.”

Elizabeth giggled at his disclaimer. “Well, I’m still getting a house call from you. So, that makes me luckier than the luckiest wives…” She looked between the two men. “Because *for once*…I’m getting all the attention from the adoring husbands.”

Ian frowned at her observation. “Well, neither of the wives have vomit on their face, Lizzy, and because of that they’ll both probably get kissed by their husbands tonight. So, I’m guessing that puts your good luck in better perspective for you… despite the split loyalty in attention right now.”

“Hey…” Wally gave him a protesting nudge. “That wasn’t nice.”

Mary shook her head at him. “And we’re off…”

Betty Jo chuckled.

Elizabeth grinned at Wally’s disapproval and more brazenly egged Ian on. “Well don’t forget that I’ve been kissed by the husbands, too, so maybe that adds balance to your kissing perspective.” Her eyes bounced between them. “I’ve also had sex with the husbands. Hot… passionate sex… *more than once*.” She giggled with her admission. “So, there’s an even more telling perspective for the lucky wives to ponder. Your bare bodies thrusting in ecstasy on top of my naked body…”

Ian scowled back at her. “That’s just not funny, Lizzy.” He collected her hair in his hands to keep it from falling in her face.

“Well, maybe I’m not funny anymore because I’m so sad.” She dropped her face onto the toilet seat with a sulky sigh.

Ian flushed the toilet paper. “Well, we can’t help you with that, Lizzy, because you bring it on yourself. And frankly, the sadness is often well deserved.”

“Hey…” Wally gouged him in the back again. “Cut it out!”

Ian shrugged back at him without offering a retraction.

Elizabeth lifted her head from the toilet to hold a pouty stare on Ian. “And now you’re just acting hateful.” She relaxed into his arms.

“Hey… sit up…” Ian moved her more upright away from his torso. “I’m sorry you feel like I’m being hateful, but that’s not my fault, Lizzy, because you make it so damn easy for me to act that way with you.”

“Dude!” Wally thumped him a lot harder. “Can you honestly not censor what comes out of your mouth? She already told you that she’s feeling sad, so stop adding to her misery.”

"You know what, Wally..." Ian blew off his scolding as he adjusted the heaviness of Elizabeth's body against his own crouching frame. "I do a better job of censoring myself when there's a judge in the room, as opposed to a nearly passed out drunk who is intent on ruining my family and breaking our daughter's heart."

"Well, then why don't you just be quiet and let me take over?" Wally did exactly that with unfaltering authority. "Elizabeth, honey..." he tenderly stroked his palm down her cheek. "We need to know how much you had to drink? Was it just a few glasses?"

"Or the whole damn bottle?" Ian added what was more likely.

Elizabeth responded to Wally, not Ian. "Maybe three glasses...tops. No pills." She closed her eyes and melted into Ian's body. "I think I'm just tired. It's been a hard week."

Ian tapped her face awake. "It's not your bedtime, Lizzy. So, we're not going to let you sleep." He turned to face Mary. "Can you get me a wet washcloth?"

"Sure." She went to a cupboard and found one to wet down for him. "Here..."

Ian took it from her hand and held it on Elizabeth's forehead. "Come on, Lizzy, open your eyes and fight with me... because that's what we're good at, and that's what I need you to do now so you can stay awake."

She giggled at his suggestion. "We do fight good. But I don't want to fight you anymore." She reached for his hand and apologetically brought it to her lips to kiss it with drunken emotion. "I'm sorry I made you mad. My heart is breaking because of it. That's why I'm drunk. Because you won't forgive me. *For anything*. Even what you let go a long time ago. But I promise I can do better if you give me another chance. I won't fight you anymore. I'll be nice. You can trust me, Ian. I wouldn't lie about that."

Ian huffed with doubt. "You don't know how *not* to lie, Lizzy. And nice is an unknown concept for you. So, let's not go there tonight."

Wally thumped him in the back. "Stop it."

"Please..." Elizabeth looked between them. "Just give me one more chance, Ian."

He exhaled with detached determination that came naturally to him when he was dealing with Elizabeth. "Are you done vomiting? Let's stay focused on what we're here for tonight."

Wally settled a commanding set of eyes on him. “Come on. She asked nicely and she said she’s sorry. And it sounded sincere to me. So, it’s your turn now… Say something back to her. And be nice about it.”

Ian held his stare for a defiant minute, but Wally held an equally determined glower back on him. “Fine.” Ian exhaled in defeat and wiped the cloth over Elizabeth’s face. “Truce accepted.” He rebelliously dropped a kiss onto her forehead to surrender on his own terms. “Okay?”

Elizabeth giggled. “That was the sweetest ceasefire you’ve done in years, Ian…”

He returned his eyes to Wally. “You see how nice I can be?” He looked back at Elizabeth with exasperated patience. “And now you can even brag into your hangover tomorrow that you also got kissed by one of the husbands tonight.”

“Thank you.” Elizabeth reached for his hand to hold it in hers. “You always find a way to say the nicest things in the meanest way. And I appreciate the analytical precision it takes to do that.”

They all chuckled at her observation which encouraged Elizabeth to add more. “That shows how much you still love me. It’s the proof that’s in my pudding.”

Ian huffed off her observation. “I think you’re eating out of the wrong bowl of pudding.”

“Nonetheless…” Mary injected herself into his surrender. “It’s too bad you had to smash your phone up, Ian, before you could get there in your head. Perhaps this can be a reminder for you in future days not to let yourself go berserk.”

“Dude…” Wally gasped at Mary’s observation. “You smashed your phone up?”

“I know…” Ian shrugged off his mistake. “From time to time I surprise myself with my own inability to maintain self-control.”

“You broke your phone over me?” Elizabeth opened her eyes to swoon into his face. “That’s so sweet, Ian.” Her focus moved onto Wally. “It’s a sign of how much he cares, even when I make him crazy.”

Ian chuckled at that. “You do make me crazy.”

“But you still love me, right?” She opened her eyes to stare into his. “Just admit it, Ian. Say you love me.”

Ian held a resistant gaze on her before he gave into the expectant pressure of everyone waiting for him to say something nice to her. "Sure. In a painful sort of unloving way."

They all laughed at that, and Wally changed the subject. "It doesn't seem like she's going to be sick anymore, so let's get her outside for some fresh air…" He braced himself by Ian's side to help him lift her body.

"On the count of three…" Wally took the lead in her drunken care and particularly stayed focused on supporting her broken wrist as they prepared to raise her. "Ready, Elizabeth? One… two… three…." They lifted her to her feet and Wally stayed in charge like a doctor conducting a medical exam. "Good girl, Elizabeth, and now I want you to walk with us. It'll make you feel better if we can get you moving outside in the fresh air. Can you help us out a little?"

"Sure." She giggled as they guided her into taking a first step. "I've got this, boys… no worries…" She drunkenly giggled. "But don't let go. I like the feel of your bodies next to mine." She laughed with her tease and wrapped her arms around them. "My two favorite men…"

When they had her out of the bathroom, she turned a somber focus on Ian. "How come you hate me so much now?"

Ian dropped his eyes on her. "I don't hate you, Lizzy. It just feels that way sometimes." He adjusted his grip on her as they walked her through Jenny's flat, into the kitchen towards the door between houses. "You make me mad when you stop thinking about others, like your own daughter, and only think about yourself."

"Never mind." Elizabeth shut him down in a brittle voice. "I don't really want to know why you hate me."

"He doesn't hate you mommy." Jenny surprisingly picked up on what Ian was saying as they made their way through the doorway between houses. "He's only a little bit mad at you because you want to take my Cinderella baby away from me. And that's mean. And daddy doesn't want you to be mean to me. Because he's my daddy. And daddies protect their princesses even from mean mommies."

Ian turned to look at her astounded by her understanding of what had been going on between them. "That's exactly the problem, Jenny. Right now, I'm just very frustrated about your mother wanting to infringe on your parenting rights."

Elizabeth didn't say anything but Jenny stayed focused on the conversation. "You can't take my Cinderella baby away from me, mommy. She's mine. The lady said so."

Ian returned his eyes to Jenny. "The social worker told you that?"

Jenny nodded in answer. "The lady who talked to me. She said I'm Cinderella's mommy, and I'm a good mommy. So, I get to keep Cinderella as long as I stay a good mommy. And nobody can take her away from me."

Ian smiled with guarded relief. "Well, that's a good sign if she actually told you that."

"She did." Jenny proudly nodded her head. "And she said I'm in charge of who visits Cinderella. That's my choice. Not mom's choice. And not yours." Jenny corrected herself in regard to Ian. "Just a little bit yours, daddy. Because you're my daddy."

Elizabeth turned to look at her. "I just want to help you take care of her. But your dad doesn't want me to help."

Jenny walked beside them in silent contemplation, then she shared an idea with them. "Okay. You can help be her mommy on one Saturday and one Sunday every month." She looked to Ian for approval. "Right daddy? Not the weekend beside the one when Ricky's mom and dad have Cinderella. Because you will miss her too much, daddy. And she will miss me. But another weekend. The one in the middle of the month. Then everyone can be a mom and dad for her. We can share her one weekend, mom. But not Christmas. And not Halloween. Because she will want to be with me."

Ian looked between Elizabeth and Jenny, apprehensive as to where that idea originated. "Did you put her up to that?" He settled his eyes on Elizabeth, with quiet suspicion. He did not want Elizabeth secretly manipulating Jenny into doing her bidding.

Elizabeth shook her head in answer. "But at least one weekend a month would be something."

Ian moved his attention onto Jenny. "Did your mother put you up to that? Tell me the truth. Was that her suggestion?"

Jenny shook her head at him. "No, daddy. That's my suggestion. Because I'm a smart mommy. And then we can all be friends again. And mommy can see Cinderella and be happy. And you don't have to break your phone again and say bad words because you're so mad."

Ian chuckled at that as he thought about her idea. It wasn't a completely bad suggestion. And he liked that it was Jenny's idea. And because it was similar to what they had worked out with Ricky's parents, who usually had Ellie at their house on the last weekend of every month, it seemed like a fair offer to make to Elizabeth. And it would still allow Ellie to have a stable family life with her pseudo-siblings because one weekend a month *felt* like grandparent time, not a shared custody rotation.

"You know what, Jenny…" Ian kept Elizabeth walking beside him, in step with Wally's calculated pace on their way to the front door. "I think that's a good idea." He reached for the door handle and pulled it open. "And from now on we're going to let you help us work out the visitations. Because you're right. You *are* a good mom, and Ellie is your daughter. So, you get to make these decisions on her behalf." He adjusted Elizabeth in his arms as they stepped outside onto the front porch.

"How's that sound to you, Lizzy?" Ian held her more securely to help her down the porch stairs. "Careful how you step down…"

Wally followed behind them as Elizabeth shot Ian a happy grin. "That sounds good to me." She slightly tripped but Ian held her steady, then she caught her breath and shivered in his arms. "Whew… it's cold out here."

She was dressed as usual, in a body clinging tee shirt that didn't cover her mid-drift, skin tight pants, and delicate sandals.

"Exactly what you need for a few minutes." Wally glanced over at Mary, who was trailing along behind them with Betty Jo by her side. "Can you find a blanket or jacket for her?"

"Sure." Mary stepped back inside.

Wally turned to face Jenny. "You know what, Jenny? I think you're the smartest person in your family because you were able to solve what your mom and dad couldn't solve for themselves. They were ready to fight over visitation in an ugly court battle that was going to cost both of them tons of money, when all they had to do was ask you what you wanted them to do. So, the next time your mom and dad start fighting over your daughter, you need to remind them to buckle down and stay in their own lanes, and stop trying to tell you what to do with your child."

Jenny high-fived his suggestion with excited approval. "That's what I'm going to do, Dr. Weldon. I'm going to tell them to buckle down and stay in their own lane."

Ian chuckled at that. “And now I’ve got the good doctor breaching childhood loyalties, telling Jenny to mouth off to *me*. Thanks for the advice, doc. That’s what I needed in my life: more back-talk.”

Wally laughed at his teasing. “How are you feeling, Elizabeth?”

“Whew… much better.”

She looked it.

Mary returned with a jacket for her. “It might be a bit big, but it’ll keep you warm…”

Elizabeth happily accepted it. “Thanks. I love wearing Ian’s clothes…” She eagerly let the guys help her into it. “There’s nothing that compares to the feel of your man’s coat on your shoulders…”

Mary shook her head at that, and Ian rolled his eyes. Elizabeth stepped back into his body and wrapped her arms around him. “I don’t know why I got so drunk tonight. I didn’t think I was drinking that much… maybe it was because I was so upset about our silly fight. But now I feel better… and I promise it won’t happen again… now that you’re not mad at me.” She unexpectedly stepped up onto her wobbly toes and kissed him on the lips with sloppy emotion. “I’m sorry for acting bad. Thank you for forgiving me…”

Ian silently wiped his mouth off to erase the unwanted kiss on his lips. Then he turned her in his arms to walk her down the dirt road that divided his property, guiding her as they moved, around pot holes that might trip her.

Jenny went back inside to watch the little kids with Ricky, and the four adults returned to the main house not too long behind her. Betty Jo and Wally went home after that, and Mary helped Elizabeth use the bathroom and change into a pair of Mary’s flannel pajamas. When she was dressed and ready for bed, Ian helped to get Elizabeth settled in their guest room for the night.

As soon as she was tucked in, Ian and Mary returned to the kids’ flat and did a final check on the little ones who were sleeping together on the hide-a-bed in Jenny’s living room. Then they went to the bathroom and cleaned the toilet and floor so the kids could use a clean bathroom in the morning. With that behind them, they said goodnight to Jenny and Ricky and returned to their own quarters to clean up their dinner dishes and retire to their own bedroom.

"Well, that was a different kind of evening with friends." Ian stepped out of his shoes and crossed the bedroom to go into the bathroom. "I did not expect Elizabeth to show up here tonight." He closed the door behind him and raised his voice. "I certainly didn't expect her to pull one of her drunken episodes in front of Wally and Betty Jo."

"I know. It's been such a long time since Elizabeth's done that."

Mary dug through a dresser drawer as she continued talking to him. "Tonight, sort of felt like a high school kegger when inevitably, someone drinks too much and that becomes the focus of the party."

Ian chuckled at her observation. "Like my going away party, when you helped me walk off my drunken meltdown…"

Mary picked up on his recollection. "Except that night was less about you drinking too much and more about the forced ending of our relationship and you moving away. And for years after you left, I would lay awake at night and playback every detail of us laying in the grass together, side by side… hardly talking, just staring at each other, feeling completely crushed as we faced the horrible reality of our inevitable break-up. It was suffocating… like I could hardly breathe thinking about you leaving the next morning..."

At the bottom of the drawer that Mary was plowing through, was a purple lace negligée with matching lacy panties that she wore on their honeymoon in Hawaii.

Ian picked up on what she was recalling. "I remember feeling more wasted than I'd ever felt before... and completely incapable of functioning… not because I was drunk, though I'm sure that was a big part of it, but mostly because I was so incredibly heartbroken."

Mary nodded with understanding. "You kept wiping the tears from your eyes… and cussing because you couldn't stop crying." She was doing the same: wiping away her tears and trying to put on a brave face for him. "It literally broke my heart. I was terrified about what might happen to you after we parted. You'd never felt more fragile to me."

Ian added to her recollection. "And then that dreaded moment came when we had to go home…"

Mary found what she was looking for and quickly pulled it out of her drawer. "I've never hated a sunrise more…" She peeled her shirt and bra off and pulled on the negligée. "I remember helping you off the grass so we could walk home together, arm in arm for the last time… it felt like we were headed to the executioner's chair. I wanted so badly for us to runaway together. I regretted talking you down from that idea when you made the suggestion earlier."

Ian agreed with what she was saying. "I hated the idea of us never seeing each other again. And I remember us hugging all the way home, promising each other how we would never forget our special bond… But regardless of that vow, it broke my heart that I wasn't going to be a part of the rest of your life."

Mary slid out of her pants to slide into the sexy panties. "And then that devastating moment was suddenly upon us, when we crossed the street and stopped outside your front door. I felt like screaming out loud when we got there, but I somehow managed to hold back, though I don't know how I accomplished that. I've never felt more panicked. I did not want to say that final farewell to you."

"Nothing has ever hurt me more than that…"

"I know. It was the worst moment of my life." Mary agreed with his sentiment as she quickly tossed her discarded clothes into the hamper. "At least Wally knows now that you weren't exaggerating when you told him Elizabeth was chaos."

Mary returned to what he originally brought up as she went to the bedroom door to make sure that it was locked.

Ian flushed the toilet and went to the sink to wash his hands. "Too bad Wally didn't believe me before he got sucked in by her."

Mary opened the bathroom door and stood there in the doorway like she was wearing her frumpy flannel pajamas.

"Wow…" Ian saw her reflection in the bathroom mirror and turned to look at her. "That's one way of making sure that you get more than a kiss from your adoring husband tonight…"

Mary giggled. "And that's very presumptuous of you to assume the outcome of your case before you've offered any persuasive evidence to the jury."

Ian laughed at her feigned shut down. "I *am* presumptuous sometimes." The intricate lace pattern that adorned her chest kept Ian from raising his eyes off of the sensual curve of her breasts. What he wanted to do was take both of them in his hands. "I'm torn between brushing my teeth first and then feeling you out, or just going for it right now and brushing afterwards." She was definitely getting more than an obligatory kiss tonight.

Mary stepped into the room wearing an unusual amount of confidence – a sexy act in itself. “Again, presumptuous for you to think that the choice is even yours…”

Ian chuckled at her retort, as his eyes followed the seductive motion of her coming to stand beside him. The rounded outline of her perky breasts teasing him through the lacey purple nightie was as tempting to him today as it was back in high school when he indulged every opportunity that she allowed, for him to cop a feel of her. “You see the kind of power you still have over me…”

He reached for her hand to tug her his direction so he could cop a feel of her right now. “No matter how badly I want it, I can’t have it, unless you deliver it to me.”

Mary giggled at his difficult predicament. “That sounds like something my dad used to say to me.”

“Yep.” Ian offered the version he used to get from her father before Mary could offer the version she used to hear. “*I know how it feels to be your age, Ian, and I’m trusting you to be a gentleman with my daughter, and my expectation is that no matter how much you think you want it, you won’t pressure Mary into delivering it to you.*”

Mary chuckled and offered the version she got from her father. “*Ian’s a nice young man, but he’s at that age where he will want certain things, and a mature restraint will be difficult for him to maintain. So, it’s in your hands to help him behave. Just because he wants it, doesn’t mean you have to deliver it. It’s up to you to remember at all times to unequivocally say no to him. If you don’t, he’ll just keep asking.*”

Ian chuckled at the last line of her father’s advice. “Guilty as charged.”

Mary giggled with him. “Well, I was never very good at the unequivocal denial, and you were far better at taking my no, than I was at delivering that no to you.”

Ian smiled at her perspective. “I never understood the logic in your argument when you would tell me, *if you don’t stop, I’m going to let you.* In my head I’m thinking… okay, so I won’t stop.”

Mary laughed at his funny observation. “I can see how that warning might send the wrong message. But again, it was always hard to say no to you.”

Ian grinned at what she admitted as he took her face into his hands to give her a sweet kiss. “So, what you’re saying tonight is that there's a good chance that you'll still find it hard to say no to my physical persuasion?"

Mary pulled her smiling face away from the kiss he was giving her. "Hands off, wild child..." She reached for their toothbrushes and handed him his brush. "You're getting ahead of yourself."

Ian chuckled at her choice of words as he ran his eyes down the purple lace that was barely concealing the natural beauty of her body. "Is that a threat..." Her round bottom obscured by the lacy pattern that was stretched tightly over it, was as alluring to his eyes as the smaller mounds on her chest that were peeking through the delicate material that was covering them; and what he really wanted to do was reach down to her rear end with both hands, to clasp her butt cheeks into the palms of his hands to turn her around, flush against his torso, so he could lock her in a tight embrace that might never end. "Or an invitation?"

Mary squirted toothpaste on both of their brushes. "My experience is that both will get the same reaction out of you."

Ian smiled at her quick answer. He was already there in his head making sweet love to her, and the anticipatory flush of passion was rushing through him. "Then maybe I'll abstain tonight to avoid predictability." He teasingly focused on brushing his teeth while he thought about rubbing the palms of his hands all over her body, from the soft round plumpness of her breasts and firm nipples, down to the mounds of squeezy butt cheeks... and everywhere in between.

"No, you won't." Mary brushed her teeth and spit into the sink before adding more. "You'll be begging me to let you in."

Ian laughed at her prediction as he spit into the sink and wiped his mouth. Then he rinsed his brush and dropped it into the holder in sweet surrender to her forecast. "And now I just want to put my hands all over you." He took Mary's toothbrush from her hand and ran it under the running water before he dropped it into the holder next to his own brush and turned the water off. Then he swiped away the toothpaste that was still on her lips and turned her his direction.

Mary giggled at his clean up gesture. "Nice that wasn't vomit... huh?"

Ian pulled her into his body. "It will certainly make our kiss more enjoyable." He wrapped his arms around her to draw her into the exploratory hold he was envisioning a moment ago. "You locked the bedroom door?"

His lips touched down on hers before she could answer, and he softly munched on them with a lover's delight. "Because I definitely want you tonight, despite the fact that I thought I was pretty tired when we left the kitchen to come to bed."

"The door's locked..." Mary slid her tongue inside his mouth. "How can this feel so incredibly exciting... after so many years? Why doesn't this feel like boring, uninteresting sex with my dumpy partner of way too long?"

Ian chuckled. "I have awesome *Lover Powers...*" He traced his hand down the length of her spine in a slow lover's dance, and drew it down lower until his palm rested on her bottom, where he squeezed a butt cheek with sexual desire. "I don't think I've seen you in this outfit since our honeymoon..." He pressed both palms into her bottom to encourage her to step closer into the heat of his body and the expectation of his pelvis.

"You haven't." Mary dissolved into his embrace. "Wake up call to self... husband might like to see you in something other than comfort clothing..."

Ian moved a palm slowly back up her torso with gentle appreciation for the feel of her curves as he traced the lace covered flesh between her hip bone and breasts. "And I was going to say, *look at you... wearing your sexy honeymoon lingerie like the foxy, hot ma' ma you are today, notwithstanding the fact that you grew two babies inside your belly.*" His wandering palm drifted back down the other side of her body with delicate delight.

Mary giggled at his touch. "Well, it's a little snug..." She shrugged self-consciously as he slid his fingers back up her body, softly over her rib cage until he got another giggle out of her.

"It's beautiful." Ian held his undivided focus on her face. "*You're* beautiful." He ran his other palm delicately up the other side of her torso over the bones of her rib cage and softly back down to the curve of her waist, until his thumb drifted over the sensitive spot on her hip bone where he knew he would entice another sexy giggle out of her.

Mary dropped her head against his chest and quietly exhaled. "My gosh, this feels good..."

Ian smiled with satisfaction. "That's how come it was so hard to say no to me in high school..." He squeezed his arms around her in a gentle lover's cradle, and tenderly kissed the top of her head.

Mary settled her eyes on him with the unconditional love of a soulmate. "Nice for both of us that we no longer have to say no to each other."

Ian tipped her face up to kiss her with passion that had only grown deeper from his years of loving her. "Nice indeed…" He loved how their lifelong journey allowed them to look back through the years together, and so many important memories and feelings. "So, tonight's a different thing for us than all those years ago when you struggled to say no to me…" He ran his hands up and down both sides of her torso in a lover's persuasive dance.

Mary shuddered with desire. "Yeah… you're definitely getting laid tonight." She giggled with her confession and her need to be taken by him.

Ian chuckled at her stated condition. "Thanks-be, to my awesome lover powers… huh?"

Mary giggled at his boasting and stepped onto her toes to kiss him on the lips. "You're a good man, Charlie Brown…" She slid her own palms up under the back of his tee shirt and over the smooth flesh of his warm torso in a needy caress that sent tingling prickles all over Ian's body.

"Despite your hot temper when it comes to your ex-…" Mary's lips met his and she added more to her scolding in the break between kisses. "And your loose, venomous tongue that knows no boundaries…and says the most regrettable things."

Ian slid his loose, venomous tongue inside her mouth to stop her reprimand as the blood rushing through him noticeably increased his internal body temperature. "And I appreciate what a good wife I have, considering your tolerance for my ex- who makes me crazy, and demands the kind of attention that would surely get other husbands in trouble with their wives."

Mary chuckled with appreciation as she offered him a playful tease. "Well, being so tolerant of your ex-wife puts me in a good bartering position with you… because how can you deny me anything when I'm so graciously putting up with all that drama, not to mention her constant effort to suck you back in – coupled with her regular reminders of the hot, passionate sex she's had with you?"

Ian smiled at her observation as he moved a palm around the backside of her body, so he could slide it inside her sexy, scant panties of purple lace, that were beckoning for his attention. "Let me balance the bartering scales with some persuasive handiwork for you…"

Mary dropped her forehead into his chest and exhaled with needy passion. "Your fingers are in my underpants…"

"Yep." Ian chuckled with his admission as he tipped her face up for a kiss. "Puts me in a good position to barter for hot, passionate sex with you…"

Mary chuckled at his confident stance. "This hand in the underpants thing has been a bad habit that you've been indulging since high school…"

"Well, you've never complained before…" He softly kissed her lips. "And ever since you first caught my eye… I've wanted to be your guy." His other palm slid up her body with appreciative delight as he moved it across a breast to fondle a nipple. "So, my hand in your underpants would just be my way of keeping you interested, while perfecting my bartering skills…"

Mary chuckled at his confession. "I don't think your bartering skills have any room for improvement..."

Ian drew his hand out of her underwear and grabbed her by the palm of her hand to lead her into the bedroom where he gently removed her nightie and her sexy lacy panties. "And now I just want to feel your warm, silky flesh tucked securely beneath my own naked body…"

****

Ian woke the next morning to his ringing cell phone. "You've got to be kidding me…" He glanced at this watch and rolled to his side to reach for his phone. It was only 8:00 am and that was way too early for a phone call from a friend.

"Hello?"

Mary's discarded negligée and lacy purple panties were still on the floor where he tossed them last night when he peeled them off of her body after their sexy foreplay. His own discarded clothes were dumped in a messy heap beside them.

"Hey Powers…"

"What's up, Wally?" Ian stopped eyeing the evidence of their lovemaking to focus on Wally's wake-up call.

"I just wanted to thank you guys for last night. We had a great time… except for… you know, but that wasn't your fault."

Ian dropped his head back onto his pillow and closed his eyes. He needed to remember to pick up the discarded clothing before any of their kids came bounding into their room this morning. He did not want Mary to get embarrassed by the kids noticing her sexy purple nightie and heavenly, lacy panties on the floor.

"Yeah, I actually had a pretty good time myself last night… but that was after you went home." Ian chuckled with the tease that he couldn't stop himself from saying, even though it immaturely implied that he got laid last night. "My wife definitely got kissed..." There was just something about Wally being on the other end of the phone that made Ian do this.

He opened his eyes to steal a peak at his sleeping beauty. Her hair was in a messy tangle spread out across her pillow and she looked absolutely gorgeous, peacefully breathing beside him.

Wally chuckled in his ear. "I honestly don't want to hear the details of your good time activities."

Ian laughed at that. "Yeah, I'll leave that to your wildest imagination."

Wally chuckled off his teasing. "I just hope you didn't leave her all marked up like you did in high school."

Ian smiled with nostalgia. It was even fun to look back through the years with Wally. It kept their life journey alive in all of their hearts. "So, what's really on your mind? Because I know you didn't call me at 8:00 am on a Sunday morning to thank me for dinner."

Wally went where Ian guided him. "Actually, you're right. Betty Jo and I were talking last night, and she wants to take Elizabeth under her wing. She's been working with some substance abuse groups, and she wants to clean Elizabeth up."

Ian snorted at that. "More power to her for wanting to take on that noble cause, but I don't have high expectations for her success in that regard."

"Seriously…" Wally stayed focused. "Why can't you just be nice when it comes to her?"

"Okay…" Ian gave the idea more respect. "I applaud your wife if she wants to take that on, especially considering your past with Lizzy, which I know from firsthand experience, can't possibly be easily overlooked by her."

Wally agreed. "We both have exceptional wives…"

Ian smiled and looked again at his own wife. “We do.” And his was the *very* best wife. He felt like the luckiest man on earth, having Mary for a wife.

“There’s more…” Wally drew Ian’s attention back to his phone call. “She wants me to offer her the job again with the stipulation that she attend AA meetings. She says that she saw enough last night to know that Elizabeth needs help. And for whatever reason, she likes Elizabeth. But as Elizabeth’s sort of ex-boyfriend, talking to her very involved ex-husband, probably the closest thing Elizabeth has right now to an actual partner, I wanted to run that by you first and see what you think.”

Ian rubbed his eyes awake then he glanced at his watch again. This was more conversation than he wanted this early on a Sunday morning while he was still laying naked in bed, before he’d ingested any caffeine or had a chance to pee. “You know what, Wally, you guys do what you want with her. It’s not my business. So, if Betty Jo wants to befriend her, and you want to hire her, I’m not going to stand in the way of any of that. Just don’t let her suck you back in again. Because that’s Elizabeth’s mode of operandi. She never gives up… as you saw last night. And she’s not above creating havoc in a marriage to try and win her cause. She will worm her way between the two of you and create all kinds of nonsensical fights if you aren’t savvy enough to see what’s happening and stop it from going further.”

Wally exhaled with determination. “So, we’re good with all that?”

“Definitely.” Ian wondered how long it would take for the flames to engulf Wally’s house. “Just remember what I told you, though Wally; Elizabeth’s picture should be in the dictionary next to the word chaos. And when you bring her up close like you’re talking about doing, there’s going to be chaos inside your house. Guaranteed.”

“Got it.” Wally chuckled and ended the call.

Ian dropped his phone to his nightstand and rolled over on his side to look at Mary. “Hey…” He tugged at some long strands of hair that hung loosely over her pillow onto his own pillow.

“Foxy jockey…” He teasingly called out to her.

“Someone is pulling my hair like this kid I knew in grade school who used to pull it.”

Ian chuckled. "Yep. That'd be me… then… and now."

Mary stirred beside him. "Were you talking to Wally just now?"

"I was."

Mary turned to look at him. "Boy, are you two becoming fast and furious buddies…"

Ian laughed at that. "Ol' Polly Wally…nerdy geek that he is…"

Mary nodded. "Who would have thought that. Right?"

"I know." Ian nodded at her observation. "It's baffling. So, guess what? He and Betty Jo are taking Elizabeth on. Betty Jo wants to save her from herself, and he's offering her the job again."

Mary wrinkled her face into a worried stare. "That sounds like a disaster in the making."

"I agree. But not my problem." Ian stroked her cheek with the tips of his fingers and quietly made the conversation more personal. "Our bedroom looks like there was some kind of wild sex party taking place in here last night."

Mary lifted herself from the mattress to see the evidence for herself. "I must admit, you had me exactly where you wanted me in the palm of your hand last night." She giggled at what she said and added more. "*Literally...* I would have begged you to do me, if you hadn't finally taken that task on for yourself."

Ian chuckled at that. "One of my better skill sets. And definitely where I like you. In the palm of my hand, begging for me to do you. And for the record, I *really* like how you feel under my body."

Mary giggled at that. "With my legs wrapped tight around your torso…"

Ian chuckled with amusement. "And now that just sounds like a come-on, I may have to accept…" He grinned at the image she sent to his head as their intimate conversation was interrupted by a knocking on their door.

"Daddy, can I have cereal?" Skylar hollered through the closed door at them.

"Sure!" Ian begrudgingly slid out of bed and scooped up the discarded nightie, the panties, and all of his clothing. "I need a minute to pee, Skylar," he raised his voice to speak to his daughter, "…and get dressed…"

"Rats…" Mary shot him a sulky expression from where he left her alone, in bed. "And here, I was hoping to climb on top of you for a morning ride into heaven…"

Ian chuckled at that. “As inviting as it sounds to have your legs wrapped around me, or you sitting on top of me taking a ride into heaven, it looks like I’m going to have to offer you a rain check on the leg-lock and joyride, because I’m apparently needed more urgently in the kitchen where I am being called upon to use my amazing *Daddy Powers* ...for the benefit of your children.”

Mary nodded with a teasing pout. “So, here’s a departing shot for you, *lover boy*: I have another honeymoon outfit in the bottom of my drawer that I am going to unearth today for a repeat performance tonight, of last night’s sex-capades. And the challenge for you now, is to try not to get too distracted by that thought while you run your very proficient gear shift through your exceptional *Daddy Powers* in the kitchen this morning.”

Ian smiled with amusement. “And here’s one for you, *foxy jockey*: how about you try and get through the day without thinking about my hand in your underpants tonight.”

Mary blushed at the thought. “And now I’m going to be thinking about that all day.”

“That’s exactly what I want you thinking about today.” Ian laughed out loud. “I’ll be out in a minute, Skylar…”

“Okay, daddy!” She hollered through the door at him. “I have to pee-pee too, and then I’m going to wake Philip and Ellie so they can eat cereal with me.”

Ian joined the kids in the kitchen a few minutes later, and poured them each cereal, then he poured himself a cup of coffee, and also a cup for Mary, which he took to her in the bedroom. “We’ve got the ride with the kids today that we promised, and then I’m thinking that Jenny and Ricky need a movie date night. I just checked the movie schedule and there’s a show playing that they might like. I can drop them off for the 5:00 pm showing, or something in that timeframe, so it doesn’t become a late night for us.”

Mary took the coffee from him. “That sounds good… as long as we get to bed early enough for our own date night.”

Ian smiled at her suggestion. “You can’t stop thinking about my persuasive finger work…”

Mary giggled. “It is going to be a long day…”

Ian laughed at that. “Yep. So, I’ll start some breakfast for us, and get Ricky and Jenny up so we can get started on barn chores.

Then we can do the ride, and get them to the theater. And while they're at the picture show we'll get the kids bathed and fed and ready for bed, so it's a smooth hand-off for Ellie when I get them back home."

"Good plan." Mary sipped her coffee and set it on her night stand. "I'll be out in a minute to help." She climbed out of bed. "I just need a quick shower…"

Ian chuckled. "You don't want to stay soiled by me?"

She laughed at his question. "Nope."

****

When she joined Ian in the kitchen, Elizabeth surfaced from the guest bedroom just a few minutes behind her.

"I do not feel like myself in Mary's flannel pajamas. They're so, I don't know, housewife comfortable?"

Mary turned to look at her. "Thanks. For a moment there, I forgot that I was the frumpy wife, and you were the glamourous wife."

Elizabeth shot her a forced smile. "I'm sorry. I didn't mean it like that."

"Yes, you did." Ian didn't let her wiggle out of it. "And quite frankly, she can make her flannel PJs look a hell of a lot sexier than you make them look. She also looks hotter in her flannel pajamas than you look in that black satin number you were wearing the other day that showed off way too much skin and left little for the imagination. Why don't you start showing some respect for yourself and hold back on your goods instead of flaunting what you have, like you're part of the free market place? And honestly, the whole young adult thing that you're trying to pull off with the belly piercing and tight clothes isn't nearly as becoming as you think it is, because you're not in your twenties anymore, and the wear and tear from your hard knocks living, is beginning to show…"

"Okay…" Mary shot him a thankful smile. "That's enough, Ian. I appreciate you standing up for me, and I'm guessing she got your point… which I take to be that you don't appreciate her putting me down. So, I don't think she needs to hear any more of whatever you might feel inclined to say to her this morning."

"I'm sorry." Elizabeth moved her eyes between the two of them. "Sincerely."

Ian nodded at her superficial effort, unpersuaded by the forced apology. "You crashed my dinner party last night, Lizzy."

Elizabeth settled her eyes on him. "I'm sorry…"

He nodded with a dismissive stare. "You vomited all over my daughter's bathroom floor… and left *that* mess for Mary and me to clean."

Elizabeth dropped her head in shame. "I'm sorry, Ian. I won't do that again."

He huffed with robotic detachment. "What does that *mean*, Lizzy? I'm not sure what I'm supposed to do with that… *you're sorry*… So what? Of course, you'll do it again. Because that's what you do. You drink, you vomit, and then you pass out like a kid who doesn't know better, or an alcoholic that can't stop drinking. So, which is it? Because you're not a kid who doesn't know better…"

She looked between them with a hurt expression. "What do you want me to say to that?"

"Just answer the question…" Ian held a focused stare on her with determination he wasn't going to lose. He might as well try and help Wally and Betty Jo out with their effort to fix her…

She nodded her head in answer. "I know. I should probably stop drinking."

"Yep… that's what I'd do if I were you." Ian nodded confirmation. "Because, notwithstanding Jenny's offer of weekend grandparenting time, I am not letting you have Ellie at your place if you don't stop drinking. And it *is* in my power to say no to that. I have no doubt about that."

"I understand."

"Do you?" Ian glanced at his watch, ready to wind-up the come-to-Jesus moment with her. "Because I have my doubts, Lizzy."

"I know. And not without reason."

"With incredibly persuasive reason." Ian nodded confirmation. "All of my reservations are based upon your past actions, some of which aren't too far in the past, unfortunately."

He let that sink in for a moment, before offering her a rundown of what he knew was coming later. "For whatever reason, *beyond my comprehension and against my sound advice,* my understanding is that Betty Jo and Wally want to help you out. I think they're courting disaster by making the effort, and I've warned them against doing so, but that's not my business, so they get to do this if they want to."

He settled his eyes on Elizabeth with a serious expression. "I believe Wally's going to offer you that job again, with the understanding that you have to attend AA meetings if you want to accept the offer." Ian let the idea percolate in her head before saying any more. "What do you think about that?"

Elizabeth shrugged like a shamed child. "Sounds like something I should probably do."

"Yep. I think so." Ian nodded at her surrender. "So, I'll watch from the sidelines to see how that goes for you. In the meantime, we're going to have some breakfast now, then we're going on a ride with the kids. You're invited to breakfast, if you feel up to eating."

She chuckled at that. "I'll pass on the food. But if you have a ginger ale or something similar, I'll take that."

Mary went to the refrigerator and found one for her.

"Thanks." Elizabeth popped the tab and drank a good portion of it. Then she settled her eyes on Ian and offered him a more sincere sounding apology. "I'm sorry for crashing your dinner party and for throwing up on the kids' floor. I never meant do that. And I'm sorry for offending Mary this morning. Sometimes I can't help myself." Her eyes darted nervously between them. "Honestly, I'm jealous of her having you now. And I wish that it was me who you loved instead."

Ian shook his head in quiet objection. "Well, that one is fully on you, Lizzy. Because I gave you a second chance with me, and I gave it my all... and you know what you did to me in return."

Elizabeth dropped her head in shame and looked away from him.

Ian nodded at her silence and left the kitchen to rattle the big kids out of bed.

When he returned, he addressed the rest of what she said with a more charitable heart. "Thank you for the apologies. I'm sorry I didn't graciously accept them without the backhanded slap across the face. My bad for not leaving that one in the past. I'll try not to do that again."

Elizabeth shook her head at him. "You don't have to apologize for pointing out the truth. That was a fair observation and I deserve your bitter anger."

Ian could easily agree with her on that one but he recognized that there was no benefit to any of them in keeping the hostilities going. So, he did the right thing and offered her a more palatable perspective.

"You know what, Lizzy, we were in a bad spell when all that happened, and honestly, if Mary had walked into my life at *any* time while we were married, especially when we were at each other's throats, there's a good chance that I may very well have become the bad actor instead of you. Because I would not have been able to walk away from Mary. I'd like to believe that I wouldn't have cheated on you to be with her, but who's to say what really would have happened, when all we're talking about right now is a hypothetical."

Elizabeth glanced at Mary with a wounded expression before returning her eyes to Ian. "Thanks… I guess." She shot him a pained smile. "There's another example of you saying the nicest thing in the meanest way..."

He shrugged off the truth in her generous observation. "So, instead of us regurgitating all the things that went wrong between us, from now on I'm going to try and focus on the fact that we made a commitment to each other on a good day, and we decided to have a child together, and for the sake of our child and the grandchild we both love, I'm going to try and show you more respect from now on. Regardless of everything that subsequently went wrong between us, I chose you to be my daughter's mother, so I need to start showing you the kind of respect that the mother of my child deserves."

Elizabeth fell into a contented grin. "Thank you, Ian." She giggled with happiness. "And, wow… you didn't even say any of that in a mean way."

He chuckled at that as Elizabeth added more. "And I'll start working on the parts of me that need improvement so it's not so hard for you to show me that respect."

"It's a deal." Ian went to shake her hand on that, then he impulsively pulled her into a friendly hug and a forgiving peck on the lips. "You need to hydrate yourself today."

****

They ate breakfast together, Elizabeth went home, and the four adults plus the three little kids went on a fun ride through the back hills of Ian's ranch. Ian and Mary each rode a child in front of them on their horses, and Ian led the third child on Donkey using a lead line for control. It was a fun ride, and a jolly time for all of them.

The little kids took turns riding Donkey, the big kids rode off on their own for a bit, then they all finally ended their ride, and returned to the barn.

When they were back in the house with their barn chores done, the older kids cleaned up for their fun date night, and Ian drove them to the theater. "You guys have enough money on Ricky's bank card for the movie and food. So, get something in the lobby for dinner before you go into the theater. The movie is in theater number two, so make sure you go into the right one. I'll be back to pick you up when the movie is over. I'll wait for you where I always pick you up outside."

"Okay, daddy!" Jenny reached for Ricky's hand and they skipped off together, out of sight.

Ian returned to the house to help Mary with the little kids.

"I'm back…" He hollered out to her as he stepped inside. "When was the last time you drove your car through a car wash?"

Mary hurriedly joined him in the entry. "The kids are in the tub, there's water everywhere, and I just scorched the potatoes."

Ian shook his head with amusement. "A normal Sunday night."

Mary gestured that she needed to return to the kids. "You know I don't do the carwash thing because I'm afraid that I'll damage the car by doing something wrong."

Ian laughed at that. "I don't know how you can be such a smart attorney, and yet you can't figure out how to do something as simple as drive your car through the car wash..." He chuckled with his teasing. "I filled your gas tank so you don't have to do that tomorrow, and I drove your car through the carwash for you. So, it's clean now."

"Thank you." Mary gave him a quick peck on the lips before returning to the master bathroom to oversee the water fight taking place in their oversized jetted bathtub.

Ian trailed along behind her as his phone rang in his pocket. "Hello?" He grabbed it following her, without looking at the caller ID.

"Hi Ian…"

It was Ricky's mother.

"Hey, Pat… what's up?"

She asked how everyone was, and Ian shared that he had just dropped the kids off for a movie date night. “We’re good. The kids are good.”

“You do such a fantastic job with them.” She offered the compliment, then she got to the reason for her call. “We had a surprise visit yesterday from a social worker…”

“You did?” Ian handed Mary a towel to wipe the water off of the floor.

“So, I thought I had better check in with you today to see what’s going on? Anything we ought to know about?”

Ian offered her a quick rundown. “She came by our house, too.” He went to the linen cabinet to get clean towels for the kids. “Elizabeth apparently called them as part of a ploy on her part to try and force some grandparenting time with Ellie that was more than what I felt appropriate, considering Elizabeth was asking for a rotating custody schedule like she was a displaced parent. But I think we’ve resolved that issue for now. So, I’m not expecting that problem to resurface. How did the visit with the social worker go?”

“It was fine. We of course, told her what a great job you and Mary do with the kids, and with Ellie and your own kids and she seemed satisfied with what we said. But the whole visit made me worried, and I thought I had better run it by you. I assumed you knew about it.”

“I think she’s just doing her due diligence before closing her file on us.”

“Great. I thought that might be the case… that it was a misunderstanding. You’ll let us know if anything else happens?”

“Of course.”

She said goodbye, and Ian ended the call.

They finished bathing the kids and fed them dinner, but not the scorched potatoes. Ian made new potatoes while Mary was dressing the kids for bed. After that, they played a board game with them, they read bedtime stories, and Ian left to pick the big kids up from their movie.

When he returned, they passed Ellie off to Jenny and Ricky, they tucked their own kids into bed, and Ian and Mary retired to their own room.

"So," Ian pulled Mary into his arms after he locked the bedroom door behind them. "Was that a white negligée that I'm remembering from our honeymoon?"

Mary shot him a happy smile. "It is, and I can still put it on for you, but..." she squinted into a tease, "After hearing you dress Elizabeth down for showing off too much skin... I'm thinking maybe the flannel PJs might be a better turn on for you..."

Ian grinned at that. "Put the classy white number on... I've been thinking about the feel of that satin between my fingertips all day."

"Sure... I can do that." Mary giggled with her offer, "But it seems like a wasted effort, considering you're just going to take it off of me."

Ian smiled at her tease. "It's the art of the removal that keeps it from becoming a wasted effort."

Mary laughingly agreed as she left his arms to go into the bathroom to change into the nightie.

"I'm thinking about those matching panties..." Ian called out to her from the other side of the closed bathroom door. "Because you know that's my specialty..."

Mary giggled as she stepped back into the bedroom with him a few minutes later. "Is there a bad-boy in the house? Someone who stole my virginity in the back of his beat-up Chevy van, days before he rolled out of town, not to be seen again for many years?"

He chuckled at her tease. "Arguably the best night of my life."

"Agreed..." Mary stepped into his arms and Ian wrapped himself around her.

"And I'd argue in my own defense, that the Officer's daughter stole *my* virginity that night when she couldn't force herself to say no to me..."

Mary laughed at his counter opinion. "A fair argument..."

Ian held her between his arms and slowly rocked her to-and-fro to music in his head. "I'm almost tempted to drag you out back in your virginal white nightie, to the Chevy van behind our house, that Ricky parked cock-eyed in the backyard where it's not supposed to be parked..." He dropped a kiss on her lips. "You interested in some very outdated 70s waterbed action on the floorboards of an old Chevy van?"

Mary chuckled at his tease. "Well, I'm certainly dressed differently tonight than that memorable night when we lost our virginity together on that disgusting mattress on the floorboards of your beat-up Chevy van."

"Yep, you are." Ian chuckled. He had purchased the van in the backyard a few years ago, complete with a waterbed on the floorboards, when he found it by chance, and thought it resembled the one that he owned in high school. He drove it himself for a few fun dates with Mary when he first got it, then he gave it to Ricky so that Ricky could learn how to drive on their property. He wasn't allowed to drive it anywhere else, but Ricky could drive it up and down the road on Ian's property, and for fun Ricky sometimes drove Jenny around in it. So, it was a nice way of letting the two adult kids feel grown-up.

"Well, we'd need to have that same soundtrack going if we did go out there…" Mary moved against Ian's body in a sexy attempt to trigger a sultry kiss out of him. "You'd have to queue up our whole song list from that night."

Ian indulged her with a kiss, then he reached into his pants pocket to pull out his phone. "Just a minute…" He googled one of their songs, and when it started, he set his phone down on the night stand by his side of the bed. "A little *Chevy Van* to set the mood…"

Mary swayed in his arms to their signature tune, one of their favorites that they were listening to during their first love making. "As nostalgic as this song feels, with its celebration of carefree love… as sexy as it sounds for us to be getting our groove on outside on that waterbed…"

"On the floorboards of an old Chevy van…" Ian nodded at where she was going in her head. "I'll take the comfort of our king size bed instead…"

Mary giggled. "Yep… nice we can now indulge that kind of luxury…"

They leisurely made love with a joint appreciation for their life long journey and when their passion was spent, they drifted off to sleep wrapped in each other's arms.

****

Ian woke sometime later to the doorbell ringing. "What the…" He reached for his phone and glanced at the time. "One o'clock in the morning…"

The doorbell rang again, and he climbed out of bed.

Mary sat up to look at him. “Who would be ringing our doorbell at this hour?”

Ian went for his robe. “I have no idea.” He pulled his robe on and left the bedroom.

****

When he opened the front door, Jenny and Ricky stood on the other side of it.

“What are you guys doing outside?” They were barefoot in pajamas.

“We can’t tell you daddy.” Jenny giggled and blushed. “It’s too embarrassing.”

“No, it’s not.” Ricky took her hand in his. “Cinderella was in our bed and I wanted to have sex. I took control of my life.”

“Honey-bear…” Jenny giggled as she looked away from him. “He took me outside to the Chevy van, daddy. There's a bed in it.”

“And we had sex out there.” Ricky matter-of-factly finished what she was saying. “It’s a waterbed.”

Ian chuckled at their confession. “I know there's a bed in it, Jenny.” His eyes moved onto Ricky. “And I know it’s a waterbed.”

“It felt good.” Ricky kissed Jenny on the lips. “I like the waterbed. And I love my wife.”

Ian shook his head with amusement. “So, why did I have to come let you in?”

“The door locked us out, daddy.” Jenny answered his question.

Ricky expanded on what she said. “We didn’t have a key.”

“And the emergency key was not under the rock, daddy.” Jenny finished his explanation.

“The van was not locked.” Ricky added to what Jenny said. “But the door on the house locked us out. I didn’t know it could do that.”

Ian chuckled at their funny predicament. “Sounds like we need to find the emergency key, so, the next time you guys want to make love in the van, I don’t have to get up in the middle of the night to let you back in.”

Jenny giggled. “It's in Ricky's pocket, daddy. The key. In his jeans in our bedroom. He got locked out Friday and forgot to put it back.”

Ian waved them inside. "So, let's make sure that Ricky puts the key under the rock tomorrow."

"Okay, daddy."

"I will, Ian."

They left him in the entry and laughingly scooted off to their own house.

Ian closed the door behind them and made his way back to his own bedroom, chuckling all the way.

"What was it?" Mary sat up when she saw him come in.

Ian couldn't stop laughing as he closed the bedroom door. "The kids are now having sex in the Chevy van."

"What?" Mary gasped with disbelief. "Are you kidding?"

Ian grinned at her surprise. "I guess Ricky has ostensibly taken my advice to take control of his life," the thought of which made Ian chuckle with self-deprecating humor, "Which may have been bad advice on my part…"

Mary chuckled with him and Ian continued with his story.

"So, anyway, I guess he wanted to get laid but Ellie had crawled into their bed, so he took control of his life and dragged Jenny out to the van to get himself laid out there."

Mary laughed at the way Ian said that. "Good thing you didn't drag me out there tonight…"

"Yeah, that might have become an awkward moment." Ian came to his side of the bed to remove his robe and slide in beside Mary, but before he started to disrobe himself, he realized that Skylar had joined them while he was at the front door. "What is she doing in here?" He shook his head at her sleeping form with jolly acceptance of their own nighttime interruptions.

"I think the doorbell woke her." Mary offered an explanation.

"Yep, it probably did." Ian settled his eyes on Mary as he lifted Skylar off of the mattress to take her back to her own bedroom. "Good thing this one didn't wander in here earlier… because I might have considered more seriously, taking you out back to get myself laid in that Chevy van."

He carried Skylar back to her bedroom and returned to join Mary in bed. "We are going to be ridiculously tired tomorrow at work."

****

When Ian came home from work the next day, the house was quiet, and Mary had dinner ready. He stepped into the kitchen to give her a hello kiss. "I was tired all day. How about you?"

"Yep. I was exhausted." She returned a kiss to his lips. "You have mail from Social Services…"

Ian stopped kissing her to step over to where they always dropped their mail when they came in at night. "You didn't open it?"

Mary shook her head in answer. "That's a felony… opening mail that's not addressed to me." She laughed with her teasing answer as Ian found the letter.

"I'm assuming this is going to be good news, not bad news…"

Mary turned the oven off. "My assumption too." She came to look over his shoulder.

Ian ripped the envelope open and pulled the letter out. His eyes scanned the words until he found what he wanted to see… "She closed the case." He exhaled with relief. "Thank goodness that one's behind us now."

Mary stepped onto her toes to give him a more leisurely kiss. "I knew you'd survive this one."

Ian wrapped his arms around her to make her kiss last longer than she planned. "Where have you hidden our kids?" He teasingly realized that nobody had leapt into his arms yet, or demanded his divided attention. In fact, the house was *too* quiet.

"Jenny has them at her place. She made them dinner all by herself, and they're watching a movie now before bed."

"Jenny made them dinner?" Ian was surprised by that. "What'd she make them?"

"Macaroni and cheese…"

He smiled at that. "My favorite… and one of her favorites." When Ian was raising Jenny on his own, that had been one of his go-to meals when he came home late from work and had to quickly fix dinner for her.

"And peas and hotdogs."

Ian shook his head with happy pride. "Well, peas were a staple when she was little, because I could get her to eat them. But hotdogs were never a favorite of mine… but she liked them. And it's a good effort on her part tonight."

"I know. I was so proud of her tonight when she read me the directions on the Mac & Cheese box, and confirmed how she was going to make it when she went back to her kitchen – right down to which measuring cup she was going to use."

Ian smiled with pride. "Jenny *is* a good mother… despite her limitations. And she's getting better at it every day." He glanced to the closed door between houses. "How long has it been since the two of us were able to come home from work without having to do the whole drawn out evening kid routine?"

Mary chuckled. "I know. It feels like it's been ages since it was just the two of us in the house. Since before all the kids were born, after you got Jenny and Ricky set up in her flat."

Ian slow-kissed her lips. "For however long it lasts tonight… I feel liberated."

Mary grinned with his observation. "I'd offer you a booty call during this brief liberation that you're celebrating… but we've been having so much sex lately, you'd think we were newlyweds or infatuated kids…"

Ian laughed at that. "So, tell me how that's a problem, Ms. Edwards, and I'll use my persuasive *Lover Powers* to talk you down from that misguided thinking…"

###

About the Author

Suzanne has been writing fiction and romance novels since the early '80s. She enjoys getting to know the characters that travel through her. She finds their lives enriching, and claims to learn a lot about life from her characters and their experiences.

Suzanne likes to write stories about people falling in love, and often write stories involving married couples whose love is tested. She gets inspired by her own characters when they survive difficult circumstances and fall back in love. It reminds her that love is fragile but also resilient. Most surprising is how strong love can feel after its most challenging moments.

Suzanne's stories often include a military or legal theme because she's a military veteran (also a military brat, wife, and mother) plus, she has a law degree.

She's been fortunate enough to live in England and Germany, and eight different American states. She's also had a varied professional career working in the medical field, the legal field, education... and years ago, she was a waitress.... So, she has a lot of life experience that falls into her writing.

She and her husband have three children and a growing number of grandchildren which keeps them busy. When she has down time she likes to garden, swim, ski, and run. She also enjoys family time, dancing and making wine with her husband, hanging with her children, and playing with her grandchildren. They've also done a lot of home remodeling lately!

Suzanne has a bachelor's degree from Saint Mary's College of California and a Juris Doctor degree from JFK University. She's a member of the National Women's Book Association, Women's Fiction Writers Association, the Author's Guild, Goodreads, Bookbub, and Romance Writers of America.

Books by this author

Something to Remember
(First Book in the *Second Chance* Series)

Something to Cherish
(Second Book in the *Second Chance* Series)

Something to Navigate
(Third Book in the *Second Chance* Series)

Travesty of Justice
(First Book in the *Starting Over* Series)

In Cadence Love
(First Book in the *Freedom Fighters* Series)

Bend in the Circle
(First Book in the *Enduring Love* Series)

Follow Suzanne on Amazon, Bookbub, and Goodreads for Release Dates for these Upcoming Books:

A Political Affair
(Projected Spring 2021)

Return of the Seasons
(Second Book in the *Enduring Love* Series)
(Projected Summer 2021)

We Don't Call Them Deadbeats
(Projected Fall 2021)

Call of the Emerald Isle (Second Book in the *Starting Over* Series)
(Projected Winter 2022)

Something to Surrender
(Fourth Books in the *Second Chance* Series)
(Projected Spring 2022)

CONNECT WITH THE AUTHOR

I really appreciate you reading my book!

Here's how you can connect with me:

Visit my website: http://www.suzannepederson.com/ and subscribe to my newsletter.

Follow me on Instagram: https://www.instagram.com/authorspederson/

Follow me on Twitter: https://twitter.com/authorspederson

Like my page on Facebook: https://www.facebook.com/talesfromtheheartandsoul/

Follow my Amazon Author Platform: https://www.amazon.com/Suzanne-Pederson/e/B07PGKYM1K?ref_=dbs_p_pbk_r00_abau_000000

I can also be found on
Pinterest, Bookbub, Smashwords, and in the Author's Guild Member Directory.

Don't forget to leave a review!

DISCUSSION GUIDE

1. In what ways did the alternating male points of view drive this story forward?
2. In what ways did the alternating points of view support or contradict each other?
3. In what ways does Ian's practiced detachment seem to fail him?
4. Which scenes might indicate that Ian is hiding unexposed insecurities?
5. In what ways did Wally's childhood and high school experiences with Ian and Mary drive his adult interactions with them?
6. In what ways did Ian's childhood and high school experiences with Wally drive his adult interactions with him?
7. In what ways did the males' childhood and high school rivalry drive their adult interactions with Elizabeth?
8. Which flashback memories are most revealing of teenage personalities?
9. Which flashback memories provide the most insight into the adult personalities?
10. Which scenes might best illustrate the unresolved tensions between each of the characters?
11. In what ways did Wally show character growth in the story?
12. In what ways did Mary's character develop in the story?
13. In what ways did Elizabeth's character develop in the story?
14. In what ways did Ian show character growth?
15. In what ways did Betty Jo's character develop in the story?
16. In what ways did Jenny and Ricky show character growth?

Made in the USA
Columbia, SC
27 October 2021

47879001R00143